Call the Dead Again

Call the Dead Again

Ann Granger

St. Martin's Press
New York

Library of Congress Cataloging-in-Publication Data

Granger, Ann.
    Call the dead again / Ann Granger. – 1st U.S. ed.
    p. cm.
    ISBN 0-312-20505-8
    I. Title.
PR6057.R259C35   1999b
823'.914—dc21
                                   99-19150
                                     CIP

First published in Great Britain by Headline Book Publishing, a division of Hodder Headline PLC

First U.S. Edition: May 1999

10 9 8 7 6 5 4 3 2 1

O cruel Death, what havock hast thou made?
Low in the dust his Mortal Body laid,
His Soul with every good to Heaven is call'd
Tho to its native dust the Body fall.
His friends in grief survived us all in vain
No sighs nor tears can all the Dead again.

—Epitaph in a Cornish churchyard, 1820

CHAPTER ONE

'I want to get to Bamford tonight. Is anyone going that way?'

The voice was well articulated and carried a faintly imperious note. The men clustered around the grimy mobile snack bar turned their heads as one. Even Wally, owner and chef, was intrigued. He placed both palms on the chain-suspended greasy counter projecting from the side of the vehicle, and leaned across to see who'd spoken.

With the shift of his not inconsiderable weight, the little white van quivered and there was an echoing jingle among its contents. A pyramid of packeted snacks slid apart and spread blue, red and green messages across the counter. *Cheese and Onion flavour – Barbecue Beef – Chicken Tikka.* One fell over the edge to the ground. A customer, at whose feet it landed, picked it up and stuck it in the pocket of his leather blouson jacket. Wally was never so distracted that he missed something like that. He rolled a bloodshot eye and the customer hastily fumbled for loose change and dropped a jumble of coins on the counter. Immediately he returned his gaze to the speaker.

The isolated lay-by was cluttered with parked trucks. Wally's was a regular revictualling stop for the long-distance lorry drivers. He dispensed hot drinks, burned sausages, wedges of heavy pastry stuffed with potato and swede and euphemistically named 'pasties', bacon butties and squares of curranty bread pudding. Wally's proud boast was that his food 'filled you up'. It not only filled, it made the customer feel he'd never need to eat again. Wally's prices were low, his hygiene sketchy, he worked all hours. He saw, as he later told Sergeant Prescott, 'life. Just about everyfing.'

What he saw on this occasion was a girl he judged about eighteen or nineteen, slender in build, wearing jeans. She also wore a tweedy jacket of the sort Wally associated with the leathery men and women who occasionally descended from the cabs of horseboxes and loudly demanded service as if he'd been the ruddy Ritz. She was standing a short distance away, surveying them all in a critical fashion.

1

'And,' added Wally in the course of that later conversation, 'she was a stunner. Just like one of them models. Tall, bit on the thin side, but hair like you never saw. Masses of the stuff.' Here Wally sounded a little wistful and passed a hand over his thinning pate. 'Wonderful colour. Out of a bottle, I suppose. But marvellous, it was. Sort of goldy bronze. She wasn't your usual run-of-the-mill hitchhiker nor your ordinary tart. She had class.' He sounded reverential.

Similar thoughts ran through the mind of Eddie Evans. He was on his way home with an unladen lorry. An empty rig was bad business but there'd been a bit of a mix-up and an owner-driver like Eddie, a self-employed one-man band as he termed it, was likely to be out of pocket. The weather had remained dull all day although it was supposed to be springtime. This year winter seemed reluctant to give way to any warmer season. The sun was obscured by a thick wadding of cloud and temperatures were unseasonably low. The trees and hedgerows were only slowly coming into bud, the spring flowers were all late.

The grey mood had permeated Eddie's very being. He'd drawn into the lay-by at the sight of Wally's van, emblazoned with promises of hot and cold refreshments, not because he needed a cup of tarry tea to refresh the body, but seeking enlivening company to refresh the soul. Other drivers, several of whom he knew, gathered there at this time of day, a little after four in the afternoon. He felt like taking a break and chatting to someone.

He didn't, as a general rule, pick up hitchhikers, male or female. He knew of a fellow who'd had a lot of trouble from doing that. He – Eddie's acquaintance – had given a lift to a girl who'd later turned up dead in a ditch at the other end of the country. The police had tracked down everyone who'd seen the kid or taken her along in his cab and there'd been hell to pay. There was no one to run Eddie's business or pay off his mortgage if he was held for questioning and his schedules went out of the window. He ignored the hitchers standing forlornly by the wayside clutching their scraps of card printed with the names of distant cities.

But Wally's tea hadn't dispersed the feeling of depression caused by steely skies and lost business. Instead it had substituted a reluctance to leave the sociable huddle around the van. A simple human need for company led Eddie on this one occasion to break his rule.

Almost without thinking, he heard himself say, 'I can take you most of the way, ducks, drop you at the Bamford turning. You'll have to hitch yourself another ride from there.'

2

Faces which had been gawping at the girl, turned to gawp at him instead. They all knew Eddie Evans never took pity on a hitchhiker.

In the silence Wally's tea urn hissed and gurgled. Wally, silent and disapproving, withdrew his head, picked up the coins placed on the counter in payment for the crisps and put them in his elderly, spring-operated till.

The girl was waiting. No one else made a better offer. No one else said anything but their thoughts hung in the air like the steam escaping from the pressure pot of the urn.

The girl turned to Eddie and said crisply, 'Right. Thanks.'

She picked up the old khaki haversack which lay on the ground by her feet and slung it over her shoulder. Clearly, she wasn't one to hang about. Her attitude was more that of someone who'd hailed a taxi than one who'd begged a lift from a trucker.

Eddie, prompted by her impatience, tossed his empty polystyrene cup into the battered wire rubbish basket. There was a murmur of amusement as he strode through the group and made for his rig.

Wally had already turned his attention to his spluttering urn. His remaining clientele expressed the opinion among themselves that Eddie had got himself trouble. Privately Wally was minded to agree but he never allowed himself to be drawn into wayside arguments.

Then someone asked, 'Who brought her here?'

There was a silence followed by a buzz of question and denial.

'She must have got here somehow. She couldn't have come from nowhere!' insisted the first questioner. 'Look!' he added, throwing out a brawny arm to encompass the surrounding fields. 'Miles from bleedin' anywhere!'

But no one claimed responsibility for bringing the girl thus far, and no one had even seen her arrive.

'Like she come out of thin air,' said someone, and Wally, not a superstitious man, felt a sudden chill even in the stuffy heat of his van.

Eddie was already having second thoughts by the time he'd reached his rig. He climbed into the cab with a stab of doubt at his heart. The familiarity of the cab's interior, the slightly sweaty smell, the Cornish pixie mascot, the snapshot of his wife Sellotaped alongside the speedometer, all these things failed to reassure him. They seemed instead to be reminding him that he'd broken his rule.

The girl scrambled nimbly up to join him. He took a surreptitious look at her as she stowed her khaki bag under her seat. She was about the age of his own daughter. Gina, too, had long hair and wore it tied back like that. But there resemblance ended. There was something about this girl, an air, a touch of something indefinable which Gina lacked. Proud of his own girl as he was, Eddie felt vaguely resentful.

It wasn't as though this girl was fancily dressed. She wore the usual jeans and funny tan leather ankle boots. Not the lace-up sort, but old-fashioned elastic-sided jobs which probably cost a packet. Gina went in for these fashion fads and they were always overpriced. These looked good quality, not cheaply produced in the Far East or South America to cater for a passing trend. Her jacket, dark brown tweed with leather elbow patches, was quality, too. She wore a dark shirt of some sort underneath it and a man's yellow wool scarf round her neck. He watched her remove it to sit with it crumpled in her hand.

The hair was in glorious contrast to all this plainness. In the dull light it seemed to have an inner glow. He thought of a polished brass candlestick in a church reflecting the dancing flames all around it. It was bunched at the nape of her neck with a piece of ribbon and spilled down her back and over one shoulder. A lock had escaped and hung down by her face. It didn't look untidy. It just looked as if it were meant to be like that. She had beautiful skin. Gina had spots and spent a fortune on acne cures.

He drew out of the lay-by, conscious of watching eyes from the direction of Wally's snack bar. He said, 'I got a daughter about your age. Her name's Gina.'

'Oh? Right.' The reply was carelessly polite.

Niggled, he asked, 'What's your name, then?'

'Kate.'

It bloomin' would be, thought Eddie glumly. Their acquaintance was only minutes old, and already he felt as if twenty-five years or so had been stripped from his life. He was an awkward youngster again, trying to chat up a girl in a pub or at a party, a girl who'd arrived with a different crowd from his own. A girl he was realising belonged in a different crowd from his.

'You live in Bamford, then?' he asked with a jollity which fooled neither of them.

'No, I'm going to see a friend.'

'Come far today?'

'Far enough.' A pause. 'London.' She raised a hand and scraped back a hank of mermaid's hair from her long, white, unlined neck.

4

Sorrier than ever that he'd put himself in this situation, Eddie took refuge in fatherly advice.

'Hitching can be tricky for a young girl!' he said censoriously, wrenching at the wheel.

Widely spaced grey eyes turned to him. 'I'm careful.'

His mouth seemed dry. It was that tea of Wally's. You could paint a ship's timbers with that tea.

'You a student, then?' he asked hoarsely.

'Mmm . . .' She settled back and stared dreamily through the windscreen down the road ahead.

'Gina, my girl, she's a nursery nurse.' He could hear the desperation in his own voice.

'Great . . .' She sounded faraway.

Fair enough, he thought. She doesn't want my conversation and I'm digging a pit for myself trying to chat her up like this. I should have stuck to my own rule. The sooner I can get rid of her, the better. What's she doing, hitching, anyway? She must have money.

But money was often nothing to do with it. It struck him in an unpleasant moment's insight, that she was playing some sort of game. He hadn't picked her up. She had picked him up.

'This friend of yours in Bamford,' he said. 'He – she – expecting you?'

'I don't know,' she murmured. 'But he ought to be, even if he isn't.' She turned her head towards him again and smiled, quite nicely. 'It's to be a surprise,' she said.

He set her down, as promised, at the Bamford turn. By now the natural light had faded and mist had crept across the fields. The trees were spectres in the early dusk. You'd have thought it was still winter. He'd been looking forward to parting from her, getting rid of her, not to put too fine a point on it! Yet Eddie still felt compunction at setting down a young girl, any woman, in this deserted spot, all alone at this time of the evening. He glanced at the dashboard clock. But it was still only twenty past six and not so late after all. However, it was chilly out there. The cold breeze swept in through the open door.

'You going to be all right, love?'

'Sure!' she called up to him. Only her head was visible as she stood in the road.

She made to slam the cab door but he leaned across and held it open. 'I'd turn off and take you right to where you was going – but I don't want to run late. My old lady will be waiting for me at home.'

'No need.' She sounded so calmly confident that he was almost embarrassed at his own fretting. She was moving away already, the khaki haversack slung across her shoulders, obscuring the mane of hair.

'Thanks!' she called back and raised her hand briefly in farewell. It was a sliver of alabaster white in the gloom. He watched her disappear into the twilight, her form growing fuzzy, indistinct and finally invisible. All the remainder of his drive home he was unable to rid himself of the feeling that he had somehow connived in something wrong.

Meredith Mitchell caught up with the lorry as it pulled away from the Bamford turn. Its rear lights glowed like angry red eyes as it roared off into the gathering dusk of a now deserted countryside. She wondered why it had stopped there. Perhaps the driver had been lost, confused, wanted to consult a road map. Perhaps he'd clambered out to scramble up into the hedge in response to a call of nature.

She forgot it as she turned on to the Bamford road and felt her heart lift. She was on the last stretch of her homeward journey. She'd been away from her Foreign Office desk, acting as one of the instructors on a week's course, pleasantly set among the South Downs. In theory, the course was to conclude tomorrow, Friday, at lunchtime, to enable all attending, whether as lecturers or audience, to set off for their scattered homes. In practice virtually everyone had deserted the place tonight, Thursday.

Meredith had joined the lemming exodus, seeing little point in remaining at her post like that doomed sentry at the gates of Pompeii. The few attendees who were down to listen to her on Friday morning had accepted with visible relief her suggestion that an extra half-hour on today's schedule would deal quite well with remaining matters and let them all go home.

She'd rung Alan before leaving and told him of the change in timetable. They'd arranged that she should go straight to his place, not her own. He'd try and get away from work early and meet her there. They'd crack open a bottle of wine and put the world to rights.

Pleasure at escaping the course and looking forward to a convivial evening was tempered by the fact that she didn't like driving at this time of the evening. She didn't mind in the true night when the headlights cut bright swathes to illuminate the road ahead and set light against dark in a clear distinction. But at twilight, the headlights vied with what remained of the waning daylight and

6

roadside shapes became misshapen and took on anthropomorphic life. She was always reminded of the scene in *The Wizard of Oz* when Dorothy, stopping to pick an apple from a wayside tree, is disconcerted by the tree snatching it back.

Ahead of her was something in the road. It moved over to the verge as the headlights picked it up. At first she thought it might be an animal. Muntjak deer roamed the plantations to the side of the road, having escaped long ago from someone's park and thrived. But this, she soon saw, was a human shape and a real one, not something from her overwrought imagination. Someone was walking along the roadside, out here, three miles at least from the first houses of the country town. Someone from a farm, perhaps?

Then, as she swept past, she saw it was a girl, saddled with a small backpack of some sort. It was late for a hitchhiker, although to be fair, the girl hadn't signalled she wanted a lift. Perhaps because of that Meredith pressed her foot on the brake. As she waited for the walker to catch up, she switched on the car's internal light so that the girl could see it was a woman waiting up there ahead of her, not some oaf fancying his chances.

Having the light on inside the car, however, made it difficult to see anything reflected in the rear mirror. It tilted the odds against the car driver, whose former advantage was lost. Now it was Meredith who sat here alone, illuminated, feeling as if she were in a fishbowl, while out there was an unseen walker – or prowler. Only one? There might have been two, and Meredith simply hadn't seen the other. She would have done better, perhaps, not to have heeded instinct and stopped. The impulse to play Good Samaritan might end with being mugged by a pair of wandering hippies. She almost drove on, but if the walker were genuinely in need of help, that would appear a cruel prank. Meredith waited.

When the walker finally caught up with the car and appeared at the passenger window, it was as such a sudden apparition that Meredith was caught unawares. She was glad to see that the girl was, apparently, alone after all.

Meredith rallied, let down the window and called out, 'I'm going into Bamford if you want a lift!'

'I don't want to go all the way into town, just to the edge.' It was an educated voice. Not that that meant anything these days.

'Fine, I'll drop you off.'

The girl sat on the passenger seat, her haversack on her knees. She stared straight ahead out of the window, watching the yellow beam of the car lights, and stayed silent.

The complete lack of any attempt at communication was unnerving. Meredith was prompted to ask, 'Do you live in Bamford?'

'No.' Courteous but firm. Not your business, indicated the tone.

Fair enough, thought Meredith, who also disliked being quizzed by strangers. She confined her next remark to a necessary, 'Whereabouts do you want to be dropped off? Do you know exactly?'

The girl turned her head at last towards the speaker. 'It's called Tudor Lodge. I believe – it was described to me – it's located on the edge of town, almost the first house.'

'I know it. It belongs to the Penhallows.'

'Yes.'

'I know Carla Penhallow. Are you a friend of Luke's?'

There was another silence and Meredith felt that somehow the question had thrown her companion.

'No.' The reply was bald, as before, but lacked the closed composure of the earlier monosyllables.

Well, Meredith reminded herself, her business *is* her business. If she doesn't want to tell me, it's for me to shut up.

But her curiosity was aroused and it won over discretion. She heard herself persist with, 'If you haven't visited the house before, you'll be surprised. It's very old and rather beautiful in a patchwork sort of way.'

'Patchwork?' At last the girl's voice echoed curiosity of her own. Meredith thought, *human at last.*

'The oldest bit, Elizabethan, is to the left, as you look at the house from the street. There's a later Georgian addition to the right. The stone porch is a Victorian addition in Tudor style. But it all works somehow. I rather envy Andrew and Carla that house.'

'It sounds nice . . .' There was the faintest encouragement in the other's voice. The girl approved this line of conversation. She wanted to know more.

But now it was Meredith who was suddenly reluctant to part with information. Who the dickens was this kid, anyhow? She appeared about nineteen, well educated, cool as a cucumber and—

Here Meredith belatedly put two and two together. The girl must have got out of that lorry, back there at the turn. She'd hitched this far from wherever she'd started. And it didn't make sense. It would have made sense if she'd been some friend of Luke's, the Penhallows' son. Another student, hard up as they all were. But if she were a friend of the parents', of Andrew or Carla's, perhaps someone from Carla's publisher or the television people who produced Carla's popular science programmes, well, she ought to have a car.

The town's name gleamed fluorescently on a road sign together with that of the obscure French town with which it was twinned. The car passed the last hedgerows and the lights picked out a petrol station forecourt, untidy but well lit, bright and reassuring, then a terrace of stone cottages, followed by a patch of trees. They'd reached the first streetlamps, just flickering into ochre-coloured life. And there was Tudor Lodge, set back from the road behind iron railings, its tall chimneys and pointed gables still distinguishable as shapes against the battleship-grey sky.

Meredith pulled over. 'There it is—'

She broke off. The girl was already sliding out of the car.

'Thanks for the lift!' She slung her haversack over her shoulder and turned on the narrow pavement to face the car, waiting for Meredith to drive away. Out of courtesy to her benefactor?

No, Meredith thought. Because she doesn't want me to see her walk up to the door. There was something wrong, she knew there was. But if so, it was difficult to think what. The girl seemed really rather upmarket. At this time of the day when people were returning to their homes it was unlikely that a burglar would make for a target or, even less, let someone else know about it.

Meredith forced a brief smile, returned the farewell salute and prepared to drive off.

'Your trouble,' she told herself, 'is you hang around with a copper and it's made you suspicious.'

In the mirror, she saw the slender form turn towards Tudor Lodge, pass through the front gate, and merge into the gloom of the gardens. She didn't hear the blackbird, always the last of a garden's feathered inhabitants to retire for the night. As it made its dusk patrol of its territory it spied the intruder and fled, shrieking its loud, repetitive warning.

It was as well she hadn't heard it. For despite her attempt to put aside her fears, Meredith, as Eddie Evans earlier, had been left with the disquieting feeling that she'd conspired in some mischief.

9

CHAPTER TWO

Andrew Penhallow tapped at the bedroom door and asked softly, 'How are you now?'

From within, his wife's voice mumbled a pain-filled reply. He pushed the door slightly open. The curtains were drawn, blocking what little remained of the daylight. The bedroom furniture emerged as shapes in gloom. On the bed in the centre of the room he could discern a hump which was Carla, curled up in a heap of misery.

'Sorry,' he said helplessly. 'Want anything?'

'Death . . .' groaned the hump.

'Aspirin?'

'No . . . Go away . . . Thanks . . .'

He shut the door softly and made his way back down the creaking oak staircase. There was a warm, muffled stillness about the house. It had often struck him that twilight in this ancient building appeared a moment of time suspended. It was as if the ghosts of all those who'd passed their earthly lives under this roof came out of the woodwork for a sort of happy hour, swapping tales of old adventures and lost loves. Having a good whinge about being dead, perhaps, or having fun criticising the present inhabitants. He wondered, in a flight of baroque fancy, if he'd join them one day. Perhaps he'd have a favourite haunt, just there by the carved newel post, watching his successors toil up and down and jeering at them, unseen and unheard. Once you were dead, Andrew supposed, you had to make your consolations as you could. The options were, he imagined, limited.

He was eighteen months short of his fiftieth birthday. The big Five-O was looming uncomfortably close. It didn't depress him so much as make him resentful. He feared he was beginning to understand those cranky old folk who grumbled incessantly about modern youth. What they were really grumbling about was being no longer young themselves. Wasn't it George Bernard Shaw who'd moaned about youth being wasted on the young? He would, thought Andrew. But any man who grew a beard like

11

that and went around in knickerbockers must long have been a stranger to youthful fancies.

He paused at the foot of the stairs and allowed himself the momentary vanity of studying his clean-shaven reflection in the mirror. He'd never been handsome. Over the years he'd gained a little weight but he fancied it lent him presence, *gravitas*, the aura of the successful man. He didn't, he thought, look too bad. Some of his contemporaries had fared worse. Godlings in youth, with the years they'd lost their hair, their waistlines, their sex drive. *Sans teeth, sans eyes, sans taste, sans everything.*

'That's right, Will old son,' murmured Andrew with a smirk at the looking-glass. 'You said it. But not me, not yet, eh?'

He gave his reflection a last satisfied nod. It was followed by a twinge of guilt, not at having caught himself out in a moment's vanity, but at the thought of his wife. Here he was thinking about himself, and Carla, poor old thing, was lying up there on her bed of pain. Absolute blighter of an affliction, migraine. Knocked her out without warning. She must have eaten something which triggered it. That was usually, though not always, the case. She'd lunched in London today, some writers' beano, and come back with the first throbbing signs of it, pale-faced and feeling sick. With a wail of 'Bloody chocolate mousse!' she'd stumbled upstairs and collapsed on the bed and that had been that.

He often had twinges of guilt about Carla. He assuaged them by reflecting that she was a very successful woman in her own right. She had her own professional life, which had quite made her a household name, and certainly had no time to be bored. He sometimes wondered, however, if what she'd always really wanted was a successful life with him, but that it had eluded them both.

He, like many men who were really deeply conventional, had dreamed of adventure, travel and, what he'd liked to think had been challenges. They'd been the cravings of a stodgy, bookish child translated into a sort of game-playing cleverness in adulthood.

Now the onset of middle age had brought with it the first disconcerting whispers of an unpalatable truth. That it had all remained fantasy. He'd done nothing that others hadn't done before him. He'd trodden a path beaten by generations of basically boring men. And somewhere along that way, between fantasy and reality, he'd done Carla a terrible injustice.

Again he quietened conscience easily enough. They'd been married twenty-five years, for crying out loud! You couldn't say the marriage hadn't worked. Amongst their friends and acquaintances, a quarter-century spent with the same spouse counted as something of a record.

So he had the evening and the house to himself. Three days still before he went back to Brussels. Three days during which he really ought to settle outstanding matters. The trouble with long-term arrangements was that, when they came to an inevitable end at last, no one had prepared for what to do next. He'd been shocked, almost aggrieved, at how complicated it had turned out. Not being able to show or share the sorrow, that was difficult, too, and after so many years, it had been very sad.

Inconvenient conscience nudged again and pointed out that regret, in his case, had been tempered with relief. What had been no trouble at all when he'd been younger had become rather a Herculean effort as he got older. Not the sex side of it, he told himself hastily. No, the subterfuge. The juggling of story lines, trying not to slip up. The one thing he had never wanted to do, he told himself as all selfish men do, was hurt Carla. He had always taken endless trouble not to hurt his wife.

Feeling quite virtuous, Andrew made his way to the kitchen and switched on the electric kettle, truncated thoughts following one another through his brain like the neon messages on certain types of public hoardings. *Make a cup of tea, watch a bit of telly, glance at the newspaper, go to bed. Sleep in the spare room and leave poor old Carla to her misery. Shame.*

As the kettle whispered to itself, he went to the window and peered out into the back garden. The funny thing about this house was that it did – by tradition – have a ghost, but not an indoor one. An outdoor one. He'd never seen it.

Mrs Flack the cleaner, of course, could tell you umpteen tales of people who had. She herself had on an occasion she'd come in to help out the hired caterers at a dinner party. She normally worked mornings to mid-afternoons only. But she was possessive about the kitchen and liked to be on hand to supervise the caterers, declaring darkly and unfairly that it was, 'in case they break anything or take a fancy to the spoons. You never know with strangers.' On going outside that evening to throw out the scrapings from the plates of the main course, she'd sensed a cold draught down her neck as she stood at the dustbin in the gathering dusk.

'I could've sworn, Mr P, that there was someone behind me, real as anything. I turned round and fully expected to see someone there. And do you know what? Not a sausage. But there was this overpowering sense of grief. I really can't explain it.'

Andrew could. Mrs Flack had sampled the wine. They'd got through a lot that night and she couldn't blame the caterers for everything.

He must have shown his disbelief because Mrs Flack had bridled and informed him that 'plenty of others have seen the poor girl'. The poor girl was a maiden in Puritan dress, an echo of the house's turbulent history. Bamford nowadays, as far as Andrew could judge, was short of Puritans. No wonder the ghost wandered around distraught.

He chuckled and turned back to make his cup of tea. He put it on a tray and feeling like a schoolboy raiding a tuckbox, added a wedge of fruit cake. He prepared to make his way to the living room.

At that moment, someone tapped at the back door.

Andrew put down his tray, surprised. Who the dickens was that? Perhaps it wasn't anyone, perhaps something had knocked against the door, a spray of foliage. It was late, no one was expected and anyway, callers came to the front door.

The tapping sounded again, more insistent. Someone *was* there. What had happened, he supposed, was that the front of the house was unlit and someone had come round the back, seen the kitchen light, and was trying to attract attention here.

He didn't like the idea of anyone prowling round the grounds at dusk. He must remember to switch on the alarm system when he went to bed. He went back to the window and looked out but couldn't see who was at the door. Outside a greyish pall hung over the garden, but it certainly wasn't dark. It wasn't too late for a visitor, after all.

He called out, 'Just a sec!' and went to open the door. A cool breeze wafted in. For a moment his eyes couldn't adjust to the loss of electric lighting. Then a shape formed in the half-light, moving, coming towards him. A slim female form stood there, tendrils of hair quivering in the movement of air.

At first superstition seized him in a paralysing grip, and then Andrew gasped, 'What the devil do *you* want?'

Alan's house was totally in darkness when Meredith drew up before it, which was no more than she'd expected. She let herself in with her own key and stepped on to a pile of post. She scooped it up and went down the narrow hall to the kitchen. On the threshold, she switched on the light and groaned.

Evidently his cleaning woman hadn't come that morning. Burned toast lay where it had been abandoned on the draining board.

14

Assorted mugs held the dried dregs of tea or coffee. The garbage bin was filled to overflowing. The latest edition of *The Garden*, the magazine of the Royal Horticultural Society, lay open on the table surrounded by a scattering of crumbs.

'I object,' said Meredith aloud, depositing his mail by the magazine 'to doing someone else's housework.'

She wasn't that keen on her own household chores. But once she'd made herself a cup of tea, there might be a long wait. There was no telling how long it would be before he got home. He might have been held up by a new case. It was the sort of thing which happened and which regularly led her to curse policework.

To be fair, her own career had led to sudden changes of plan before now. She hung her shoulder bag on the back of a chair, switched on the electric kettle, and set to work to tidy up.

She'd just got the place straight and drunk her tea, when she heard the key in the door and a stamp of feet out in the hall. Alan, fair hair unusually unkempt and his long, narrow face flushed, burst into the kitchen. She stifled the impulse to laugh because he managed to combine eagerness with diffidence in a way which was entirely his own. His clear blue eyes were, as ever, alight with intelligent curiosity, as if he expected something of others, some display of equal intelligence. He never, she reflected wryly, even in the most extreme circumstances, lost a natural air of distinction. Standing there he reminded her of an agitated Afghan hound, lifting its thin face, tossing its glossy coat and wheeling around on slender legs as if they were all about to embark on some adventure.

'Well timed!' she informed him, going towards him and lifting her arms to twine round his neck.

He looked pleased but mildly surprised because she wasn't, by nature, demonstrative.

'I'm sorry . . .' he gasped, kissing her hurriedly. 'I tried to get away early. But I'd no sooner put down the phone after you rang, than things started happening, one after the other—'

'Don't worry about it.' She felt a pang of conscience. 'It's all stolen time, anyway. I wasn't supposed to leave until tomorrow midday. I told you, I've skived off early. How's your week been?'

'Dull. How was the course?'

Meredith gave that question due consideration. 'Much as those occasions usually are. A good group of people on the whole, but most of them looking on it as a week off with a few chores thrown in.'

'Then take the same attitude.' Alan made for the wine rack.

'It did involve me in a lot of work with the preparation . . .' Seeing he'd selected a wine and had turned towards her holding the bottle interrogatively, Meredith dismissed the rest of her sentence. Who cared, after all? She'd done her bit.

'Fair enough. Yes, that wine by all means.' She stretched her arms above her head and, catlike, relaxed. 'The weekend starts here! It was a quiet drive home, anyway. I came straight through, no hold-ups, nothing. It'll be worse tomorrow afternoon with the Friday night traffic to contend with. Nearly everyone leaving the course tonight made that an excuse.'

'I tell you what,' he said, wrestling with the corkscrew. 'Give me twenty minutes to take a shower and change and we'll go to the new Greek restaurant. They say it's very good.'

'That sounds fine. No rush, take your time. It's the weekend! Only, I suppose, you'll be working tomorrow?'

He grimaced. 'Probably. But I might be able to get away lunchtime. I'll do my best. We'll think of something special to do, something different. Make a break in the routine.'

Meredith shuddered. Routine, that was the dreaded word. Life was getting to be predictable. She'd successfully avoided the abyss for thirty-six years and now the prospect of a regular lifestyle, holding no more surprises, was creeping up relentlessly. The role she'd been playing over the last few days had encouraged the feeling.

Aloud she said, more to reassure herself than by way of information, 'I broke a rule tonight. I picked up a hitchhiker.'

A police-type scowl. 'Very unwise.'

'It was a girl.'

'Violence doesn't have to be masculine. The girls are getting to be worse than the boys,' he informed her glumly.

'This one was very well spoken, attractive – she was on her way to Tudor Lodge.'

That caught his attention. He put down the opened wine unpoured. 'And hitching? Must be a student friend of young Luke's.'

'I asked her that, but she said she wasn't. I was surprised. Of course, she might have been lying.' It struck Meredith that was perhaps an odd thing to say and she hastened to justify it. 'She did appear to hesitate before denying it. But then, she was rather a strange young woman, but strikingly good-looking with magnificent hair. Very self-confident, too, even a touch haughty.' She grimaced apologetically at what might sound an old-fashioned word, but it seemed apt. 'She had a very grand manner for one so young!' she explained, adding thoughtfully, 'She must have got out of the lorry.' Meredith put up a hand to push aside a hank of dark brown bobbed hair in an absent-minded gesture.

'What lorry?' Alan was sidetracked until he remembered the wine. He poured them a glass apiece.

'Thanks, cheers!' She raised her glass, then took a sip. 'Lovely. Well, there was a lorry up at the turn and I think, just deducing, that she must have got out of that. She was walking along the road with a small-ish backpack, not signalling for a lift. I thought it was getting a bit dark and it was lonely out there. I decided to play Good Samaritan.' She paused. 'I don't think she'd ever been to the house before. I wonder whether they were expecting her. I got the distinct impression they weren't. I don't mind telling you, the whole thing left me feeling very uneasy.'

Alan grunted. 'Andrew home this week?'

'I think so. I saw Carla last week. She was expecting Andrew that evening. Half the time she doesn't know when he'll turn up. They keep him busy. She was rather upset that he's had no time earlier this year to watch Luke play rugby. She went over to Cambridge to watch a couple of games, but I think the boy would've preferred his father to be there. Andrew minded too, of course. I suppose they've got used to that sort of thing. Andrew's worked for years in Brussels or Strasbourg or wherever the EU pitches its tents. It must have played havoc with their family life.'

'I wouldn't mind having a good old chinwag with him,' Alan mused. 'I haven't really talked to the man since God knows when, or even set eyes on him for a twelvemonth, which is disgraceful considering we live so near.'

'We were both invited to dinner there in the New Year,' Meredith reminded him. 'But you had to go haring off on that forgery thing and cried off.'

'We'll put it right. Find out from Carla when Andrew's next coming home and we'll all go out somewhere and have a slap-up meal. Reminisce.'

She pulled a face. 'Old School yarns? You were his contemporary, weren't you?'

'He was a year ahead of me. Seniors didn't fraternise with juniors in my day so he wasn't a pal. I recall him as a plump kid with his nose stuck in a book most of the day, middle-aged before his time. Fourteen going on forty, you know the type. Headed for university with the school rubbing its hands at the prospects of a scholarship winner. He could be relied upon to roll out a Latin grace without a stumble. Useless at sports.' He frowned. 'Wonder who the mysterious girl was? They *must* have been expecting her.'

'I'm pretty sure they weren't. There was something—' Meredith paused, seeking the best word. 'Something furtive about her. I don't mean she crept along, hiding her face. I told you, she was rather self-confident, if anything. It was just that I got a funny feeling about it. I suppose I did the right thing, taking her there?' She began to sound worried.

He hastened to reassure her. 'If she was on her way to the Penhallows', she'd have got there sooner or later with or without your help!'

Meredith's eye fell on the open copy of *The Garden*. It showed a picture of a traditional cottage garden, an untidy riot of shape and colour. She touched it with her finger. 'Did you know,' she asked, 'that the Penhallows have a ghost in their garden?'

'Makes a change from a couple of gnomes with fishing rods.'

'On the level. Not making it up. It's been there since the English Civil War, 1640s. I say "it", but I should say "she". It's, she's a young woman.'

'And Carla's seen this ghastly apparition, has she? Before or after a wee dram of a nightcap?'

'You,' Meredith informed him, 'are too cynical. It's all that police work. It's a sad tale of star-crossed lovers. Load of rubbish, I suppose, but sort of nice for all that.'

He leaned across the table and chinked the rim of his glass against hers. 'I always suspected that behind that hard-boiled exterior lay a romantic heart.'

'I am *not* hard-boiled!' She was deeply indignant, hazel eyes sparkling. 'Nor, come to that, particularly romantic, I admit. But I like a bit of local history and this should appeal to you. It's a tale of bloody murder.'

He sat back. 'Go on, then.'

'Well, the family who lived in the house declared for Parliament, Roundheads. But the sixteen-year-old daughter had a sweetheart and he was from a neighbouring family which was Royalist. So, when the King's cause appeared lost, the young man's family arranged for their son to flee to France. But he wanted to see his beloved one more time. He sent a message by a trusted servant, that she should meet him in the garden of her home at dusk. But the servant betrayed him and on the way there he was ambushed by Roundhead troops and killed. Now, whenever disaster threatens the owners of the house, she's to be seen at twilight, roaming in the garden, waiting for her lost love.'

'When disaster threatens, eh?' said Alan the unbeliever with a grin. 'Let's hope no one has spotted her recently, eh?' His grin grew broader. 'Unless she's changed her style, got herself a thoroughly modern backpack and has taking to hitching lifts to get there!'

CHAPTER THREE

Not knowing what to do, Andrew had dealt with his surprise by taking refuge in trivial courtesies. He had poured his visitor a cup of tea and offered her a piece of fruit cake. It gave him time to think but little else. He was no nearer coming to terms with his predicament.

She'd accepted the tea, but not the cake, and now sat in a Windsor chair by the table, waiting. Her hands rested lightly on the curved wooden arms. By her feet lay a disreputable khaki bag, the sort of small backpack sold by army surplus stores. Her smooth calm face, expressionless within its frame of glorious hair, put him in mind of a Botticelli Venus. She had him completely in her power. It wasn't a situation he relished or intended should last. There was always a way out. He was a lawyer by training and finding loopholes ought to be second nature to him. It was an unpleasant novelty to find himself temporarily defenceless.

Andrew, crumbling cake nervously between fingers made even stickier with sweat, said, 'You oughtn't to have come here, Kate.'

'Aren't you pleased to see me?' She stirred at last, to his great relief, but only to pick up her cup and sip a minute quantity of tea. He wondered if she'd drunk any at all or had simply gone through the motions, pretending.

There was an episode, wasn't there, in *The Count of Monte Cristo*? The disguised hero, intent on tracking down those who have wronged him, visits the house of one of them but gives away the clue to his real identity by refusing to eat or drink anything. To break bread with one's enemy's would be to deny oneself the luxury of revenge.

Was that what she wanted? Some sort of revenge? Andrew wanted to ask her but dared not. At the same time he told himself this was nonsense. She'd merely wished to see him.

'Of course I'm pleased to see you, darling,' he said. 'But not here – I mean, my w—' He couldn't say the word in front of her. 'Carla's upstairs.'

21

'Ah!' Mockery danced in her grey eyes. 'She might come down and surprise us? Discover your guilty secret?'

'She's sick!' he said coldly. 'She suffers from migraine. She won't come down and really, Kate, I don't care for the way you expressed that. There is no question of a guilty secret.'

'She knows?'

Andrew grew flustered and, with it, cross. 'No! I've never— There was no need.'

'Then it's a secret.'

'All right, it's a secret, if you like. But not— There's no question of guilt.'

He knew at once he'd made a mistake. Some cursed Freudian impulse had put the word in his mouth. If there were no question of guilt, why mention it at all? Why sound defensive when there was nothing to justify? If he'd been some wretched malefactor in the dock, a halfway decent barrister would have leaped on that slip of the tongue and torn his evidence apart!

He suddenly had the unpleasant sensation of being an onlooker, just as if he'd joined one of the ghosts he'd been imagining earlier, seeing himself sitting here, sweating and stumbling over his words. How ridiculous he must look and sound. The fine image he'd created of himself, only a brief time before, gave way to the unflattering picture of a bumbling pompous twerp. Cold with fear, he wondered if that was what she saw when she looked at him. She couldn't have missed that fatal word. He was horribly afraid she was going to laugh.

But she said, suddenly brisk, 'You didn't get in touch.'

So that was it. He almost cried with relief. She'd come here in a fit of pique. He had words all ready to deal with that.

'Look, darling, I meant to. But I've been damn busy. I am a very busy man and people expect to have my full attention. I have a great deal on my mind, very serious responsibilities.'

Oh hell, he'd done it again! The wrong words kept insisting on speaking themselves. He shouldn't have mentioned responsibilities. Rather weakly, he concluded, 'You know I spend half my time travelling back and forth to the Continent and when I do finally get a few days between, I'm frankly just about knackered.'

'Let's see,' she said. 'How long does it take to write a postcard? While you're sitting in a plane, or in Eurostar, you must have lots of time to do that. While you're going through the Channel Tunnel, for instance. How long does that take? Twenty minutes or so? Yes, plenty of time to write a card.' The mockery in her voice increased.

Belatedly he made an attempt to grab the moral high ground. 'That's enough, Kate!' he said sharply. 'There's no need to be flippant. I admit I should have written or called you. But you should have let me know you were coming here, not just turned up like this.'

'I could have phoned the house,' she said. 'And Carla might have picked up the phone. I could have told her I was your secretary.'

Genuinely bewildered, Andrew asked, 'Why are you being so cruel? When have you ever lacked anything? I've done my level best for you.'

She leaned forward and there was expression now in her grey eyes. Hatred. He was appalled to see it.

'You dumped me.'

'I didn't – I haven't . . .' he gasped. 'I've been trying to tell you how busy I've been. As it happens, I was going to write or phone as soon as I got back to Brussels. And incidentally, you've changed your London address twice. I did ring you, not so long ago, and got a complete stranger.' That was better. It wasn't his fault. His voice grew cool with righteousness. It wasn't allowed to last.

'I've been in my present flat four months,' she said coldly. 'I wrote and gave you the address and the phone number.'

'I don't know why you let the cottage go,' he muttered.

'Because I didn't want to live there, right? Stuck down in Cornwall, miles from anyone. But you'd like that, wouldn't you? Buried in the country where no one could stumble over me. That was the way you always liked it, wasn't it?'

In a cool tight voice, Andrew said, 'That is inaccurate and unjust.' It was his official manner and it usually worked to good effect. But not, he was dismayed to see, on her.

She relaxed in the Windsor chair, shrugging away his pompous protestations. 'I've met Luke, by the way.'

'L-Luke . . .' At the mention of his son's name Andrew flinched as if he'd been shot. 'Where?'

'At a party, after a rugger match. I went along with some friends to see the game and we sort of cadged an invitation to the party afterwards. He's frightfully fit, isn't he? Rather good-looking.'

'You didn't tell him?' Andrew's voice was dead with fear.

'Course not. Not but what the poor guy might like to know. But I wasn't ready to tell him – yet. They were all celebrating a win and pretty well tanked up. Anything I'd said wouldn't have registered. I've got a pic. Want to see it?'

She reached down to the canvas bag and took out the sort of yellow folder in which developed negatives come back from the chemist. She shuffled through the contents and handed one to him.

'Here, you can keep this one if you like.' She handed him one and dropped the rest and the folder on the table.

This couldn't be happening to him. It was never meant to happen – things were never meant to turn out like this. He'd been so stupid. He should have foreseen. This was a nightmare. Carla upstairs, wrestling with her headache and nausea, wasn't suffering more than he was. But thank God for her migraine. At least she wouldn't come downstairs and walk in on this. How would he explain it? How could he offer any explanation which wouldn't sound weaselly? He felt physically sick. Why hadn't he been frank all along, told them all, told them everything?

The snapshot was a good one. A crowd of happy young people, healthy, beautiful, the world their oyster. Someone brandishing a bottle of champagne. But most of the men were drunk, you could see that, even Luke. Andrew was relieved to see it because it meant Luke was unlikely to remember much detail about the occasion. Then Andrew felt a spurt of envy because he'd never been the sporting type, yet had always envied the camaraderie, the post-match horsing around, the confidence which had blessed the athletically gifted.

After the second's envy, his reaction was of anger, not only with her but with himself and his job. He'd been held up in Europe and quite genuinely so for most of the earlier part of the year. It wasn't the first time he'd been unable to make the touchline at matches, both during Luke's time at university and before that during his schooldays. But this time his absence from the scene had mattered in a way it'd never mattered before. If he'd been there, he'd have stopped this. He wouldn't have allowed it. He'd have seen her and, somehow, kept them apart. Damn the European Union. Damn his career. Damn his success, damn everything. It was all turning to dross.

Andrew had never felt older, more vulnerable, so alien from all around him. There was a world out there in which he'd imagined he cut a distinguished swathe – an important man. In fact, he didn't even belong in it. It had nothing for him and he nothing for it. He dropped the photo on the pile on the table.

'This is a very silly game, Kate,' he said coldly. 'You know he's— It's quite impossible. My God, it's unthinkable! I won't have Luke hurt! I mean that! I shall tell him myself. I shall write to him tomorrow. And in the meantime, you, young woman, will stay away from him.'

'We were getting on really well,' she said. 'He is quite nice.'

He almost struck her. 'You will stay away from my son!'

He'd snapped the words without thinking and had hurt her more than he'd intended or even imagined he could. She almost reeled back, then leaned forward and with equal venom, returned, 'I'll do what I bloody well like! You don't have any right to give me orders!'

They had been raising their voices and both suddenly seemed to become aware of it. An awkward silence fell.

It gave Andrew time to regroup his forces. Normally he was pretty good at thinking on his feet. Don't fight on ground which suits the opponent, he calculated. Get her out of the house. Talk to her when you've had time to work out what to say and she's had time to calm down. She's obviously upset because you didn't – you were slow to call her. She should understand how busy you are.

Aloud he said, 'It's getting late. Obviously you can't stay here. There's a place in Bamford, The Crown, which has rooms. It's reasonable. Give me a moment to check on Carla. Then I'll drive you there. How are you for cash?'

'Broke,' she said.

'I'll see to that. If you needed money, you should have let me know. What have you done with your allowance?'

'It's not a fortune,' she said scornfully. 'I spent it. I went to a party and needed a proper evening dress. I got a nice one. It cost six hundred quid. But that's not bad, you know. Pretty cheap, really.'

'Not bad?' He goggled at her. 'Six hundred pounds? For a dress you'll probably only wear once?'

'What did you want me to do? Go along to Oxfam and get one for fifteen quid? Never mind the sweat stains under the arms?' She gave a little hiss of exasperation. 'Oh, come on, I got it on sale. Reduced twice, an absolute bargain.'

'Six hundred was the *sale* price? Where on earth did you buy this frock?'

'Gown,' she corrected him. 'Harvey Nichols.'

'Between Oxfam and Knightsbridge,' Andrew said with emotion, 'there are a host of other stores. Middle-of-the-range ones.'

'Selling frumpy old designs, thanks.'

He couldn't win this one. It was a woman's logic. But he didn't mind. He was just relieved that at long last they were squabbling about a trivial subject like a new dress. He got up. 'I'll check on Carla. Wait here.'

He climbed cautiously back upstairs and opened the door of the bedroom a crack. There was no sound. 'Sweetheart? I'm just nipping into Bamford to the off-licence. We're low on gin.'

No reply. The light from the landing, entering the room in a narrow band, illuminated the small bottle on the bedside table. She must have taken one of her pills and they usually sent her off to sleep. She wouldn't wake till morning. Good.

He returned to the kitchen and found with relief that Kate was still there. She was rummaging in the fridge.

'Leave that!' he snapped. 'I'll give you money to buy dinner at The Crown.'

'OK.'

Her tone was careless. She was being more reasonable. She'd wanted to give him a fright and she had. Now she was prepared to be sensible. It was going to be all right. Andrew smiled at her and patted her shoulder.

'You'll be very comfortable at The Crown.'

He realised as soon as they got to the place that he'd been overoptimistic. He'd never frequented The Crown himself, although it was prominently placed in the town centre and you couldn't miss it. He'd always thought it looked quite a nice old place from outside.

Inside, he had second thoughts. It was old, certainly. It had last been fitted out in the mid-thirties, by the look of things. It was the sort of place travelling salesmen stayed – or people whose cars broke down and left them stranded late at night. The reception area was dark and smelled of nicotine and beer fumes from the open door to the bar.

Beside him, Kate was looking around with open disgust on her face. She slung the khaki bag over her shoulder and asked, 'Is this it, then?'

'It's all right. Upstairs is all right,' he said in as positive a tone as he could, bearing in mind he'd never been upstairs in the place.

A youngster, thin-faced and sharp-eyed, clad in black trousers, shirtsleeves, bow tie and fancy waistcoat emerged from the bar, attracted by their voices.

'Good evening, sir, can I help?'

Andrew, already irritated by the sight and smell of the place, was further annoyed by this young man's general air and appearance, particularly by his hair, which stuck up like a porcupine's quills. Andrew snapped, 'I want to book a room! Isn't anyone on duty? Look here, you'll do.'

'Sorry, sir, I'm the barman.' This was accompanied by a sly look as though the youth had guessed Andrew's opinion and was taking a subtle revenge. 'Receptionist will be with you in a tick!'

The barman gave him a brisk nod and cast Kate a longer, more appraising look before returning to duty among the optics and glasses.

'Ignorant young lout . . .' muttered Andrew.

A young girl had at last arrived, wandering out of an office to stand behind the reception desk, staring at them.

Andrew cleared his throat and began again. 'Have you a room free?'

'Double?' she chirped, glancing from him to Kate and back again.

'No, single!'

'Oh, right.' The girl looked mildly surprised. She turned and surveyed a row of keys. 'We only got double left.'

'Then double!' Andrew fairly yelled at her. 'Good God, what's the matter with everyone in this place? Why did you ask if you knew you'd only got a double room?'

She pushed a small printed form towards them. 'Register here, please!' she snapped.

'Let me,' Andrew muttered to Kate. 'I'll register for you. Better not put your name and address.'

Kate shrugged, disdainful. Again he felt humiliated. It was fast becoming a disagreeable habit. Now he wanted to be rid of her company as fast as could decently be arranged.

With officious fingers he took out his wallet and extricated a credit card. 'Charge the room to this card. And everything else, meals and the rest of it.'

The receptionist wrote out the card's number laboriously. Then she turned and unhooked a large, old-fashioned key.

'Number Six, upstairs, first floor, end of the corridor.'

There was no porter at The Crown. You carried your own luggage and tracked down your room yourself. Or perhaps the receptionist was just taking a surly revenge.

He and Kate went up the dark stairs and along the narrow

corridor. The door of Number Six, when they reached it, yielded to the key after a few moments' wrestling with the antiquated lock.

'Seedy!' Kate condemned it, walking in and throwing her bag on the bed.

'It's not bad!' Andrew said defensively.

In all honesty, it could have been a lot worse. It was a large room, with a double bed. They probably had no single rooms thought Andrew vengefully. The girl had just asked on principle.

There was a big, old-fashioned wardrobe, a monster of a TV, a curtained recess with a washbasin. A tray on the table held tea and coffee sachets, pots of UHT milk and an electric kettle. There were two reproductions of Victorian cartoons on the wall, both on a fox-hunting theme. One was entitled 'Riding Out' and showed horse and man setting off, animal full of beans, rider a dandy in a red coat. The other was called 'Walking Home' and showed the same pairing, the horse muddy and dispirited, the man dishevelled and afoot, making their slow way back. Its message mocked Andrew.

'The bathroom must be along the corridor,' he said hastily. He'd vaguely noticed it as they passed. 'But you'll be comfortable enough here. Have dinner here tonight.' He glanced at his watch. 'I dare say they go on serving until nine. Tomorrow I'll meet you in the lounge downstairs around ten thirty, all right? We can have a nice long chat.'

'Sure.' She sat on the edge of the bed and bounced experimentally.

Andrew took out his wallet again. 'Any bill you run up here will go on my card – but here's some cash in case you need it.' He pulled out thirty pounds, all he had on him.

She pocketed it without thanks.

'But you shouldn't need it. I want you to stay in the hotel,' Andrew went on. 'I don't want you wandering around Bamford. It's a strange town to you and you – might get lost or something.'

'You mean, I might meet up with someone in a pub and start telling him all the sordid little details!' She was back in wounding mode.

'I do not mean that. For goodness' sake, Kate! You know I only have your best interests at heart.' He wanted to say 'I love you' but he knew she'd scorn the words. He said, 'You are very, very dear to me.'

She said, very quietly, 'I used to love you. I thought you the most wonderful man in the world.'

Andrew asked, 'Used to?'
But she didn't answer.
He muttered, 'Good night. See you tomorrow!' and hurried out of the room.

Downstairs the receptionist yawned as she watched him stride past. It was a little before eight. She went off duty at eight and the night porter came on. She thought it funny that the fat geezer wasn't staying with his bit on the side. He'd probably got a wife and was hurrying home to her. At The Crown, they'd seen it all before.

As for Andrew, switching on the ignition, he failed, preoccupied as he was, to notice his daily cleaner, Mrs Flack, enter The Crown carrying a biscuit tin. Mrs Flack, her mind on the meeting she was about to attend, didn't see him. If either one of them had spotted the other, it might have led to explanations and made a difference. But there again, it might not.

'The sweaters for Bosnia were very well received,' said Irene Flack. 'What we need now is a summer project.'

The ladies of the Knitting Circle shuffled about and rattled empty cups. There were two digestive biscuits left on a plate but no one was bold-faced enough to take one. They met in one of the private rooms of The Crown which were hired out to any organisation requiring a meeting place. This room, the smallest, was east-facing, chilly and rather dusty. It was used as a store by the hotel, and extra chairs were stacked up one on top of another in unsteady towers around the walls. But it was cheap, central and The Crown provided the tea, all in the cost of hire. The ladies took it in turns to bring in biscuits. Tonight Mrs Flack had brought the digestives and some custard creams. The custard creams had gone first.

Someone offered, 'We could make more blankets. The charities are always asking for blankets and it uses up all the odd wool.'

'I can't face knitting all those squares again,' objected Mrs Warburton. 'Anyway, we all used up our odd bits of wool knitting the last lot.'

'Tea cosies don't seem so welcome nowadays,' said an elderly knitter sorrowfully. 'Such a pity. I have a very pretty pattern, like a crinolined lady. You know, the cosy is the skirt and you send away for the little china lady's body to put in the top.'

'If you've lost all you possess in a Bangladeshi flood,' said Mrs Warburton, 'the last thing you need is a tea cosy.'

Mrs Flack, always the peace-maker, observed, 'Clothes and blankets do seem the most popular with the charities. I did have one little idea.'

They all stared at her, Mrs Warburton combatively.

Irene flushed and uttered the word, 'Layettes.'

There was a silence. Mrs Warburton said slowly, 'Baby clothes. You know, Irene, that's a very good idea. All those refugees seem to have dozens of babies.'

'Babies outgrow their clothes so quickly,' put in another knitter eagerly. 'I've got lots of patterns.'

'Baby wool is a bit pricey.' Mrs Warburton could be relied upon to find a snag, even if she approved the principle.

'You can get it very reasonably in the market, in big bags,' said Mrs Flack. 'We could do the most popular things, matinée jackets, little bonnets.'

'In those hot countries,' asked the eldery knitter, 'do the babies wear woolly bonnets? I should have thought it very bad for their poor little heads.'

Mrs Warburton said she'd seen pictures of babies in Africa, all wearing bonnets. Perhaps it got chilly at night.

'During the day,' suggested someone else, 'the bonnets would keep the sun off. It's very important to keep the sun off babies' heads.'

One way and another it was decided that if the Knitting Circle didn't get to work quickly, the babies of the Third World would be left suffering either from cold or heat, and both sets of circumstances could be dealt with by supplying woolly caps and matinée jackets. Shawls were considered and rejected as being too labour intensive and taking too much wool.

This decided, the meeting came to an end. There was a general move towards clearing up. Someone stacked the cups ready for the hotel to take away. Mrs Flack looked for her biscuit dish and saw that it was now empty. She looked hard at Mrs Warburton, but that lady had a singularly bland expression – and biscuit crumbs lodged in the bow of her ivory crepe blouse.

Irene offered a lift home to any knitter without transport, but Mrs Warburton was taking along the elderly knitter with her, and all the others had someone coming to collect them.

They parted company. It was a quarter past nine.

Irene's little car was old and had recently developed an ominous clank. She hoped it wasn't going to give up the ghost entirely.

She relied on it. She was a widow, living alone in one of the terraced cottages at the edge of town, beyond Tudor Lodge and just before the garage forecourt. It was very convenient to live so near the house where she worked as 'daily housekeeper' to the Penhallows. 'Daily housekeeper' sounded better than 'daily woman', which conjured up an image of scrubbing brushes and Jeyes Fluid. She could walk to work. But walking into town was a tidy step and in bad weather highly unpleasant, which was why she needed the old car. There was no bus.

The car grumbled in its usual way as she turned out of the market square and set off along the main road out of town. The street lighting wasn't all it could be. Luckily there wasn't too much traffic about at this time of night in Bamford. She didn't like driving in traffic. There were few pedestrians, too, because nowadays people didn't walk about much after dark even in this country town. Well, thought Mrs Flack, young people did. But not the older ones, not her generation. None of the Knitting Circle would have dreamed of setting out through dark streets. The thought made her sad because she was a Bamford woman, born and bred. But there you were, it was a sign of the times.

The car was rattling along quite nicely now, filling her with the optimistic hope that the clank didn't mean anything serious. She'd nearly reached Tudor Lodge already. Mrs Flack frowned and peered through the windscreen. Just when she'd been thinking that no one would be out on foot, there was someone who was, walking ahead of her in the same direction as she was travelling, striding out confidently in the darkness. A girl, she could now see, and all alone at this time of night. Mrs Flack tut-tutted to herself. Had she not been nearly home, she might even have stopped and offered the girl a lift although, as a rule, she didn't pick up hitchhikers. One never knew.

She caught up with the girl and took a curious glance at her. Difficult to make her out but definitely young, walking with a light springy step. She had very long hair, trousers or jeans, a jacket of some sort. Mrs Flack overtook her by the gate of Tudor Lodge.

She swept past and reached the terrace of cottages. She lived in the one at the far end and parked her car in a useful piece of open ground between her property and the garage forecourt. She had an idea the ground belonged to the garage, but Harry Sawyer had never objected to her leaving her car there. She was grateful to Harry for this and for keeping her car on the road, always willing to tinker about with it and charging her very little, sometimes nothing.

She got out, locked up carefully, and set off down the pavement to her own front door. She could see ahead, back into Bamford, quite well, what with the lighting from the garage behind her. She really did appreciate the garage being here. Its lights, which stayed on all night, were such a comfort. She was looking for the girl she'd passed near Tudor Lodge. The walker ought to have reached the terraced cottages by now and Mrs Flack was interested to see which one, if any, she went into. But the pavement was empty.

'How odd . . .' she murmured.

Where could the girl have gone? Surely she hadn't managed to get here and indoors so quickly? Mrs Flack glanced mistrustfully at the other three cottages. They all looked well sealed up against the night. Mrs Flack applied a process of elimination.

Old Mrs Joss at the other end of the terrace, the end nearest to Tudor Lodge, went to bed early and never opened the door after dark. The girl couldn't have gone in there. She'd certainly never seen that girl visit her immediate neighbours, with whom Mrs Flack 'didn't get on'. As for the cottage between Mrs Joss and the people with whom Irene didn't get along, that belonged to weekenders, city people who turned up now and again and were not, by the look of the place, there at the moment. It was in darkness and besides, you always knew when they were there because they'd a large red car, very expensive, which they parked outside. The car was protected by an alarm which was always going off in the middle of the night. No mistaking when they were in residence, all right! That left only Tudor Lodge itself and Mrs Flack knew that no young girl was staying there. Mrs Penhallow would have asked her, Mrs Flack, to make up a bed and get everything ready. It was as if the girl had vanished into thin air.

A cool breeze touched Mrs Flack's neck. She shivered and pushed the key into the lock and hurried indoors. She didn't like the idea of strangers wandering about. Still less the inexplicable fashion in which the walking girl had apparently dematerialised. It quite gave her a funny feeling, rather like that very odd experience she'd had out by the Penhallows' back door that night. Mr Penhallow had been very rude about it and inclined to mock in a hurtful way, suggesting she'd had a glass of wine (which, incidentally, she had, but only the one). There'd been someone in the garden that night, she'd been sure of it.

'There are more things,' quoted Mrs Flack uncertainly, 'in heaven and earth than . . . than something.' She didn't know the end of it. Than you reckoned there were, something to that effect.

She put the security chain across and checked all the windows and the back door before she went to bed.

She hadn't retired long, and was still propped on pillows reading her library book, when she heard the cry. Irene, immersed in the story – it had got to a thrilling point – sat up with a jolt of alarm.

She glanced at her bedside clock. The hands had just passed ten. Had she imagined it? She didn't think so. It had definitely been a shout or yell, not near at hand but not so very far away either. She strained her ears but it wasn't repeated. She wondered about the girl she'd seen, but it hadn't sounded like a woman's cry. If it had been a female scream, she'd have got out of bed and called the police. It had been a very odd sort of cry altogether and she wondered briefly if it had been made by a fox. They made odd noises, strangled yelps and shrieks, especially when mating, which they sometimes did in full view of the house, out there in the back garden at night.

She felt resentful. She'd been unsettled on arriving home at the way that girl had vanished, and now this. Her pleasure in her book was spoiled. She closed it carefully on a bookmark and put it on the bedside table. Sliding out of bed, her toes felt for her slippers. She pulled on her old dressing gown and padded over to one of the two windows.

They gave views in different directions. This one overlooked the back of the house and the narrow strip of garden. Thanks to the permanent illumination of Sawyer's garage, it was never quite dark out there. The lawn was a pale carpet on which the shrubs formed blunt black shapes. She could see nothing moving, not even a cat.

Irene, steadily more annoyed, transferred herself to the smaller window in the end wall of the house. It gave her a view of her own car, parked on the spare land, and the garage itself. Behind the garage stood Harry's bungalow. That was in darkness. He lived there alone now. He'd been married but his wife had upped and gone off with a double-glazing salesman, which Irene had found not only immoral but improvident. It seemed to her that a hard-working husband with a bricks-and-mortar business like the garage, ought to have more to offer a woman than a man who went round knocking on folks' doors, trying to sell home improvements no one could afford.

Poor Harry, but he'd got over it. Mostly, thought Irene, by working even harder! Even as she watched, she saw him emerge from the back of the garage's workshop and hurry towards his bungalow. He opened his front door. A light came on inside and she had a brief glimpse of his old dog, wagging its tail, before he disappeared. Working late, poor man, and no wife there to make a cup of tea or get him a bit of supper. She tutted to herself before padding back to her warm bed.

Probably the 'cry' hadn't been any such thing, but a mechanical screech from the direction of the workshop as Harry opened or shut the big metal doors. Or, she thought, if it had been a yell, it very likely came from some late-night film on next door's television. They showed very noisy action films once it got late and the people next door must be deaf, she reckoned, to have the sound turned up like they did. She'd spoken to them about it several times and got a very surly reply. It was one of the reasons they didn't get along. They, too, were members of the Joss clan, a son and grandchildren of old Mrs Joss at the end. The Josses were bad news and always had been.

Or yet again, it might have been further off than she'd thought. Some young men horsing about on their way home from the pubs. It was so quiet out here that any sound carried on the night air. Really, Bamford wasn't the peaceful place it used to be, concluded Mrs Flack, thoroughly put out. But with so many reasons to choose from to explain the disturbance, she was able to dismiss it from her mind.

She snuggled down into the welcome warmth, pulled the blankets over her ears and shut out the unsatisfactory modern world.

Andrew had reached home at eight thirty and put the car in the garage, wondering whether Carla would have heard him drive out or back. He must remember, should she ask, that he was supposed to have been at the off-licence.

But no one called down the stairway as he entered the hall. She must still be asleep. He breathed a sigh of relief and crept upstairs to check on his wife again. Yes, asleep. It looked as if she hadn't moved since he'd looked in earlier.

He would definitely make up a bed in a spare room so as not to disturb her. He went along the landing to the airing cupboard and found sheets and a pillowcase. He decided on Luke's room because there was a duvet on the bed in there. Their son sometimes turned up without announcing his imminent arrival and so they didn't pack the duvet away. Andrew dragged a sheet over the mattress and threw another on top, under the duvet. He couldn't be bothered with a duvet cover. He could never get the wretched things on. The bed felt a bit damp but that was probably only cold. There was a hot-water bottle in the bathroom.

He went along the corridor to the bathroom in question (the main bedroom where Carla lay had ensuite facilities). He showered, feeling much of the stress and strain of mind and body flow away with the hot rain trickling down his body. Securely wrapped up in a towelling robe, he found the water bottle in a cupboard and went downstairs to switch on the kettle to fill this cosy little leftover from an age before central heating, electric blankets and duvets. The activity, being in control, making these simple decisions, organising his bedtime, had restored his equilibrium.

So much so, indeed, that he went to the little sitting room which they called the 'TV room' because it was a refuge for anyone who wanted to watch a programme when others preferred to sit and chat or play cards. It had come into being when Luke had been younger and given to watching endless car-chase and tough-cop series. His parents had exiled him here. Then Andrew had discovered how useful it was when he wanted to watch something political, undisturbed. He'd installed a small drinks cabinet and went to it now to pour a nightcap. He switched on the TV intending to watch *News at Ten* as he sipped his malt. Soon he found his head was nodding. It had been a tiring day. He switched off the television and made for the kitchen.

There his lightened mood was immediately dashed by the sight of the two empty teacups which reminded him of his visitor. He hoped she would have had the sense to stay in The Crown. He thought it unlikely that she would wander round town, seeing it was so late and not a pleasant night. On the other hand, thought Andrew uneasily, she might have decided to go down to the hotel's bar. He remembered the sharp-faced youth with the fancy waistcoat. That barman, he was the sort who'd chat up a pretty girl like Kate, wanting to know all about her.

He glanced at the mobile phone lying on the kitchen dresser and wondered whether to call The Crown. But if he checked on her, she'd be furious – and let's face it, he didn't need her angrier than she already was.

'Though why she's in such a wretched bad mood, I don't know!' he muttered.

The cake, or most of it, still lay uneaten on his plate. He didn't fancy it now. He picked it up and tipped it into the waste-bin. He left the cups. Mrs Flack could wash them in the morning.

The kettle boiled. Andrew filled his bottle, and with it glowing warm and comforting in his arms, went towards the door into the hall. He stretched out his hand to the light switch, reminding himself as he did that he must remember to set the burglar alarm which was at the foot of the stairs. It was as he was like that, with his hand just touching the light switch but not yet having flicked it off, that his attention was unexpectedly taken.

Someone tapped urgently at the back door.

Andrew whirled round, hardly able to believe his ears. Not again? Such was his disbelief that for a moment he didn't move. Then anger swept over him. He should have known she wasn't in the mood to do as she was told. He marched to the door and threw it open. The cool night air rushed in as he stared out.

'Look here!' he snapped. 'You can just bloody well go back where you came from!'

There was no reply and there was no one there. Had he imagined it? Andrew stepped out into the back garden, hesitating. He wasn't dressed for the chill outdoors. Dew had already formed on the grass and seeped through his slippers, striking cold on his bare feet. It was underlined by the warmth of the rubber bottle which he still clasped as he moved unhappily a little further into the darkness. He peered about him.

'Kate? If you're there, show yourself. We can go indoors and talk it through if you insist. But stop playing around like this. I'll get bloody pneumonia!'

Too late he heard a movement behind him. A heavy object smashed into the back of his skull. The rubber bottle fell to the ground and bounced. Andrew uttered a high-pitched shriek which was less a cry of surprise, fear or pain, than the rush of air expelled from his lungs. Then he fell forward in a dead weight on to the dampening grass.

He was dazed but still conscious, *compos mentis* enough to realise he was under attack but momentarily unable to do anything about it. He lay on the wet turf, moaning. Whoever had assailed him was coming closer. He knew he ought to do something about it, defend himself. Yet he could only think this must be some horrible mistake. A form was bending over him. He opened his eyes, seeing only a vague dark shape against the indigo night sky. He raised an arm with superhuman effort and held it weakly, uselessly, between himself and his assailant.

He managed to whisper, 'Stop – please – you've got it wrong—'

because he was still convinced in a muddled way that this was a mistake and the other person hadn't realised it yet.

Then another blow smashed into his temple, triggering a firework display of coloured lights accompanied by searing pain. He knew then it was no mistake. That this was intended and it wasn't finished. It wouldn't finish until he was dead. Shock, pain, a dulling of his senses, all paralysed him. A fog was gathering inside his head. Too late he rallied and in one last desperate effort tried to roll aside. Another blow cut short his pitiable attempt at escape. Face down, wet grass stalks rubbing against his teeth, fingers clawing at the ground, he uttered a last, mumbling groan before a final blow obliterated consciousness for ever.

CHAPTER FOUR

Alan Markby put his hand on the gate of Tudor Lodge and hesitated. The scene ahead of him wasn't unfamiliar. In fact, it was all too familiar. At the house itself shutters and curtains had been drawn across, at least overlooking the street, in the traditional sign of a death in the house. In these prying days it was also an indication of a desire for privacy, to be spared the intrusive lens of the news photographer, the grimacing face of the reporter brandishing his notebook or tape recorder.

There were a few of *them*, he'd already noted with disapproval, hanging about in the street. They did so in the manner of seasoned hacks. Lord alone knew how they'd got the news so fast. A local stringer probably, phoning through. They clustered in small groups, sipping hot drinks from vacuum flasks, munching thick sandwiches and gossiping, all the while keeping a sharp eye open for signs of any newsworthy development. Each of them was under pressure to take back a story. The human angle. The curious detail. Above all, the macabre. The public loved to feel its skin crawl.

A little further down the road, by some cottages, a private ambulance waited discreetly.

One or two overoptimistic souls among the waiting journalists had dared to hail Markby as he got out of his car. He'd dealt with them firmly and courteously in practised manner. They accepted his refusal to talk without too much fuss. They were aware, in any case, that having just arrived he knew little more than they did. The time to ambush him would be later, when he left. He had recognised at least one of them as being from a top-circulation broadsheet. That would be because of the political angle. The rest he judged tabloid men. That was because they scented scandal.

Markby sighed and pushed open the gate. It creaked teeth-grindingly as if sharing his mood. It was a little after ten in the morning. The sun was shining fitfully from behind scudding clouds. They might get a little rain later. They could do with it. The gardens were dry. He glanced at this one. Ground rock-hard, which meant little chance of footprints. Otherwise the garden gave the air of being adequately kept. The lawns to either side of the narrow path were neat. There were some shrubs, the low-maintenance sort. Up at the house, either side of the front door, were wooden troughs which, he guessed, would be filled with potted flowers once the danger of frost was over.

All this neatness was spoiled by the tracks which, despite the unyielding soil, had been made by the passage and repassage of feet and equipment since early light. The turf, not yet recovered from winter, was now bruised and scarred with a visible path leading round the side of the house. He followed it, ducking under the blue and white plastic tape which had been tied from a post driven into the ground at the corner of the house, across the lawn to the front railings, signifying that beyond that lay police business and the public should keep out.

As he rounded the house into the back garden, he heard voices. There was another lawn here, running away into the distance and surrounded by a high, old dry-stone wall. Overgrown shrubs clustered in dark, cobwebby clumps at the base of the wall. Three or four well-established plum trees, probably donkey's years old by Markby's judgement, spread their branches over a cluster of figures around a white tent. Markby experienced a moment's nostalgia, remembering, as a child, being allowed to camp out of a summer night in a relative's orchard. A uniformed constable holding a mug saw him coming and dithered with his coffee before setting it down by one of the trees and coming to meet him.

'Good morning,' Markby greeted him, producing his identification. He didn't know this young man, and by like token, the young officer wouldn't know him by sight, though probably by reputation.

'Morning, sir!' The youngster straightened his slouching stance. 'Inspector Pearce is in there.' He pointed self-consciously at the tent. He had limited experience, and had been on the scene of some fatal accidents before now but never on the scene of an out-and-out murder. He knew the drill, of course, but couldn't quite repress his excitement. His gesture tentwards was overdramatic and owed something to television.

'The doc's been and gone,' he added.

'Scene-of-crime crew here?'

'Yessir, and Detective Sergeant Prescott.'

And Uncle Tom Cobbleigh and all. Mustn't be flippant, Markby thought. But he wasn't joking. He was steeling himself. This one was going to be nasty.

Markby made his way to the tent, pushed aside the flap, ducked his head and went inside.

'Hullo, sir,' Pearce greeted him. 'Just waiting for the taskforce to arrive to search the grounds. Looks like he died here though, where he fell. Blunt instrument. No sign yet of a weapon.'

It was a bit of a crush in the tent. The floorspace was taken up mostly by the body, decently covered now with a sheet. Sergeant Prescott, the third person present, was a large young man and Dave Pearce fairly sturdy. With Markby's arrival one of them risked trampling on the deceased. Prescott cleared his throat tactfully.

'Morning, sir. I'll just wait outside, shall I?'

The tent heaved and shook and threatened to collapse around them and the body. Pearce half raised an arm as if to ward off falling canvas. Luckily Prescott extricated himself without disaster. Once he was gone, the other two shifted around and made themselves marginally more comfortable.

'Deceased is Andrew Penhallow, owner of the house,' Pearce began. 'Mrs Penhallow suffers from migraine, apparently. She had a turn of it last night and went to bed early, dosed up to the eyeballs with sleeping pills. Slept like a log all night and didn't realise her husband hadn't come to bed until she woke up this morning. That was around seven thirty. She got up and searched the house for him. Then came out here in the garden and found him like that. She didn't hear a thing, but then she wouldn't, she says. Knocked out by drugs. Nuisance, that.'

Markby reflected that for the murderer, it had been highly convenient.

'Let's have a look, then.' He stooped and turned back the sheet.

It was Andrew Penhallow, all right. He lay face down. One arm was doubled beneath him. The other lay slightly outstretched. He was wearing a towelling dressing gown and had been wearing slippers but they'd fallen off and lay some distance away. His bare white feet showed broken veins at the ankle and a couple of corns. Feet, hands, elbows . . . they always show up someone's age, thought Markby ruefully.

The hair at the back of the dead man's head was matted with gore. More dried blood and bone had already formed a sticky crust over another wound on the temple. A small black beetle had slipped under the sheeting and was crawling towards the moist scab, feelers waving. Markby stretched out his hand and flipped the insect away with his fingernail. In stooping to do this, he came in closer proximity to the corpse and the acrid stench of stale urine struck his nostrils. Death accorded no dignity, he thought. He dropped the sheet back.

'Looks as if he'd been on his way to bed when something caused him to come outside here,' Pearce said. 'We found a full hot-water bottle nearby, as if he'd been carrying it when he was struck. The water in it was stone-cold when found. I reckon three or four blows.'

The superintendent only grunted, peering at the battered head. 'We'll have to await the post-mortem report to find out whether he was killed outright or whether he might have been saved if he'd been found in time.'

'One blow could've hit the spot. Lucky, as it were,' said Pearce, and then obviously realised, to his dismay, that 'lucky' was hardly the best word to have chosen. He hurried on, before the superintendent could chide him, 'He might have bled to death.'

'He certainly bled profusely,' Markby retorted.

Pearce realised he was being warned not to anticipate the post-mortem examination. He gave a rueful nod of assent.

Markby hadn't missed the unfortunate use of 'lucky' earlier, but there was no point in jumping down Dave's throat over it. Dave wasn't callous by nature. He'd just spoken carelessly.

'Who identified the body?' Markby asked. Used as he was to sights like this, he found this one particularly repulsive as he'd feared he would. He kept his voice deliberately neutral.

'His doctor, Pringle. He was called to Mrs Penhallow and he stayed to confirm death for us.'

'Who called him to Mrs Penhallow? You?'

Pearce shook his head. 'The cleaning woman. She arrived after Mrs P found her husband's body. It was between seven thirty and a quarter to eight this morning that the cleaner turned up. She's called Mrs Flack and says Mrs Penhallow was sitting on the lawn by the body, just wailing and screaming in a terrible state. She tried to get her indoors but failed, so ran and phoned the doctor. After that she phoned the police. She seems a sensible sort of woman, kept her head. She also confirms that it's Penhallow.'

'OK. They can take him away.' This time Markby's voice wavered slightly, betraying how shaken he was inwardly. He'd seen enough dead bodies, many in worse condition than this one. But Penhallow had been a contemporary many years ago in his schooldays, and his death stirred distant, poignant memories. *I knew him, Horatio . . .*

The loss of those of your own generation, those close to you whom

42

you've seen grow up, does more than arouse a natural sorrow. It stirs a deep-seated awareness of mortality. Markby wasn't immune to it. He thought, Damn, who'd have ever imagined Penhallow would've ended like this? He was such a harmless blighter as a kid.

Pearce had put his head out of the tent to relay the order to the constable, who set off importantly to the private ambulance down the road.

'We took a look at the windows and doors of the house for signs of anyone trying to break in,' Pearce said. 'Didn't find anything. The place does have a security system but it wasn't switched on. He probably meant to switch it on when he went to bed. What puzzles me is that he was struck from behind. If he came out here to investigate something he'd heard or even glimpsed through the window, and then confronted the hypothetical visitor, I'd expect him to be struck from the front. A fleeing intruder wouldn't be likely to come up and hit him from behind. He'd just run like the clappers to get out of the garden before the householder saw him. Or he might knock him over and then scarper. He wouldn't stay to bash his head repeatedly.'

There was sound of movement outside. By common accord the men in the tent removed themselves and let the morticians take the body of Andrew Penhallow from his own garden with as much dignity as was possible in the circumstances.

They watched it go in silence, eventually broken by Markby who said, 'I knew him slightly. That is to say, I was at school with him.'

Consternation showed on Pearce's face. 'Oh, sorry, sir. Didn't realise he was a friend of yours. Nasty for you.'

'I can't say he was a friend.' Markby's respect for words extended to the term 'friend'. He didn't like to hear it bandied around and used when all that was meant was 'colleague' or 'acquaintance'. It indicated a degree of intimacy which didn't exist and could lead to mistaken assumptions, as had Pearce's use of 'bled to death' ahead of the autopsy findings.

'He was just someone I knew – and had known for a long time, but never closely. I took a marginal interest in his career as you do when you hear about someone you remember as a spotty teenager. A very bright kid, mind you.' Markby cast his mind back and conjured up a fuzzy image of a pasty youngster with spectacles. 'Not much good at games.' He'd told Meredith that. Funny how one remembered such things.

'Bit of a swot, eh? What was his line, I mean his profession?'

'He was a recognised authority on international law. He worked in Brussels, at the European Commission. He travelled back and forth a lot. It didn't, I suppose, leave him much time for a social life in this country.'

This, too, struck a familiar, poignant note. Markby reminisced, 'Though he wasn't good at sports, he always tried. Pity really. Sports are always a road to popularity. I don't think Penhallow had many close pals even back then. But he was liked well enough – tolerated, I suppose. No one ragged him more than most or gave him a bad time. I wasn't surprised he took up the law. He was a pedantic sort of youngster. He might not have been much good at games but he knew all the rules, even the most obscure. But then, in my day, it was the sort of school which turned out a lot of lawyers and parsons.'

Pearce privately considered that living it up in Brussels must be a desirable exchange for Bamford's nightlife. He reflected that at the school he'd attended, if even one of the pupils had made it to either of the professions named, it'd have made headlines in the local paper.

The superintendent was saying briskly, 'Our paths didn't cross much over the last few years. As I said, he was away from home a lot. I saw him occasionally as I still live in Bamford and it's a small town. Meredith, Miss Mitchell, knows Carla Penhallow, his wife. She – Carla – is quite well known. You may have seen her on the telly. She's a chemist by training, but does those popular science programmes and had written several books along the same lines.'

Pearce asked awkwardly, 'I suppose we know the lady's suffered migraine attacks before?'

It was a perfectly legitimate query and one which would have to be followed up. But Markby was able to say, 'I'd heard Carla suffered from migraines. Meredith mentioned to me that she'd read an article on the affliction by Carla Penhallow in some women's magazine. You could check with her doctor. Have you seen her?'

'Only to introduce myself,' Pearce admitted. 'She'd calmed down a bit but wasn't up to answering questions. I thought she looked familiar and now you mention it, I remember seeing her on the box.' Pearce paused before adding courteously, 'I dare say she might be able to answer a few questions now, if you'd like to go and see her, sir.'

Markby reflected wryly that Pearce seemed doomed to pick the wrong words this morning. 'Like', for example, wasn't quite the word he'd have chosen in the circumstances. But he certainly ought to speak to Andrew's wife himself, if only to express his personal shock and condolences, and not leave it to someone else. Carla would appreciate that – and certainly think it odd if he didn't. He looked towards the house. 'Anyone else at home, other than Mrs Penhallow?'

'The cleaner, Mrs Flack. That's all, no other family. There's a son but he's away from home at the moment. He's been informed.'

A distant discreet purr marked the ambulance engine starting up. Sergeant Prescott, who had taken himself off on his own line of inquiry, was approaching them.

'One of the undertakers,' he said diffidently, 'has been chatting to an old woman down at the cottages, while he waited.'

'Chatting?' snapped Inspector Pearce suspiciously.

'She came out and offered them some tea,' Prescott explained. 'And then she said, amongst a lot of general oh-dear and how-dreadful, that there was a lot of to-ing and fro-ing from Tudor Lodge last night. She knows because she turns in early but her bedroom has a little window which overlooks the gardens here. It's a row of terrace houses, as you'll see, and this woman's – a Mrs Joss – hers is the end one nearest Tudor Lodge. When cars turn in or out of Tudor Lodge's garage drive, the headlights sweep across her window, so that's how she knows. I thought I'd go and have a word with her in a minute.'

Markby nodded. 'Yes, but watch out for the press. Work your way round the back of the cottages, if you can – oh, and tell Mrs Joss not to "chat" to anyone else!'

Prescott strode athletically across the lawn. Inactivity was anathema to him.

Markby made his own way slowly towards the back door of the house.

The taskforce hurriedly put together to search the grounds had arrived by now and were being briefed by Pearce. Markby raised a hand to tap at the kitchen door, changed his mind, and went to the window alongside it. He peered through.

The kitchen appeared to be empty. It was a large, old-fashioned room with heavy wooden dressers and shelves, but with an ultra-modern stove of traditional type plus a microwave oven, also a dishwasher. There were the usual bits and pieces hanging around: bunches of dried herbs and flowers, antique serving dishes fixed to the walls. There was a touch of *Homes & Gardens* about it all. That look cost money. But no one would doubt the people who lived here had money. The house would be a natural target for a burglar.

Markby was about to leave the window when his eye was caught by a streak of colour on a straggling hebe bush growing against the wall. He stooped and took a closer look. A thread of yellow woollen fibre had snagged on a twig.

He walked back to Pearce and asked, 'Seen this?'

Pearce came to view the thread. 'Doesn't look as if it's been there long, does it? I'll get it bagged up. The windowsill and the glass have been dusted for prints.'

There was a movement behind the glass panes as he spoke and they both looked up guiltily. A middle-aged woman now stood in the kitchen and looked out at them. She raised her eyebrows.

'The cleaner,' murmured Pearce.

'I'll leave you to your job,' Markby replied, and moved towards the back door.

It opened to admit him before he knocked. He smiled at the woman and asked, 'Mrs Flack?'

'Yes,' she retorted briskly. 'And you're Chief Inspector Markby who used to be in charge over at Bamford. Have you come back again?'

He interpreted this as meaning had he returned to his old job, not had he returned to this house. He explained diffidently that he now ranked superintendent and worked from Regional HQ.

'Hmm,' said Mrs Flack, casting a shrewd glance over him as she digested the news of his promotion. 'Well, I'm glad it's you, anyway, because she's in a terrible state and she needs careful handling. At least you'll be polite, I dare hope.'

Mrs Flack didn't appear to have a great opinion of the ways of the constabulary, reflected Markby.

He edged into the kitchen, murmuring, 'How is she?'

'I've just been up to see her. She's lying down. She's stopped that awful wailing. But she's not herself – well, you wouldn't expect it, would you?' Mrs Flack's gaze met his defiantly.

'Mind if I sit down?' Markby sat down before Mrs Flack denied him the chance. 'Perhaps, before I have a word with Car— with Mrs Penhallow, you could spare me a moment or two?'

'I don't know anything about it!' She stared at him, shocked. 'He was as dead as mutton when I got here this morning, laid out there on the lawn, all covered in dew. He must've been there all night, poor soul. And she was sitting beside him in her nightgown, might've caught pneumonia, and carrying on something terrible. It frightened me. I thought she'd gone right out of her mind so I ran in and called Dr Pringle. Then I called the police,' she added.

'That was very clear-headed of you.'

The compliment mollified her but she was an honest woman. 'Dr Pringle told me to do it.'

'But I dare say you'd have done so, anyway. Was the electric light on here in the kitchen when you arrived?'

She nodded. 'Yes. Very dark kitchen this, of a morning. Even in midsummer it's on the gloomy side. It's all those trees out in the garden. They take the light away.'

So he'd have to ask Carla whether the kitchen light had been on that morning when she'd come downstairs or whether she'd switched it on. He didn't relish asking Carla about anything, not if she were in the state described by Mrs Flack. Probably she wouldn't remember details.

'Perhaps you could tell me something about the routine of the house, Mrs Flack.' he said. 'What, for example, is the exact nature of your employment?'

Mrs Flack sat down in a wooden Windsor chair and folded her hands in her lap. She wore a pink checked overall and sensible shoes. Her hair was permed and tidy and had been, he guessed, treated to a colour rinse. It was a foxy brown-red.

'I'm daily housekeeper,' she said firmly. 'Not daily woman, that's different.'

'I understand,' he said humbly.

She nodded. 'I come in every day at seven thirty and I get the breakfast. Not that Mrs Penhallow eats much breakfast, but if Mr—' She faltered slightly at the prospect of talking of her late employer, but pulled herself together. 'If Mr Penhallow or the young fellow, their son, were here, I'd cook a bit of bacon. Mrs Penhallow has fruit and yoghurt. Then I wash up the breakfast things—'

Markby's gaze drifted to the dishwasher. Mrs Flack said loudly, 'I don't bother with that contraption. What's wrong with a bowl of hot water and a good washing-up liquid?'

'Nothing!' Markby was reminded of his old nanny. There'd been no arguing with her, either.

'Then I load up the washing machine, make the beds, dust, put the Hoover round . . .' Mrs Flack listed these domestic chores rapidly.

'Cook lunch?' he asked.

She shook her head. 'Not what I'd call a proper lunch. Often there's no one here to eat it anyway. Mrs Penhallow goes up to London a lot. Mr Penhallow is – was – away on the Continent and the boy is a student. But if Mrs Penhallow is here, I make a simple lunch, salad or a home-made soup. I make a good soup.' She paused for this to be appreciated and he nodded. 'Then I clear it away. Do a bit of ironing, maybe. If Mrs Penhallow is home, I might bake a batch of little cakes and then, four o'clock, I take her a cup of tea and after that, I go home.' She pointed across the room over his shoulder and explained this puzzling gesture with, 'I live down in the terrace. It's only a step.'

'You're never here of an evening?'

'If there's company I come in extra.'

'And cook?'

She shook her head with a touch of regret. 'More to keep an eye on things. They like that fancy dinner party stuff and get caterers to bring it in. What it costs I wouldn't like to think and you've got strangers meddling in your kitchen. I'm a plain cook and not a bad one, but Mrs Penhallow's never asked me to cook, not proper meals. For day-to-day, she buys a lot of frozen stuff, what you just pop in that microwave oven. It's a very expensive way of doing things, to my mind, nearly as bad as those caterers, and I often wonder whether it's really healthy.' She seemed to reflect this sounded like criticism of her employer and pressed her lips together before going on, 'I didn't come in last night. I had no cause to. Last night,' said Mrs Flack, raising her voice slightly, 'was my knitting circle and you can check that. Several people saw me there.'

Markby hid a smile. Clearly Mrs Flack believed that everyone in the vicinity of a murder was immediately asked by the police to provide an alibi.

All the same, despite her insistence on an evening innocently spent, he sensed Mrs Flack had suddenly become uneasy. It was as if something had jogged her memory. So, thought Markby, what new element had been introduced to the conversation?

'Fine,' he said. 'Ah, what time did you get back from your knitting circle?'

Now she was visibly ill at ease. 'It'd be around half-past nine. We meet at The Crown.' Lest he should think this indicated a night carousing, she added hastily, 'In one of the upstairs rooms. They provide tea for us. That's all. We take our own biscuits.'

'And you walked back? It's a long way.'

'No, I drove my little car.' She fell silent. With her right hand she began to fiddle with the wedding ring on her left third finger.

Markby asked gently, 'And you saw something odd as you passed Tudor Lodge?' It was a leading question and a barrister wouldn't be allowed to put it in court, but there was something this woman wanted to tell him. She didn't know how to begin and needed urging.

Now she leaned forward and began in a rush, 'Well, now you mention it, I'd forgotten – what with all the trouble this morning and the police coming and everything. Perhaps it's nothing. It will sound silly and I'm not a silly woman—'

'No, you're a very sensible person and that's why I'd like to hear anything you can tell us,' he interrupted.

'Oh well, then . . .' She smoothed her apron. 'It's two things. I mean, I saw one and heard one, but not at the same time. The thing I saw, it was a girl. She was walking along the pavement, so late at night and all by herself! I passed her in my car just before I got to Tudor Lodge. When I got home, I looked back, but I couldn't see her. She'd vanished. I did wonder, well, if she'd turned in here.'

Markby concealed a rush of interest. Careful now, don't put her off. 'Can you describe this girl?'

But Mrs Flack was doubtful. 'I only caught a glimpse. Long hair and wearing trousers or jeans. She walked very straight, confident. But why? Why would she come calling so late? She wasn't staying here, I'd know about that. Although—'

She looked flustered. 'Mrs Penhallow hadn't asked me to make up a bed. But someone had made up a bed in young Luke's room. I looked in there this morning, the door was open, and someone had put sheets . . . but I thought maybe Mr Penhallow. If he came home late, or if she had one of her bad heads, he sometimes slept in another room. And she did have a bad head last night. She told us so this morning. She took her sleeping pills and didn't hear—' Mrs Flack fell silent and pulled out a handkerchief from her overall pocket.

'And what was the other thing?' asked Markby sympathetically, as she dabbed at her eyes.

'What?' She blinked and put away the handkerchief. 'Oh yes, I'd gone on to bed and I heard a funny yell. Not a proper scream but a shout of some sort. I thought it might be next door's telly, or foxes, or just lads larking about in town. It'd be just after ten. I looked at my alarm clock.'

Markby considered this. Prescott would have to ask at the terraced cottages whether anyone else had heard anything. Returning to the matter of the girl, he asked, 'There's no sign of a visitor's luggage upstairs? Or of anyone else being in the house?'

Again she paused, then shook her head firmly. 'No luggage. But – well, there were two cups on the table here this morning. But I thought Mr Penhallow had made tea for himself and Mrs Penhallow.'

With sinking heart, Markby asked, 'Where are the cups now?'

'Washed up,' she declared as he'd guessed she would. 'I don't leave dirty crocks lying about my kitchen, no matter what's going on!'

More's the pity, he thought, but didn't say. Yet the woman still looked ill at ease as if there was something she wanted to get off her chest, but hesitated to put into words for fear of what? Disbelief? Ridicule?

He leaned forward again. 'Is something else worrying you, Mrs Flack?'

She threw him a look which was part guilt and part relief. 'You said I was sensible just now,' she said. 'I wouldn't want to spoil your good opinion of me.' She gave a nervous, girlish giggle.

'Nothing you'd say will do that,' he told her.

She flushed. 'Well, the thing is – just for the moment I had such a silly idea. The way the girl just – just vanished. You see, there's an old story, about this house . . .'

'Ah!' he exclaimed. 'The ghost! As a matter of fact, someone was telling me about that only recently.'

'You've heard it?' She was clearly pleased. 'Then I don't have to explain. Of course, normally I don't pay any attention to old yarns, superstitions. I'm a practical sort of body myself. But you can't help it sometimes. There was one evening when I'd stayed late to help out because the Penhallows had a big dinner party. I went outside here to the dustbin around nine o'clock and I could've sworn there was someone standing right behind me. But when I turned round, there was nothing. Yet it was so real.' She shook her head. 'Mr Penhallow, he just made fun of me when I told him.'

Markby sat back and considered this. 'How long ago did this happen?'

'Must be at least six months. Let's see, it was last October if I recall right. Yes, because it was coming up Hallowe'en and Mr Penhallow did say if anyone was out there it'd be kids playing a prank. But no kids come right out here. It's miles from any housing estates or what you'd call residential areas. Anyway, they jump out and shout, "Trick or treat!" They don't go fading away into nothing.'

They sat in silence for a moment. Then Mrs Flack asked, 'Would you like me to go up and see how Mrs Penhallow's doing now? She might be able to talk to you.'

Markby stirred. 'Yes, thank you. Tell her it's Alan Markby. She has met me before.'

Mrs Flack got up and hurried out. He could hear her climbing the stairs and calling out, 'Mrs Penhallow, dear? Are you fit for a visitor? It's a gentleman you know . . .'

He repressed a wry smile. Unintentionally Mrs Flack had veiled her words with innuendo and made his call sound seedy. He looked around the kitchen, interested to see it closer to hand. Mrs Flack didn't cook of an evening and from the sound of it neither did Carla, or very little. But if Andrew had been away so much on EU business, she and the boy, Luke, had probably made do with simple meals on a tray for much of the time.

For the occasional grand dinner party, according to Mrs Flack, the housekeeper was called back as extra help but only, it seemed, to supervise the professional caterers. Otherwise Carla made good use of the microwave and there were plenty of ready-made dinners available for that. Yet there was a forest of culinary aids hanging from hooks on the wall, every kind of mixer, masher, scraper, peeler, corkscrew and slice. A large, expensive and up-to-date food processor stood on a worktop. Glossy cookbooks were stacked neatly nearby and all of it, it seemed, for show. The cookbooks didn't look as if they'd been disturbed or opened in a long time. The processor appeared hardly used. It still had a shop-new gleam to it. Meals here probably veered between something on toast and beef Wellington, according to circumstances. It occurred to him to wonder just what sort of a family life the Penhallows had led.

Mrs Flack was returning. 'She's coming downstairs, sir.' She took up position by the door into the hall and made a formal gesture. 'Will you come through, sir? She'll receive you in the drawing room.'

The proprieties, after all, were to be observed.

CHAPTER FIVE

Markby stood on the drawing-room threshold and saw that Mrs Flack had managed some adroit manoeuvring. Carla Penhallow had arrived before him. First encounter with the bereaved was always difficult and this time personal acquaintance hindered rather than helped. Consequently he was left a stranded, embarrassed observer of the scene before him.

The curtains had been drawn creating a twilit gloom at mid-morning. To compensate for the loss of daylight a table lamp had been switched on. Its muted glow, through a heavy, old-fashioned parchment shade on an onyx base, illuminated deep-cushioned sofa and chairs upholstered in a cornflower-blue cretonne with a floral design. His gaze took in a Victorian card table, piano, several family photos in expensive frames and a painting hanging above the hearth.

The scene, in oils, was by an above-average though not, to his eye, outstanding artist. It depicted fishing boats crammed in a tiny harbour against a background of cluttered white-washed cottages and overhanging hillsides. A community clinging to the land and making its living from the sea. Although nowadays probably making its living from tourism, Markby thought wryly. The painting radiated that peculiar light which identified the location as Cornwall.

In these comfortable surroundings, Andrew's widow, as he had to think of her, was standing by the window, half turned away from him. She appeared to be looking at, rather than through, a gap in the drawn velvet curtains. Had she looked through, she'd have seen the garden where the diligent search was being conducted for the weapon which had killed her husband. He guessed she saw nothing. She was lost in her misery and oblivious to all else, even to his arrival.

He cleared his throat. She started, then turned and came quickly towards him, holding out both hands.

'Oh, Alan!'

He gripped her outstretched fingers in a manner he hoped was

53

reassuring and sympathetic. 'I'm very sorry, Carla.' Her fingers were ice-cold and her gold wedding band and another ring with a large square-cut emerald pressed into his flesh.

She detached herself and made an effort at self-control. She was dressed in tan wool trousers and a beige knitted top. The sweater hung loosely on her thin frame. Her face was drawn with despair and her short-cut hair, which contributed to her well-known elfin looks, stuck up like a schoolboy's. She wore no make-up. He supposed her forty-five, but even in her distress she'd pass easily for thirty-something. She wasn't a beautiful woman or even a conventionally pretty one, but she had the sort of face which attracted instant attention and, once seen, was not easily forgotten.

'I'm so glad it's you,' she said almost inaudibly but with a heart-wrenching dignity. 'Andrew would have wished for you to come.'

He felt he had to put the record straight before they went any further. 'I'm glad I was able to come but I can't claim the decision was mine. I was on hand when the call came in. I'm in charge for the time being. But I – I may have to hand over to someone else at a later date. Because I knew him – know you both.'

There had been a brief, hurried phone conversation with the chief constable. 'You knew the man, Alan, and it may help us. On the other hand, if things get close to home, you're aware how it is – your knowing him will hinder things. I'll rely on you to decide if it's time to hand over to someone else.'

'I didn't know him all that well,' Markby had replied. 'Since we were kids I must have seen him a dozen or so times. I know he had a house in Bamford but he was seldom in it. Anyway, I don't know why, but we just didn't keep up the acquaintance.'

'There's a security aspect, too,' the chief constable said gloomily. 'Though terrorists generally like bullets and bombs, not blunt instruments. But we mustn't forget he was an EU mandarin and, of course, the European Union arouses quite a bit of passion these days. Fishermen, beef farmers, small businessmen – they've all got an axe to grind. These Eurocrats give the impression of living off the fat of the land at our expense, but when it's *our* lives, they can appear unsympathetic. It's all rules and regulations with them, everything done by the book according to fifty subclauses in small print.'

'It's getting that way with police work,' Markby had replied.

He heard the chief snort derisively. 'Tell me about it! Do your best.'

* * *

Now, not wishing to sound overofficial and soulless, Markby said, 'We'll get to the bottom of this, Carla. I hope we won't have to cause you too much distress and upheaval. But there will be a certain amount. It's unavoidable. I – and my officers – will have to ask questions, some of them very personal. All investigations are cruel intrusions into private lives.'

'A murder,' she said, 'is a cruel intrusion by its very nature, isn't it?'

That threw him momentarily and he could only nod.

She moved away and stooped to take a cigarette from a small brass box on a table. She turned towards him, holding out the open box.

He shook his head. 'Thanks. I haven't smoked in fifteen years.'

She returned the box to the table and lit her own cigarette. Drawing on it, she said, 'Andrew wanted me to give up. I had cut down. Right now, I don't care what it's doing to my lungs. Don't you ever long for a cigarette, Alan, even after fifteen years? In your job, you must have many stressful moments.'

He was obliged to be honest. 'Yes, sometimes I think I'd like a smoke. But I don't feel it so strongly I've ever given in and lit up. I've got used to not smoking, put it that way. I don't want to start again.'

She sank down on a soft-cushioned armchair and indicated he should take the matching chair opposite. 'I saw the little ambulance leave. That was – they were taking him away?'

'Yes.'

'And there'll be an autopsy? Yes, of course there will be. You must forgive me if I talk a lot of rubbish. My head's all over the place. Will they, I mean, before we get him back to bury him, will they – tidy him up again?'

'They'll do a good job.' He hesitated. 'I can come back later, Carla.'

She shook her head firmly. 'No. I want to talk. I need to talk to someone. It'll stop me worrying about Luke.'

'Your son?' he raised his eyebrows. 'What's wrong with him?'

'Nothing, only that he's driving down here from Cambridge. They've not told him his father is dead, only that there's been a incident. I just hope he's driving carefully and not going hell for leather, risking an accident or losing his licence or anything. I'll be so pleased when he gets here safe and sound. But poor boy, it will be such a terrible thing to find . . .'

She leaned over the arm of the chair and stubbed out the half-smoked cigarette. 'Bloody migraine,' she said.

'You're still suffering?'

'No, not now. But I was, last night. I went up to town, to London I mean, yesterday, for a business meeting over lunch. We're discussing a new series for TV. The last series went well but we don't want just to repeat the old formula—' She broke off and grimaced. 'Listen, still talking shop at a time like this! Is that the sign of an entrenched old hack or what?'

'Not an old hack. Meredith watched your last series and told me at the time how much she enjoyed it.'

'Thanks. All unsolicited testimonials welcome. The thing is, someone had ordered the lunch beforehand and it was fine until the pud and that turned out to be chocolate mousse. Chocolate is one of the foodstuffs which trigger my migraine and I try to avoid it. But we were all talking and before I knew it, the waitress had plonked down this mousse in front of me. It was only a dinky little glass bowl of the stuff so I thought it'd be all right and I ate it. The migraine started on my way home. Luckily I wasn't driving. I took a cab back from the station, staggered upstairs and just fell on the bed. And there I stayed . . .'

She put her hands over her face. In the silence which followed, a phone could be heard ringing. After a while, it was answered by a man. He guessed Pearce had told Mrs Flack to leave answering all phone calls to one of the attendant police officers.

The sound of the distant one-sided phone conversation seemed to recall his companion to matters in hand. Carla looked into his face and said quietly, 'I might have saved him, mightn't I? If I'd hadn't been sick. If I hadn't eaten a stupid dish of chocolate mousse? It's so – so trivial a thing and it had such a – a dreadful result. And I ought to have known! Chocolate nearly always—'

'Don't blame yourself, Carla!' he said quickly. 'You couldn't know a killer was lurking around and even if you'd been downstairs, you couldn't necessarily have prevented what happened. You might have become a victim, too.'

She leaned back in the chair, resting her long white fingers on its arms. In the lamplight he could see how dark blue veins crisscrossed the alabaster skin of the back of her hands.

'What can I tell you?' she asked hopelessly.

He adopted a brisk manner because he found that usually witnesses found it reassuring. Their world was falling apart but at least someone sounded as if he were in control. 'Inspector Pearce will be coming to talk to you later. He's a good man and you can have every confidence in him. This chat, it's just a preliminary. I really only have a couple of questions. What time did you arrive home and did you see Andrew at all last night?'

'Yes, I saw him when I got home. That would be about five fifteen. I caught an early afternoon train because I knew one of my heads was coming on and I just wanted to get home. I told him I had migraine and I went straight upstairs.'

'Was anyone else here? Mrs Flack? Any visitors?'

She shook her head.

'Did he bring you a cup of tea or anything?'

Another shake of her head. 'No. I don't want anything when I've got one of my heads. Andrew knows that. I generally take aspirin or something similar. But last night I found a couple of sleeping tablets left from when I had a bout of insomnia around Christmastime. I took one of those and it sent me off to sleep.' She gave a brief gesture of resignation. 'It seemed a good idea at the time.'

'So you had no further communication with Andrew after telling him you were going to bed immediately with migraine?'

She hesitated. 'I think he may have put his head round the door and asked how I was. That would be just before I took the sleeping pill. I'm hazy about it. Migraine, I don't know if you're a sufferer, but it just blots everything out. All you know is, you're miserable and in pain.' She broke off and took her hands from the chair arms to twist her fingers together. 'I sound self-pitying, don't I? I was just ill. Andrew was – was fighting for his life.'

'No, you don't sound self-pitying,' he told her. 'You're telling me exactly how it was, and that's what I want.' He glanced up at the painting over the hearth. 'Cornwall?'

'What?' She followed his gaze. 'Oh, yes. Andrew's birthplace, Port Isaac. Not that Andrew was especially obsessed with being a Cornishman. He liked to drop it into conversation if he thought it would gain him a brownie point or two.'

Markby, who'd known a few 'professional' Welsh or Scotsmen of this type in his time, nodded.

He moved the conversation gently back to its previous course. 'Had Andrew been in England long on this visit?'

'Only a few days. He usually stayed a week or so. You and Meredith were supposed to come to dinner the last time he was home, if you remember.'

'I know,' he apologised. 'I was called out and that was it, I'm afraid. Sorry.'

'He has – had – a flat in Brussels.' Carla paused. 'I suppose I could have gone over there and we could've set up house there. But, you see, I have my own career and being stuck in Belgium wouldn't have suited things at all. Besides, there was Luke. If I stayed here at least he had one parent in the country.'

It seemed to Markby she hesitated again, barely perceptibly. It put him in mind of Mrs Flack earlier. Was there something Carla had thought of and then decided he needn't know?

'He didn't mention any problems? Nothing seemed to be worrying him?'

'Not more than usual. He has – had – a responsible position and he took it seriously. Nothing out of the ordinary, though. He hadn't been threatened or anything, or I don't think so. He mightn't have told me, I suppose, but I think I would have guessed if there were something like that on his mind. Besides, surely, that has nothing to do with it? What happened to Andrew, it was a nasty, vicious act done by a professional criminal, a burglar. Andrew must have confronted him.'

Markby glanced round the room again. 'Nothing appears to be disturbed in here.' A thought struck him. 'Mrs Flack hasn't tidied up, has she?' It was the sort of thing the woman would have done, as witness those washed teacups.

But Carla, thank goodness, was shaking her head. 'No, she's had no chance.' She stared at the objects around her in a bewildered way. 'It's all fine,' she said, as if she couldn't believe her eyes.

'You mean nothing, as far as you can see, either here or elsewhere, is missing?'

'I haven't looked!' she retorted, then shook her head. 'I'd have noticed if drawers were pulled out, that sort of thing. But we don't keep large sums of money in the house. I suppose—' She jumped nervously to her feet and darted past him out of the room calling, 'Irene!'

Mrs Flack's voice was heard immediately in reply. She must have been lurking nearby ready to dash in and protect her employer from police bullying. There was a murmured exchange of words.

Carla reappeared, flushed. 'Irene says everything's in its place, or she thinks so. The silver is still on a sideboard in the dining room. It's a Georgian tea service. The good knives and forks are still in the drawer there. Irene looked particularly, after she'd phoned the police.' Carla smiled sadly. 'Irene's what used to be called a treasure. She cares about us all, she—'

She faltered and looked down at her hands, gripped so tightly the knucklebones seemed to be forcing their way through the skin.

Markby murmured, 'I know. Take it easy, Carla.'

She raised her head and met his concerned gaze with a look of defiance. 'It had to be a burglar! Someone Andrew disturbed as he was trying to get into the house and who lashed out . . . The man then panicked and ran off when he saw – he saw what he'd done.'

She collapsed into her former chair and tears welled in her eyes. 'No one else would hurt Andrew! Why should they?'

The tears were a worrying indication that this interview couldn't go on much longer. Markby made more soothing noises but persisted gently, 'When you came downstairs this morning Mrs Flack hadn't yet arrived, is that right?'

A furious shake of the head. 'No, she came after— Oh, poor Irene. She must have been so frightened. Not just by seeing Andrew – like that. But because I'd lost it completely. I was just sitting there, she tells me, and howling like a dog. I have to go by what she tells me because I don't remember myself. Dr Pringle came along a little later. I calmed down a bit after they got me indoors.'

'Carla,' Markby asked tentatively, 'how much do you remember of the moments before you found Andrew?'

She gave a little jump and stared at him. The tears had been fought back but lent a suspicious brightness to her eyes, which looked huge and frightened in her drawn face.

'I mean,' he went on, 'can you tell me exactly what you did from the moment you got out of bed until you went out into the garden?'

'Oh,' she frowned. 'Yes, I think I can. I got up and I saw Andrew wasn't there in the bedroom but I wasn't surprised because he often slept in another room when I had migraine. I remember looking at the alarm clock.' She nodded, assuring herself that her memory was working well. 'I thought Mrs Flack would be along shortly. I went out into the corridor and looked in Luke's room because I thought Andrew would've crashed out in there. The bed was made up but no one had slept in it. That's . . .' she paused. 'It seemed odd. I didn't think anything was wrong, but I was puzzled. I thought, perhaps he dozed off on the sofa down here.' She indicated the sofa nearby. 'I came downstairs, looked in here and then, when I saw he wasn't here, went into the kitchen.'

Markby leaned forward. 'Can you describe the kitchen?'

'Describe it? It was just as it always is.' She blinked nervously. 'What do you want me to say, Alan?'

'I don't want you to say anything but what you remember!' He smiled encouragingly. 'I don't want to put ideas in your mind, Carla. But, well, the back door, was it open or shut? The electric light, switched on or off?'

She screwed up her face in concentration, trying to piece together the scene.

'The back door was shut and the light switched off,' she said dully. 'I switched it on. I opened the back door. I'd realised Andrew wasn't in the house and I thought he might have gone out already, to pick up some milk or something. I thought I'd go out to the garage and see if the car had gone . . . But I didn't get that far . . .'

Her voice tailed away and he said sympathetically, 'I am truly very sorry, Carla.'

She gave a little sigh. 'It's so horrible it oughtn't to be able to get worse. But things can always get worse, can't they? There are pressmen out there, Irene Flack said. Just like carrion crows all hovering over the road when some rabbit's been squashed by a car.'

He leaned forward and touched her arm. 'Take it easy, Carla. Get some rest. Let us take care of the press. Inspector Pearce will come and see you perhaps this evening, or even tomorrow if you're not up to it. If you remember anything at all, tell him, even if it's something you can't swear to because you'd taken a sleeping tablet. And especially, anything you can recall Andrew saying or doing which was even slightly out of the ordinary.'

She took her hands from her face, calm again. 'Yes, of course. Thank you, Alan.'

Back in the kitchen, he found Mrs Flack had been waiting for him. She jumped out at him from behind the fridge as he walked in. 'You haven't gone and got her all upset, have you?' she accused.

'No,' Markby promised and got a mistrustful look in return. He looked round. There were two light switches, one by the door from the hall, the other by the back door. Suddenly he asked, 'Have you a key, for when you arrive in the morning?'

'Of course,' said Mrs Flack starchily.

'Then don't you set off the burglar alarm?'

'Generally one of the family's already switched it off, but if need be, I know the combination,' she said. 'Only this morning, of course, it wasn't necessary.'

Because Andrew Penhallow had never had the chance to set it the previous night, thought Markby. Something which might have entered into his assailant's calculations.

'I'd be obliged,' he said, 'if you'd check round the house again, really thoroughly in every room, to make sure nothing's disturbed or missing. Mrs Penhallow really isn't in a state to do it at the moment.'

'I know that,' snapped Mrs Flack. 'I sometimes wonder what you policemen think you're doing, bothering people only hours after a poor soul like Mr P has been called to his Maker. Asking lots of questions and expecting sensible answers. I know you have a job to do,' she concluded, according him the right to be there at all, 'but there's decency, you know, even at a time like this.'

He didn't argue because it was pointless. But she was wrong. Decency was one of the first victims in an investigation.

An unexpected free day at home means you can catch up with the odd jobs. Defrost the fridge. Clean the kitchen cupboards. Take down the bedroom curtains and put them through the wash. Take the car to the out-of-town superstore and stock up. Tidy up the patch of rear garden.

Meredith sat at her kitchen table eating a leisurely brunch and reflecting that all these worthy chores were likely to remain untackled. The very thought of any one of them caused a distinct lowering of her spirits, already low enough. This wasn't how she had imagined the forthcoming weekend.

She'd entertained the pleasing notion that she and Alan might go away for a couple of days. Not far, since time was limited. A country club with a good restaurant, perhaps, and a health spa with a heated pool and sauna. A restful, restorative break would set them both to rights. Her real reason for slipping away from the course had been to spend the time with Alan. Last night, at the Greek restaurant, her plan even seemed to be working. He'd agreed the weekend away was a good idea. He was going to check this morning, first thing as soon as he got into work, and let her know if it were feasible. He hadn't rung and he hadn't let her know. She suspected the worst.

But he should have rung, even if only to tell her it was out of the question. Meredith got up from the kitchen table and made purposefully for the telephone.

But at Regional HQ they told her Superintendent Markby wasn't available.

'You mean, he's there but busy, or he's not in the building?' Experience had taught her to ask this question.

But she got the reply she didn't want. He wasn't there. He'd been called out.

'Thanks,' she said gloomily, dropping the handset into its cradle. 'Thanks a bundle!'

Called out meant a new case. A new case meant farewell to any idea of going off to a country club hotel despite the fact that he'd reached the rank which ought to have guaranteed he had weekends free. But knowing Alan, if something had cropped up on Friday, as it seemed it had, he'd be loath to go away. He'd want to be here, just in case . . .

Meredith stared down at the phone, memory stirred. There was someone else she ought perhaps to call. The Penhallows. She hadn't forgotten the mystery hitchhiker. It had worried her intermittently ever since she'd picked her up. Now, running through the events of the previous evening rapidly in her mind, she felt sure the visit the mystery girl had been about to pay Tudor Lodge had been an unexpected one. That carried certain possibilities where the Penhallows were concerned, which mightn't apply for other people. Andrew, for instance, had an important and possibly sensitive job. Carla was a 'celebrity', known from her appearances on the TV popular science programmes. Andrew and Carla between them were in the market to attract a versatile range of oddballs: the overenthusiastic fan, alien-spotter, Eurocrank or, given their joint high income, the criminal – sane or otherwise.

Meredith riffled through her address book and found the number for Tudor Lodge.

The phone rang for so long at the other end she thought they must all be out. She was about to replace the receiver when someone answered. It was a male voice but certainly not Andrew.

'Yes?' it said discouragingly.

'Is that Tudor Lodge?' Perhaps she'd got a wrong connection.

'Yes.'

'Could I speak to either Mr or Mrs Penhallow?'

'Sorry, madam,' said the voice firmly. 'Neither of them is available.'

'Not available' seemed to be the answer she was getting today. Obstinately, Meredith asked, 'When can I speak to either of them?'

'May I ask who is calling?' asked the voice with a wooden formality which confirmed a growing suspicion in her mind.

With incredulity and some alarm, Meredith asked, 'Are you a police officer, by any chance?'

That had turned the tables. Now he sounded surprised. 'Why do you ask that, madam?'

'No one,' she informed him with asperity, 'calls women "madam" but the police. Unless you're a butler and I don't remember the Penhallows having a butler. Is there something wrong at the Penhallows?' Her voice rose on an anxious note.

'I'm afraid I'm not in a position to give out any information,' said the irritating voice. 'I suggest you ring tomorrow.'

'Blow tomorrow!' snapped Meredith. 'What's going on there? My name is Mitchell, Meredith Mitchell. I'm a friend of Mrs Pen—'

She was interrupted. The voice exclaimed, 'Is that you, then, Miss Mitchell?' It had lost its official note and sounded surprised and pleased. 'It's Dave Pearce here. You trying to get in touch with his nibs?'

'Inspector Pearce? Good God! I mean, why? What's happening there? What do you mean, in touch with him? Is he there?'

Alan, at Tudor Lodge, at – she glanced at her wristwatch – a little before midday. Her heart sank. It must be serious. Not just a break-in or something.

'Inspector?' she asked, filled with dread. 'What's going on?' Inwardly she was cursing the fact that she'd done nothing last night to ensure all was well at Tudor Lodge. She'd told Alan about the hitcher, certainly, but she ought to have insisted that on their way to the restaurant they'd detoured by the Penhallows' and checked all was well. Or even just picked up the phone and asked.

Pearce's voice, lowered to a confidential whisper, sounded in her ear. 'I can't tell you now, not over the phone. I'll tell him to give you a call. It's – it's a serious matter, yes. But Mrs Penhallow is all right.'

Relief surged through her. 'Thank goodness for that!' Then the implication struck her. 'And Andrew, Mr Penhallow?'

''Fraid not. I'll get the superintendent to call you, all right, Miss Mitchell?' Dave Pearce's voice was firm again. That was as much as she was going to get by way of information.

'Thanks,' she said yet again, and put the phone down.

For a moment or two she stood irresolutely in the hallway. What she'd like to do was run straight over there and see for herself. But if the police were there they wouldn't like that at all and she'd get short shrift.

A faint noise from the kitchen caught her ear and brought her out of her reverie. There it was again. Had she left the window or door open? Meredith walked towards the door between kitchen and hall which she had shut behind her on coming out here to telephone. She twisted the handle and threw it open.

Almost at the same moment the outside door, from kitchen into her small backyard, clicked shut. She had a brief impression of an outline against the frosted glass panel and then heard a swift patter of light, running feet.

She dashed to the window over the sink unit and was just in time to catch a glimpse of a boy of about thirteen or fourteen, in the ubiquitous jeans and bomber jacket, white training shoes, but with a telltale head of cropped ginger hair. He scrambled up and over the wall bounding the property to the rear with the alacrity of a cat, and dropped down. As he did he turned his body towards her and she glimpsed his face before he was gone. He looked neither scared at having found someone unexpectedly at home, nor jubilant at his escape. He looked like someone repeating an action made many times before, so often, it had become routine, as it probably had. Before he'd dropped to the ground on the far side, the encounter would already have been written off in his mind.

Meredith ran out into the yard and across the paved area to the door in the wall. It was locked. She wrestled angrily with it and gave up. The key was indoors, hanging on a hook in the kitchen. She never used this back entry and so kept it secure at all times. But not secure enough, it seemed. On the other side, as she and her intruder had known, was a narrow alley, just wide enough to take one person. It ran along the back of all the properties in the Victorian terrace and connected to a jumble of odd passageways and alleys linking the older buildings of the town.

She returned to the kitchen, and this time locked her back door carefully. In broad daylight, she thought! He didn't lack nerve, her youthful sneak thief. But he'd probably kept an eye on this house all week while she'd been away at the course and satisfied himself the occupant was away. He'd had no way of knowing that she'd returned. No doubt he'd have broken a window to get in, but he'd tried the back door as a matter of routine – people were often very careless – and he'd got lucky.

She searched around the kitchen to see if anything had been taken. She couldn't see any gaps and he'd had both hands free to scale the wall. Her purse, thank goodness, was upstairs in the bedroom. But it had been a close and unsettling thing. His being young didn't mean he wasn't dangerous. The kitchen was full of likely weapons. Two sharp vegetable knives lay on the draining board. Had she confronted him face to face, he might have snatched one up and—

She drove away the image and resolved to keep the door shut and try to warn her next-door neighbours to do the same, without alarming them. Both were elderly.

An intruder. To herself she whispered aloud, 'What *has* happened at Tudor Lodge?'

*   *   *

Markby found Pearce waiting for him outside. The inspector was watching the search of the garden, his hands in his pockets, and a disconsolate expression on his face. Poor Dave, thought Markby, knew his weekend plans were ruined. He was probably trying to think up some way of making things up to and with Tessa, his still fairly new wife. Tessa would learn, in time, that to be married to a policeman was to share her man with an implacable mistress. Work would always come first. No wonder police marriages often bit the dust. Markby's own marriage had done so. Even his relationship with Meredith . . . Markby suppressed a sigh.

The superintendent approached his junior and asked with some sympathy, 'Find anything?' He nodded towards the overalled figures.

'Not yet,' mumbled Pearce. 'No such luck . . .' he added. He pulled himself together to ask, 'You see the widow?'

'Yes. She's very distressed.' Markby summarised the interview. 'We'll have to check it all out. Only Penhallow was at home when she got back last night, but Mrs Penhallow took a taxi from the station and the driver may remember her. She is fairly well known. Check the train times. The business lunch should be easy to verify and its menu. You shouldn't have any trouble with that. Get SOCO to dust the light switch just inside the back door and the other switch too for good measure. If they haven't already done it, both sides of the back doorhandle need to be dusted too. Mrs Penhallow says the kitchen was in darkness this morning and she switched on the light, presumably at the switch by the hall door. She also says the back door was shut. So who shut it? And did the same person take the precaution of switching off the light at the same time?'

'Right,' said Pearce. 'Prescott will be asking a lot of questions at those cottages and at the garage! He's down there now. He's gone to see the old lady who's so chatty, Mrs Joss. Oh, Miss Mitchell called just now. She's worried about what's going on here. I said you'd call her back.'

'Oh damn, I should have called her,' Markby said wearily, then frowned at a memory. 'The hitchhiker,' he said. 'She was worried about that hitcher and quite possibly she was right to be!'

Dave was looking at him, puzzled, so Markby explained.

'Meredith picked up a young female hitchhiker yesterday and dropped her off at Tudor Lodge. That would've been some time before seven. Carla says no one but Andrew was in the house when she got here from the rail station at five fifteen. But Carla went up to bed immediately and took a sleeping tablet. So if the girl came later, she wouldn't have known of it.

'Mrs Flack found two cups on the kitchen table this morning. Andrew made tea for someone and it wasn't his wife. A pity Mrs Flack is such an efficient washer of dishes!' He sighed. 'We might've got a really good set of prints. Now, note this! The housekeeper saw a girl walking near Tudor Lodge, coming from the direction of the town later, around nine thirty. Irene Flack says the girl disappeared suddenly and it's quite possible she turned into the grounds of this house. So, the question for us is, was this the same girl or another one?'

'It sounds a promising lead!' Pearce said excitedly, clearly hoping this whole matter would be cleared up now without too much trouble.

Markby dampened his enthusiasm. 'Let's say it's a mystery. Either Penhallow received two separate visits from two distinct young women, or he received two separate visits from the same one. If it was the same girl, why did she leave, only to return? Where was she coming back from? How had she spent her time in the interval? What time did she leave this house after her first visit? And here's something else. Meredith got the impression the Penhallows weren't expecting the girl. So, if Andrew got a surprise visit the first time, how surprised was he to see her the second time? Had he arranged with her that she should come back again? If he had, knowing she had no transport, why didn't he fetch her? Or go to *her*, wherever she was, and discuss their business, whatever *that* was, in some mutually convenient spot?'

He hissed in exasperation. 'We've got to find her, or both of them if there are two girls, if only to eliminate both from inquiries. So hold your horses, Dave. It may not be a lead, only a time-wasting red herring.' Consolingly he added, 'I agree it's possible, at the very least, the hitcher was the last person to speak to Andrew alive.'

'And the last person to see the victim . . .' Pearce murmured Mephisto-like.

'Quite. It would take strength to inflict the injuries to his head, but a healthy young woman, why not? By the way, let's not mention the girl to Mrs Penhallow yet. Let's see if we can find out something about her first.' He glanced at his watch. 'I'll go over to Meredith's place now and see what she can remember about the girl she picked up. She did tell me but I wasn't paying too much attention at the time, to be honest. I was opening a bottle of wine.'

'You think this chap Penhallow had got a bit on the side?' Pearce was dealing with the obvious first.

Why not? Dave, ever the plain speaker, had put it bluntly but reasonably. Markby conceded the possibility.

'If he was playing away from home, he certainly wouldn't be the first. All those legitimate trips to the Continent would give ample opportunity. But for God's sake, don't start a wild rumour. The press would get hold of it and the tabloid pack in full cry after a secret mistress isn't what we want! In no time at all we'd be reading banner headlines which would not only cause extreme distress to the family but foul up our investigations completely. Either they'd get to her first and the next thing we'd know she'd be selling her story and posing topless, or she'd take fright, bolt and lie low, possibly even leave the country. Of course—' Markby interrupted this lurid scenario – 'we are supposing that she exists.'

Pearce said tentatively, 'We could perhaps just ask Mrs Penhallow if they were expecting anyone, or whether the young chap, Luke, has a girlfriend—'

They were interrupted by a shout and both looked up.

Striding across the lawn towards them was a fit-looking, ruddy-faced and tousle-haired young man in jeans, his burly shoulders stretching a rugby shirt.

'And, I fancy, here he is,' murmured Markby. 'Right on cue . . .'

'Oy!' Luke Penhallow stood feet apart and hands on hips and addressed them pugnaciously. 'You the police? What the hell's going on here? What's happened to my father? And where's my mum?'

67

CHAPTER SIX

'There you are then, dear,' said Mrs Joss, and handed Sergeant Prescott a large rose-patterned mug of murky tea.

If there was one thing Prescott couldn't stomach, it was thick, stewed tea. 'Thank you, madam,' he said, putting it down with every intention of forgetting it.

'Oh my,' said Mrs Joss with a hoarse chuckle. 'Madam, eh? Teach you nice manners, don't they, in the police?'

Prescott wondered just how soon he could get answers to a few questions, issue his warning about gossiping, and get out of here. The tiny room was filled with furniture and bric-à-brac, making it almost impossible to move at all without knocking over a china lady in a flounced crinoline or pottery spaniel. Every flat surface and the backs of all the chairs were covered with embroidered cloths edged with hand-made lace. Decorative plates studded the walls.

Three cats, two white with tabby patches and one striped all over, slumbered about the place. The white pair were entwined on the windowsill and the striped one crouched by the hearth whence it fixed him with a baleful yellow glare. Prescott, topping six foot in height and solid in build, perched uncomfortably on his chair with his elbows clamped to his sides. The phrase 'bull in a china shop' sprang unflatteringly to his mind.

'How are they getting on, then? Found out yet who dunnit?'

It was quite evident that Mrs Joss was having the time of her life. The murder of Andrew Penhallow had affected her daily routine as winning the lottery might have done, transforming it from predictable tedium to mind-boggling excitement in a trice.

Her apparent lack of either grief or sympathy made Prescott genuinely curious. He asked, 'Did you know Mr Penhallow?'

'Of course I knew him,' said Mrs Joss. 'He was my neighbour. Though he and I didn't speak, apart from "good morning", that sort of thing. He was a bit of a grand gentleman, wasn't he? Or thought himself one, which isn't always the same thing!'

Prescott regarded her with some disfavour. She was as brown as a

69

walnut, a shrivelled beldame with iron-grey plaits looped up over her ears from which dangled large gold rings. She also had a moustache. An earlier age would've burned her on sight, with or without that evil-looking moggy glowering at him from the fireplace. He was certain she had a crystal ball and a pack of tarot cards hidden about the place somewhere.

'You spoke to him often?'

'He wasn't here often,' said Mrs Joss in a decidedly sinister way. 'He was away in foreign countries. He went off on them missions.' She nodded as one who tipped the wink to an insider.

'I think,' said Prescott, 'you mean he worked at the European Commission.' He had earlier acquired this information from Mrs Flack.

'Same thing, isn't it?' Mrs Joss demanded.

'No,' said Prescott bluntly. 'He was a pen-pusher of some sort, not the Man from U.N.C.L.E.'

She brightened. 'I like all them old telly programmes. They don't make no programmes like that any more. But like I say, he wasn't hardly ever at home. Nor more is she. She works in London. Funny sort of arrangement, if you ask me. Not what I call a marriage. When I was married, my hubby and I lived together under one roof till he died. If my hubby had gone off to foreign parts like it, coming and going, I'd have wanted to know what he was up to! Well, my hubby went off during the war, but that's because the navy took him. But I knew where he was. He was on a ship. I never had cause to grumble about my husband,' said Mrs Joss in the manner of one summing up an irrefutable argument, 'not to the day he was called to his Maker, twenty year ago last Christmas. He fell out of a tree.'

Prescott managed to prevent himself asking whether it had been a Christmas tree.

'It was his living,' continued Mrs Joss, perhaps sensing that an explanation was called for. 'He was a tree-surgeon. They had this tree up on the main road and it was dangerous. A big branch was hanging off. So he had to go up and cut it off. But he slipped on account of the frost.'

'I'm sorry,' said Prescott, suddenly ashamed of himself.

'It was quick,' said Mrs Joss. 'I hope I go as quick when it's my turn. We had a grand funeral. I hope my family give me a good send-off. You know, lots of flowers and a good old knees-up afterwards.'

'Mrs Joss,' said Prescott firmly, 'did you happen to see or hear anything last night? Anything out of the ordinary?'

'Ah, now,' she said. 'I can't say I heard anything you'd call strange.' She paused and frowned. Her gold earrings swung. He noticed that her ear lobes were withered like soft leather and the holes pierced to take the earrings had stretched with age to dark slits in the crinkled skin. ''Cepting a car's brakes.'

Prescott leaned forward. 'How do you mean?'

She gestured with a brown, large-knuckled hand. 'I heard a sort of squeal like when a car brakes sudden. I thought it might be them joy-riders. Or it could've been down at Sawyer's garage. He's got a door what makes a nasty screech. I keep telling him, he ought to oil it. It's not as though he hasn't got enough oil, not down there in a garage. He works very late and the electricity he burns, it's a wonder the country don't run out of the stuff.'

'What time was this squeal?'.

'Oh, late,' she said. 'I'd gone to bed. I go to bed early. I've only got my pension. I can't be burning electricity all night or keeping the fire in. Up with the sun and to bed with the sun. That's how I was brought up. I don't need no clocks.'

Oh great, thought Prescott. That's really helpful. 'I understand,' he said, 'that you noticed some activity at Tudor Lodge during the evening.'

'What, do you mean them cars going in and out?' asked Mrs Joss with a frown, after due deliberation.

'If that's what you saw.' Prescott clung to his patience.

'I never saw them,' said Mrs Joss. 'I saw their lights. I'd gone to bed. But whenever a car goes in or out of the drive up to their garage, the headlights goes past my bedroom window. I got two bedroom windows and one of them gives out on the side, looks towards Tudor Lodge. Those cars was going up and down all the time last night.'

'How often?' asked Prescott, pen poised over his notepad.

'Dozens of times,' said Mrs Joss confidently.

Pressed more closely, Mrs Joss became flustered and revised this estimate to three or four times. Yet more quizzing elicited that not all these lights had gone in or out of Tudor Lodge. Only twice, could Mrs Joss say, that had been the case.

'But there's Irene Flack,' said Mrs Joss, keen to show that there had been other traffic about. 'She's got a car. She goes out to her knitting group of a Thursday night. I heard her car come back and the lights went past. Her car makes a funny noise, sort of clunkety-clunk. I reckon there's something wrong with it.'

Useless, thought Prescott with an inward sigh. The old girl's evidence was utterly useless. She didn't or couldn't tell the time by

71

a clock. She couldn't count. She couldn't be precise about anything. By his reckoning, she'd been disturbed three times by cars. It hardly amounted to the Wacky Races out there.

'If you'd like to read what I've written here, Mrs Joss.' Wearily he proffered his notebook with the sparse information he'd jotted down. 'Tell me whether you agree with it. You might sign at the bottom, if you agree it's right.'

She gave him a strange, almost coy, look. 'I don't hold much with reading and writing, dear. I never went near no school.'

'What, never?' asked Prescott impolitely. 'Not even when you were a little girl?'

'No, dear. We was on the road. My parents were travelling people.'

'Mrs Joss,' he asked tentatively, 'may I ask how old you are?'

'Eighty-three,' she said. 'Don't go thinking I don't know how old I am, young man! I got eleven children living and two dead. Twenty-one grandchildren and three great-grandchildren. That's not bad, is it? Not for someone who never went near no school?' And she burst into raucous laughter.

Despite himself, Prescott found he was laughing with her. 'All right, Mrs Joss. Thank you for your time. Now, you won't go chattering to people about any of this, will you?'

He had to warn her, but really, it hardly mattered, she was useless as a witness and nothing significant could be said to have come out of his visit. As it happened, Prescott was wrong about this, but he didn't know it at the time.

He put away his notebook and was about to take his leave when the back door slammed and a voice called out, 'Gran?'

The door to the room opened and a thin-faced young man of about twenty appeared. Though of puny build, he carried himself with brash style. He wore jeans and a black bomber jacket with silver flashes on the sleeves. His dark hair gleamed with gel and had been combed straight up into a forest of spikes. At the sight of Prescott he stopped and for a moment appeared about to turn and run. Then he pulled himself together and entered the room cautiously.

'Hullo, Gran,' he said, stooping to kiss her leathery cheek, but keeping one eye on the sergeant. 'Got a gentleman friend, have you?'

She cackled with pleasure. 'This is my grandson, Lemuel,' she said proudly. 'He's my Dan's middle boy.'

'Lee!' The young man turned a fiery red which worsened the appearance of his acne-scarred skin. He turned to Prescott, insisting, 'I'm called Lee, not Lem— not what Gran said.'

'What's wrong with Lemuel?' snapped his granny. 'It was your granddad's name!'

'Nothing, Gran!' To cover his embarrassment, he leaned against the table in an exaggeratedly nonchalant fashion, folding his arms. He wore an expensive wristwatch.

Presott was fully aware that more than a difference of opinion over Lemuel versus Lee was worrying the newcomer. The cause of Lee's unease was that he'd immediately realised the visitor was a police officer. And what, mused Prescott, have you been up to, that you want to make yourself scarce at first sight of the law? How did you pay for that watch, I wonder, *if* you paid for it?

'So you're Lee Joss?' Prescott was himself young enough to sympathise with the newcomer over the name his thoughtless parents had bestowed on him. Lemuel, would you credit it? Traveller families liked old names, the sergeant knew. But Lemuel . . .

Lee's grandmother answered for him. 'I told you, he's Dan's boy. They live just along here, next door but one, next to Irene Flack.'

Prescott felt a tingle of interest. 'You live nearby? Good, so perhaps you noticed or heard something last night, Mr Joss?'

Panic showed briefly in Lee's eyes. 'I was working last night. I'm barman at The Crown. You ask them. I started work six thirty and I never closed up the bar till ten thirty and then I was clearing up. I didn't get back home till midnight.'

'Walk back?' asked Prescott.

Lee looked startled. 'Course not! Gotta motorbike.'

'I heard that and all,' said his grandma quickly. 'That makes an awful racket, that does, so I know Lemuel come home the usual time. I allus hear him and I heard him last night. This gentleman is a police officer, Lemuel, and his name is Sergeant Prescott. He's here because of poor Mr Penhallow.'

'Oh, that,' said Lee, clearly relieved. 'I heard about that.' A gleam had entered his eyes which Prescott hadn't failed to notice. But he wasn't sure what it meant. For a moment it had almost been as if Lee Joss had thought of some joke but decided against making it. 'Got croaked, didn't he?' Now that the inquiry didn't concern him or his family, Lee's manner had relaxed.

'Where did you hear about Mr Penhallow's death?' Prescott asked suspiciously.

'I dunno,' was the wary reply. 'They're all talking about it down the town.'

But that gleam of laughter was back behind Lee's dark eyes, despite the caution of his words. Making a fool of me, thought

Prescott, irritated. What does the little squirt know that's so damn funny?

'Make good money working behind the bar at The Crown?' he asked. Though not unhandsome, Prescott's looks had suffered from an addiction to collison sports, on the rugby field and in the amateur ring, which had left him with the air of a fairground bruiser. He could, when need be, appear quite alarming, as now.

The laughter faded in Lee's eyes. 'Fair enough. Could be better. What's it to you?'

'Motorbikes cost money.'

'Yeah, well, my dad let me have some money towards it.' He shrugged and adopted an air of bravado, asking truculently, 'What's this got to do with old Penhallow?'

'*Old* Penhallow?' Prescott seized on the familiarity. He knew he'd got the boy walking nicely into a trap. 'You knew him well? Had dealings with him, had you?'

Lee unfolded his arms and moved away from the table. 'No, well, I knew him by sight. Tubby bloke, always looked pleased with himself. Suppose he would, being well off like he was.'

'You think Mr Penhallow was wealthy?'

'Oh, come on!' Lee burst out. 'Look at that big house! And his old lady always on the telly. She must make a packet! Course he'd got money! Both him and his missus driving flash cars, and he'd got a real stunner of a girlfriend—' He broke off, but too late.

'Tell me,' said Prescott, reopening his notebook. 'Tell me about Mr Penhallow's girlfriend. You've seen her?'

'Yes, Lemuel!' urged his grandmother. 'I never knew he had no fancy woman! You tell us all about it!'

'I'm sorry about the weekend,' Alan said.

As he drew up before her tiny terraced house, the door had been jerked open and she had catapulted out to meet him before he'd managed to get out of the car.

It was a pity that she'd rung Tudor Lodge like that and spoken to Pearce. She already knew something was wrong and there was little he could do but blurt out the horrid truth. Nevertheless, he sought to blunt the shock by an indirect approach. But he should have known better. Indirect approaches seldom worked well with Meredith, who tended to regard them as shillyshallying and an insult to her intelligence.

'Oh, the weekend . . .' She waved the topic away as irrelevant now. 'What's happened at Tudor Lodge? Why wouldn't Pearce tell me?' She scraped at a hank of glossy brown hair and fixed him with anxious hazel eyes.

He picked his words carefully as he followed her into the house. 'There was an – incident – last night.'

'I know something bad has happened,' she said impatiently. 'Stop treating me like an idiot, Alan.'

'I wouldn't dare. I'm afraid it concerns Andrew. Don't blame Dave. He could hardly give out details over the phone.'

'Has Andrew been hurt?' Meredith answered her own question immediately, seeing reality in his expression. She collapsed on to the nearest chair. 'Oh no.' She closed her eyes. 'He's dead.' She opened her eyes again and stared full at him. 'He is dead, isn't he, Alan?'

'Yes, and I'm sorry to have to tell you he died violently.'

He pulled out a nearby chair and sat down with a sigh. 'It seems to be common knowledge already. Nothing travels like bad news. The police were seen arriving at Tudor Lodge this morning, I suppose, followed by the death wagon. It wouldn't take a Sherlock Holmes to work it out. But God knows how the press got on to it so fast.'

'When did he die?' she asked bleakly.

'We're not sure yet. Probably some time last night, say late evening, around bedtime? He was dressed in pyjamas and dressing gown but was found outside the house, in the back garden.' Memory threw up a poignant image. 'A hot-water bottle was lying on the ground nearby.'

Meredith was listening, outwardly calm, but he knew she was badly shaken. She'd paled and he could see the pulse jumping in her neck.

Alan got up and went to fetch a small glass of brandy from the drinks cabinet. 'Here . . .'

She took it, sipped it and set it down. 'Did he disturb a burglar?'

'People always ask that first,' he reflected. 'We can't say. As for cause of death, we'll know more after the post mortem. Right now, all we know is, he was struck repeatedly on the head.'

'Oh my God,' she said, 'Carla! Was she hurt? Did she see the intruder?'

'She wasn't hurt, but she is very shocked. No, she didn't see or hear anything. She had a migraine and had taken a sleeping tablet. She found him this morning. He was outside the house in the garden.'

'In his pyjamas?' Meredith frowned as she recalled this point.

'He may have gone outside to investigate a noise.'

She was silent for a moment. When she spoke it was to disconcert him by asking, 'Was there a torch near the body?'

'One's not been found yet.' He eyed her warily.

'You don't go outside at night,' she argued, 'in the dark, into your garden, to investigate strange noises, without a torch or some kind of flashlight. You don't just go out there holding a hot-water bottle!'

'We're searching the grounds.' This wasn't good enough, he knew, and added more briskly, 'Look, he was found this morning, by his wife, laid out on the back lawn, at around seven fifteen. His wife had hysterics. The cleaner arrived around seven thirty and found them both. She called the doctor and the police. All the usual things had to be done before the body was removed and it's only now that we're getting down to going over the place inch by inch. You can't expect miracles!'

'I'm not asking for miracles, I'm asking if there was a torch near the body!' The colour had come back into her face now. She was her normal combative self. On the one hand he was pleased to see it, on the other, he could do without the inquisition.

'How about some kind of defensive weapon, something he would have taken out into the garden with him?' she continued.

'We've found no weapon of any sort yet. You don't know he took a defensive weapon, as you call it, with him.'

'Right, he took a hot-water bottle, I was forgetting. When attacked by a nocturnal intruder, beat him off with a flexible container full of hot water, probably covered with a plush jacket in warm red, electric blue or even disguised as a teddy bear!'

Alan sat back in his chair. 'You know, sarcasm does not become you. Moreover, if you don't mind my saying so, it's inappropriate in the circumstances. I actually came here to see if you could help, not just to bring you the bad news. But you aren't helping by sitting there accusing me of not knowing my job!'

She was unrepentant. 'I'm not accusing you of anything. I want to know what happened to Andrew! I'm just asking the obvious. Look, for example, you might've found his gun lying by the body.'

'Gun?' Markby felt a chill hand laid on his heart. 'He had a gun?'

'A shotgun. He'd have got the licence for it from Bamford police so they must know that! Once when I called round there, young Luke had got it all in bits on the kitchen table on newspaper, cleaning it.'

She appeared to find all this information self-evident and was regarding him with the air of a righteous citizen whose taxes were being shamefully misapplied to support an incompetent police force.

'Wait, wait a minute . . .' He made a palm-outward movement with both hands, stemming the flow of words. 'May I use
your phone?

'Shotgun!' he snapped down the line moments later to Pearce. 'Or
there may even be a pair, probably in a gun cupboard. Even if the
cupboard appears locked and there are no obvious marks of a forced
entry, get a key and get the weapon or weapons out of the house.
Send them over to forensics. Yes, I know he wasn't shot! Look,
you'd better just be praying the things are there in the cupboard,
and not in the hands of some lout running round the countryside
with them!

'Gun,' he said, when he came back to where Meredith sat waiting.
'If someone knew there were guns in the house, he might have
thought it worth burgling just for that.' He paused. 'Although
there's no sign of forced entry to the house itself, or we haven't
found any yet.'

Meredith had drunk the remainder of the glass of brandy while
Alan had been on the phone. 'So what help can I give? You said you
came here to see if I could help. I'm sorry if I was being sarcastic.
It was the shock. And I still think they were logical and pertinent
questions.' She swept her hands over her head, settling her untidy
hair. 'Go on, then, ask.'

'You're in the wrong job,' he said unwisely. 'You should have
taken up the law. You'd have been a very good barrister.'

She looked positively fierce. 'I know I'm in the wrong job. It's
taken me fifteen years to find out, but believe me, I know it now.
I don't need anyone to tell me.' She gazed gloomily into the empty
brandy glass.

He reached out and removed it from her grip before she got the
idea of having another. One snifter for the shock was fine, but it was
too early in the day to start knocking the stuff back seriously.

'Never mind your stalled career, if that's what it is. Turn your
mind to my inquiry before that gets stalled as well. You remember
the girl you picked up last night?'

'What's that got to do with it?' Something like panic briefly
invaded her hazel eyes. 'Alan, don't tell me that girl . . . I knew
it, I knew it!' She didn't so much wring her hands as wave them in
frustration.

'Whoa! Wait a bit, will you? I don't know if the girl has anything
to do with it. But I want to know everything that happened yesterday
in and around Tudor Lodge. Tell me again, all of it. Everything you
saw, everything she said, every impression you got.'

She told it again, slowly and carefully, from the moment she saw the lorry parked at the Bamford turn to her last sight of her passenger, disappearing into the gloom of Tudor Lodge gardens.

When she'd finished, they both sat in silence for a while. 'Hmm,' Alan said eventually. 'I wonder.'

'I should have called the house when I got home and checked that everything was all right,' she said with a sigh. 'I knew, just *knew* in my bones, that something was odd about that kid. She was a beautiful girl, mind you, and very well spoken and upmarket generally. I suppose that put me off. If she'd been a grubby dropout with purple hair and a skull and crossbones stencilled on the back of her jacket or even a cheeky young kid like—'

She broke off and he raised an eyebrow.

'I mean, that sort of person,' she said. But he was sure that wasn't what she'd been going to say. Cheeky young kid like . . . ? Perhaps she'd tell him later. He hadn't, in any case, time to worry about anything else at the moment.

'The point is,' continued Meredith, 'that if she'd looked scruffy, spoken badly, been less confident, I'd have got out of the car and walked to the door of Tudor Lodge with her. I would've said I was taking the opportunity to call on a friend. It would have been so easy for me to do, to check her out like that. But I didn't do it. I thought her behaviour curious but not criminal. Appearances mislead, don't they?' She spoke the last words in tones of deep depression.

'We don't know that her behaviour was with criminal intent,' he pointed out. 'You could be tormenting yourself over nothing. She could've been a totally legitimate caller.'

She ignored this defence, clenching her fists and striking them on her knees. 'I, of all people, should know better. I've dealt with hundreds of emergencies and I've lost count of how many different kinds of people. I ought to know better by now than judge by a hacking jacket and a private-education accent! How could I be so dim?'

'Hey, you are not dim! Don't start blaming yourself. Carla is already doing that.' He saw her enquiring look and added, 'Because she slept through it all. She didn't rush out and save him.'

'Oh Lord, Carla! She must be out of her mind with grief! Who's with her, apart from the coppers? The cleaning woman, is she still there?' Meredith had half risen to her feet.

He told her that Luke Penhallow had just arrived as he was leaving. 'If you're thinking of going over there to see her,' he added, 'I suggest to go tomorrow, not today. There are enough people trampling round the place today.'

The phone broke shrilly into the conversation. 'That'll be Pearce, ringing back about the gun.' Alan got to his feet and went to answer.

Meredith, from her chair, listened to the one-sided conversation.

'What, two of 'em? Both still there? Thank God for that.'

'Amen!' she muttered. But Pearce was clearly relaying further information. It had a remarkable effect.

'The Crown?' Alan shouted, the words ringing around the tiny hallway. 'You mean, that pub up in town? Yes, I know it lets rooms. Joss? The barman? When? Well, has Prescott gone to The Crown to pick her up? Why not? Get him over there before she cuts and runs, if she hasn't done so already!'

The phone was slammed down. He reappeared, grabbed his ancient Barbour, which he'd thrown on a chair, and began to struggle into it. 'Got to go! Your protégée of the roadside may have turned up! If the barman of The Crown is right, she was booked into the hotel last night, around seven forty-five – by Andrew Penhallow, no less!'

CHAPTER SEVEN

It was late lunch time when Prescott reached The Crown. He wasn't acquainted with the place, never even had a drink here. It looked a bit run down to him, the sort of hotel which didn't ask too many questions of its guests. Penhallow might have chosen it for that reason.

Diners were beginning to drift away from the restaurant. The smell of frying, boiled vegetables and coffee mingled not unpleasantly in the air. From somewhere in the far reaches of the hotel, crockery rattled and voices were raised, trolley wheels squeaked. It all reminded Prescott, who had a healthy appetite, that he hadn't eaten. He wondered, if the girl should prove to have scarpered, he could take time to have a bar meal before reporting back.

He leaned on the reception desk and explained his purpose to a trim young woman whose attention appeared to be taken up entirely with examining her purple-lacquered fingernails. The pert receptionist looked unimpressed, merely twitched a finely drawn eyebrow.

'You'll have to see the manager,' she said. 'And he's not here. Not till after two o'clock.' She drew his attention with a purple talon to the old-fashioned wall-clock behind her. After two, meant after two by that clock and no other. Prescott need not consult his wristwatch.

The hands stood at a quarter to two on the clock's enamelled face. The image of the bar sandwich danced tantalisingly in Prescott's brain. But business first. A quarter of an hour might make all the difference. He wouldn't fancy explaining to the superintendent that a suspect had slipped away while he, the sergeant, munched ham sandwiches washed down with a pint. Moreover, the receptionist's dismissive manner had annoyed him a little. He ignored a plaintive rumble from the region of his stomach.

'I've an enquiry about a hotel guest,' he said sternly. 'You can tell me what I want to know, I expect.'

'I don't deal with the police,' she retorted, parrying the thrust neatly. 'The manager does that.'

81

Various scenarios ran around Prescott's brain and threatened to distract him from his purpose. How often did the police come here, for goodness' sake, that the manager *always* dealt with them? What den of vice was represented by this run-down small-town hostelry? And what did this snappy female mean, she didn't deal with 'the police'?

Used as he was to being abused by the unruly element of the town's youth, this was going too far. Prescott felt strongly that a smart young woman in a business suit ought to be supporting the guardians of the law, grateful to him – them – even. What was wrong with the police in her eyes, for goodness' sake? The look she was giving him suggested he was contagious.

'Pity he's not here, then. You'll have to do,' he said heavily. He had the satisfaction of seeing her flush and bridle. Whatever her intention, it hadn't been to imply she was in any way second-best to the absent manager.

He adopted an official manner which wouldn't have disgraced the policeman in Toytown and enquired sonorously, 'Last night a middle-aged man and a young woman came in here and booked a room. Were you on duty then?'

He knew the answer from the sudden gleam of comprehension in her mascara-lined eyes. She leaned forward and declared vehemently, 'Dirty old devil!'

'I beg your pardon?' For a moment Prescott thought she meant him and his majestic stance deserted him.

'The old bloke. I knew he was up to no good, even though he didn't stay. It was about a quarter to eight, just before I go off. He booked the room for her and took her up there. But he didn't stay up there long – not long enough, if you know what I mean?'

She gave him a meaningful look. Prescott, to his mortification, felt himself blush. He took refuge in renewed gruffness.

'What name did he give? Can you describe the man – or the woman?'

'Course I can. Tubby bloke, name of Penhallow. Here . . .' She fished out a card. 'Here's his registration. He said to charge everything to him. Well, he wouldn't do that for no reason, would he? He must have money, I suppose, because he didn't have any looks and he wasn't that young. She's young.'

The receptionist sounded disapproving. It wasn't the supposed immorality which bothered her, it was the disparity in the age of the illicit pair.

But Prescott had seized on the present tense. 'She's still here?'

He was unable to keep the eagerness from his voice, nor the surprise. He'd really thought the mystery woman would've cleared out by now.

'As far as I know. Want to know her name or do you already know it?'

'What is it?' snapped Prescott.

'All right, keep your hair on. It's a funny one. Drago. Never come across that before, myself. You ever hear it? Even though he registered, Penhallow, see? Here . . .' She tapped the card. 'She, the girl, she told the night porter her name when she was going out yesterday evening. She asked him about being able to get back in again if she came late back.'

'What time?' Prescott demanded. 'What time did she go out?'

'You'll have to ask Andy, the night porter. He's not here now. I go off duty at eight so it'll have been after that.'

Prescott glanced at the gloomy staircase. 'Which room? Is she up there now, do you know?'

'She might've come down for lunch, if you want to look in the dining room first. You can't miss her. She's got lots of long goldy-red hair. Don't know if it's natural, it might be. The colour, I mean.'

The receptionist paused to consider whether the guest's hair might be dyed. Clearly this was of more interest to her than anything which might have brought the police to the hotel. Prescott cleared his throat and reluctantly she brought her mind back to matters in hand.

'If she's not there, she'll be up in her room, Number Six. Want me to ring up?'

'No,' said Prescott, as the receptionist stretched a hand towards the switchboard. 'No, I'll announce myself, thanks.'

A glance into the dining room and another through the lounge door revealed no golden-haired young woman. A business rep was consulting a road map in the latter and three morose diners were finishing their meals in the former.

Prescott ascended the dark staircase. The treads creaked beneath his weight. He supposed the place was very old. The walls were lined with yellowed Anaglypta. The stair-carpet was frayed and quite dangerous in parts. The first door in the corridor in which he found himself was labelled 'Bathroom'. He rattled the handle experimentally. The door swung open and revealed a huge, ancient bathtub, a wooden towel-rack and a white-painted chair. He sniffed. There was a faint scent of some floral soap or bath essence.

The door of Room Four was open and allowed a band of light to flood the otherwise dim corridor. A maid was stripping down the bed. She glanced up incuriously as he passed. The room didn't appear very inviting to Prescott's eye. All right if you just wanted somewhere to crash out for the night, but hardly luxurious. The Crown seemed an odd choice of place for an assignation. But he supposed Bamford didn't offer much in that line.

He found himself before Room Six and paused. Through the door panels he could hear the faint sound of a television set. She was watching telly, was she? Catch her unawares. He smiled and knocked at the door.

'Come back later!' called a female voice.

He knocked again and fancied he heard a hiss of annoyance. Footsteps approached and the door was thrown open.

Prescott wasn't familiar with the expression *coup de foudre* but that was what he experienced.

She was the most beautiful girl he'd ever set eyes on. She was younger than he'd expected, only about nineteen. Her magnificent hair, which everyone seemed to remember, cascaded unbound round her pale, oval face and over her shoulders in Pre-Raphaelite splendour. She had large grey eyes fringed with dark lashes and they sent shivers up and down his spine.

'Yes?' she asked coldly.

Prescott realised he was gawping. He fumbled for his identity card. 'Police . . .' he said weakly. 'Er, Sergeant Prescott . . .'

She didn't even glance at the card. He probably had 'Police' stamped on his forehead.

'Yes?' she repeated.

'Miss, er, Drago?' He struggled to pull himself together and take the initiative.

'Yes,' she said for a third time, defeating his intent. A touch of impatience added to her tone indicated he was being especially slow.

'I'd like to talk to you,' he mumbled.

Oh God, no! he thought in agony. Couldn't I have phrased it better than that? Men must constantly indicate they wanted to talk to her. He felt huge, clumsy, foolish.

'What about?' Eyebrows were raised. The grey eyes expressed mild curiosity. At least she hadn't simply slammed the door in the face of yet another graceless oaf scraping an acquaintance.

'About Mr Andrew Penhallow,' Prescott said, and the situation took an irrevocable step forward.

Until that moment the body in the garden had been no more than the subject of an investigation. He hadn't known Penhallow personally. One couldn't strike up an acquaintance with a corpse. He'd felt the usual decent respect and sympathy for the victim of a violent assault. It was all changed. Now, quite suddenly and even in death, Andrew Penhallow became a rival.

With tumult in his breast, Prescott realised that the man had been close, as close as it was possible to be, to this wonderful girl. Penhallow had brought her to this dingy, tatty hotel and installed her in these miserable surroundings when she was deserving of the very best. It had probably been just another in a series of surreptitious small-hotel trysts and unfashionable restaurant lunches. And she, presumably, had given him in return all that loveliness and youth. The inequality of the exchange seemed criminal. At that moment, Prescott hated Andrew Penhallow.

But something of a kindred emotion showed briefly in the girl's eyes. 'He sent the police to warn me off?' she gasped. She seemed to flinch at the idea and then rally, and with a toss of her sunburst mane became a Valkyrie.

Grey eyes snapping, she advanced on Prescott, who retreated into the corridor. '*He sent you?* He sent *you* to tell me to leave him alone? Is *that* why he didn't turn up this morning as he promised?'

The awful scorn in her voice broke the initial spell under which he'd been suffering. Though still overwhelmed by her as a person, Prescott's training came to his aid. It restored him to being a police officer in the course of his duty and shielded him from the withering effect of her contempt.

'Miss Drago,' he said firmly, standing his ground. 'Can I come in? I need to have a word with you. Or we can go down to the lounge but really it needs to be in private.'

The maid had emerged from Room Four at the sound of their voices to stand in the corridor, a bundle of sheets in her arms, and stare at them both.

The girl glanced at the woman and then at Prescott. 'Right,' she said irritably. 'Come in, then. I've no intention of being a sideshow.'

Room Six was as dreary as Room Four in fixtures and fittings, but illuminated by her presence. She marched across to the television and switched it off. Then she flung herself into the one armchair and sat there with one jeansed leg propped across the other and her arms lying on the chair arms. She didn't invite him to find himself a seat.

85

Prescott shut the door with unnecessary care and looked around. Unfortunately most of the floor space was taken up by the double bed. Try as he might, he couldn't avoid looking at it. There was a very small upright chair by the dressing table and he took that. He knew he looked ludicrous, worse than in Mrs Joss's sitting room. She said nothing and, thank God, didn't laugh.

He asked awkwardly, 'May I know your full name?'

'Katherine Louise Drago. Are you going to write it down?' She raised her eyebrows and there was just the faintest twitch at the corner of her full lips.

Prescott, who'd fumbled for his notepad, turned brick red. 'Have you got some means of identification, Miss Drago?'

She thought about that. 'No. Why should you want any?'

'Driving licence? Even an envelope addressed to you?'

She looked round the room and seeing a khaki haversack lying in one corner, pointed to it. 'I might have something in there.'

Prescott began to be nettled by her casual attitude. 'Would you look, please?'

She got up and fetched the bag. After rummaging in it, she produced a small book with the double heart logo of the blood transfusion service on it. Prescott took it. It gave no address but it did give the name Katherine Drago, together with her blood group and the information that she was a regular donor. He returned it to her.

'May I ask what you're doing here in Bamford, Miss Drago?'

'Of course you may ask,' she said sweetly. 'And I may equally decline to answer.' She dropped the transfusion record card back into her bag.

'Why should you do that, Miss Drago?'

'Why should you want to know, Sergeant – I've forgotten your name?'

'Prescott,' he said, sweating.

'Well, Sergeant Prescott, I'm in Bamford on business of my own which concerns no one but myself.'

Wrong! he thought. 'I understand you came here last night with Mr Andrew Penhallow.'

She didn't reply, merely looked straight at him as if he'd committed some horrendous social *faux pas*.

This, Prescott told himself sternly, is at the very least a witness, and quite possibly a suspect, in a murder case. He tried to harden his heart, but ever perfidious, it refused to comply. She couldn't be involved, could she? Not this wonderful creature?

'How long have you known Mr Penhallow?' He was as much asking the question for himself as for the record.

She didn't answer at once. He was aware that her expression had changed, become more wary. She put up a hand and smoothed back one hank of bronze hair as her grey eyes studied him. He recognised a time-wasting gesture and it both encouraged and discouraged him. She was tempted to prevaricate, which indicated she did have something to hide. On the other hand, *what* did she have to hide? Not, he almost prayed, surely not guilt?

'I really don't think,' she said, 'I have to say anything unless you tell me why.'

Now it was Prescott's turn to sit silent. She fidgeted and suddenly her serene self-control snapped. She leaned forward, grey eyes alight with passion. '*Did* he send you? *Did* he phone the police and set you on me? I've done nothing illegal. I'm a free citizen and can go and come as I damn well want!'

'But you're in a hotel room registered in the name of Mr Penhallow,' Prescott said. 'And that's of great interest to us, I'm afraid.' He put his notebook away and stood up. 'I'm sorry you won't co-operate, Miss Drago. I'm afraid I must ask you to come with me.'

'And I decline.' She settled back again. 'I don't have to go with you. Accompanying the police to the station is a purely voluntary action. It's enough that you know where to find me. And you can find me here. Unless, of course, you are arresting me, which is a different matter. Are you arresting me?'

'Please,' Prescott begged, 'don't make things more difficult than they already are and please don't waste my time. This is a serious investigation and you could be in serious trouble, Miss Drago.'

She was bright and needed no more than a hint. The air between them seemed to shiver in horrified anticipation.

She turned red and then white. 'What's happened?' she whispered. 'What's happened to him?'

'Let's wait until we get—'

She leaped out of the chair and threw herself at him, pummelling at his chest with both fists. 'Damn you, you – you stupid great ox of a copper! What's happened to him?'

Prescott gripped her wrists and held her off. She tried wrestling with him briefly and then relaxed, though she was still panting.

'If I come with you,' she gasped hoarsely through a tangled mass of bronze curls, 'will you tell me exactly what's happened?'

'Superintendent Markby or Inspector Pearce will tell you,' said

Prescott unhappily. He looked at her wrists and was dismayed to see the red marks of his own fingers on them. 'I hope I didn't hurt you,' he muttered.

'Oh, for goodness' sake!' she exclaimed. She turned, grabbed the haversack and slung it over her shoulder. 'Well, go on then. Lead me off to your local dungeon! Why're we hanging about here?'

Since Bamford police station was nearer than Regional HQ, they'd taken Kate Drago there for a first interview. The interview itself was to be conducted by Dave Pearce, but Markby sat in on it as observer.

Prescott, who'd brought the girl in, lurked unhappily in the background. He'd shown a tendency to hover protectively over the witness, which hadn't gone unremarked by the superintendent. He'd need to keep an eye on that situation. Young police officers were as vulnerable as any other young men and this girl was startlingly beautiful.

Markby glanced round the interview room, familiar to him from his time at Bamford. He thought critically that it could do with a lick of paint. It was quite nice to be back, albeit in unwished circumstances. He returned his attention to the girl. She was to all appearances unworried by her surroundings or the company of so many officers. He was made curious by her apparent self-possession. Could anyone be quite so unmoved in these circumstances? Give no sign of nervousness as they all sat here looking at her? It hardly seemed natural. Or was it merely a front? If so, she was a consummate actress. He glanced surreptitiously at his wristwatch. They were waiting for a woman officer to be found to sit in. Things were likely to get a bit fraught. She was, so Prescott had indicated, a difficult person to question. When she found out Penhallow was dead – supposing she were not already aware of this – she might collapse. That sort of icy control, in his experience, sometimes snapped with quite terrifying result.

They'd established that she was Katherine Drago, called Kate, and had a London address. She was a student at a college of fashion and design. She was nineteen years old and though technically of age, she had been asked whether she wanted a friend or relative to be contacted and brought here. To this she'd replied with a terse negative.

The door opened and the woman officer came in. It was now crowded in the little room.

'Right, Sergeant,' said Pearce to Prescott, 'you can go.'

For a moment, Markby thought the young man was really going to argue. But Prescott went, not without a last glance at the girl, who ignored him.

Oh dear, thought Markby. Cupid's arrow, tricky little dart that it was, had pierced the stalwart Prescott's hide. He'd have to snap out of that or be taken off the case.

The policewoman took a seat. Kate Drago glanced at her and turned to Inspector Pearce. 'Now you've got everyone here you want, you can tell me what all this is about.'

'We're inquiring,' Pearce said tentatively, after he'd identified himself and the other two officers present for the benefit of the interviewee and the tape recorder, 'into events at Tudor Lodge, Bamford, during the past twenty-four hours. You answer the description of a young woman who hitched a lift from the Bamford turn to the house between six and seven last night. You later checked into The Crown Hotel in the company of Andrew Penhallow, of Tudor Lodge—'

'He booked me in and then left me there,' she interrupted.

Unperturbed, Pearce continued, 'We'd like you to tell us what your relationship was with Mr Penhallow, why you visited him and what your intention was in remaining in Bamford.'

The interview room became so quiet Markby could hear the ticking of the clock on the wall and the soft breathing of the policewoman who was sitting not far from him.

In a strangled voice, Kate Drago asked, 'Why do you ask what my relationship with him *was?* Why not *is?* What's happened to him?'

'All in good time,' Pearce told her. 'Why don't you go on telling us about last night?'

She jumped to her feet and thrust her pale impassioned face at Pearce, who recoiled. 'Don't dare patronise me! Your sergeant made it clear something's happened to him and I'm not telling you anything until you tell me what! Is he hurt? Is he in hospital?'

Pearce didn't answer and she sank back in her chair, all colour drained from her face. Her grey eyes looked huge and for the first time since her arrival, frightened. 'Is he – has he—'

Pearce, flushed, straightened his tie and twitched his shoulders inside his tweed jacket. 'Mr Penhallow is dead!' he told her with perhaps unnecessary energy.

She swayed in the chair. The policewoman scrambled to her feet. The movement seemed to rally the witness who waved at the officer to signify she should stay back and whispered, 'I'm all right.'

But you don't look it, thought Markby. Whatever the relationship with the late Andrew Penhallow, it had been a close one.

Pearce was thinking the same thing. 'Would you like some water, Miss Drago? You seem very distressed at the news.'

'Of course I'm bloody distressed!' she burst out. The near-shouted words fractured the tense atmosphere. She leaned across the table, bronze hair rippling. 'You don't understand! Look – you must have got it wrong. He can't be dead! I've got to see him! I've got to talk to him! We haven't – hadn't – sorted out anything and there's so much—' The words spilling out of her came to an abrupt halt as speech seemed suddenly beyond her capability.

'I'm afraid he *is* dead, Miss Drago. You understand why we're anxious to trace both his movements and those of anyone who might have spoken to him or seen him within the last twenty-four hours. It's important that you are frank. Just tell us what you've been doing and with a bit of luck, we can eliminate you from our inquiries. I ask again, what was your relationship with Mr Penhallow?'

She sat back in her chair, put up both hands and swept back her tangled hair. In a low clear voice she said, 'There's little point in denying it now. Not that I ever denied it before. He was the one who didn't want— But it doesn't matter now what he wanted, does it? Or what I wanted? It's all wiped out, isn't it, by death? All that silly secrecy. In the end, it didn't matter.' She gave a mirthless little croak of laughter.

'That's right,' said Pearce, his voice touched by curiosity. 'It's not the time to be keeping secrets now. Were you lovers?'

'What?' She stared at him, apparently genuinely startled. Then, regaining her composure, she sat up straight, fixed Pearce with a fierce stare and demanded, 'Good grief, do you always ask that kind of question?'

In a handbag? thought Markby. She was either a very grand young woman or, as he'd already suspected, a very good actress. He wondered whether she was acquainted with Wilde's play.

The policewoman also hid a smile, caught Markby's eye, and looked guilty.

'I'm afraid,' said the unfortunate Pearce, reddening again, 'that I'm obliged to ask all kinds of awkward and embarrassing questions. Were you and Andrew Penhallow – were you his mistress?'

'You plods must be sleaze-obsessed! Of course I'm not – I wasn't – his mistress, you idiot!' The grey eyes sparked with anger. 'I'm his daughter!'

CHAPTER EIGHT

'Have they all gone?' Carla Penhallow raised her hand and turned her gaze towards her son's silhouette in the doorway.

'Yes, all of 'em, the police and Mrs Flack. I had to push her out of the door. She felt you needed a woman's presence to support you. I said we'd manage fine.' Luke squinted anxiously at his mother as if he wasn't as sure of this as he'd like to be.

The single table-lamp was still the only electric light in the drawing room, just as when Markby had seen it. But since his visit Mrs Flack had been busy and lit the log fire in the open hearth, filling the air with the scent of resin and the crackle of splitting wood fibres.

'Shock calls for warmth!' she had declared. 'And there's nothing so comforting as the sight of a real fire.'

Not only heat but light emanated from the hearth. The glow drew the contents of the room inward in cosy intimacy. Distorted shadows danced on the walls and ceiling. The logs whispered as the flames took hold and occasionally sent out a long hiss as if they'd been told a secret.

Carla huddled before them, an empty coffee mug at her feet. She leaned forward and peered intently into the flames, as children do when seeking pictures in the fire. She sat so close, Luke wondered she didn't burn her face. Yet despite the heat blasting from the hearth, she had donned an old cardigan of his father's over her sweater and drawn it tightly around her thin body, pushing her hands into the baggy sleeves in the manner of a mandarin.

He came further into the room. He was over six foot tall and powerfully built. The flames gave a rosy hue to his blunt, weather-tanned, good-natured features. In the setting of this old house, an observer might have thought him the very image of an eighteenth-century squire, just returned from riding around his land.

'How are you feeling now, Mum?'

She ignored his question to put a fretful one of her own.

'What were you all talking about? You were all arguing. I heard you.'

He frowned. 'Nothing. It was just a bit of police bureaucracy. Nothing to worry you.'

She looked up, suspicion in her face, so he was obliged to add, 'They wanted to remove Dad's guns. That's to say, they did remove them and I couldn't stop them, I'm afraid. First they made me take them out of the cupboard, though it was all locked up and I couldn't see the point of it. Then, when they wanted to take them away altogether, I told them pretty bluntly I couldn't see why. He had a perfectly good gun licence. I showed it to them. The guns were in a metal cupboard bolted to the wall and hadn't been fired in ages. Anyone could tell that. But they said that now he – that the licence had been issued to Dad and now it would have to be renewed in my name or yours if we wanted to keep them and we'd have to apply again. They ground on about regulations. They gave me a receipt. The police mind is beyond me. To think they'd waste time with that . . .' He broke off, resentment in his voice and face.

But her curiosity satisfied, his mother had returned to staring into the flickering logs. They crackled, spat and sent up a shower of orange sparks.

Luke balanced on his heels before her, picked up the empty mug and turned it between his palms. 'Mum, you really ought to eat something. You've had nothing all day, Irene Flack told me. Let me bring you something on a tray.'

She gave him a wan smile and reached out a thin hand to ruffle his hair. 'I don't fancy anything, darling.'

'You must have something!' he insisted.

'Well, a glass of whisky wouldn't go amiss!' she confessed.

'Not without something to eat as well. Look, I make a mean omelette, honestly. How about that with a couple of slices of toast?'

'Oh, Luke!' She gave a choked little laugh. 'What a fusspot you are. This is all wrong. I should be the one fussing around you. You've had such a shock, and the long drive, and dealing with the police . . . What a lousy mother I am.'

'Hey!' he protested. 'You're the best! I'm not a kid, you know.'

'Yes, I do know. But it seems so little time ago that you were just a small chap pedalling a trike round the garden – all right! I won't go on. I won't embarrass you with baby stories! Even though there's no one to overhear—' She broke off to put her face in her hands. 'No one . . .' Her voice was muffled through her fingers.

Luke got up, perched on the arm of her chair and put his brawny arm round her thin shoulders. 'I'm here,' he said.

They sat together in silence for a while, then Carla said calmly, 'I will have the omelette, then; we'll both have something to eat. That would be nice. Only do let's have a whisky first!'

He laughed, patted her arm and said, 'That's the ticket, Mum!'

A little later, when they'd eaten and Luke had piled the dishes into the sink to await Mrs Flack in the morning, he handed his mother another whisky.

'It's all right,' he said. 'I'm not trying to turn you into an alcoholic. It's a nightcap. Drink it down and get off to bed.'

Carla held the glass up to the firelight and its contents glowed like molten bronze. 'Drink it down? My dear boy, this is your father's precious eighteen-year-old Macallan. It should be treated with reverence.'

He grinned and threw himself into a nearby chair. The logs had burned down to blackened, crumbling skeletons, fringed with white ash which fell away with soft sighs into the embers. Carla tilted the whisky glass and watched the contents slide from side to side.

'Luke, dear, we have to brace ourselves. We're in for a very difficult time. No – let me finish. We've got to keep each other going. Your father's death, the manner of it—' She paused then resumed, 'It means that this house and everyone in it will be under a spotlight. It's going to be quite horrid. I don't mean the police, poking and prying, I mean the press, cameras . . . We shan't be able to go in and out freely. We shan't be able to talk to people.' She frowned. 'I really must have a word with Irene Flack in the morning. She mustn't gossip.'

'I think the police have warned her about that,' he said.

'Yes, but that's not the same thing as you or me telling her. It's a family thing, you see. Death is a family matter and Irene is a sort of family member. Or a household member if you prefer. Either way, she's worked here a dozen years and what she doesn't know about us—'

Luke interrupted earnestly, 'You really don't have to worry about old Irene, Mum. But I'll talk to her in the morning if it makes you happier.'

She looked at him with a firmness of expression he hadn't seen all day. 'It's not just your father's death which will be looked into.

There's his life – that will be taken apart, everything looked at. You've got to be prepared for that, Luke.'

Puzzled, he asked, 'What are they going to find?'

'I don't know. Probably nothing. But I've seen it happen before. Deaths, funerals, they release secrets. What I'm trying to say, Luke, dear, is that we mustn't let anything we learn change the way we think of Dad. Do you understand me? Whatever comes out – should there be anything – it mustn't sully our memories of him. That's very important. You do understand, don't you, Luke?'

He nodded unhappily, wondering why this over-heated room suddenly felt so chill.

His mother stood up and stooped to kiss his forehead. 'Good night, dear. Don't sit up too late. I dare say the police will be back first thing in the morning. I wonder if Alan Markby will come? You met him earlier, didn't you? He knew Dad as a boy. I hope they'll let him stay in charge of things but perhaps they won't.'

She walked to the door where she turned and repeated, 'Good night.'

'Good night, Mum.' He watched her go before turning back to the fire. It rustled in a way which seemed to be mocking him, and collapsed in upon itself in a puff of white ash. He had a premonition, which he couldn't fight off, that everything he'd taken for granted, his whole world, was about to follow it.

Kate Drago's claim to be the victim's daughter caused considerable consternation. Whatever they'd been waiting for, it hadn't been that. As Inspector Pearce afterwards put it, 'That put the cat among the pigeons, all right!' At that precise moment the unfortunate Pearce appeared flummoxed, unsure how to continue the questioning.

After the initial stunned silence, Markby got to his feet and moved towards the interview table. He could no longer remain only observer. Silently, the woman officer vacated her chair, surrendering it to him, and occupying his former seat in the corner. Pearce pushed his chair back, throwing Markby a glance almost of gratitude, clearly more than happy if the superintendent took over.

So, what did he ask? Markby wondered. Demand she prove it? Tackle that one later, he decided. Go along for the moment. He smiled at the girl.

'We didn't know that, Miss Drago.'

'No,' she said shortly. 'Very few people did. He didn't – there's his wife, you see. She doesn't know and he didn't want her to

94

find out.' A tiny frown mark briefly puckered her brows then smoothed out and she almost smiled. 'She'll have to find out now, won't she?'

'Yes, she'll have to be told.' Markby wondered what the girl was thinking. Her question had been put with a slight lift of tone as if she rather relished the prospect of Carla being told. Or was relieved by it? Not, at any rate, worried.

'Perhaps,' he encouraged, 'you'd like to tell us about it?'

When she looked doubtful, he added, 'I should tell you I knew Andrew Penhallow when we were boys, we were at school together.'

Pearce looked resigned at the fresh mention of Markby's schooldays and wondered what had led the other man to join the force. If he'd wanted a career in the law, why hadn't he gone for being a barrister or a judge or something? That's what that sort of public school background usually led to.

It's being out there where the action is, thought Pearce, answering his own question with a flash of insight. He doesn't like being brought in at the end, he wants to be there in the middle of it all. And he doesn't care about prestige. Look at the fight he put up to avoid being promoted to superintendent!

'I knew he was a Cornishman,' Markby was saying. 'That's to say, his parents lived in Cornwall and he thought of it as home. Or he did then. Later, I dare say, after he started travelling about so much, he thought of himself as a more cosmopolitan figure.'

'I suppose he did,' Kate said. 'He certainly didn't think of himself as a Cornishman, as you said. Well, a bit of a Cornishman. It's in the blood. You don't lose it.'

She settled back as if she'd decided to tell them everything and the atmosphere in the room became perceptibly less tense. They all relaxed. The policewoman crossed her ankles. Pearce looked as if he wished he had a cigarette but didn't like to ask if anyone minded. She probably would, the witness, and she'd tell him so.

'My mother's name was Helen and she's dead. You'll be wondering about that.' They all nodded in varying degrees of embarrassment. She went on briskly, 'He and my mother were childhood sweethearts. He went away to school, as you were saying, from an early age and she'd stayed at home. But their parents were neighbours and friends. So they'd always known one another.' She paused and fixed Markby with a direct questioning look. 'Tell me, honestly, do you think he'd have turned out a

95

different sort of person if he hadn't been sent away to school so young? Did you? Turn out differently, I mean.'

'I don't know,' Markby said. 'One can't know. I was packed off to boarding school at a very early age largely because my father had been sent. As it happened, my uncle, who was unmarried and the rector of Westerfield near here at the time, offered to chip in to pay the fees. My parents felt they couldn't turn a good offer down.' He paused. 'I don't think they ever questioned that it was a good offer.'

Uncle Henry had been quite a legend for his tight-fistedness. No wonder the offer hadn't been refused. It wouldn't have been repeated.

'Oh.' She thought about this and shrugged. 'Well, anyway, although my parents were always close, from childhood, they recognised they each wanted something different from life. He wanted to be famous and have a "proper" career. You know, cut a swathe in the world, that's what my mother always said.'

She paused again to consider her words. 'He was a very dull man, really. I suppose he just dreamed of being a pirate. Cornwall has a long tradition of pirates, smugglers, wreckers, that sort of thing. Like I said, it's in the blood. Mum, on the other hand, was an artist. She loved the North Cornwall coast and never wanted to leave it. It inspired her. She always said that when she was away for any length of time, she felt suffocated, as if she really couldn't breathe properly if it wasn't Cornish air. Another Cornish tradition is artists' colonies. So that's where she settled, in a nest of painters and potters. It suited her down to the ground.'

Kate's clear, grey, disconcerting gaze rested on Markby's face. 'So they each did what they wanted. They arranged it, while they were still both very young, just teenagers. He would go away and she would stay. That's what they did. He had his high-powered career and in due time a high-profile wife. She had her painting and me.'

She fell into abrupt silence. Markby wisely didn't interrupt and when he saw Pearce open his mouth to ask something, signalled him to wait. She needed time to gather up her memories and sort them through. It was a painful process for her. The line of her jaw was taut and the pulse twitched in her long white neck. He wondered whether the artist mother, or any of her painter friends, had ever used Kate as a model.

She began again. 'Mum told me they hadn't planned me, but when she found she was pregnant, they were both delighted. She really believed that. I believe her, as far as her own feelings went. She really loved me. I'm less sure about him. I doubt he was nearly as chuffed as he liked to make out, but well, he went along with it. He wouldn't have wanted to upset her by suggesting she get rid of me. Anyway, he trusted her to be discreet and keep me down there with her in Cornwall. But I'm sure that from the start I was a complication he could well have done without! Oh, he never said anything, to her or to me,' Kate added hurriedly. 'Don't get me wrong. But you don't fool a child. A child always sees through adult pretence.'

'Yes,' Markby said. 'A child does always suss out a fake.'

He thought of his sister's children and the terrifying ability they all had to read the adult mind, especially Emma, the eldest.

Suddenly he realised what it was about this girl worried him. It was the similarity to his niece. Emma, outwardly a doughty, capable young lady of thirteen, was inwardly a sensitive little soul. It's so easy to damage children like that, to be unaware that they are struggling when they appear to be coping. Perhaps, he thought, what both Emma and Kate here lack is a sense of humour. They are both so deadly serious. He wished he hadn't used the word 'deadly'.

Kate was talking again. 'After I was born he took a sort of financial responsibility for me. He never paid money directly to her. He was too clever for that. But he took care to pay something because even Mum might've kicked up a fuss if he hadn't. She had no money and a baby costs a lot. He helped her buy a small picture gallery – a bit of a tourist trap – and from then on made regular business loans which were never repaid. She thought that was fair. She was so trusting. She thought he was doing his best. Later he paid for my private education. It was at a local day school, a convent. Mum liked it that way, to have me coming home at the end of every day. But really, I wasn't to be sent away, you see, because at a boarding school anywhere there'd be a chance I might meet up with a daughter of one of his colleagues.' Her mouth twisted in derision. 'He wasn't a fool.'

Markby didn't altogether agree with the last statement, but didn't say so. If not a fool, then Penhallow had been extremely short-sighted. Surely he'd realised that sooner or later a day of reckoning must dawn, the whole story emerge? He'd apparently done nothing to prepare for it, trusting in the deviousness of earlier arrangements.

Kate's mind was running on the same lines. 'I don't know what he thought would happen when Mum got older or when I grew up. I don't think he wanted to think about it. Even when Mum's cancer was diagnosed he didn't seem to grasp how serious it was. It was discovered too late for really effective treatment. She made the choice to stop all treatment when it became clear she wasn't going to get better. "All that pain," she said. "For nothing. I don't want to die in a hospital bed. I want to die at home, where I can see the sea from my bedroom window and hear and smell the waves." So that's what she did.'

The speaker's voice was cool and taut but the trauma of her mother's final pain-filled weeks had burned itself deep into her being. Markby wondered whether she'd had a chance to grieve properly, let it all out and have a good cry, sob on an understanding shoulder. Not on Andrew's at any rate. And with the buried grief was buried anger. A desire to blame someone for Fate's cruelty. What more obvious a hate-figure than the man who'd loved but left?

'He didn't come to her funeral,' Kate said. 'He was away in Europe and so sorry he couldn't make it. He sent a splendid wreath with a formal card attached. "Dear friend of childhood", it read. I don't suppose I'd have expected him to write, "dear lover" or "dear mistress" or "dear mother of my child", but I do think he could have done a bit better, don't you?'

Yes, thought Markby. She's hurt, bitter and very, very angry.

'He did drive down to see me a couple of weeks afterwards. He took me out for a pub lunch and asked me what my plans were.' Kate drew a deep breath. 'He was so casual, as if I wasn't his own flesh, for crying out loud! It made me so bloody mad! I gave him a really dirty look and asked him, what did *he* intend to do about me now?

'That shook him. He turned pale then red.' Kate's voice held the first note of amusement, but it was an unkind mirth. 'He had to order another whisky. Then he made a speech, a pompous one. He pointed out I'd reached eighteen, the legal age of majority, and completed my schooling for which he'd paid. He didn't see what more he could do. Surely I didn't expect him to go on paying for my upkeep – that was his word, as if I were a house, not a person – for ever? I should get a job. The gallery had been closed down during Mum's illness but perhaps I could reopen it? Branch out? Do coffees and Cornish cream teas.'

She leaned forward so suddenly that her audience started back. 'He was saying I should carry on where Mum had left off, stay down there in Cornwall, out of his way, for ever! They'd buried my mother and he was trying to bury me! I thought, you bastard. No, you don't, you don't dump me like that! I told him I wasn't trained for any career and I thought I ought to get some qualifications. But to do that, I'd have to go to college somewhere, and I'd need some financial support.' She gave a brisk nod.

Markby had a vision of the two of them, huddled in the corner of some cosy pub, Kate outlining her terms while Andrew listened helpless and aghast.

'He said,' Kate was continuing, 'after he'd had another good swig of whisky, that he realised the circumstances were unusual. He meant my mother's death. He agreed it was a sensible idea for me get some qualifications. I could see his mind working, you know, thinking it out. If I were qualified in some way, I'd get a better paid job and be less likely to keep coming to him. So, he said, if I needed a couple of years to get myself organised, then he was prepared to pay me a modest allowance until I reached twenty-one, the old age of majority. But I was to keep quiet about it. If asked, I was to say it was money left to me by my mother. I thought, you mean old bugger!'

Markby, devil's advocate, prompted, 'You thought he should have made a better financial settlement on you?'

She jumped up, the chair scraping on the floor and rocking, and Pearce moved forward now in alarm. Markby waved him back.

Kate shouted, 'Are you really so stupid? I didn't want his *money*!'

'No,' Markby said quietly. 'You wanted public recognition.'

She sank back into the wooden chair. 'Yes! I'm – I was – his daughter! I wanted to hear him say it to the world!'

'But that was something he felt he couldn't do,' Markby pointed out. 'Nor was it part of the original deal he made with your mother.'

'He didn't make a deal with *me*!' she said coldly. 'You say he *couldn't* declare it, I say he *wouldn't*. So I decided to force his hand. Looking back, the whole thing had been on his terms from the start of his affair with my mother. It was high time someone else called the shots.'

'Now wait a moment,' Markby contradicted her gently. 'You said yourself your mother wanted it that way. She wanted to stay at home and paint, and she did. She was able to do that largely because he financed it. It's hard to make a living from painting otherwise.'

Certainly, in his view, her parents had been equally selfish. But Kate wasn't prepared to hear criticism of her mother.

'She wanted to stay in Cornwall,' Kate said patiently, as if he were especially obtuse. 'But anything they'd fixed up had to change once she'd had his child, didn't it? He had responsibilities.'

'He paid your school fees, and that in addition to the money he gave towards the gallery. It represented a considerable financial outlay for him.'

Markby frowned as he heard himself speak the words. Yes, a lot of money over the years. And was it possible his wife had never suspected? Never noticed that there was never quite as much money as there ought to be?

Kate was looking impatient again. 'Mum wasn't a business-woman. She wasn't practical at all. Of course she was happy enough to accept the "business loan" arrangement. That's how he paid my school fees, not directly. Just increased the business loans. What Mum didn't grasp was that there was no formal recognition implied in that. Nothing she could hold him to. It was voluntary on his part. Nothing legal. No written agreement. No ink on paper acknowledgement I was his child. He could simply have discontinued the arrangement if she'd tried to change the rules. Or even called the money in, if she'd been really difficult, tried to move away from Cornwall, for example. But she trusted him and anyway, she was an artist, she didn't worry about money. If it was there, fine. If it wasn't, well, wait till it turned up. So long as there was enough to pay the electricity bill, for food and the odd bottle of wine, most of all for the painting necessities!' Kate smiled but the smile faded quickly.

'Even her death fell convenient for him, just as I reached eighteen! You see, I think he'd long tired of the affair and he meant to discontinue all payments once I was eighteen, not just the money for me, but all the money. He was going to dump her. There's nothing good about cancer, but at least poor Mum was spared any showdown with him over money and, even worse, being abandoned after so many years. That would have destroyed her. But she'd have let him off the hook, you know, let him walk away, just forget us. But I'm not like my mother . . .' Kate's eyes met Markby's again and the colour of them now was akin to burnished steel. 'I wasn't going to allow him to forget *me!*'

'Phew!' muttered Pearce.

It was impossible, thought Markby wryly, not to feel a little sorry for the hapless Penhallow, even if he had been author of his own misfortunes! But he felt sorry for all three people in the case. What a mess people made of their lives and of their children's lives.

With real interest he asked, 'Did you see much of him while you were growing up?'

'When I was small, yes. He came fairly frequently. He and Mum, they were still, you know, still actively lovers then. He always brought expensive presents. I got a foreign doll in a silk dress, a little pink bike, a silver-backed hairbrush and mirror, little girl presents. The sort of things a man like that imagines a girl will want. I never liked dolls. I liked the bike best. Later on I'd have liked a computer but by then he'd given up trying to find gifts and just gave me a tenner when he saw me. At the same time, I don't want you to think there wasn't any fun! He was always very jolly in those days. He made Mum happy. She glowed when he was there. We laughed a lot and played silly games and went down to the beach hunting for shells and coins and things.'

Almost inaudibly she concluded, 'I always knew he was my father. I wanted desperately for him to like me. I always suspected that really, in his heart, he didn't like me and that's why he gave me the presents. It was guilt.'

'You may be wrong on that one,' Markby told her.

'Love doesn't set conditions,' Kate said bleakly. 'It doesn't say, look, I love you but there are all these rules . . .'

'You're wrong on that one, too,' Markby said.

The policewoman, in her corner, lifted her head and gave the superintendent a curious look.

More briskly, Markby invited, 'Tell us about your visit to Tudor Lodge. Your intention was to confront him in the bosom of his family, is that it? Cause a scene?'

'No! No, not cause a scene!' She frowned. 'I'm not – not like that. I'm not the hysterical type. I wanted to embarrass him, yes. I thought, it might force him to come clean and tell them who I was.'

'Showing scant regard for their feelings,' he suggested.

She flushed and thought about that for a moment. 'Yes, I suppose, if you put it like that, it wouldn't have been very nice for them and after all, they never did me any wrong.'

'"They" being his wife and son, Luke?'

'Yes.' For a moment she seemed about to add something but changed her mind.

'You'd never met or spoken to either of them?'

'I've never met or spoken to Carla. I've seen her on television.' Reluctantly she added, 'I have met Luke. But he didn't know who I was at the time. It was at a party. I sort of wangled my way there. I was curious to see my half-brother. I don't know if Luke even remembers me. Probably not. I was just a girl. I did get myself into a couple of photos, though. I rather hoped my father might see one of them, but apparently he didn't because nothing was said. So I got hold of some copies and decided to take them to Bamford and show him them myself! I hitched here. I was lucky and found a lorry driver at a lay-by, having some coffee at one of those mobile snack bars. He took me most of the way and dropped me where the road turns off. A woman car driver picked me up after that and took me right to the door of Tudor Lodge. Actually, I wasn't too pleased about that. She knew the family and was curious, dying to ask me questions, really nosy. But I didn't encourage her and she gave up, thank goodness!'

Markby suppressed a smile.

Kate shook her bronze mane. 'But that's why I came, to show him the snaps. I thought that would really push him into doing something.'

'And did it?'

She didn't answer but her complexion whitened and her mouth twitched as if the question had really touched a nerve. Whatever Andrew's reaction had been, it hadn't been the one she'd wanted. But what had she wanted? That he accept what he'd always refused to do, just like that, in a moment? Shout out to the whole household that his illegitimate daughter had arrived and they should all come and meet her? No, she hadn't really thought it through.

As if to confirm this, Kate said stiffly, 'I don't know how I thought he'd tell them.' She pushed back her hair. 'But anyway, as it turned out, they weren't there. That is, Carla was in the house but she was upstairs lying down. Migraine, he said.' She fell silent.

As Markby didn't speak, Pearce took up the questioning, surer of his ground now. 'When you arrived at the house, did you go to the front door?'

'What?' It was as if she'd forgotten Pearce. She stared at him for a moment with a blank expression before rallying. 'Oh no, to the kitchen door.' She made a moue of irony. 'To the tradesmen's entrance! There was no light on in the front of the house so I walked around the back and there was a light in the kitchen. I peeped in the window and I saw my father. He was making a cup of tea. Why am I telling you this? I've explained who I am and why I came to this horrible little town.'

'You just carry on,' Pearce invited, an edge to his normally pleasant voice. 'What happened next?'

'All right!' She glowered at Pearce. 'I knocked at the door. He opened it. He was surprised but invited me in. He was afraid, I suppose, that if he tried to keep me out and I raised my voice, his wife might hear.' She stopped and showed no sign of going on.

'And . . .' prompted Pearce.

'You know,' she said, 'this really is none of your business. It's got nothing to do with whatever you're inquiring into. And listen, you haven't yet told me how he – died. What's your interest? Why've I been dragged in here?' A scowl puckered her fine eyebrows.

'We're treating his death as suspicious,' Pearce snapped. 'That makes everything our business.'

Markby realised Dave was thoroughly fed up. The girl had managed to throw him off his stroke. Well, he was going to have to put up with a lot more hassle from this witness before the matter was settled. He'd just have to learn to handle it, thought Markby unkindly.

The girl's pale complexion had taken on a greyish tinge. In a rush, she said, 'My father asked me in, gave me a cup of tea, then bundled me out of the house. He left me in that dreary hotel where your sergeant found me. He was alive when I last saw him, all right? He was fine!' She drew a steadying breath. 'So that's it. Can I go now? Or do I have to sign something?'

'All in good time!' snapped Pearce. 'What time did Penhallow leave you at the hotel?'

Kate had already half risen from her seat. 'I don't know, eight, maybe? There was a receptionist, she can tell you if you check.'

'Miss Drago,' Pearce sounded just a little triumphant, 'we have a report of a young woman answering your general description who was seen in the vicinity of Tudor Lodge some time after nine yesterday evening. The young woman was walking briskly from the direction of the town centre. Could that have been you? Did you return later?'

She sat down again and for only the second time in the entire interview so far Markby sensed fear. She muttered, 'It was the pits, that hotel. What was I supposed to do? Just hang around there until he'd thought of some way of getting rid of me? I went down to the dining room and had a disgusting meal, a nameless fish in a floury sauce and steamed vegetables. It was all they had left. I probably did the hotel cat out of his dinner.'

Markby sympathised. The Crown wasn't noted for its cuisine.

'I put my head round the door of the bar,' Kate went on. 'The barman gave me what he imagined was a sexy look. I didn't fancy him or sitting there being ogled by him and all the lowlife infesting the place, so what was I to do? Sit in that grubby bedroom watching TV? I was angry. I don't like being dumped. I thought, I'll go back, try again. I walked because there wasn't any bus and there wasn't a sign of a taxi. It didn't take all that long, about twenty minutes. When I got there I saw the kitchen light was still on so I did as I'd done the first time, walked around to the back of the house. I could see my father through the window, just as I did the last time but this time he was filling a hot-water bottle.'

Kate looked down at her hands. 'It was such an ordinary thing to be doing. It made him look, I don't know, somehow older and more vulnerable. He was wearing a dressing gown and just looked like an old gent getting ready to go to bed. I even felt a bit ashamed of harrying him.' She rallied and attempted to cover up this admission of momentary weakness. 'I wasn't harrying him, really, but it was just the sight of the hot-water bottle, you know . . .'

They all nodded. Markby asked, 'He didn't notice you?'

'No. I stood there for a bit, not certain what to do and then—'

She began to fidget and look unhappy. Pearce sat up straight. Was a confession about to be delivered?

One was, but not the one Dave Pearce hoped for.

'Look,' Kate said, leaning forward confidentially. 'This will sound really weird. But as I stood there I had the oddest feeling. As if I wasn't alone in the garden. It was really scary. I peered about and got the shock of my life. I saw someone standing at the far corner of the house, just watching me. I froze. I didn't know what to do, who it was . . .'

'What did this newcomer look like?' Markby asked her.

Kate shifted unhappily on her chair. 'I can't tell you. I don't even know which sex it was. It was just a shape, but definitely human. It just stood and watched making no sound, as if waiting to see what I'd do. I couldn't see any features. Frankly, it was unearthly. I was stressed out and perhaps it was my imagination, but oh damn, I just turned and fled, all right? It was a really stupid thing to do and telling you now, in the cold light of day, it sounds so feeble and – cowardly, I suppose. But I was in a pretty upset state and it was just the last straw.'

'And went where?'

She gave Pearce an exasperated look. 'Back to the hotel from hell, where else?' She put her clasped hands on the table and added in a firm voice, 'And that's it, all of it. Believe me or not, that's what happened. If you want to talk to me any more, I'd like a solicitor present. I do know one, as it happens. His name is Frederick Green and he lives in London, Hampstead, so you'll have to wait until he can get here and that won't be before tomorrow, I imagine.' A spark of malice showed in her grey eyes. 'So, end of conversation, right?'

End of conversation, right, thought Markby. Until the legal eagle got here. In the meantime, what to do with her?

'If you're released, will you undertake to remain at the hotel until we need you?' he asked.

'Who's paying?' she asked rudely. 'It costs money.'

'We can accommodate you in the cells overnight, if you like!' snapped the goaded Pearce, who'd had enough.

She leaned forward, 'No you damn well can't! Not unless you charge me first! I've co-operated fully with you and all your stupid questions! I've not been charged with anything and unless you mean to change that, I'm leaving!' She jumped to her feet, clearly furious.

'And we've not finished questioning you, Miss Drago!' Pearce retorted.

She sat down again, folded her arms and gave him a glacial smile. 'Go ahead, then. Lock me in your dungeon. Freddie Green will have me out of there in five seconds when he gets to hear of it!'

'We appreciate your frank co-operation, Miss Drago,' Markby interpolated, glancing at Pearce. 'But as the inspector says, we would be fully entitled to hold you overnight in the circumstances. However, I realise that your relationship to the dead man means this is a very stressful business for you, and so, I'll ask you again whether you will undertake to stay at The Crown until your solicitor gets here?'

'All right,' she conceded. 'I'll stay at the wretched hotel. I've just about got the money.'

Markby asked mildly, 'Did you bring a change of clothes with you?' She must have had something in that knapsack.

'How thoughtful of you,' she said sarcastically, mistaking his purpose in asking the question. 'I can manage.'

'You misunderstand.' He was obliged to make it clear. 'We shall need the clothes you're wearing. This officer—' he indicated the policewoman – 'she'll accompany you to the hotel and collect your outer clothing, including shoes and that yellow scarf.'

Kate's hand strayed to the scarf. 'Why? What the hell is this?' She broke off and the flush which had stained her cheeks drained away to leave them grey. 'You're looking for blood and stuff!' The words were croaked, the true horror of her situation striking her with physical force, snatching her breath.

Markby did his best to reassure her. 'It's routine. Don't worry, you'll get them all back but not for a day or two. So, do you have a change of clothing?'

The girl opposite him shifted miserably on her chair. 'I – not exactly a change of clothes. I brought a pair of black silky trousers and a striped silk top. Shoes? Yes, just a pair of patent slip-ons to wear with the other things. The clothes pack up small and don't crease. I – I thought I might need to dress up for something.'

Her face was burning by now and Markby could guess the reason. She was being humiliated. What the girl had hoped, of course, was that her father would present her to his family, that she'd be welcomed, invited to dinner perhaps? And there would be need for some smarter, fancier gear. Pathetically, as it now seemed, or perhaps it had been defiantly, she had packed her party clothes.

She thrust aside her embarrassment and fought back. 'I should damn well hope you won't keep them long! I can't go around in silk pants and top all day like a tart!' She gave Pearce a malicious look. 'Well, Freddie's an old friend. He can bring me down some clothes. In the meantime, I'm not saying another word until he gets here, right?'

'We're taking a risk, aren't we?' Pearce asked, when Kate had left. 'Letting her walk out of here like that?'

He was looking sullen, which was unlike Dave, normally a placid individual. It was something about the girl, thought Markby. First Prescott, now Pearce. It's nothing to do with police work, it's just biology. Prescott's smitten and Dave, even though happily married, is rattled.

Firmly he said, 'Possibly, but I don't think so. Look at it this way, she's a highly articulate and intelligent young woman. If we incarcerate her in a police cell overnight, she'll take her revenge by being as awkward as possible from now on. And she's asked for her solicitor, so we can't question her any more now until he turns up.'

'She's awkward now!' fumed Pearce. 'When this smart-aleck solicitor arrives, there'll be two of 'em!'

'Come on, Dave. She has co-operated, as she said, very well in the circumstances. I don't think she'll take off. She came here for a purpose, remember! To get her father to acknowledge her before his family! Nothing so far has indicated she's given up that goal.'

'But he's dead, her father,' objected Pearce. 'So if that was her plan, it's scotched! And we haven't established she's telling us the truth about that, being his daughter, I mean. It's the sort of thing she can say now that both he and her mother are dead. Who's to prove it or disprove it?'

'Penhallow is dead,' Markby replied. 'But Carla and the boy, Luke, are still very much here. So, as far as Kate Drago is concerned, the plan's still achievable.'

'You mean, she'll hang around until she can find a way to confront *them*?' Pearce looked horrified. 'And we'll let her? Surely that's hardly fair on them?'

'Nothing's fair about murder, Dave. I believe that Kate Drago will stay here for as long as there's the slightest chance of meeting the Penhallows. Her coming here was with the purpose of being introduced to them. She even brought along a smart outfit in case she got an invitation to stay. She's not a girl to give up a long-held determination at the first serious hurdle. She's a fighter, Dave, not a bolter. When she does meet up with them it may lead, as they say, to developments! Her story was presented convincingly just now, but perhaps she's a good actress. I want to know a lot more about her, and we'll learn more at this stage by letting her loose, than by keeping her incommunicado in a cell.'

Pearce chewed his lower lip mutinously. 'She tells a pretty thin story. She came back, she saw the old chap Penhallow—'

Markby cleared his throat and murmured that he and the late Andrew Penhallow had been more or less contemporaries.

'I didn't mean old as in *old* . . .' Pearce made good his *faux pas*. 'I mean, you know, it's a turn of phrase, isn't it? I was going to say, she saw old – she saw the late Mr Penhallow through the window. He was alone. I go along with all that. But then her story enters fairyland. She saw a mysterious shadowy form, can't say whether male or female, and promptly takes to her heels and this, mind you, after she's walked all the way from The Crown back to Tudor Lodge with the purpose of having a second interview with him! It doesn't sound right, not to me.'

Markby thought about it. 'I admit she's vague about the shadowy form she says she saw in the garden. As to whether it'd be enough to spook her into running . . . She was very strung up and it was late. She'd counted on finding her father alone as on the first occasion. If she'd thought someone else was approaching the house, she might have decided to cut and run on impulse. Don't forget, if she was able to spy on her father through the kitchen window, then anyone else in the back gardens could have done the same. Perhaps someone else was hanging around, contemplating breaking in and then, very conveniently, Andrew Penhallow opened the door! Mind you,' Markby added, 'Tudor Lodge is reputed to have a ghost!'

'Ghosts don't bash people's heads in!' said Pearce.

Markby found Prescott in the canteen, hunched gloomily over some cooling coffee and a half-eaten doughnut. Fortunately, there was only one other person there, one of the civilian employees who was sitting with her back to the room.

Markby put his hand on the chair opposite the sergeant and asked, 'Mind if I join you?'

'Go ahead . . .' mumbled Prescott without looking up. As Markby sat down, he raised his head and belatedly saw who had spoken. His chair scraped noisily as he half rose to his feet. 'Sorry, sir! Didn't realise . . .'

The superintendent waved him back to his seat. 'I don't want to disturb you or hold you up. You'll be going off duty I dare say.'

'Been off duty for the last half-hour,' confessed Prescott.

Markby smiled. 'In no hurry to get home? The canteen staff will be flattered.'

Prescott looked embarrassed and shifty.

'Or possibly,' Markby went on mildly, 'waiting to hear how the interview with Miss Drago turned out?'

There was no need for the unfortunate Prescott to answer that. He turned brick red and knocked the doughnut off the table.

Markby waited while Prescott retrieved the pastry from the floor and pushed it and the crockery aside.

'We've released the lady,' said Markby. 'So I'm afraid if you were waiting here in the hope of a sighting, she's already left.

She was driven back to The Crown where she's undertaken to stay at least until her solicitor gets here from London – which will be first thing tomorrow morning. She's spoken with him on the phone. She'll be back with him to answer further questions.'

Prescott looked apprehensive. 'How did it go? The interview?'

'Oh, she was fairly frank and helpful. She admits returning to the house later yesterday evening, but says she was frightened off by a prowler in the gardens.'

Prescott brightened. 'Someone else was there!'

'So she says. Even if it's true, it doesn't mean she didn't do it.' Markby crushed the sergeant's clear hope. 'So if you think she didn't, just try and keep an open mind, anyway. I've met some charming murderers in my time.'

He felt sorry for the younger man, but it was true. Villains who'd looked like angels . . . he could think of several.

Brusquely, he ordered, 'At the moment, the finger is pointing squarely at her. You can start with checking her story regarding her journey to Bamford. We know she was set down at the gate of Tudor Lodge around six fifty. We have that witness, and incidentally, the witness also remarked on her curious manner long before we had any reason to think anything was going wrong at Tudor Lodge.'

Prescott, with the air of a man risking his career, murmured, 'Do I check that witness out again, sir?'

'You know as well as I do, the witness is Miss Mitchell. She's an observant person and, as a witness, reliable. She'll give her evidence again any time. Incidentally, she saw a lorry had stopped at the Bamford turn which supports the girl's claim to have been given a lift in a lorry. What I suggest you do is start at the beginning, which means find that trucker. Get Kate Drago to describe the spot where she was picked up. Find who brought her that far from London, if you can. I'd like to trace her back to her own doorstep, though probably we shan't be able to do it. But we certainly ought – or you ought – to be able to find the lorry in which she travelled the last leg of the way.'

'Yessir!' said Prescott enthusiastically.

Markby detained him as he was about to bolt for the door. 'And when you've done that, find the night porter at The Crown – you can track him down at home. He saw her go out and he should have seen her come back from her second visit to the house. Find out what time she came back and if she looked distressed.'

'He'll have heard all about the murder by now,' objected Prescott glumly. 'And he'll know all about Kate, about Miss Drago, too. He'll say she came back covered in blood, with her eyes rolling, brandishing a knife.'

Markby, who knew that witnesses liked to be wise after the event, suppressed a smile. 'So, be prepared, and bring him back to reality. Incidentally, forensics are looking at her jacket, jeans and boots. If they do find Penhallow's blood . . .'

'I know her blood group,' Prescott said unexpectedly. 'I saw her blood donor's card. It's A negative, that's unusual, isn't it?'

'She's an unusual young woman.' Markby got to his feet. 'So just remember, you're a copper, right? That doesn't mean you don't have feelings, but if they get in the way of your job, then it's time to speak out and say so! No one will hold it against you. I'll get someone else to do the work.'

The young man flushed a dusky red. 'I know my job, sir.'

'Fine. So now go home and get some rest. Tomorrow,' said Markby, 'is likely to be a very busy day for all of us!'

And that included himself. Of course, he wasn't obliged to give up his Saturday, but he couldn't leave things now, not simmering away as they were, and especially not with Kate's solicitor arriving in the morning. That was an interview at which he needed to be present.

He hoped Meredith would appreciate this argument, but he had a feeling she probably wouldn't.

CHAPTER NINE

Mrs Crouch set down the teapot and patted its gaily striped woolly jacket. It was a gesture which seemed to reassure her. 'You'll have a bit of sponge cake?' she asked.

Meredith held out her plate. Mrs Crouch's sponge cakes weren't to be refused. It was the traditional hour of 'elevenses', though technically only ten thirty on Saturday morning. Moreover, although coffee was the usual drink at mid-morning, at the Crouches' they drank tea. It was something to do with Mrs Crouch's mistrust of the coffee percolator and Barney Crouch's refusal to drink the instant variety.

It had been on Meredith's mind that she should warn her elderly neighbours about the possibility of a sneak thief. She knew that they were lax about locking doors during the daytime. Mrs Crouch was inclined to keep to country habits acquired in youth and more trusting times. Barney wouldn't even think about it. As Alan had rung late the previous evening and explained that he'd be tied up at least during Saturday morning, Meredith had been given a good moment to call round with her news.

As she'd expected, other news had preceded hers. Andrew Penhallow's violent death was the talk of Bamford. It put Meredith in a tricky position. She didn't particularly want to discuss it. She certainly didn't want to reveal her acquaintance with Carla Penhallow. That would lead to eager demands for information from the horse's mouth, information she couldn't provide (and wouldn't, if she could).

After listening to the Crouches' version of the murder (highly coloured and including several digressions of their own invention), she attempted to divert their attention with her own tale of the youthful burglar. She was, however, too late. News travelled fast in the town, leaving Meredith hopelessly in its wake. At the moment, Bamford was doing unusually well for outrageous news. Moving effortlessly from one subject to another, the Crouches informed her that an elderly neighbour had already discovered the presence of the young prowler.

'Mrs Etheridge,' said Mrs Crouch. She reflected. 'It would be her, wouldn't it? You know what she's like. Mind you, she was a nervous girl, as I recall. When we were at school, the boys used to drop slugs down the back of her dress to hear her scream. And she could scream, could Janet. Fit to bust your eardrums.'

The idea of the dragon-like Mrs Etheridge she knew as a nervous youngster proved beyond Meredith's powers of imagination. But her lack of response was unnoticed by Mrs Crouch, who flowed on.

'Young devil. If I caught him I'd give him a bit of my mind.'

'Give old Janet something new to complain about,' mumbled Barney Crouch disrespectfully from his fireside chair. 'Once she's over the shock of it, she'll be telling the tale for months.'

His wife shook a teaspoon at him. 'As it happens Janet and I are of an age. We've got birthdays only a week apart. So don't you be making so much of the "old". And it's nothing to be taking lightly. If it happened to you, you'd have plenty to say!' She turned back to her visitor. 'Honestly, Meredith, I don't know what young people are coming to. It was never like it in my day.'

'Yes, it was!' argued Barney. 'There have always been child thieves. Make good thieves, kids. Small and nimble, that's it. Squeeze through a tiny gap, wriggle out of your grip and then look like butter wouldn't melt in their mouths. Adult rogues have always used kids. Charles Dickens wrote about it. The Artful Dodger and all the rest of them.'

'Oh, in London!' Mrs Crouch dismissed his interruption as irrelevant. 'I dare say in London, or a big place like that. But not in Bamford!'

Barney rolled his eyes at Meredith and then winked. Seeing suspicion on his wife's plump features, he promptly buried his nose in his cup.

'Well,' Mrs Crouch continued her story, but keeping her eye firmly on the miscreant, 'she'd been out shopping, had Janet Etheridge, and brought quite a lot back, some of it in her shopping trolley and some in a plastic carrier bag. She got to the door and she noticed there was a kid hanging about in the road kicking a can. But that's not unusual, the way the youngsters hang around now with nothing to do. I don't know what's wrong with them. They don't seem able to entertain themselves, except by doing wrong. It's all those computers. That's what I say.'

'I used to climb over folks' walls and pinch apples and plums,' said Barney.

'You would!' she snapped. 'Well, Janet opened her front door and carried the plastic carrier into her hall. Then she went back for her trolley, and do you know what?' She paused dramatically.

'No,' said Meredith, as she was expected to.

'Of course she doesn't,' growled Barney, 'if you haven't told her yet!'

'I know you do it to annoy me and I shall just ignore it, there, so you needn't bother!' Mrs Crouch informed her husband loftily. She returned her attention to Meredith and took up her tale. 'Just in those few moments she'd had her back turned, he'd nipped over her front wall and grabbed her purse. She'd left it on the top of her trolley. She turned back just in time to see him jump over the wall back into the road and set off full pelt. Course, she couldn't catch him.'

'Oh dear,' Meredith sympathised. 'It was unwise of her to leave her purse unattended like that.'

'You don't think someone's going to pinch it when you're only a few feet away, do you?' argued Mrs Crouch. 'She'd only turned her back a minute and when she turned back, there it was – gone!'

'How can it be there when it's gone?' asked Barney pedantically. 'I do wish you wouldn't misuse the English language the way you do!'

The Crouches hadn't been married all that long. Mrs Crouch, formerly Mrs Pride, was a local woman and had been a widow. Barney was an 'incomer', a Londoner by birth and a scriptwriter in his day. He'd retired to a lonely house near Bamford with the intention, as he was wont to tell people, of peacefully drinking his days away. 'And then I met a good woman! Before I knew it, I was married and domesticated.'

'And very comfortable,' his wife would add. 'You'd be crippled with rheumatism by now in that damp old house, to say nothing of your liver gone to pieces with whisky.'

The Crouches wrangled all day and, as Meredith realised, took considerable pleasure in the verbal fencing.

'It's money, I suppose,' Mrs Crouch was saying. 'They just look out for any bit of cash lying around. I mean, they couldn't take *things*. If a child like that turned up with a new radio, say, or a valuable piece of silver, questions would be asked.'

'Kids like that,' muttered Barney, 'know where to find a fence.'

'Not in Bamford,' his wife repeated. 'It's all very well you talking about London, Barney, but the only fences we've got in Bamford are made of wood and wire and go round folks' gardens.'

'You'd think, wouldn't you,' Barney addressed Meredith, 'that this town was innocence personified?'

This was definitely not a suitable remark in view of recent events. Mrs Crouch looked grim and observed that in her young day, people weren't battered to death in their own homes, not in Bamford. Barney managed to restrain himself from pointing out that Penhallow hadn't been inside his house, but outside it. Meredith agreed it was a shocking thing and edged the conversation back to the youthful intruder.

'Do you think Mrs Etheridge could describe the boy? It would be worth knowing if it were the same one.'

'A gang?' cried Mrs Crouch.

'Go and ask her,' suggested Barney. 'She'll be pleased to see you.' He gave a suppressed chuckle. 'More'n that. She'll be delighted!'

'I do believe,' said Mrs Etheridge calmly, 'that the world is coming to an end.'

There was, Meredith reflected, no answer to that. Visiting Mrs Etheridge didn't mean comfortable chairs, pots of tea and homemade cake. Meredith sat stiffly on an upright chair, sprung so fiercely it might have served as a primitive ejector seat. She had been offered, with clear reluctance, a cup of watery instant coffee and a Bourbon biscuit. Nevertheless, Mrs Etheridge was keen to talk about her recent alarming experience, as Barney had rightly guessed. She did so at some length, putting her own particular spin on events.

'There are signs of it everywhere,' continued Mrs Etheridge. 'Even here in Bamford. Decay and corruption all around. Only look at what happened over at Tudor Lodge, that poor Mr Penhallow. But chickens do come home to roost, don't they?'

This seemed such a *non sequitur* that Meredith was seduced from her resolve not to discuss the murder and asked, 'What do you mean?'

Mrs Etheridge leaned forward. 'Haven't you heard? They do say Mr Penhallow's past caught up with him. He'd been keeping two families, you know, and neither one knew about the other, there! Whether he married both women or not, I couldn't say.

But if he did, he'd be a bigamist, wouldn't he? Or if he didn't, I don't know that it makes it any better. What's more, one of his illegitimate children has turned up. It stands to reason a thing like that is going to cause trouble.'

The coffee slopped in Meredith's cup and she saved it from spilling in the nick of time. She realised her mouth was gaping and closed it hurriedly.

To say this was a new development would be putting it mildly! If true, it would prove shattering. When she'd last spoken to Alan, the girl had been no more than a hitchhiker, mysterious perhaps, but nothing had suggested a revelation like this! A daughter? Had Andrew really been leading a double life?

She shook her head to clear it. Gossip ran around small communities like wildfire. The Penhallows, though long resident in Bamford, could not be said to be well known in the town and what probably had been seen as their aloofness had fed the rumour. Andrew's frequent absences, especially his spending so much time on the Continent, Carla with her high-powered career and TV appearances – it was natural enough that the townsfolk were prepared to believe almost anything of them.

Supporting this, Mrs Etheridge observed, 'It's too much money. It leads people into temptation. All that coming and going. But there, that's modern ways for you.'

Meredith merely mumbled, her mind running on furiously. It couldn't be true. Yet that girl had been unforgettable, the oddness of her manner, that mix of assurance and guile. Marching up to Tudor Lodge unexpected and, presumably, uninvited, but so certain that she'd a right to do it. If she were Andrew's daughter, it would explain it. Add to that the unwillingness to explain herself to Meredith. Although, thought Meredith, why should she unburden herself to a stranger merely because that Good Samaritan had offered her a lift?

She shifted on her chair and wondered how quickly she could escape from here. The urge to see Alan as soon as possible was overwhelming. He'd give her the facts. What Mrs Etheridge was telling her could turn out to be quite wrong. It *had* to be wrong, surely?

'You look a bit took aback,' observed Mrs Etheridge. 'You haven't drunk your coffee.'

'Oh, sorry.' Meredith sipped guiltily at the pale brew and remembered her original purpose in calling here. She rallied and forced herself to attend to her original design.

115

'Er, the boy who took your purse – I believe you got a good look at him.'

Mrs Etheridge considered her reply, fidgeting with the cuffs of her hand-knitted beige cardigan. 'He was messing around in the street when I came home and kicking a can along. I called out to him to stop making such a row and to put his empty can in a bin somewhere, or take it home. He just ignored me, of course. They have no manners these days. He just carried on kicking this tin up and down. It made a terrible noise. I'd got rather a lot of shopping that day. My knees have been playing up and I've not been out much. I opened my door and just carried my plastic carrier bag inside – only just inside, mind, a few feet. I wasn't far from the shopping trolley, even though I'd left it just outside the front step.'

She looked and sounded defensive. Her negligence had played a part in her misfortune but she was unwilling to admit it. 'I heard a scraping noise and someone breathing. I turned round quick – but not quick enough. He was scrambling back over the wall and away he went down the street – with my purse!' She was breathing heavily herself by now with indignation. 'I phoned the police.'

'And?' Meredith waited but there was a perceptible pause before she got an answer.

'They were far from helpful,' said Mrs Etheridge stiffly and pressed her lips together.

'Oh, I'm sorry. Did you, er, lose much money? Or anything valuable?'

'Not a lot of money,' the woman conceded. 'Seeing as I'd finished my shopping and I always pay the proper way, with cash. I don't have one of them plastic cards. The only other thing in the purse was my library ticket and the library's issued me a replacement one. I only hope the young monkey doesn't go taking lots of library books out on the old one. The girl at the library said they'd keep an eye out for that. I mean, as I said, if he did that and kept them all, I'd have to pay, wouldn't I?'

Meredith assured her that since she'd informed the library, they'd be well aware of the risk. 'Could you describe him? Because a young boy tried to get into my kitchen. I frightened him off but I'd like to know if it was the same.'

'Kitchen?' Mrs Etheridge looked alarmed. 'Excuse me, dear.' She got up and hurried into the rear of the house, leaving Meredith in the cheerless parlour. There was an unfriendly-looking,

116

green-spiked sansevieria growing in a pot nearby. Meredith hàstily emptied her coffee into the compost.

Mrs Etheridge was coming back, panting slightly and with a flush on her pale cheeks. 'I just went to lock my back door, Meredith, seeing as you said he'd tried to get in that way. What a terrible thing it is, not safe in your own home. But you chased him off, you say, before he took anything?' She sounded a little resentful that Meredith had not suffered any loss. 'I don't know that I can describe him well. All the youngsters look the same to me. They all seem to dress alike, jeans and one of those jackets with a zip, those big clumsy white shoes. This one was stocky, about fourteen? Perhaps a bit younger, I really couldn't tell. He had a very short haircut, that I did notice, but not so short I couldn't see he was a real carrot top. He'd red hair, I mean. More coffee?'

'Thanks, no, I must go. But that certainly sounds like the same boy.' Meredith got hastily to her feet.

'All I can say is,' Mrs Etheridge offered on the doorstep, 'that whoever he is, he's on the road to ruin.' She gave a satisfied nod and shut the door.

'Good morning, good morning!' trilled Dr Fuller happily, waving a shiny surgical instrument at his visitor. 'Come to see what I've got for you?'

Alan Markby was not having a good morning. This was a side of his business he disliked intensely. Consequently, he'd seen no reason why, if he had to give up part of the free weekend to which his exalted rank entitled him, it should be spent attending the autopsy on Andrew Penhallow. He'd deputed Pearce. 'I knew the fellow,' he'd explained. 'I don't fancy watching him being opened up.'

Pearce had looked glum. No one relished attending autopsies, though it was customary for at least one of the investigating officers to be on hand. However, Pearce had duly stood by during the grisly business and was now off somewhere restoring his flagging spirits with a different kind of spirit. Markby was here, in the aftermath, to find out what had been discovered.

'We don't see much of you these days,' Dr Fuller greeted him. 'Too grand for this sort of thing, eh?'

Markby mumbled an excuse and added that he'd had some personal acquaintance with the victim.

'Your man,' Fuller went on cheerfully (he was invariably a sunny soul), 'had a quite remarkably thin skull.' He set down the scalpel to Markby's great relief and proceeded to peel off his thin rubber gloves. 'Very interesting. I've seen a couple like it before, but still it's rare, yes, I'd say rare.' He beckoned. 'Now over here . . .'

'It's all right!' Markby said, knowing he felt and sounded pusillanimous. But Fuller was leading him towards something he probably wouldn't want to see and not being a medical man, wouldn't understand. 'I take your word for it. So the blows to the head were the cause of death?'

'Yes.' Fuller looked over the upper rim of his spectacles. 'They left interesting impressions. One, on the left temple, was particularly clear. It made a very unusual pattern and I couldn't suggest to you what caused it, other than a heavy instrument. These marks can fade so I got your photographer to take some pictures before I did anything else. I've got 'em over here. Come and look.' He whirled about and set off in a different direction.

Looking at photographs was an impersonal thing. Greatly relieved, Markby followed the pathologist into a small, cluttered office. Various close-ups of Penhallow's wounds were spread across the desk. He stooped over them.

'They're still tacky, don't touch 'em!' Fuller warned. 'You can see quite clearly,' he pointed with a Biro, 'the impression of the weapon, here . . . and here.' He moved to a different photograph.

'Yes, I do see . . .' Markby's professional interest eliminated the last vestige of queasiness. This wasn't the bruised and broken skull of the man he'd known as a child. This was just a piece of evidence.

The curious mark referred to by Fuller was a round depression scarred with red punch-holes . . . or at least that was how it looked to Markby, who asked, 'You say you don't recognise them and no more do I. Have you got any idea what could've made those marks?'

Fuller shrugged. 'Only, as I said, some heavy article which could be wielded and left a regular pattern, deeply incised enough to leave a print on the skin. An ornament? A garden one? Or some gardening tool? You're the gardener, mean anything to you?'

'Not a thing at the moment.' Markby squinted at the photo. He put it down and picked up the second image to which Fuller had drawn his attention. 'Is it possible to say which blow killed him?' he asked.

Fuller looked cagey. 'Well, normally I'd have said one at the base of the skull or one at the temple, but in view of the unusual fragility of the skull itself, any of the other blows might have done the trick. They all caused extensive internal damage and bleeding.'

'What about his hands?' Markby asked, setting down the photographs and straightening up. 'I couldn't see any injuries to them.'

'I agree he doesn't appear to have put up much of a fight. But scrapings from beneath his nails might yet yield some information. So far I've identified soil, which the lab can check is from the garden, and just a trace of pale blue-coloured fibre. The lab boys will also have to take a look at that.'

'Soil . . .' Markby frowned. 'So possibly he fell and scrabbled in the dirt trying to rise?'

'He might have crawled a short way, dazed . . .' Fuller suggested. 'Any tracks or bloodstains around the body?'

Markby sighed. 'The ground was too hard for prints, but the grass was bruised with any number of tracks. First his wife, who found him, trampled all around and then the daily housekeeper came out and further disturbed the scene. Finally the local GP, called to attend the hysterical wife, took a look at the body, although he says he took great care where he put his feet and I believe him. But the grass was already pretty well trampled by then and he couldn't help but add to it. We didn't find any bloodstains at a distance from the body but they could have been rubbed off and carried away on footwear.' He paused to make a mental note to check whether Carla's slippers, Mrs Flack's and the doctor's shoes had been examined.

'Were there any yellow fibres?' he asked suddenly.

'No, just blue.' Fuller raised his eyebrows. 'Why?'

'We found yellow fibres elsewhere. Well, thanks, I'll wait for your report. He was a fit person, otherwise, would you say?'

'Fit for his age,' Fuller nodded. 'Though showing signs of a sedentary lifestyle and rather a few too many good meals. The thin skull, that was a bit of bad luck really. He wouldn't have known about that, I mean, how vulnerable he was.'

Vulnerable, thought Markby. None of us knows how vulnerable he is. Yet Penhallow, with his tangled private life, ought to have felt vulnerable. Or had he believed he could keep juggling the elements of his double life indefinitely? He'd been an intelligent and successful man. Also arrogant? At the very least foolish in underestimating what his daughter might do. He should have seen Kate as the element in the situation which he couldn't control.

'His Achilles heel!' he said aloud.

'Nothing wrong with his feet,' said Fuller pedantically. 'It was his head.'

'No, I meant – oh, never mind. Could a woman, say, a young fit woman have inflicted those blows?'

'Don't see why not,' said Fuller. 'They used to say poison was a woman's weapon, but these days . . .' He paused and added firmly, 'Not that I could imagine one of *my* daughters doing something like this.'

Nor had the unfortunate Penhallow imagined any daughter of his likely to do it. Had he been wrong?

Markby drove back to Regional HQ through the quiet byways, ignoring the motorway with its thundering traffic. Even on country roads nowadays one met a fair amount but he was in luck and saw few other road-users.

Spring was late. The hedges should be bursting with bud but still appeared bare and lifeless. Pasture hadn't picked up yet, the sheep tearing at it with determination and a touch of desperation. From the corner of his eye he glimpsed a hovering dark shape, a sparrowhawk. He wondered what kind of luck the hunter was having.

He drove past the entrance to some kind of smallholding. A hand-printed board propped by the roadside listed various vegetables for sale to the passing public. All produce, proclaimed the board, was organically grown. That was new, he thought. A few years ago, organic methods were considered uneconomic, now they were seen as some sort of salvation. This led him to think of his sister, Laura, and her family.

Like him, Laura had chosen the law, but a different area of it. She was a partner in a well-known local firm of solicitors. Her husband, Paul, wrote, lectured and broadcast on cookery. Which was why the sign he'd just passed prompted Markby's memory. Paul had long been an advocate of home-grown produce but of late, his interests in all things 'green' had extended into other aspects of lifestyle. The result of this was that Paul had embraced pedal power and was to be seen doggedly cycling around Bamford. Markby's private opinion was that Paul himself was a hazard on the roads and a danger to the environment all round, but he sympathised.

As if in response to his thoughts, when Markby rounded the next corner, he saw ahead of him an eccentric figure. It pedalled along, head down, towing behind the bike a purpose-made mini-trailer, a box on wheels attached by a curved arm to the cycle frame. Smiling, Markby overtook the cyclist with a tap on the horn, and drew into a field entrance further along the road. He got out and waited.

A few minutes later, a yellow cyclist's helmet bent over handlebars appeared. The equipage reached Markby and halted. The wearer of the yellow helmet raised his purple, sweating face and puffed, 'Hullo, Alan! What are you doing out here?'

'I might ask you the same,' Markby replied. 'But if I had to guess, I'd say you've been shopping.'

'Not for nothing they made you superintendent, eh?' Paul dismounted and propped the cycle against the five-bar gate behind them. 'Come and see what I've bought!'

Markby followed him to the red-painted wheeled box. Paul opened it with a flourish and declared, 'There!'

'Carrots,' said Markby. 'Parsnips. Broccoli.'

Paul extracted a muddy vegetable and patted it lovingly. 'You'll appreciate this, Alan, being a gardener. Now anyone with a bit of garden can grow something like this.'

'Yes, well, I haven't got a garden, only a patio.' Markby gazed at the contents of the box with some resentment. 'My gardening is in tubs and a greenhouse. Though everyone today seems to think I must be an expert!'

'You grew very good tomatoes in that greenhouse last year,' said his brother-in-law generously. He locked up the box and straightened up. 'Can you come to dinner, you and Meredith?'

'Not this weekend, sorry. Busy.' That wasn't quite true, but he'd decided to take Meredith out somewhere really special tonight, to make up for the loss of part of the weekend.

'That'll be the Penhallow business, I suppose?' Paul nodded. 'Word around the town has it he was a bigamist.'

'Word is wrong, at least as far as I know. He married but once. He did, however, maintain two separate families.'

'Seems like doubling up the trouble to me,' said Paul. 'The man must have been a glutton for punishment. How about next Saturday? Ask Meredith.'

'I will. Sorry I can't give you a lift or help you with any of that stuff. I'm on my way back to HQ.'

'Oh don't you worry about me,' Paul declared nobly, preparing to remount his bicycle. 'I'll be home in no time.'

Markby drove off, seeing in his mirror the yellow helmet recede

121

until it was lost from view. Dissatisfaction nibbled at his soul. There was another life out there, beyond police work. He wondered if he'd ever get a chance to enjoy it.

Discontent with life seemed to be Sergeant Prescott's lot this morning. On arrival at Regional HQ, Markby found him looming large and gloomy outside the main entrance, indulging in a furtive cigarette.

'Surprised to see a sporting type like you addicted to the weed,' Markby said. 'And aren't you supposed to be checking out Kate Drago's story?'

Prescott ground out the cigarette with his heel and looked gloomier than ever. 'Yessir, just going. I rang her local nick. I mean, the one nearest to her London address, and they're checking the flat for me. I showed her a road map and she pointed out the spot she reckons she got the lorry to pick her up and I'll drive down there now. She's waiting upstairs, by the way.' Prescott jerked his thumb over his shoulder. 'She came in about half an hour ago and – um – she's got her solicitor with her.'

'That was quick work!' Markby observed. 'He must have driven down first thing or caught an early train.'

'If you ask me, he's a quick worker all right!' growled Prescott.

Kate sat on a chair in a corridor in a shaft of pale sunlight. She wasn't wearing the party outfit but jeans, which looked new, and matching denim jacket which looked old but needn't necessarily be so. Markby knew from his niece that clothes were sold in that beat-up condition. Mr Green had presumably brought the clothes with him or the girl might have a credit card. She had claimed to have no money, but that might have meant no more than she had no ready cash. Or the claim to have no money might have been part of her plan to force her father to take responsibility for her board and lodging. His gaze took in her feet, which were shod in smart little black lace-up boots. All this new gear or the money for it had come from somewhere. He wondered just how good a liar she was.

Kate herself looked composed. Her glorious mane of hair had been twisted into a knot on top of her head. Russet strands escaped to frame her pale, frozen features. Markby thought her like a statue, sitting there, not moving, apparently neither seeing nor hearing.

In contrast to his client's immobility, Frederick Green, solicitor, paced the corridor, clearly out of humour. Markby had been curious to see Freddie Green and now that he did, he thought he understood Prescott's misgivings. Green was young, no more than thirty, and everything about him spoke of assurance and ambition. Though he must have risen at an early hour to make his journey, his appearance hadn't suffered a jot. His hair, a little long, had clearly been trimmed by a top men's stylist. No matter how often he turned his head, the groomed strands did no more than ripple, the shape remained intact. His suit was Italian, doubtless a designer label, and his shoes hand-made. Even his briefcase, propped on a chair beside Kate, gleamed as if freshly polished. It was obvious from his expression he thought himself in a nest of rural plods and he expected little from them in the way of efficiency or even rudimentary knowledge of the law.

His glance, however, when it took in Markby, changed from truculent to wary.

'Good morning, Miss Drago,' Markby addressed the girl first. 'How are you today?'

She moved her head slightly to cast him the briefest of glances. 'As well as can be expected, considering my father's been murdered; I've spent a hellish night on a lumpy mattress over collapsed springs; and am sitting here waiting to be interrogated by you and your thugs.'

Before Markby could answer, Green had moved forward, frowning at his client to indicate she should speak only when he gave permission. He then turned his attention to the new arrival.

'Superintendent Markby, I take it? Green . . .' He thrust out his hand.

Markby shook it briefly. The solicitor's grip was firm. Though a dedicated follower of fashion and lacking height, he was a chunky young man and fit. He probably worked out at a gym. Markby supposed him good-looking in a predatory way. No wonder Prescott had been driven to light a cigarette to calm his nerves after seeing his rival.

'I would like to say, before we begin,' Green informed him, 'that my client and I appreciate your not keeping her in a cell overnight.'

Markby, who'd expected a demand to know why the pair had been kept waiting this morning, blinked. Green by name but not by nature.

'No need for that,' he returned blandly. 'We knew where to find Miss Drago.'

Kate muttered some further derogatory remark about the facilities offered by The Crown, but the mutter trailed off into silence after another minatory look from Mr Green.

It said something for this young man that he was able to control his mutinous and spirited client so well.

'Let's go into my office, shall we?' Markby invited. 'Has anyone offered you coffee or tea?'

If Green wanted to play the exchange of courtesies game, it wouldn't do any harm to go along for the moment. Doubtless Green was building up to asking for something.

They settled in his office and the tea arrived. 'When Inspector Pearce gets in, ask him to come up here,' Markby told the tea-bearer.

Kate picked up her polystyrene cup and nestled it in her hands, as if for warmth. Green looked at his tea with horror and made no move to touch the cup.

'Miss Drago,' he said, 'is very distressed, as you'll appreciate. She's suffered a shocking bereavement in terrible circumstances. Despite this, I understand she co-operated fully with you yesterday, answering all your questions frankly.' He paused but Markby said nothing, forcing the solicitor to continue. 'She has given the matter great thought overnight—'

'Couldn't sleep a wink!' said Kate.

'Quite!' The warning glance. 'Despite having racked her brains and turned the matter over and over in her mind, she is unable to come up with any further details which might be of use to you. She has, in short, told you everything she knows.'

'People usually believe they have,' said Markby. 'But it's surprising what little details slip the mind in moments of stress, and re-emerge later.'

'This isn't later,' said Green. 'It's only the next day. I don't think anything can be gained by putting her through the ordeal again so soon, do you?'

Markby twitched an eyebrow. Green flushed and hurried on, 'I understand you've kept clothing belonging to my client. May I ask why?'

'Certainly. Forensics are taking a look at the items. That's quite normal in the circumstances.'

Green pounced. 'Have their tests revealed anything?'

'Shouldn't think they've had a chance to look yet.' Markby turned to Kate. 'Glad to see you've been able to find some suitable clothes for the time being.'

'Freddie brought most of it.' She tugged at her denim jacket.

'I got the boots this morning, on my card. It's an expense I could well have done without!'

Green, for all his question, couldn't have been unaware of the significance of the police keeping Kate's clothing. He now moved on to something else. 'If it comes to footprints, then I would remind you that my client made two visits to the house and walked round it to the back door on both occasions. Also, when my client last saw her father he was alive and well, Superintendent.'

'And when was that?' Markby looked at Kate, but Green replied. 'When she saw him through the window on her second brief visit. He was filling a hot-water bottle. Not the action of a worried or injured man.'

'You're sure, Miss Drago, that you didn't speak to your father on that occasion?' Markby asked her. 'You didn't attract his attention, say, by tapping on the windowpane? You're sure he didn't see you?'

'He didn't see me,' she said in a dull voice. 'I didn't tap at the window. I told you, I chickened out and fled.'

'Understandably,' interpolated Green smoothly. 'Miss Drago was frightened by an apparent loiterer in the garden. I assume you are following up that lead?'

There was a knock at this door which made them all jump and cut off what would have been a terse reply from Markby. It opened to admit Dave Pearce. Proceedings were interrupted while introductions were made. Though Green was a bright and capable young man, thought Markby, he still had a lot to learn. His expression, for example, when sizing up Pearce, betrayed that he clearly dismissed him as an irrelevance. Freddie Green dealt with the top men.

'To resume, my client has told you,' the solicitor went on when Pearce had found a seat, 'she had the distinct impression someone else was in the garden and watched her as she stood by the rear window.'

'Yes, she did.' Markby leaned back and wondered how Green would take to the legend of the Puritan ghost. Badly, he decided. To Kate, he said, 'You're still unable to describe this person you think was lurking in the garden?'

'I didn't actually see whoever it was, I just felt a presence . . . and I seemed to make out a shape, a person standing about, oh, twice the width of this room away.' Kate paused and added bleakly, 'I was frightened.'

'As you will well understand!' put in Green. He cleared his

throat. 'Superintendent, is it really necessary to detain Miss Drago in Bamford? She would like to return to London. It would be easy for her to come back if you need her again. She would be staying at her flat and you have the address, I believe? She's enrolled on a college course and is missing lectures. She has only the minumum luggage with her here. She has commitments elsewhere.'

'And I,' Markby said mildly, 'have a murder to solve. If it's any consolation, it's messed up my Saturday, too. I appreciate Miss Drago's predicament but unfortunately, it's the nature of our inquiries to inconvenience people. I must ask her to stay in Bamford for the moment.'

'You mean,' Kate burst out, 'I've got to stay in that horrible hotel?'

Green made rapid shushing noises and paddled his hands to quieten her. 'Do you intend to charge my client?'

'We're awaiting the result of forensic examinations. Until we know a little more, we have no plans to charge any particular person.'

The solicitor said coolly, 'You cannot, therefore, prevent her return to London.'

'No.' Markby looked at Kate.

'But it will look uncooperative if I do?' Kate challenged, her voice crisp with resentment. 'I get the message. Don't bother, Freddie. It seems I have to sit it out here.'

'You don't!' said Green viciously, glaring at Markby.

He recovered almost at once, but Markby had witnessed the slip of the mask, and it told him this suave young man was at heart a street fighter.

To Kate, Markby said, 'You don't have to stay, of course, Miss Drago. But we'd appreciate it. There may be things we need to ask you about quickly, items we may need you to identify. We don't know. To have you miles away in London really wouldn't be helpful.' He returned his gaze to Green. 'Miss Drago's come in for interview voluntarily and it's appreciated. But we could, if we think it helpful, hold her for twenty-four hours without a court order, and if I decide it necessary, extend that period to thirty-six hours. After that, as you will know, a magistrate's authorisation is required.'

'And I don't doubt,' Green said nastily, 'that you feel sure a magistrate would oblige. Very well, Kate . . .' he turned to his client, 'you'd better stay on for a few days. But if during that time they want to interview you again, let me know and I'll come back at once. Remember, not a question do you answer unless I'm there!'

When the pair had left the building, Pearce said hesitantly, 'You know, sir, I still think we should have kept her in the cells overnight when we had the chance, before that smarmy little tyke got here. She is our chief suspect.'

'It was my decision!' Markby retorted irritably, before adding more mildly, 'You may be right, Dave. But I'm gambling on her being more forthcoming if we leave her free.'

'They'll cook up something between them, that solicitor and her,' was Pearce's comment. 'I reckon in the end she'll do what he says. She looks on him as a friend.'

Markby snorted. 'Did you check out those fingerprints on the back door handle and light switches?'

'We did. No luck. Both kitchen switches showed the prints of Mrs Penhallow and Mrs Flack, as you'd expect. The back door showed prints or part-prints of Mrs Penhallow, Mrs Flack and Dr Pringle.' Pearce hesitated, seeing Markby frown. 'You think it's important?'

'It would've been nice to find some prints other than those of the doctor and the members of the household. Kate Drago's for example, or any strange prints. There isn't even any smudging to suggest a gloved hand or any attempt to wipe off prints . . . Look, Penhallow went out into the garden to see or search for someone. He was carrying a hot-water bottle but no torch. We can assume, I think, that was because sufficient light beamed out from the kitchen behind him through the open door to illuminate the immediate area by the house. But when Mrs Penhallow came downstairs in the morning, the light was switched off and the back door shut. So someone switched it off and closed the door, very neatly. It has to be the killer. A light left on all night might have been noticed and invited attention. Or someone looking out of a bedroom window could've seen Andrew's body lying on the lawn. So the light was switched off.'

'They're simple flip-up-and-down switches,' said Pearce. 'You can operate them with your elbow. As for the door, if there were prints, by the time Mrs Penhallow had opened up in the morning and the cleaner and the doctor had run in and out to the telephone and the body, well, no chance.'

'Shows a certain clarity of thought on the part of the killer, though,' mused Markby. 'He or she didn't panic.'

'That girl,' said Pearce darkly. 'She's a cool one. She wouldn't panic. She'd remember to switch off the light and shut the door.'

'Very likely,' Markby was forced to agree. 'Did you find any trace of anyone else having been in the garden where Kate says she saw someone lurking?'

'There are some broken sprays on a rose bush but it's difficult to say when the damage was done.' Reluctantly Dave added, 'Perhaps even during the search of the grounds. You know how it is.' Rallying, he went on, 'But that girl's a quick thinker. She had to come up with a reason to support her story about running away. So she says she saw someone. What more obvious? Of course, she can't describe the person. If he – or she – was that difficult to make out, then ten to one "the person", if she saw anything at all, was a bush or a shadow from the house in the moonlight.'

'Or the ghost?' murmured Markby.

Pearce gave him a nervous look, clearly unsure whether the superintendent was making a joke or was going a bit soft in the head.

'Don't forget,' Markby had seen the doubtful expression, 'that Mrs Flack reports a presence in the garden on previous occasions. Unless you choose to believe in spooks, it could be that someone was watching the place over a period of months? Now, why?'

'She did it,' said Pearce, reducing speculation to the simple answer. 'People get killed by family members all the time. He wouldn't do what she wanted and she lost her temper and attacked him. I'd put a tenner on it,' he concluded.

It would have interested Pearce to overhear the conversation taking place at the same moment, in the privacy of Freddie Green's car.

'I'm sorry, Kate,' the young man said. He pushed the key into the ignition but hesitated to switch on, turning his head to peer up at her as she sat beside him.

'It's all right, Freddie, you did your best and I'm grateful.' Kate folded her hands in her lap. 'As I said back there, I'll have to sweat it out here.'

'Yes . . .' The engine still didn't spring into life. Green was fidgeting about and looking considerably less assured than he had earlier. 'Look, Kate, it might be a good idea, when I get back to London, for me to have an informal word with Sir Montague Ling.'

Shock infused her pale features. 'The barrister? You're briefing counsel?'

'No, no, nothing so formal!' he hastened to reassure her. 'The old chap's a family friend, a crony of my dad's. I could just, well, mention our predicament . . . that is, your situation . . .'

She interrupted, blood rushing into her alabaster skin and staining her cheeks an angry red. 'You think they're going to arrest me, Freddie, don't you? You think they're just putting their case together and then they'll pounce on me! You really believe I'm going to stand trial for killing my father!'

'If everything happened the way you told it, Kate, of course they won't arrest you. Circumstantial evidence isn't enough. They haven't found the weapon. But let's face it, you had motive, you were there probably only a very short time before he was attacked, one of the last people to see him alive . . . and your returning to the house a second time, after he'd taken you to a hotel and told you to stay there, well, it does look bad.'

'I thought you were a friend!' she gasped.

'I am! Kate, not only as a friend but as your solicitor I'm trying to look ahead, be ready for them, do what's best. You must see that?' He was almost pleading.

'What I see,' she said in a low, quivering voice, 'is that you think I did it, just as they do. You think I killed my father.'

CHAPTER TEN

The gate gave a low creak of protest as Meredith's hand pushed it open. Ahead of her lay Tudor Lodge. The stone blocks of its fabric, in the afternoon sunshine which blessed them today, glowed with deep honey tones. The bright light also emphasised their worn and pitted surface and made it obvious where later Victorian additions had been tacked on to the earlier fabric.

In contrast, the house's background of trees and shrubs loomed as a tangle of dark shadows. It would be so easy, she thought, to hide in the gardens here and watch the back of the house. To watch the front of the house would be much more difficult. It would involve standing on the open lawn, visible to all, or out in the road.

She tried to visualise the house as she'd seen it on Thursday evening when she'd stopped to drop off her passenger. No lights had been showing then in the front of the place but a glow to the backing trees had suggested a source of light at the rear, probably the kitchen.

Meredith glanced towards the row of terraced cottages further down the road. The nearest one had a window overlooking Tudor Lodge. That would be the house belonging to the old lady, Mrs Joss, who, Markby had told her, had left Sergeant Prescott firmly in the belief that he'd interviewed the local witch. If Mrs Joss had got up during the night and looked out of her bedroom window, would she have been able to see over the wall into the back garden of the Lodge? No, thought Meredith, the trees would've been in the way.

She sighed to herself. An independent witness would be just what was needed. Yet she herself was a witness, who'd delivered up the strange visitor to the Lodge. More than ever, Meredith regretted that she hadn't waited at least to see whether the girl made for the front or back of the place. But the last she could remember of her was that brisk figure marching confidently up the path.

Far less confidently, Meredith set off up the path herself. But as she reached the front door, someone came round the corner of the building and called out, 'Good afternoon! Can I help?'

131

She turned, thinking it might be a police officer, to find herself being observed warily by a young man in jeans and sweater.

'It's Luke, isn't it?' she said, recognising him. 'I'm Meredith Mitchell. Do you remember me? We have met.'

The frown on his weather-tanned face smoothed. He came forward holding out his hand. His grip was firm and his palm leathery. 'Yes, of course I remember you. Sorry if I sounded sharp. I thought for a moment you might be press. They've been hanging around.' He accompanied the last remark with an expressive grimace.

Meredith asked, 'How's Carla? I didn't know whether to call or not. I can go away if you think I should.'

Luke hunched his broad shoulders. 'She's doing pretty well in the circumstances. No, don't leave. She'll be pleased to see you and she needs to talk to someone. Perhaps you can bring her out a bit. The trouble is, she doesn't want to put more worries on me, as she sees it, so she just tries to reassure me when what I'm trying to do is reassure her!' There was a note of despair in his voice.

Meredith chose her words with care. 'There's some pretty wild gossip going round town. I don't know whether you've heard any of it. It's inevitable, and unpleasant, and you should be forewarned.'

'If you mean my father's secret family, that's not gossip, that's fact!' Luke's voice cracked. He drew a deep breath. 'It's been a helluva shock. Apparently I've even met her, my half-sister as I suppose she is. It was at some party and to be honest, I really don't recall her in too much detail. I seem to remember a girl, a very attractive girl, who was keen to be in some photos being taken at the time. But you know how it is . . .' His open features reddened. 'I'd had a couple of drinks.'

Meredith smiled in sympathy before asking more soberly, 'How has your mother taken the news?'

'She went silent when they told her. To be frank, I don't know how she's taking it because she won't discuss it with me and refuses to hear a word of criticism of Dad. Things,' said Luke bitterly, 'are a bit awkward all round at the moment.' He lifted his head and looked directly at Meredith. 'How could he do it? Dad, I mean? How could he deceive her – both of us – all those years? *Why* did he do it? He and Mum were so happy and so well suited, or so it always seemed to me. It wasn't as if they quarrelled or didn't care about one another.'

'People get their lives in a mess, Luke,' Meredith told him. 'They don't mean to do it, they just do.'

To herself she was thinking, He's only just finding that out. It's a cruel experience.

But not a unique one. Her own memories stirred painfully in their half-sleep. She said, 'I'll go and see your mother, then.'

Carla looked tired and drawn but at least not weeping as Meredith had feared. Normally she'd have judged Carla pretty tough, but murder had a way of cruelly stripping a veneer of toughness to the fragile bone.

'Tea or gin and tonic?' Carla asked as soon as Meredith had taken a seat. A little defensively, she added, 'I'm not on the bottle. Luke keeps too close an eye on me for that.'

'Fine, G and T. I've been drinking tea with my neighbours.'

Carla went to the drinks cabinet and busied herself. Her back turned, she asked, 'Ice and lemon? I'll have to get it from the kitchen. Excuse me.'

Meredith opened her mouth to say not to bother with the ice but her hostess had already disappeared. Minutes later she brought both drinks to where Meredith sat, sliding down into the adjoining chair and lifting her glass in salute.

'To the memory of better days!' She sounded bitter and Meredith couldn't join in the dark toast.

'They'll find out who did it, Carla.' It was a lame attempt at reassurance and Meredith had never been more aware of the finality of death. So what if the killer were caught? Andrew had gone for ever. She added, 'I saw Luke outside.'

'Poor boy. His world's shattered. He idolised his father.' Without warning, Carla added, 'I knew, of course. Luke thinks I didn't, but I did.'

Now really thrown off balance, Meredith murmured, 'Oh, did you?' before rallying to ask almost incredulously, 'I think I know what you're talking about, but I've got to ask, are we referring to the same thing?'

'About this kid, this daughter of Andrew's who's turned up out of the blue? Yes.'

'He told you?'

Carla laughed, a curiously harsh sound. 'Andrew? Lord, no! He'd never have done that. He would have wanted to protect me. That's how he'd have phrased it in his own mind. Not to upset me or cause a scene. Andrew hated scenes and the person he was protecting was himself. No, I knew because in the end, a wife always knows, doesn't she?'

'I've never been a wife,' Meredith said drily.

'Your fault. That handsome copper of yours is pining to whisk you up the aisle. You ought to nail him while you can. He won't wait for ever, you know. Men don't. They haven't got the patience to wear willow as the old saying goes.'

There was nothing Meredith felt she could reply to that, so she didn't try. Luckily, it had been a temporary diversion on Carla's part. She leaned forward now, cupping the gin glass.

'It wasn't switching to a new aftershave or money draining out of a joint account, the usual sort of giveaways. We always had separate personal accounts plus a joint housekeeping account. Provided the money in that stayed at its usual level, I had no way of telling what Andrew did with the money in his personal account . . . any more than he knew what I did with mine!'

Carla looked up, a gleam in her eyes. 'But I didn't have a long-term, or even a short-term, lover, that's the difference! No, I think the giveaway was in the nature of the gifts he bought me. He'd come back from the Continent not just with a few decent bottles of wine or maybe some perfume. No, he brought ridiculous things which I couldn't possibly use but were always fearfully expensive. I knew early on they were bad-conscience gifts, the product of guilt. Andrew had a tender conscience and whenever it gave him a jolt, he appeased it by spending money. So I assumed he had a mistress in Brussels. I wasn't surprised. After all, we spent a lot of time apart. I wasn't too worried because well, they manage these things on the Continent so much better than we do in England. I trusted him to be discreet. But one day a colleague who'd just returned from a surfing holiday in Newquay told me he could have sworn he'd seen Andrew in a country pub just outside the town. Andrew was supposed to be abroad at the time and I said so. The colleague joked about it, saying Andrew must have a double.'

Carla sipped the gin. 'That was the first time. I dismissed it. We're all supposed to have a double somewhere, aren't we? Then about six months later it happened again. Different colleague, different Cornish resort – Tintagel this time. Someone the spitting image of Andrew was seen walking on the cliffs towards Arthur's castle with a woman and a little girl.'

Carla gave a rueful smile. 'I've worked as a telejournalist and I've been around newsroom people. Their sixth sense for this sort of thing must have rubbed off on me. I knew instinctively something was seriously amiss. After that I kept a lookout. I rang him in Brussels a couple of times and he wasn't there, not at his flat nor at his desk. His secretary parroted out some reason or other. But I thought, merry hell, he's not even in Belgium! He's scooted off to Cornwall! I went down there and nosed around. I knew where he'd been born and I started there. I didn't have to look too far. Everybody knew about him, local boy made good. Everybody knew he was a sort of partner in a souvenir shop run by his old childhood friend. The childhood sweetheart turned out to be my age, good-looking in an arts and crafts sort of way, and mother of a ten-year-old girl. No father of the kid in evidence, just a few knowing smiles and indulgent nods of the head.'

Carla shook her own head. 'Poor Andrew. He was so naïve. I think they all knew down there, at least, all the older people who remembered him from a boy. But they were discreet, you know.'

'You never faced him with the truth?' Meredith asked curiously. 'Or never even thought about doing that?'

Carla didn't answer at once. She put down the emptied gin glass with a rattle on the side table and plucked absently at strands of her short-cropped hair. 'Need a damn haircut,' she said. 'And a rinse. Thought I might go a shade or two lighter? What do you think?'

She surely didn't expect an answer to this tangential question and Meredith gave none.

After a moment Carla stopped fiddling with her hair and said briskly, 'Yes, I thought about confronting him with it. But then I thought, what about Luke? Luke was only a little older than the kid in Cornwall. It's the heck of a tender age to find out your dad has an alternative family and you have a half-sister much your age. And then I thought, why rock the boat? My career's going well, so is his. He comes home. We have a good time. He's not going to leave me. If he'd ever meant to do that, he'd have done it by now. He's in the public eye and he can't afford a scandal. Why not just let things drift on? Who's suffering, after all?'

'You were,' said Meredith crisply. Cool detached reasoning can only go so far. Surely Carla didn't expect her to buy this explanation lock, stock and barrel? There had to be another reason she'd gone along with her husband's deception.

Carla looked up with that gleam back in her eye. 'Don't fool you, do I? But all I've said's true. There was another reason, though. Don't forget, I'm in the public eye, too. I just couldn't face being made to look a fool. Can you imagine the tabloids? The banner headlines? *TV SCIENCE GIRL DISCOVERS HUSBAND'S LOVE NEST*? So I closed my eyes and let it go on.

'After a while, I realised that whatever he had down there in Cornwall, it was no more than a sort of hobby, a nostalgia trip down childhood's memory lane. What he really wanted, what mattered most to him, was here in Bamford, me and Luke. So what could I have said to him? That he should make a choice? He'd made it. He'd chosen us. I felt a bit sorry for the woman in Cornwall because she had to play second fiddle and pretend all the time. I saw that really Andrew loved me and Luke. And we were very happy, Meredith. That's the truth. Why spoil it? Why force him to give up the other woman or divorce him, when it would ruin the very happy family life we had here?'

Carla smiled. 'There was something about Andrew, you know, that was very childlike. He wanted all the sweets in the shop.'

They were interrupted by the sound of some altercation outside the window. Luke's voice could be distinguished raised in anger and another male voice protesting and wheedling. Then silence fell, broken by the creak of the gate.

'Press,' said Carla. 'Luke's acting as a very effective guard dog!'

'So what now?' Meredith asked.

'Now I sit here and do as the police say. I have made one decision, though. It's about the girl, Andrew's daughter.'

Meredith eyed her warily. Carla had a triumphant look about her, the look of someone about to spring a surprise and take delight in it.

'I'm going to ask her to come and stay here at Tudor Lodge, with Luke and me.'

There were several things Meredith could have said, all of them wise and tactful. What she actually found herself blurting was, 'You must be out of your head!'

'Most people would agree with you.' Carla nodded. 'But when all's said and done, she's Andrew's girl. Andrew took care of her, more or less, while she was growing up and were he still – were he still with us—' Carla's voice faltered slightly – 'then he'd want to go on looking after her. So I must do it for him. Besides, she's staying at The Crown and it can't be very comfortable. The kid's lost her mother, as I understand it, and now she's lost her father, just as Luke has. She's Luke's half-sister.'

Carla's calm façade cracked. 'Meredith, my husband's been murdered! He hasn't just had an accident or died of illness. Someone came here and killed him! It's torn our world apart, mine, Luke's and Kate's too! We've got to try and help one another, pull together! Oh, I know it's a mess. But, don't you see, I'm trying to straighten it out? Do the right thing? Try and build this family up again.'

You're trying to do, thought Meredith, what Andrew signally failed to do! Bring order to this irregular situation. But it wouldn't be that easy. Had it not occurred to Carla that Kate Drago had been the last person – as far as anyone knew – to see Andrew alive before the intervention of his killer? And that, as everyone knew, presupposed there was another person involved in his death. To bring the girl here might not only prove ultimately a hideous embarrassment but dangerous. It had all the makings of a tragic error.

She tried to express a little of this in the most tactful way. 'You don't know the girl, Carla. You only know who she is. I've met her. Admittedly only briefly, but the impression I got was that she's very capable and rather deep. Besides, what does Luke think about it?'

'He feels, like me, that we should do as Andrew would have wanted,' came the firm response.

That wasn't the impression Meredith had got from her brief meeting with Luke outside the house. She had sensed a bitter resentment towards his father's memory. 'Think it over,' she begged. 'Talk to Alan. After all, the police may think it unwise. It could complicate their inquiries.'

'On the contrary, I'm sure it will make things simpler.' Carla had that obstinate tone of someone whose mind is made up and who isn't prepared to listen to a reasoned argument of any kind. 'You know, Meredith, I feel almost as if Andrew were still here with us in this house. I think he approves of my decision. This morning, as I walked down the main stair I almost thought I saw him. I certainly felt his presence, watching me.'

'Watching over you, may be!' Meredith muttered.

Carla's hearing was acute. 'I know what's on your mind, Meredith. But I don't think she attacked Andrew. If I thought that, of course I wouldn't have her here. But why should she have done such a thing? And if none of that convinces you, and I can see it doesn't, don't forget the newshounds slavering at my door. I understand they've been hanging around The Crown, too. Mrs Flack tells me that they've even offered Kate money for her story but she's turned them down. Of course, that may only be rumour. Irene Flack says she got it from Lee Joss who works as barman there. His grandmother lives in one of those cottages between us and Sawyer's garage. It makes good sense for Kate to be here with us so we can protect her – and thereby ourselves – from the tabloid press. It's not fair to leave a young girl all alone to deal with reporters.'

'Yes, I can imagine how the grapevine's buzzing!' Meredith said grimly. 'But let's face it, Carla. We don't yet know who attacked Andrew and until we do—'

'Burglars!' Carla didn't let her finish. 'I don't know why people won't accept the obvious. There are yobs hanging around looking for places to break into. This house is a natural target. They thought Andrew had gone to bed – and he hadn't. There was a hot-water bottle in the garden near his body. He must have felt cold in Luke's room. After all, the bed hadn't been slept in for a few weeks. So he came downstairs, filled the bottle and disturbed the intruders. They ran out and he ran after them . . .' Carla's voice trembled but her tone remained adamant.

'I know there are petty thieves of one kind and another hanging around,' Meredith admitted, 'because one tried to get into my kitchen and did succeed in snatching my neighbour's purse—'

'You see!' Carla fairly bounced out of her chair. 'You've told Alan?'

'As a matter of fact, no,' Meredith admitted.

Carla gazed at her in dismay. 'But why on earth not? This could explain everything. The same person or people could've tried to break in here—'

'Carla,' Meredith protested. 'It was just a kid. I saw him with my own eyes and I'm not mistaken. He was no more than thirteen. Perhaps only twelve. He does his pilfering in broad daylight and he's an opportunist thief. He runs away if disturbed. He couldn't have anything to do with what happened here.'

'But you must tell Alan!' Carla insisted. 'It still proves what I'm saying. It doesn't have to be the same thief, but it shows that there are thieves about in Bamford!'

'Fine, I'll tell him. I didn't before because it's petty, a local matter for the local police. But, Carla, until it's been established just what happened here on Thursday night—'

'On Thursday night,' Carla interrupted, 'Andrew was attacked by an intruder. He was killed defending this house and me. I think, don't you, that rather than criticise anything else he may have done, he ought to be given credit for being so brave and losing his life so – so gallantly!'

Outside the house again, Meredith looked round for Luke but he was nowhere to be seen. She hesitated. It wasn't her business to interfere, yet she had been the one to bring Kate Drago to Tudor Lodge and she couldn't just walk away now, certain in her own mind that Carla was about to make a serious error of judgement. Indeed, had already made it, because the conversation had concluded with Carla announcing that she'd already phoned The Crown and left a message for Kate, so there was no point in Meredith arguing.

But Kate wasn't in the house yet and there was still Luke to consider. Luke had considerable influence with his mother, and Meredith couldn't believe he was as keen to see Andrew's daughter in the family home as Carla apparently was. It might not be too late to prevent what could prove a disastrous move.

Perhaps, she thought, Luke was in the garden to the rear of the property. She began to walk slowly round the inner boundary along the dry-stone wall. These old walls – and this one showed signs of being very old – fascinated her. Meredith touched the weather-worn edges of the blocks and wondered how long they'd been here, stacked with skill and without mortar and held together by weight, balance and by accumulated grime and small weeds which had somehow managed to gain a hold in such poor rooting material. She had made almost a complete tour of the back gardens without seeing Luke when she came upon a place where the coping stones of the wall had crumbled. The damage had been caused by a huge horse chestnut tree which grew on the other side and stretched one of its mighty branches across, resting directly on the wall. Over the passage of time it had forced the upper stones from their perch and sent them tumbling down on the garden side in an untidy, grass-grown heap. The great branch reached down to ground level and offered a kind of garden seat. Meredith sat on it.

It was a pity the garden was so neglected because it offered so much. She wondered whether Luke, when young, had indulged in the autumnal hobby of collecting the conkers. She remembered doing that when she'd been a child, splitting open the spiked green husks to reveal the beautiful shiny mahogany-coloured fruits within. Then came the business of boring a hole through with the aid of a skewer borrowed from the kitchen, the threading of a string and tying of a knot to secure it and then – the conker fights!

She ran a hand over the rough bark reminiscently, then frowned. It was scored in long scraped wounds, recently made. She could smell the sap. Meredith looked up. A bird rustled in the branches. It was the only creature to see what she did. On impulse, she got up and clambered on to the branch, steadying herself with outstretched hands. One could, without difficulty, make one's way up the branch to the top of the wall. Once there, one could, with a little awkwardness and some risk of scratches, climb over and transfer oneself to another branch on the further side which tipped down towards the ground. Long unused to this kind of activity, Meredith slid and scrambled down it and landed on the further side of the wall.

She gave a low whistle of surprise and satisfaction. It needed a little agility, but the tree none the less offered a perfectly usable 'stepladder' over the wall, a way in and out of the Penhallows' garden. The scratches visible in the bark on the garden side could also be seen in the branch on the further side. Someone had climbed in and out of the garden by this route and recently. Meredith reflected that the damage could have been caused by children or by members of the police search party. But it might be worth investigating further. She looked round.

She was standing on a beaten path which led down the side of the Penhallows' property, before turning left and apparently running behind the row of terraced cottages. Meredith followed it. As she'd guessed, it ran to the rear of the cottage gardens and then debouched on an open patch of grass. Beyond it stood the garage forecourt with its petrol pumps, plate-glass windows and garish colours. But the intervening grassy space itself was occupied by an elderly car. The bonnet was open and two figures bent over it, a man and a woman, both deep in examination of the engine. As Meredith watched, the man straightened up and wiped his forehead with the back of a grimy hand.

'I'll see what I can do, Irene. But you really need to think about getting rid of this old wreck.'

The woman extricated herself from her cramped position and was revealed to be Mrs Flack, Carla's housekeeper. 'I don't say you're wrong, Harry, but I can't afford a new car, and that's it.'

'I'll keep an eye open for you,' the man said. Meredith could now see he wore work overalls and she recognised the garage owner. Sawyer was a man in his late forties with a long narrow face, straight nose and close-set large eyes, which all combined to make him look like a friendly horse. At that moment he caught sight of the newcomer. 'Hullo, where did you pop up from, then?'

Mrs Flack turned and looked surprised. 'Why, Miss Mitchell!'

A little embarrassed, Meredith walked over to them. 'I've been to see Mrs Penhallow. I just thought I'd take a little walk. There's a path . . .' She gestured behind her towards the track behind the terrace.

'Oh, that's doesn't go anywhere,' said Mrs Flack. 'Waste of your time, walking down there. It used to be a back way in to our gardens, but none of us uses it now.'

'Oh, you live here?' Meredith looked back at the cottages.

Mrs Flack indicated she lived in the one nearest to them, at the end of the row, and the furthest from Tudor Lodge. 'And I keep my little car here,' she added. 'It's handy and Harry doesn't mind.'

140

Harry Sawyer looked mildly surprised. 'Well, 'tisn't for me to mind, is it? It's not my ground.'

Now it was Irene Flack's turn to look astonished. 'Not yours, Harry? I always thought it was part of your property, all one with the garage. Sort of spare to requirements, as you might say.'

'Wish it was!' he said briefly.

Mrs Flack frowned. 'Well, I never. I never said anything to you, I know, but I thought, if you'd minded you'd have told me. Who does it belong to rightly, then?'

Harry lifted an oil-stained hand and pointed in the direction of Tudor Lodge. 'Belongs to them, don't it? Penhallows. I've been after them to sell it to me for years, but they won't. Can't see why. It's no use to them and I've offered a fair price.'

'Well, fancy that!' Irene thought over the information. 'Never knew that!' she added.

Harry Sawyer was looking at Meredith. 'You been to see Mrs Penhallow, you say? How is she, then?'

'As well as can be expected,' Meredith replied cautiously. She wondered whether Mrs Flack knew yet of Carla's plan to invite Kate Drago into the house.

But Mrs Flack only said, 'Nice to think she's got a friend to call on her. It's been a terrible shock.'

Sawyer released the support which held up the car's bonnet and closed it with a clang. 'Like I say, Irene, I'll keep a lookout for a little second-hand car for you, replace this. It'd be worth it in the long run. You can't keep repairing this one. One of these fine days it'll let you down when you need it most.'

Meredith decided to leave them to their business discussion. She said goodbye and set off, this time taking the more obvious route, walking past the front doors of the terraced cottages. She saw, when she reached the one nearest to Tudor Lodge, that its occupant, an old woman, sat at the window to watch the world go by. She leaned forward and peered at Meredith, curious to see a stranger. Meredith smiled but the old dame merely looked suspicious and rather fierce. The witch-like Mrs Joss! But then a murder practically on her doorstep would have made her nervous of anyone new.

Feeling that those dark somewhat spiteful eyes bored into her back, Meredith reached Tudor Lodge. She was just in time to see a car turn into the garage drive. The driver braked and put his head out of his window. It was Luke.

'I thought, as you were with Mum, I'd just nip into the town for a couple of things,' he said. He sounded tetchy, as if he thought Meredith had let him down.

'I haven't long left her,' Meredith assured him. 'Luke – I don't want to sound as if I'm poking my nose into your family business, but this idea she has of inviting—'

'Asking my sister into the house?' he interrupted bluntly. He sat back in his seat and stared through the windscreen at the building in front of him. 'She wants to do it. She thinks Dad would have wanted it. I can't stop her.'

'You could,' Meredith urged, 'if you really insisted. She wouldn't disregard your feelings entirely if you made them clear.'

'It's not so easy,' he said. He kept his gaze averted and she sensed the brittleness of his façade of competence. 'The state she's in – a row is the last thing we need. If it makes her happy, easier in her mind, knowing she's doing what she thinks Dad would've wanted, I'm not going to stop her. There's the press angle, too. We don't want journalists talking to her. It'll be a bit awkward, I suppose, but we'll manage somehow. After all, it's not as if Kate is going to be staying with us for long, is it?' The last words were spoken obstinately.

Meredith managed to stop herself saying, 'You don't know that!' The young man was bottling up his true feelings. That couldn't be good, but this wasn't the moment to argue the point. 'I've just been for a walk down there by the terrace. Mrs Flack is there, looking at her car with the garage owner, Sawyer, isn't it?'

'Old Harry? Yes, he keeps it on the road for her. It's a dreadful old rattletrap.'

'He says, that is I understand, you own the piece of land on the further side of the cottages, between them and his garage and he wants to buy it.'

Luke grimaced. 'That's right, and Dad always refused to sell! Did Harry tell you what he wanted to do with it?' When she shook her head, he explained, 'Harry's got ambitions. He wants to sell cars, not just fix them and sell fuel. He'd like to build a showroom and be an agent for one of the big makes. But he needs more room than he's got and so he'd like that scrap of open land. Years ago, those cottages belonged to Tudor Lodge, but they were sold off. That's how we come to own just that bit of land beyond them. It somehow got left out of the sale of the cottages. It's no use to us, I admit, but a car showroom? It's bad enough already with Harry's place shining like a beacon all night long, cars in and out, petrol tankers . . . A showroom as well would be the last straw. I like Harry and I'm sorry for him, but it's just not on. Dad was adamant and I agree.'

'I see,' Meredith said thoughtfully. 'I'll let you get back to your mother, Luke. Just pick up the phone if you need me for anything.'

She watched him drive in and made her way to where she'd left her own car. As she drove off, it struck her how little they'd all known about Tudor Lodge and its inhabitants.

This thought was immediately pushed out of her head by another. She'd made a promise, or a sort of promise, that she'd tell Alan about her intruder. She was sorry she'd told Carla she'd do it, but it had been difficult to refuse. Not being able to avoid a promise didn't make it less of a commitment.

But Meredith didn't want to tell Alan about the boy burglar. He had enough on his plate without that to worry about. Nor was it the sort of offence with which the Regional Squad bothered itself. It was a purely local matter. Meredith havered for a few minutes and then, with a sigh of resignation, turned the car in the direction of Bamford's local police station.

She hadn't been inside the building for some time but it was all too familiar. Alan had been in charge here when they'd first met. It made her feel faintly nostalgic, though she also thought critically that the place could do with a lick of paint. She wondered who was in charge now. There'd been a man called Winter for a while, but she had an idea he'd left. It didn't matter. The errand which brought her called for no one more senior than the desk sergeant.

But the desk officer was busy. Meredith hung about for a few minutes, wondering if coming into the police station counted as keeping her promise, even if she hadn't spoken to anyone. She was on the point of leaving, telling herself that she'd tried to report the matter and no one could do more, when a woman officer appeared.

'Can I help you?' She smiled at Meredith. She was young and pretty with fair hair scraped into a knot and wore regulation pullover, trousers and heavy footwear.

So she wasn't to be allowed to slip out unnoticed. Meredith explained the reason for her visit.

'You should keep your back door locked,' said the young woman severely.

'It was the middle of the day,' Meredith countered.

'Doesn't mean no one's hanging around. Burglars are like anyone else. They'd rather work regular hours, besides not risk setting off a burglar alarm. People often turn off their burglar alarms during the day. Neighbours may be out at work. An unlocked door makes it easy. All chummie has to do is walk in and help himself.'

Meredith began to appreciate how Mrs Etheridge had felt when she'd reported her encounter with the red-haired boy, apparently to unsympathetic ears. A prickle of annoyance touched her.

'Lose much?' asked the officer cheerfully.

'I didn't lose anything. I told you, I disturbed him. But it could have turned out nasty. Most of my neighbours are elderly. One of them had her purse stolen by her own front door. She reported it here. I've been talking to her and we think it may be the same boy.'

'It probably is,' said the Job's comforter in uniform. 'But if he's as young as you say, we won't be able to touch him. If anything, it'll be a case for social services. If he turns out a real tearaway and he's put in the care of the local authority, it won't stop him getting up to his tricks. Wait until he turns sixteen.'

'Great!' muttered Meredith.

'Don't blame us, our hands are tied,' said the young woman. 'We can advise you on making your home more secure, if you like. Keep a chain on the door, safety locks on the windows, don't let anyone in unless you personally know who it is or are shown some form of identity. Here . . .' She reached for a display nearby. 'Take some of these pamphlets. They might give you some ideas.'

Meredith left the station clutching her pamphlets. She was glad she hadn't mentioned it to Alan and now she certainly wouldn't.

CHAPTER ELEVEN

'You've got to stop her, Alan. Can you imagine what might happen if that girl moves herself into Tudor Lodge?'

Alan Markby paused in pouring out the wine and turned towards the speaker, the bottle held in his hand. Having finally got away from Regional HQ in the early afternoon, he was off duty now until Monday and looking forward to a pleasant and relaxing evening with Meredith. It now seemed unlikely to work out that way. It never did, he found himself thinking with some irritation. And he hadn't even had a chance to tell her his plans for the rest of their weekend yet.

The day was cool and they'd lit the fire in the hearth. His house was Victorian and still had its open fireplaces. Before Meredith had entered his life, he had seldom used this room which the original owners no doubt would've called the parlour. He had lived in the kitchen. Then Meredith had bought her own little place in Station Road. She had explained that when she came to spend the evening over at his place, she didn't expect to spend it in full sight of the sink. So the parlour had been refurbished, after a fashion. That was to say he'd painted up the walls and woodwork and bought a couple of comfortable chairs and a coffee table. His sister, Laura, had contributed a rosewood sideboard which she'd bought at auction.

'Because, Alan, I thought how perfectly it'd fit into your place, the right period, you know.'

It might be the right period, but he privately thought it a gloomy old thing which reminded him of his late Uncle Henry, that last of the Victorians, in his family, anyway. He had a private fantasy (not so private since probably anyone who knew them guessed it) that one day, Meredith would move in here, with him. He fully realised he was going to have to do better than a rosewood antique and a pair of Parker Knoll recliners before that happened.

She was sitting on the floor in front of the spitting flames, heedless of the risk of one of the tiny incendiaries landing on her clothing. Although outdoors it was still quite light, in this room the light was always poor. A boost was needed so he had switched on a small reading lamp which perched on the sideboard. Between the firelight and the lamp her face bathed in a rosy glow. Auburn highlights gleamed in her bobbed brown hair which framed her earnest face in glossy curtains. She wore a baggy and strangely patterned sweater, blue with pink pigs marching across it, and rested her arms on her bent knees. He wished, he wished . . .

'Alan?' she prompted.

'What?' He recalled that he'd been asked a question preceded by a peremptory request. He couldn't give a satisfactory reply to either.

'I can't,' he said simply.

'Can't' was a word Meredith didn't admit to her vocabulary. She gave him a severe look. 'Someone has to. I'm doing my best but if you spoke to her, you could try the official police line, for goodness' sake. After all, you aren't going to tell me you think it's right? Honestly, Alan! Kate Drago was the last person, as far as we know, to see Andrew alive and she's behaved in a very shifty way throughout.'

He finished pouring out the wine to give himself time to formulate an answer, set down the bottle and brought the two glasses over to the hearth. The ruby wine glowed as flames struggled up at last from the kindling and the log began to burn properly.

'Of course I don't think it all right,' he said as he handed one glass to her. 'I agree the girl's word may not be trusted. She is a suspect. She has to be. But she hasn't been charged with any offence. She's not under arrest. She is a relative of the family, albeit one which has unexpectedly emerged from the woodwork! It's up to Carla, in the end. She says she wants her there. I certainly understand that both Carla and Luke will want to keep the girl away from reporters.'

'She's more than just a suspect, she's your most likely suspect!' Meredith accepted and sipped her wine but kept her eyes on his face.

'Yes – and no. Frankly, I haven't got a likely suspect. All right!' He gestured to ward off the protest. 'She was the last person to see him alive, as far as we can establish. Other, that is, than his killer if she isn't his killer. I admit that. I also admit that if it weren't for the fact that she's his daughter, I might even now have her locked up in a cell. But it's a tricky business. We're talking patricide. I certainly don't believe she came to Bamford to kill her father. I believe she came here to force him to introduce her to his legitimate family. For that, he needed to be alive. She didn't want him dead, Meredith. Under questioning she's been fairly frank. She had no cause to kill the man. Without him, as far as she could know, she had no way of getting accepted into the family. He was her link.'

'On the contrary,' said Meredith argumentatively, 'while he was alive, he kept her out of his legitimate family and out of the way in Cornwall. Now he's dead it seems that she's got herself invited to stay at Tudor Lodge pretty quick. Within forty-eight hours, in fact! I call that good going and it's all come about because Andrew was murdered! She has a good motive; she may well have hated him.'

'But she couldn't know what would happen after his death,' he persisted. 'It would have been far more likely that Carla would have refused even to see her. As far as Kate's concerned, the way it's turned out is sheer luck. Incidentally, first examination of her clothing has shown up nothing suspicious. No blood, no damage as caused in a scuffle. Yellow fibres from her scarf were found near the kitchen window and bear out her story that she stood there to watch her father as he moved around the kitchen. But there are no fibres beneath his fingernails which match her jacket or any other item of clothing she wore at the time.'

She pounced on the implication. 'There are fibres, then, beneath his fingernails?'

'Sorry, that's not for public knowledge.' The decision had been made not to make public knowledge of the blue fibres, beneath Penhallow's fingernails, not while there was any chance of finding the garment from which they'd come.

She thought about that and he drank his wine as he waited for the next line of attack.

'Even,' she began, 'even if I agreed with you that Kate's not necessarily the killer, I still can't believe you think it's a good idea for her to move in with the family.'

'I don't. I admit I was hoping that Kate being left at liberty might shake up some response somewhere, but I hadn't anticipated this. If I'd known what was in Carla's mind, I'd have stepped in quick to nip the whole thing in the bud. But we didn't know she planned to ask Kate to stay and now, you say, she's done it.'

'She left a message at The Crown because Kate was out,' Meredith said. 'I suppose Kate has got it by now. I wonder where she was?' She frowned. 'I mean, why wasn't she at The Crown? You told her to stay there.'

'To make it her address in Bamford, yes. I didn't exactly forbid her to set foot out of the place, nor could I. Perhaps that smart young lawyer of hers took her out for a decent lunch somewhere before he went back to London. He probably did. He would have wanted to talk over the case and prepare his client for likely questions and explain the sort of thing we'd be doing. She – as far as we know – has never been involved in a murder inquiry. She won't know the law nor the procedures. He should. Besides, the food at The Crown isn't exactly exciting and she's been complaining about it nonstop. She does,' added Markby with some feeling, 'complain a lot.'

Meredith pushed back a hank of brown hair. 'You still haven't found a murder weapon?'

'Neither found nor even identified. Blunt object, yes. But a distinctive kind of object which left a peculiar imprint. So far it's got us foxed.'

There was a silence, but he was sure she was thinking up something new by way of attack. In fact, what she said was, 'You know there is a big old tree which reaches over the garden wall at Tudor Lodge and would make it very easy to climb over the wall in or out of the property?'

'I suppose you've tried it?' He rolled his eyes ceilingwards.

'Yes, I have, as it happens.'

'Need I have asked? *As it happens*, yes, the tree's been noted, and yes, there are marks on the bark, some of which, I'm afraid to say, were made by an overenthusiastic constable during the search. Any other marks on it could have been made by children. It's the sort of trees boys climb . . . and girls too, as I've just learned!' He paused. 'Any other discoveries during your unauthorised prowl around the gardens?'

'No. Except that, you know the man who owns the garage just a little way from Tudor Lodge, just beyond the terrace of cottages?'

'Harry Sawyer, he's a local man.'

'Well, he had been asking Andrew to sell him the patch of land between his garage and the terrace. There's a historical reason why it belongs to Tudor Lodge, it was part of the once bigger estate. Anyhow, Andrew wouldn't sell, refused point-blank. Harry wants to build a car showroom there.'

'And from whom do you have this?' Markby was irked. He hadn't known it. It mightn't be relevant, but someone ought to have turned it up. Meredith, he thought ruefully, had a habit of coming up with odd bits of information.

'From Harry himself and from Luke, who ought to know. Andrew feared that a showroom would mean extra lights and traffic in and out of the site. He was probably right and I have to say I sympathise. That garage glows like a beacon all night long anyway. Irene Flack seemed surprised to hear it, though, so I don't think it was common knowledge. Irene thought Harry had owned the land already.'

When Alan didn't reply she raised her eyebrows questioningly. 'What's on your mind?'

He set down his glass. 'I ought to say it was work, that it was the interesting information you've just provided. It *is* interesting and we'll have to look into it. But I'm trying to put the whole thing out of my mind until Monday. I rang Springwood Hall . . .'

'The hotel?'

'I thought, we'd drive over there later, have a really good dinner, stay the night . . . Make a weekend of it, or make the most of what's left of the weekend.'

Meredith smiled up at him through the untidy locks of brown hair. 'That sounds nice. I really wanted, you know, when I skived off early from that course, for us to spend some time together.'

Alan hadn't meant to say the next thing, but he said it anyway. 'I've been thinking a lot recently about us.'

She didn't play for time by pretending she didn't know what he was driving at.

'It's my fault,' she said.

'No, it's mine. The police work, as usual. But if we were together, I mean, if we shared a home, then at least we'd see something of each other.' He gave a rueful grin. 'If only in passing, dashing past one another in the mornings!'

'It's still my fault,' she said. 'Shillyshallying and not knowing my own mind.' She hesitated. 'Can't we go on as we are?'

He shook his head.

'Oh.' She looked momentarily downcast, then rallied. 'That was a stupid question. Of course we can't.'

'*I* can't,' he said. 'That's the problem. I'm sorry, but that's the way it is. Look, I wouldn't be so crass or so conceited as to issue an ultimatum. I suppose, if you insist – that is to say, if you feel this is the only way we can go on, I'll have to come to terms with it. On the other hand, I've had one marriage fail on me and I know that when things are less than satisfactory, you just have to grasp the nettle, make some hard decisions. What you can't do is just drift.'

'Carla said something of the sort. That you – that I should make up my mind.'

Markby snorted. 'In the circumstances, Carla's hardly in the position to act as counsellor on matters of the heart.'

'Perhaps she is. She admitted to me that she had realised Andrew had a mistress, but that he would never tell her. She went down to Cornwall, you know, and found out.'

'No, I didn't know that either. However, it doesn't surprise me. I'd be surprised if Carla had *denied* she even suspected what Andrew was up to. Carla's too bright to have missed the telltale signs. Over so many years, Andrew must have slipped up occasionally. She never thought of leaving him?'

'She thought about it and decided against it. He seemed to value their relationship and to want to keep his marriage going, so she let it be. There was young Luke to consider as well, and the press headlines. She let things drift on with the problem never discussed. And look where it ended up!'

'I don't anticipate anything so dramatic in our case,' he said drily. 'I realise this is a very strange way to be doing it, but I'm asking you to marry me.'

'And I realise I've taken enough time already making up my mind about us. But still, I'd really like a little more time to come up with my answer. Can you bear it, to wait just a little longer?'

'If there will be answer.'

She nodded. 'Yes, there'll be an answer. I promise.'

Sergeant Prescott had also had a busy day. He'd been checking Kate's account of her hitched journey to Bamford. He had found the lay-by and talked to Wally. He talked to any other drivers he found there and although none of them had been there on the occasion in question, several of them knew Eddie Evans. Evans, he was told, was a reliable chap and a family man. They identified Eddie's home town from which he operated his one-man haulage business.

It seemed to Prescott that Kate might have talked to Evans on the long drive. He needed in any case to speak to the man. But here he was foiled. For though tracking down Eddie's address wasn't difficult, a phone call, answered by Eddie's wife, informed him that Eddie had left at five that morning for the Continent with a load. He was certainly across the Channel by now, and wasn't expected back home until the end of the forthcoming week.

'Why so long?' asked Prescott crossly. 'Whereabouts in France has he gone?'

'I didn't say he'd gone to France,' said Mrs Evans. 'I said he'd gone to the Continent. He's taken the rig over on the ferry to Ostend. He's got a load to drop off and then he goes on to pick another up to bring back.'

Prescott acknowledged his error. 'All right, then, where exactly is he driving to, to pick up this return load?'

'Turkey,' said Mrs Evans.

Having failed to track down Eddie, Prescott had targeted Andy, the night porter at The Crown, who lived in a village about five miles from Bamford. He'd found Andy, a small, wizened man in a cap and grubby dungarees, in his garden.

To Prescott's considerable dismay, Andy had acquired a load of horse manure and was setting about digging it in as the sergeant arrived. He moved well upwind and called out his questions.

Shovelling serenely, Andy said Kate Drago had left the hotel on the night of the murder at about nine. He couldn't swear to the time, mind, but thought that was it.

'She asked me about taxis. I told her where the rank was. Only I warned her that she'd be lucky to find one that time of night. Busy time, see. People going out for a drink these days don't want to take their cars. Don't know whether she found a taxi or not. She didn't say where she was going. This is good muck, this is. I get it over at the riding stables. The secret is to let it get proper rotted.'

Gagging, Prescott asked what time she had returned. Andy was equally vague. 'It'd be after half-past ten. No, I wouldn't say she looked upset. More bad-tempered, I'd say.'

'How exactly?' Prescott shouted from the far side of the plot.

'Like she hadn't got her own way over something,' said Andy. 'What's the matter with you, then? You look a bit green.'

An hour and a half, thought Prescott as he beat a hasty retreat. Not a lot of time to get out to Tudor Lodge, attack her father, cover her tracks and get back. But time enough. 'Damn!' he said sadly.

His long and frustrating day had come eventually to an end. He was off duty at last, and making his way home. He wasn't a local man, but though he worked out of Regional HQ, he lived in the town because it offered the nearest and cheapest rented accommodation he could find. His small flat was above a shop in the High Street. The flat didn't offer a garage and he was forced to keep his car some distance away in a rented lockup. He was returning from this on foot when he came across Kate Drago herself.

She had so filled his thoughts as he walked along that he wondered if he were imagining her. But no, there she was, unmistakable, and walking away from the town's main chemist's shop with a plastic carrier bag in her hand.

The sergeant hastened his step and called out loudly, 'Hullo! Kate – Miss Drago!'

She hadn't seen him but, hearing her name, stopped and turned suspiciously, her lips forming a discouraging rebuff. When she saw who it was, she hesitated, but looked no more encouraging than before.

'Am I being trailed around town now?'

'No, of course not!' Prescott protested. 'I'm off duty.'

'Right.' She made to pass by.

Impulsively, Prescott urged, 'Wait!' and then, taking inspiration from the door of a nearby teashop, added, 'Would you like a cup of tea or coffee or – something?'

'Haven't you got anything else to do?' she asked. 'Seeing as you're off duty?'

'No,' said Prescott truthfully. He explained, 'I live along here, above the clothes shop. I'd make a cup of tea when I got indoors, anyway. I'd invite you up – but it's not much of a place.'

'I wouldn't accept your invitation anyway, Sergeant!' she retorted drily.

He flushed, 'No, I didn't expect – I wouldn't – look, the café there is quite a nice place. They have cake and so on.'

'All right!' she said unexpectedly.

Seated in the cramped interior, she put her plastic carrier on the floor and leaned her elbows on the table. They'd found a table to the rear of the café, which was fairly crowded, mostly with a clientele of respectable middle-aged women. They were the last of the 'four to five' tea-time crowd. Shortly it would thin and be replaced by the early evening 'high tea' customers, who'd order from the light meals menu. The café didn't aspire to more than that and closed at six thirty. There wasn't a great deal of room for someone the size of Prescott, who was squeezed uncomfortably against the stone wall and risked, if he moved unwisely, knocking over a vase of silk flowers on the table.

Kate Drago was watching him with mild amusement. 'Do you come here often, as they say?'

'No,' said Prescott. 'Not on my own, I wouldn't. Not exactly my sort of place.'

'So why the desire to bring me?'

'I don't know.' He attempted to justify his action. 'I thought you might be on your own. Nowhere to go but The Crown. Your solicitor gone back to London, has he?'

'Yes, he's gone back.' She ran the tip of her tongue along her upper lip as she surveyed him. 'You didn't ask me here because you though you'd do a little out-of-hours sleuthing? Gain a few brownie points with the superintendent?'

Goaded, Prescott's embarrassment faded. 'Look,' he said belligerently, 'I've been driving around all day, going from pillar to post, trying to check your journey here.'

Her gaze, which had been tolerant since coming into the café, grew wary again. 'And did you check it? Satisfactorily?'

'More or less. The trucker who gave you a lift to Bamford is out of the country.'

'What's he going to tell you, apart from confirming he set me down where the road turns off for Bamford? I didn't chatter away to him. It's not my style. He talked a bit about his daughter, gave me lots of fatherly advice about the dangers of hitching.'

'He was right,' said Prescott, aware he sounded stuffy. 'I mean, it is a bit risky for a girl like you.'

'Like me?'

'Pretty,' said Prescott, reddening.

'Oh.' She leaned back. 'Why did you join the police, Sergeant?'

'My name's Steve,' he told her.

The waitress had appeared. 'Sorry to keep you waiting. What'll it be?' Her hand was poised above her notepad.

'Er – tea, for two . . .' Prescott glanced nervously at Kate. 'Or do you prefer coffee?'

'Tea will be fine,' she said.

'Cake?' asked the waitress. 'Scones, toasted teacakes, carrot cake, and I think there's still lemon sponge. Otherwise I'm afraid it's nearly all gone. We've been busy.'

They settled for carrot cake. That was Kate's choice and Prescott followed it, although he personally thought carrots a bit odd for a cake ingredient. Admittedly ignorant of such matters, he'd always thought cakes contained things like sugar and eggs and dried fruit. Carrots went on a plate with meat and potatoes.

'Well?' Kate prompted when the waitress had left them.

'The police? I thought it'd be interesting, offer a career.' Prescott furrowed his brow, trying to come up with some reason which might make sense to her. 'It'd give me the opportunity to play sport.'

'And is it interesting?'

'Sometimes. There is a lot of routine boring stuff. But you get that in any job, don't you? You meet some interesting people—' He felt his cheeks burn.

Amusement was back in her face. 'Like me?'

'Like you,' said Prescott simply.

She took the compliment badly. Her pale pointed face flushed and became aggressive. 'The police would like to prove I killed my father.'

'No!' He was genuinely shocked. 'They – we want to find out what really happened, that's all.'

The carrot cake arrived. He was relieved to see it looked like normal cake.

She picked up her fork and stabbed her portion. 'Do you think I killed him?'

'No,' he protested, knowing that he oughtn't to be saying it, or discussing the matter with her like this, unofficially. But he wasn't sorry. She wore her hair pinned up in a knot today and he wished she had left it loose to tumble round her shoulders as it had when he'd first seen her.

The tea arrived with a clatter. 'Everything all right?' asked the waitress and was gone before either of them could tell her.

'You may like to know,' Kate said, picking up the metal teapot and pouring his tea for him, 'that my father's wife and my half-brother both believe in my innocence.'

'Do they? I mean, good!' Prescott's hand, reached out towards the milk jug, was stayed. He had been surprised she hadn't put the milk in first, but now he forgot that at the unexpected statement. Away from base all day, he hadn't heard the news of her proposed move to Tudor Lodge.

'Yes.' She fixed her eyes on his face, a mocking light gleaming in the depths of them. 'You were right in saying I was on my way back to The Crown, Sergeant – Steve. But only to pack up my gear. I'm glad to be able to tell you I'm moving out of that awful dump. I've been invited to stay at Tudor Lodge.' She indicated the plastic carrier by her feet. 'I popped out to buy some bits and pieces I'll need.' Her eyes locked with his and hers glowed with triumph. 'I'm going to stay with my family,' she said.

Added to the unexpected news, that almost tangible air of victory silenced Prescott for a full minute. Then he picked up his cup and said inelegantly, 'Blimey . . .'

The middle-aged women turned their heads inquisitively as the girl's laughter rippled around the café.

Carla paused in the kitchen doorway, a bulging plastic sack in her arms. Mrs Flack was by the sink, wiping down the draining board, her back to the door. She didn't turn, though she must have known her employer was there. The housekeeper's form radiated disapproval.

Carla said a little awkwardly, 'Thank you for making up a bed for my guest, Irene, and for giving up your Saturday to come in and help out like this.'

Mrs Flack took her time wringing out her dishcloth and draping it over the taps before she turned round at last. 'That's all right, Mrs Penhallow.' Her voice was suspiciously bland.

'Look!' Carla put down the plastic sack. 'I know some people think it odd—'

'It's not for me,' interrupted Mrs Flack, 'to pass comment, I'm sure.'

Carla sighed at the lack of encouragement and indicated the sack at her feet. 'I was turning out a couple of things and I thought of your knitting and sewing circle.'

'Oh?' Mrs Flack's interest was taken before she remembered that she was displeased and that a bribe wasn't going to win her over. Her bland tone returned. 'Very kind of you.'

'I know you unpick good hand-knits and reknit them, so there are a couple of Andrew's sweaters in there and also a couple of fleecy things which might cut up and make little bootees or toddlers' coats. You did mention, I think, that you were going to suggest baby clothes to your members?'

Carla sounded coaxing but looked as if she really thought Mrs Flack was quite right in saying it wasn't for the cleaner to pass comment.

Mrs Flack walked stiffly to the sack and picked it up. 'It'll be much appreciated. I haven't got my car so I'll just put it in the utility room till tomorrow.' She sounded marginally more gracious.

Carla waited, fidgeting about, until the housekeeper returned from stowing away the sack. 'Irene, about my husband's daughter. I can see you don't approve, but I'm sure it's the right thing to do.'

'It's your decision to make,' said Mrs Flack. 'There's no need to apologise.'

Carla flushed and added obstinately, 'It's what Andrew would have wanted.'

Mrs Flack might have declared the decision one entirely for her employer, but at this she was moved to express an opinion. 'Now that's something we can't ever say, is it? Not when talking of the dear departed. We can't ever know what *they* would've done, can we?'

Carla pressed her lips together so tightly the colour drained out of them. 'I think I know my husband's mind! I certainly know my own mind, what I want to do. I'm sorry if it will make extra work!'

It was her turn to march away, displeased.

'Well, I'll be keeping *my* eye on that young woman, never you fear!' muttered Mrs Flack. 'Too kind for your own good, that's what you are, Mrs P, and that girl's taken advantage of it! It's *not* what poor Mr Penhallow would've wanted. Don't care what you say. He can't have wanted it, or he'd have done it himself, long ago. And he didn't, did he? So there!' She gave a brisk nod, agreeing with herself.

CHAPTER TWELVE

Sunday morning and barely light. The mist curled across the open farmland around the town and hung in massed clumps in the dips between the undulating hills. The muntjak deer had emerged from the conifer plantations and tore at the rough grass of the firebreaks. There were roe deer in there too, but they had withdrawn to the inner fastnesses. Very faintly, in the absence of other sound, a muted roar marked the distant motorway.

Dave Pearce, who was a countryman by upbringing, enjoyed this time of day. He would have wished to be out with a gun, rabbiting. As it was, he was a different kind of hunter these days. He turned his car into the forecourt of Sawyer's garage. Behind him the two police cars followed suit.

The garage was still closed up. If Pearce recalled rightly, Harry did open up on a Sunday morning but closed his business at lunchtime. Presumably he didn't do enough business on a Sunday afternoon to justify paying staff.

'Wait here,' Pearce ordered the men who had clambered from the following cars.

He walked briskly around the main garage building, down the pathway which ran alongside it and across the patch of ground towards Harry's dilapidated bungalow.

When it came fully into view, Pearce paused to survey the place. He thought how strikingly it contrasted with the rest of the property. The garage itself, its pumps, forecourt and shop area were pristine, fresh with new paint and polish, and showed every sign of a hard-working and ambitious proprietor.

Not so the bungalow. Either Harry had no time or no interest in the building. It was a place to sleep, to keep his personal effects, cook his meals. Pearce and Tessa, his wife, had spent long hours decorating their first home and the sight of this forlorn dwelling filled Pearce not only with critical disapproval, but with something deeper-seated which he was reluctant to face. He knew Sawyer's wife had left years ago. Everyone knew it. Sawyer was a local man. There were Sawyers dotted around the villages of the area, all related by sometimes intricate descent to some far-off Sawyer ancestor. Pearce never used Harry's garage, but he knew of Harry by repute. But now he realised this sad dingy home represented more than the neglected bolt hole of a busy man. It represented a failed marriage, lost dreams. Perhaps it wasn't just a case of Harry having little time for the place. Perhaps he actively hated it, sublimating everything into his ceaseless efforts on behalf of his garage business.

Harry was up and about. There was a light in his kitchen. Pearce pulled himself together, crossed the remaining patch of weeds and scuffed earth, and knocked sharply at the door.

A dog barked. It sounded like an old dog and it must be deaf if it hadn't heard his approach. After a moment, the door was pulled open and Harry appeared, frowning and wiping his hands on a threadbare towel. He hadn't yet shaved and peered blearily at his visitor. Behind him could be seen an aged German shepherd. It wagged its tail uncertainly.

'What do you buggers want, then?' Sawyer asked without particular animosity.

Pearce was used to this kind of welcome. He produced his identity card.

'I know who you bloody well are,' said Sawyer, casting it the merest disparaging glance. 'I asked you, what you want? I'm not open for business yet. Eight,' he added.

'I don't want fuel,' Pearce said. 'We've come to search your premises, garage and bungalow. I've a warrant . . .' He produced it.

Sawyer showed slightly more interest in the warrant but not much. Pearce was annoyed by his casual attitude. Markby had rung the previous evening with a report of Sawyer having had some dispute with the murder victim about land. They hadn't yet found a murder weapon, not even managed to identify its type, but a repair workshop was full of tools.

'Get out there!' ordered the superintendent in the way of a man who hadn't to get out of bed early on a Sunday and go himself. In fact, it seemed, the superintendent had quite other plans for his Sunday. He had informed Pearce that he would be out of town from Saturday evening, the moment he set down the phone, to Sunday evening. He would be at the Springwood Hall Hotel and Country Club and woe betide anyone who disturbed him there.

Pearce knew what that meant. He sympathised. Fat chance he and Tessa even got to go away for a weekend these days. If the super and his ladyfriend could nip off for a bit of romance, good luck to them.

A warrant had been obtained from a none-too-happy justice of the peace on Saturday evening. Called from wrestling with his bow tie in preparation for a golf club dinner, this worthy had expressed his hope that this wasn't going to prove another wild-goose chase of which he felt there had been far too many recently on the part of the police.

Consequently, Pearce had felt himself obliged to turn out this morning in person to oversee its execution. He hadn't held the rank of inspector long enough to feel secure in it yet and the last thing he needed was a spat with the local magistrature. Sergeant Prescott, whom he trusted, was off duty today and he wouldn't feel easy leaving supervision of the search to anyone else. Neither had the call-out pleased Tessa because her sister was coming to lunch specifically to admire the newly installed fitted kitchen. 'What am I supposed to do with the roast?' had rung in his ears as he'd left the house.

The dog shuffled forwards arthritically and stretched out its white-haired muzzle to sniff at the newcomer, staring up with filmy eyes which probably saw little but a smudged outline. The garage owner's hand dropped to touch its ear and it lost interest. If its owner thought the man was all right, then the dog accepted it. It retreated and sank stiffly to the dusty hall floor with its bony rear haunches sticking out like a couple of wings.

'What are you looking for?' Harry Sawyer's gaze had sharpened, betraying that he wasn't as unmoved by the visit as he'd appeared. 'I keep everything regular. Don't do special jobs for cash, nothing like that.'

'I'm not a taxman,' said Pearce wearily.

'Then what do you bloody want? I gotta open up for business eight sharp. The girl's coming in to mind the till. Newspapers'll be dropped off any minute now. I got a business to run!' Belatedly it appeared to sink into Sawyer's brain that his day was to be entirely disrupted.

'I suppose you can sell newspapers and stuff,' said Pearce unwillingly. 'But you can't go in your repair shop.'

'I don't want your lot turning it out, leaving everything upside down!' The dog looked up, worried at the changing tone of its master's voice. It gave a soft whine.

'We'll leave it as we find it,' Pearce assured the garage owner.

'No, you bloody won't!' argued Sawyer.

Pearce was inclined to admit he was probably right. But he wasn't in the mood to waste time in dispute. He turned and set off briskly towards the rear entry to the workshop, which faced the bungalow.

Sawyer followed, expostulating as he went. 'How'm I supposed to do any work? I've gotta earn a living, you know. How long's this going to last, then? What d'you mean, as long as it takes? How long will it take is what I want to know! You can't do it, you can't lock me out of my own premises. If that's legal, then legal is bloody daft!' he added in a distant echo of Mr Bumble.

Giving minimal replies, Pearce ordered his team to start their search.

As they spread through the repair shop, he heard Sawyer's voice from behind him somewhere, muttering, 'I'm not taking this lying down, you know! I'm not going to put up with this. I got jobs in hand, people coming Monday wanting to pick up their cars. What am I supposed to tell them? Turning up unannounced and sending in the heavy mob. I've got my rights and I know what's right, too, and I'm going to see I get it! No one's entitled to cause me all this grief. Not no one, and you're bloody well not going to get away with it, not you nor no one else!'

Pearce turned smartly to face his accuser and said, 'Well, since you've got quite a bit to say, you won't mind answering a couple of questions for me, will you?'

'I've got nothing to say to you buggers.'

'I understand you wanted to buy that piece of land over there from Mr Penhallow at Tudor Lodge.'

'What if I did?' Sawyer demanded in surly tones. 'It's no secret.'

'It wasn't a well-known fact, though, was it? Irene Flack, your nearest neighbour and the Penhallows' housekeeper, didn't know it.'

'I don't go gossiping about my business,' Sawyer retorted. 'Which is not to say I got anything to hide. If Irene had asked me before, I'd have told her. I thought she did know, anyway, and that was why she always parked her little car there. I thought Mr Penhallow had given her permission. If she thought it was down to me, then that was her mistake, wasn't it?'

Doggedly, Pearce continued, 'But Mr Penhallow refused to sell. Is that right?'

Sawyer paused and rubbed the back of his hand across his mouth as his eyes assessed his questioner. 'He might've. It wasn't settled. We were still discussing it.'

'His son seems to think it was settled. His father had refused and that was that.'

'Then the young feller has got it wrong, hasn't he? It seems to me,' added Harry sarcastically, 'that a lot of people has got things arse about face around here, including you lot – or you wouldn't be here bothering me with silly questions and making a right mess of my premises!'

Pearce turned to look at his men swarming all over the repair shop. If they had got it wrong, they were going to look very silly.

At Tudor Lodge Kate Drago opened her eyes, seeing the bedroom in daylight for the first time. By the time she'd checked out of The Crown and made her way here last night, approaching darkness had necessitated switching on the lights in the house.

Now Kate sat up in bed and surveyed her surroundings with a tingle of excitement. The room was decorated in predominantly cream and forget-me-not blue. Cream paintwork, blue carpet, cream cotton curtains sprigged with tiny blue flowers and matching duvet cover. It was the sort of home in which a selection of reading matter was provided for house guests. Stacked on the bedside table were assorted paperbacks, two of them whodunnits. No one had thought to remove those.

Kate swung her legs out of bed and padded to the window. It overlooked the side of the house. She could see lawn, shrubs, a dry-stone wall, more trees and just glimpse, between them, the roofs of the terraced cottages she knew lay beyond. She couldn't see Sawyer's garage and she couldn't see the police cars.

She whispered, 'I've done it. I'm here!'

The victory remained hollow, the void stemming from the absence of the one person who should have been here to see this. *He* had cheated her, right at the end. He had cheated her by taking refuge in death. He was still here. She knew that. She had felt his presence as she'd climbed the creaking wooden stair last night. But it wasn't the same. He should have led her into this house and presented her to the others, not obliged her to come here like a refugee. Not even in her original clothes, for goodness' sake, in which she'd made the carefully planned trip to Bamford. The police had those. She'd had to go out and buy others, charging them to her credit card despite the fact that she probably wouldn't have the means to pay the account when it came through. But this, she thought bitterly, this was a rich man's house!

Kate turned and made for her khaki haversack which lay in the corner of the room. She hunted about in it and withdrew a leather folder designed to hold a pair of photographs. It was old, the once polished cover scuffed and cracking. She'd found it in a drawer in the cottage when clearing the place out.

She opened it up and studied the two portraits it contained. One was of a younger Andrew Penhallow, slimmer, good-looking. The other was of a woman with pretty, if weak, features. She had long fair hair and dangling earrings. In the photo, she was about thirty years old. She wasn't smiling, but looked very serious, even a little sad, as if she guessed the nature of the disease which was growing within her.

Kate smoothed the image with her forefinger. 'It's going all right, Mum. You'll see. It'll turn out right yet. I mean to get what's owing us, both of us. Freddie says I've got a good claim on the estate.' She closed the folder. 'They won't get rid of me so easily! I've come here for what's mine!'

From the bedroom window in the side of her terraced cottage, Irene Flack had seen the police cars parked in the garage forecourt. Puzzled and worried, she went downstairs in her dressing gown and set about preparing her breakfast. The actions involved – making toast, boiling the kettle, measuring out porridge into the pan – distracted her from what was going on at the garage, and made her think instead of what must be going on at this very moment at Tudor Lodge. Who would be performing these simple domestic chores today? She wondered whether she ought to get dressed quickly and walk up there and make breakfast for them all, although she didn't normally work at weekends and had already surrendered her Saturday. But it was no use sticking to schedules when emergencies arose and there was no denying there was an emergency at Tudor Lodge. That was Irene's firmly held opinion. She looked at the clock. It wasn't yet eight and no one would have started yet on the breakfast preparations.

Making a decision, Irene switched off the gas, ran upstairs and grabbed garments at random. As she let herself out of her cottage, she glanced back towards the garage forecourt. Harry was standing there with the girl who worked as cashier. They were deep in discussion. As Irene watched, the girl turned away, got back into her car, backed out of the premises and drove away. It looked very much as if Harry had decided not to open up this morning.

Heavy-hearted, because it seemed that this business was going to involve them all and they'd get no peace, she walked briskly past the terrace towards the Lodge. Before she got there, the door of the last cottage opened and old Mrs Joss appeared.

'Good morning!' called Irene, trying to get past before the old crone could delay her.

Mrs Joss gripped her sleeve. 'What's going on?' she asked eagerly, the gold loops swinging at her withered earlobes. 'What's going on down at Harry's place? It's all coppers! I see 'em go past.'

'I don't know!' said Mrs Flack, detaching herself firmly.

'You going up to the house, then?' asked Mrs Joss, undeterred. She meant, Irene knew, Tudor Lodge. 'I thought you didn't oblige of a Sunday.'

'They need all the help they can get right now!' Irene was provoked into saying.

Mrs Joss nodded. 'That young girl's there, ain't she? Little madam, eh? Up to no good, that one.'

Irene stared. 'Now how on earth do you know that?'

'My grandson, Lemuel!' Mrs Joss smirked with pleasure at having sprung a surprise. 'He works in the bar up at The Crown. That girl's been staying there, brassy little piece, so Lemuel reckoned, sharp as a knife. Well, last night she moved out and left a message if anyone wanted her, she was at Tudor Lodge. What's more, Mrs Penhallow, she sent the young fellow up to settle the bill.' Mrs Joss looked furtive. 'It's not what I call quite right,' she said. 'It's what I call monkey business.'

Mrs Flack couldn't help but sigh agreement. 'It's not what I call right, but it's what Mrs Penhallow wants!'

The old woman chuckled softly and it gave Irene the creeps. She could believe Mrs Joss capable of almost anything. Years ago, so it was said, and before present legislation, young girls 'in trouble' had found their way to Mrs Joss's door, and the old girl was a dab hand with herbal remedies to this day. The older folk in Bamford still turned up from time to time to buy a cough syrup or 'blood purifier'.

'Lemuel reckons the young fellow looked like thunder so I reckon he don't want her there,' Mrs Joss smirked.

But this was going too far. Mrs Flack said frostily, 'I dare say young Luke might well look like thunder with all the staff of The Crown standing round gawping at him. Seems to me they can't have enough work to do!'

Lemuel's grandmother bridled. 'My grandson is a real hard worker. They set a lot of store by our Lemmy up at The Crown.'

'Do they indeed?' retorted Mrs Flack in battle mode. 'Seems they must pay him well at any rate, since he's always got some new jacket or such and there's that noisy motorbike *and* that radio thing he walks round with, blasting everyone's ears! Not short of money,

163

your Lemuel! And there's me always thought hotel staff didn't get paid much. Just shows.'

She stalked off, leaving Mrs Joss muttering imprecations.

When Mrs Flack walked into the kitchen at Tudor Lodge, she found Luke there, carefully setting out bacon rashers on the grill pan.

'You let me do that!' she said firmly, manoeuvring him aside.

'What are you doing here, Irene?' he asked, surprised. 'You came in yesterday extra and it's really not fair on you to ask you to give up another free day. I can manage.'

'I'm not saying you can't,' said Mrs Flack. 'But you've other things on your mind and so you should. You've a guest in the house. Things being as they are, your mother can't be expected to be worried about meals and such. Nor more should you be. You ought to be thinking about yourself and your mother. You leave this to me.' Her nimble fingers buttoned her overall as she spoke.

'Thanks, Irene,' he said, and gave her a hug.

'Well,' said Mrs Flack, pleased. ''Tis only right and decent. That young woman, she'll be wanting a proper breakfast, I suppose? She's not on one of them funny diets?'

'I shouldn't think so,' said Luke dourly, 'not after having seen her tuck in last night.'

'Nothing wrong with a healthy appetite,' Mrs Flack conceded that even Kate Drago had a right to that. 'You ought to eat more, a big fellow like you. And as for your mother, what she eats wouldn't keep a sparrow going. Now, if you want to help, you'd better go and lay the breakfast in the dining room. You'll be more comfortable in there than out here with me clattering about. If you see your mother, ask her what she wants done about lunch.'

Luke made his way to the dining room and set about his task. As he placed cutlery on the table he heard a noise from the doorway and looking up, saw Kate standing there. She said, 'Good morning.'

The apparent ease of her manner stirred the embers of his resentment. She must have a metaphorical hide like a hippo, he thought. Didn't she feel the slightest embarrassment?

Yet, if any embarrasment was felt, it was felt by himself. The injustice of this made him angry but he couldn't help it. Her eyes were following his hands as he set out knives and spoons and it reminded him of an episode the previous evening.

He had collected her from the hotel, settling the bill, and driven her to Tudor Lodge in stony silence. His mother had been welcoming, but had overdone it, gushing and then, realising what she was doing, falling silent and miserable. He'd urged her to go upstairs and rest. He would fix the evening meal, such as it was. His mother had given him a grateful look and scurried upstairs.

The girl (he knew her name, of course, but he insisted on calling her 'the girl' in his head, refusing to accord her any kind of familiarity) had followed him to the kitchen. There he'd announced that he was cooking scrambled eggs for their supper and refused her offer of help. She'd hung about the kitchen as he worked (determined to make him notice her, he thought), until he'd ungraciously suggested she set the table. He hadn't told her where to find anything and a strange kitchen could be a bewildering place. Kate had opened and shut doors and drawers at random in her hunt for cutlery, salt and pepper pots, plates and cups. He saw her difficulty but steadfastly refused to indicate where anything might be found. It had been a petty act of malice on his part, and that was why he now felt ashamed. But she, equally obstinate, had refused to ask. It had led him to wonder whether obstinacy was a family trait – and then angrily to deny to himself that she was family.

Eventually she'd found enough things to set a table without having to give in. So in a sense, she'd won the silent tussle – and that had made him even angrier.

His mother had then reappeared. They'd eaten in silence after Carla had ventured to suggest a glass of wine and found no takers. Luke had refused because he was determined to do nothing which looked like celebrating. The truth was he'd felt physically sick. Good God, hadn't the girl sat in this kitchen with his father? Or so the police had said. Perhaps, for all he knew, at this very table? And how she tucked into the eggs and the mushrooms and tomatoes which had accompanied them! While his mother picked at the food and he'd almost gagged on it. He supposed she hadn't been eating well at The Crown, which was a dump, as everyone knew, but if she'd had any sensitivity . . .

'Breakfast will be soon,' he said now, forcing himself to look at her. His lips moved stiffly as if they didn't want to work and form sounds. 'Irene Flack's come in to cook it.'

Kate moved towards the table and rested her hands on the back of a chair. 'I want to talk to you,' she said in her clear voice.

'Go ahead.' His heart sank. Talk to her was the last thing he wanted to do. He really thought he couldn't manage it. He looked away but he could still see her hands, resting on the wooden bar. They looked small and fragile. Appearances were said to be deceptive. He wondered how strong those slender fingers were. The hair prickled at the nape of his neck as he imagined them gripping a weapon, raising it high . . . He turned his back to her so that she shouldn't see his face.

She took the movement as a clear snub and it rankled, cracking her armour of apparent ease.

'You might at least look at me!' she burst out.

Luke turned slowly to face her and saw that her face was white with rage beneath that sunburst of hair. At that, his own temper which he'd kept in rein with such difficulty, broke free and flared.

'Look,' he croaked. 'I didn't invite you here. My mother did. I'm going along with it because that's her decision and I'm supporting her in it. I don't know what you want. I don't bloody care. Whatever it is, it can wait. My mother's not well. I won't let you bother her or cause her any distress, have you got that? And as for playing on her soft heart, wriggling your way into her sympathies, I'll put a stop to that, too!'

She said very quietly, spacing the first words for emphasis, 'I – am – your – sister!' She added, more drily, 'You might not like the idea, but that's too bad. You're just going to have to get used to it. You and the police, all of you. If you think I'm going away again, forget it. I'm not. I'm here to stay.'

Luke let a fork drop and stooped to retrieve it. 'Is that why you turned up at the party after the match? To spin me this yarn about a fancied relationship? Incidentally, who asked you along? Or did you just gate-crash?'

She flushed. 'No! Someone invited me. Look, I admit I talked him into it. I came along to watch the match and got talking to this guy on the touchline. He said he was going to the party afterwards, did I want to come? Of course I did. I wanted to see you. I thought, if we did get into conversation, I could sort of pave the way to introducing myself properly later.'

'My mother was watching the match that day,' he said fiercely. 'Were you planning to get talking to her, too? Drop a poisonous hint or two, perhaps? Watch her go to pieces out there in the open with everyone looking on and nowhere to hide?'

She tilted her jaw, her embattled little face frozen. 'As it happens, I didn't realise your mother was there earlier. Even if I had, I wouldn't have bothered her. It was you I wanted to meet. It was time we met.' The last words slipped out as if she'd said them to herself many times before. There was a curious stubborn chanting pattern to them. This was her mantra. This was her excuse or whatever you cared to call it. This would be her answer to any criticism. He wondered briefly if she were quite sane.

What he said was: 'And that's what you told Dad when you came sneaking round here?'

'I didn't sneak!' Her eyes flashed. 'I tried—He would have agreed, if he hadn't – if it hadn't happened.'

'We'll want proof, you know,' Luke said callously. 'Proof you are who you say you are.'

Her body language had become tense. Now it relaxed. 'That's all right. If you want DNA tests, all that sort of stuff, I'm quite willing to undergo those. Besides, there are all the people who knew them, knew about the affair. Freddie Green, my solicitor, says I won't have any trouble establishing the relationship.'

'You can establish what you want!' Luke's voice rose and cracked with rage. 'Dad never acknowledged you and I won't, not ever. You're nothing to do with me, nothing to do with this family. As soon as the police say you can leave town, you can get out. You *will* get out! If you don't, whatever my mother says, I'll throw you out of this house myself!'

He saw her shocked face and was taken aback himself by his own vehemence. Had he said that? That couldn't have been him, surely? So brutal, so melodramatic and, above all, so out of control? But it was the truth, nothing but the truth, as they said in court.

He met her wide appalled grey gaze and said firmly, 'And I mean it, too.'

CHAPTER THIRTEEN

On Monday when Meredith got up and looked out of the window it was as if someone had drawn back a curtain up there in the sky. She leaned out and sniffed the air. There was no denying it. After stuttering and faltering for a month, spring had arrived.

She went out into her backyard in her dressing gown and turned her face up to the sunshine and the mild breeze and felt that special frisson in the atmosphere which signified a natural world awakening from a long winter sleep. The birds were dashing about in a positive frenzy as if realising nest-building had become a priority. There were buds and new shoots where she could have sworn there hadn't been any yesterday.

She clattered around her kitchen making coffee and toast and reflecting cheerfully that it hadn't, after all, turned out such a lost weekend. Quitting Bamford, even if going only a few miles down the road to Springwood Hall, had proved a brilliant idea on Alan's part. Away from the usual surrounds, they'd both been able to relax.

Unfortunately, this new happy mood wasn't to last. The curse of Monday struck as soon as she reached Bamford rail station. Her train was running late and, when it turned up, was packed. Not only had people who'd turned up for that train become mixed with people who'd arrived a little early for the next one, but they found carriages already packed with surly commuters who would normally have caught an earlier train which had been cancelled. Once she got to London, things didn't improve. An 'incident' had halted tube services on the line she normally took. Buses were slow, caught up in heavy traffic and roadworks. She finally arrived nearly an hour late. She was hot, dishevelled and out of sorts.

Gerald, with whom she was obliged to share an admittedly roomy office, looked up and saluted her with a coffee mug.

'Hullo, Sherlock, done it again, I see.'

'What?' she retorted, banging down her briefcase on the desk.

Gerald fished out his tabloid paper and held it up folded to display the headline.

MURDERED EUROVIP'S DOUBLE LIFE

'What's a eurovip, for goodness' sake?' Meredith wondered why setting headlines in print which looked like an eye-chart could be considered good journalism. It wasn't that she couldn't guess the substance of the story, but the manner of its presentation annoyed her. This was what Carla had feared, and with good reason.

'This bloke who got his head bashed in, down in your neck of the woods. Things do happen when you're around, don't they?' Gerald sounded wistful. 'Nothing happens around my way. Couple of old girls had a squabble Sunday morning over a poodle fouling the pavement. That was it for excitement. Did you know this euro-guy?'

'Only very slightly. I know his wife a bit better, only a bit!' she added hastily, seeing the gleam in Gerald's eye.

Too late. He leaned forward eagerly. 'Go on, let's hear all the dirty details.'

'There aren't – I don't know any. Gerald, you are definitely in the wrong job. Why didn't you take up journalism? Then you could have worked for one of those rags you read and you'd be first on the scene.'

'I've thought about that,' he returned quite seriously. 'I'd have been good at that sort of thing. You're right. I should've gone in for journalism but my mother urged me to think about a secure future.' He watched her settle down at her desk and when she didn't volunteer any details, salacious or otherwise, he changed tactics. 'Have a rotten journey? Bad luck. I'll get a cup of coffee, shall I?'

'Is that the equivalent of the open chequebook? Gerry, I don't have any details!' She put out her hand. 'Let's have a look at that report.'

He handed over the tabloid. The paper had got hold of the basic facts. They made quite a lot of Carla's TV links. She was described as 'distraught' and 'locked away inside the family's luxurious manor house'.

While she was reading it, Gerald had fetched some coffee and a Penguin chocolate biscuit. He set these before Meredith in a coaxing way like a bowerbird tempting his prospective mate.

'It's not a luxurious manor house,' said Meredith, returning the paper to its hopeful owner. 'I can set you right on that. It's a nice old house and very comfortable. But it's not exceptional, by which I mean it's not a millionaire's hideaway. Sorry, it's all I can tell you and I realise it's not worth a chocolate biscuit.'

'Keep the biscuit,' he said, now sounding like the sort of fairy-tale character who offers poisoned goodies to lost children. He had a drawer full of snacks. Gerald sometimes went on diets but they never lasted longer than a week. His doting if possessive mother repeatedly told him he was a fine figure of a man with, thanks to her advice, a good job. 'You didn't catch sight of this girl, then? The one who turned up and claimed to be his long-lost daughter? And a stunner, too, they say.'

It was her misfortune, Meredith reflected, to be inherently honest. She was a bad liar and before she could formulate a reply that would be basically true but evasive, Gerald had read her expression.

'Ah,' he said, pulling up a chair and settling down nicely. 'Go on, let's have it.'

So much was the whole thing still worrying her that even telling Gerald some of it might ease her mind. Meredith gave way to temptation. Despite his curiosity, Gerald was discreet. He liked to collect gossip but didn't pass it on. The awareness that he knew what others didn't, bolstered his deeply rooted feelings of insecurity which the prospects of a pension at the end of a day had done nothing to assuage.

'Actually, Gerry,' she began, 'you will keep this to yourself?'

Gerald drew his thumb across his throat.

'I gave her a lift on Thursday evening. I was driving home from that dreadful course—'

'Forgot about that,' he interrupted, sidetracked. 'Never mind, you can tell me about that afterwards. Go on.'

'I didn't know who she was. It was late and nearly dark. She was walking along a lonely road, a girl on her own. So I stopped and offered a lift.'

'I never come across beautiful girls wandering alone in country lanes at nightfall,' sighed Gerald.

'You don't live in the country, Gerald. You live in Golders Green. She asked me to take her to Tudor Lodge. I dropped her off there. It was getting late and I was on my way home, hoping to spend the evening with Alan. I didn't hang about to see what she did next. But I admit, I had a bad feeling about it all and that's not just hindsight. I said as much to Alan when I saw him.'

'Ah, the lovelorn copper! And what does he think about it all?'

Meredith sat up and folded her arms. 'OK, Gerry, that's it! I'm not going to tell you another word. And you can take back your chocolate biscuit, as well!'

Gerald waggled his fingers at her and danced back to his desk looking pleased with himself.

Pearce looked far from pleased with himself as he reported back to Markby on the same Monday morning. He noticed, however, that the superintendent looked positively cheerful. Well, he would, wouldn't he? growled an inner Pearce uncharitably.

'We didn't find it,' he said. 'We took away over thirty tools and bits of stuff and sent them over to forensics. They're not too pleased, you won't need me to tell you! They've told us, basically, we can whistle for the results. They'll be weeks. But frankly, none of the tools looked as if it could have caused those funny wounds. On the other hand, we'd have to examine every bit of metal in the place to be sure, and that means hundred of items! It's a repair workshop! He'd have got rid of it by now, anyhow, wouldn't he? I've got the place sealed up and Sawyer's doing his nut.'

Pearce reflected on his visit to the garage. 'Funny sort of bloke. When we first turned up he didn't seem much put out. Hardly batted an eyelid. Then, when he took in what it meant – that he wasn't going to be able to get into his own workshop or even have the run of his bungalow till we'd finished, he changed his tune. He's talking about a slur on his character and muttering about getting legal advice, by the way. He says he knows his rights and no one's going to march in jackboots over him and get away with it.'

'Did you ask him about his difference of opinion with Penhallow?' Markby wasn't too surprised that no obvious item had turned up which could have caused the patterned wound in Penhallow's skull. Beyond the garage lay open country. If he were Sawyer, and if he had just caved in a man's skull, he'd have lobbed the weapon into the middle of a bramble thicket out there, or down into the soft mud at the bottom of a stagnant pond. As for Sawyer's threats, they were par for the course. If the man were innocent, he felt sorry for him. But they had to follow it up. More than likely, however, everyone's time and effort was being wasted.

Pearce sighed. He'd missed Sunday lunch completely and when he'd finally got home, Tessa and her sister had been sitting in front of the TV, watching the Sunday evening drama, flushed with sherry and resentment.

'He doesn't deny that he approached Penhallow about buying the piece of land. Penhallow had refused but Sawyer didn't take it as final. He says he was confident he'd talk him round eventually. I don't see how we could prove or disprove that. Sawyer reckons that's how he saw the situation. The most difficult thing, he says, was getting hold of Penhallow to discuss the affair. Penhallow constantly being away in Europe, he meant.'

Markby looked up sharply. 'Did he manage to catch Penhallow during this last trip home?'

'He says he saw him at the garage one morning. Penhallow called in for fuel. Sawyer asked if Penhallow had changed his mind. Penhallow replied, quote, "Are you still on about that land, Harry? I told you, I'm not interested." Sawyer, who's either a bit of an optimist or a bit thick depending how you see it, interpreted that as not being an outright refusal. He reckoned that if he gave it time, he'd wear Penhallow down, get him interested. He thought the next time Penhallow came home, he might get him to agree.'

'Any witnesses to this conversation?'

Pearce shook his head. 'It's a possibility, though, isn't it? How's this? Sawyer decided to make an attempt to get Penhallow to agree on this last visit. Things had been dragging on long enough and he wanted them settled. He didn't know when Penhallow would come home again. So he went round to Tudor Lodge. Kate Drago told us she thought she saw someone else in the gardens, watching. She took fright and scarpered. It might have been Sawyer. The girl, according to her own story, had run off and Sawyer got his chance to talk to Penhallow alone. He stepped forward, rapped at the door, and Penhallow, believing it to be his daughter come back, opened up. Sawyer begged Penhallow to sell him the land. But Penhallow had had a rough day, what with the girl turning up out of the blue earlier, and he wasn't in the mood to listen to Sawyer. Probably told him to bugger off. Sawyer lost his temper and felled him with – with some implement we haven't yet found.' Pearce nodded. 'To me it makes a lot of sense. I'd say Sawyer was unpredictable.'

'Oh, it makes a lot of sense,' Markby agreed. 'But did he do it?'

'We could bring him in,' suggested Pearce hopefully.

'Wait until we get a report back on the tools you sent over for examination.' Markby leaned back and tapped moodily on his desk. 'We couldn't hold him on what you've got so far. Any good solicitor would have him out of here in minutes.' He stretched out his hand to the phone on his desk. 'But talking of the law, I wonder . . .'

'So, Alan, you've got yourself landed with this!' Laura leaned back in her chair and surveyed her brother tolerantly.

Today's sunshine shone through the window of her office and picked out gold lights in her fair hair, neatly swept up into a

French pleat. A sister who was a partner in the leading firm of local solicitors was a help and sometimes a hindrance. This time it was a little of both. She was handling Andrew Penhallow's estate and when a rich man was murdered, it was always worth knowing what the will contained. Hence his presence here this morning. Laura, however, anxious not to show undue favour to her brother, would probably prove as easy to get information from as the proverbial stone. Markby didn't just want the gist of the bequests. He needed a hint as to the personalities behind them. That he wouldn't get here.

The same sun's ray also showed up the dust on the bookshelves. Lawbooks, lines of 'em, thought Markby. Were they ever used for reference or were they there to impress clients? It wouldn't do to ask. His sister didn't take kindly to jocular questions of that sort.

'I didn't ask for it,' he said. 'I can still ask to be taken off the case, I suppose. On the other hand, Carla Penhallow seems satisfied that I'm in charge of investigating her husband's death. And, of course, everyone is worried about the press. A little scandal goes a long way in selling copies and there's potentially enough here to send tabloid circulation soaring for a bit.'

'Hmm . . .' Laura chose professional discretion. 'I can't comment on a client, naturally. You want to know about the will. I've been in touch with the two major beneficiaries who have no objection to my releasing the terms to you, prior to probate being granted. However, I should inform you that there may be some complications.'

'The Drago girl,' Markby said. 'She has a claim on the estate, then?'

'Oh, yes, if she is who she says she is. Once upon a time it wouldn't have been so. But now illegitimacy isn't a bar to inheritance. I've had a preliminary phone call from her solicitor, a Mr Green. Perhaps you ought to talk to him about her side of the matter.'

'So, who are the two main beneficiaries as of the present moment?'

The sun must have shown up some minuscule amount of dust on the lapel of Laura's navy-blue business suit. She smoothed it away. 'Mrs Penhallow and Luke Penhallow. There is a sizeable sum of money to Luke, in trust until he's twenty-five, by which time his father assumed he'd have finished his formal education. At twenty-five, Luke will receive whatever the trust contains. It's – it's likely to be a decent amount. That's off the record, by the way! There are small bequests to the housekeeper and one or two other people, but most goes directly to Mrs Penhallow, including the house, Tudor Lodge.'

Markby looked up sharply. 'She wasn't already a co-owner?'

'No. Mr Penhallow bought the house on the eve on his marriage and the deeds are in his name only.'

Markby frowned. Had Penhallow been having doubts, even then? Worrying whether he was marrying the right woman and seeking to protect the considerable investment represented by Tudor Lodge?

Aloud, he asked, 'There is no mention of Katherine Drago or of her mother, Helen Drago?'

'None whatsoever. But I gather from this morning's call it's likely Katherine Drago, the daughter, will wish to contest that. You really should talk to Green.'

'I've met him,' said Markby gloomily. 'Smart-aleck.'

'Again, it would be unprofessional of me to comment.'

'You wouldn't care to comment, I suppose, on the fact that your client, Mrs Carla Penhallow, has taken this alleged daughter of her husband's into the family home?'

'No, I wouldn't!' Laura snapped, flushing. Then she added, 'I'm not happy about it, Alan. But what I advised my client is privileged information.'

Her brother sighed. 'All right, thanks for your help, anyway.'

'You are coming to supper on Saturday? You and Meredith? Paul's got a whole new set of ideas on a healthy cuisine.'

'I know, I met him pedalling along on that bike of his, trailing a box of muddy veg.'

'Simple food, no fuss,' said Laura. 'I'd have thought it right up your street.'

At Tudor Lodge Monday dragged by. There was a diversion in the morning when an intrepid photojournalist established himself in a tree overlooking the garden and snapped merrily away until spotted, hauled down and sent packing by Luke.

Luke was glad of the chance to work off some energy. He felt as though he'd explode if something didn't happen soon to sort out all this mess. Their guest was keeping a low profile. She appeared at meals and disappeared immediately afterwards. Fine, he thought. Perhaps she's taken the hint at last.

Nevertheless by the evening he was tired. Not the weariness which comes from having been busy, but the exhaustion which overtakes the mind. It was only nine but Kate had gone upstairs and he supposed she wouldn't be coming down again before morning. His mother had retired to the room they called her study, where her fax machine and computer were kept.

Luke made his way there, tapped at the door, and looked round. She was sitting in front of the computer in an old green dressing gown, apparently working. There was a lamp on to boost light, but the flickering monitor illuminated her figure, giving it a strange bluish tinge.

'Hey,' he said. 'Give it a rest.'

She didn't look round from the screen. 'I'm writing letters, dear. There are so many. So many people to tell . . .'

Her hands dropped from the keyboard to rest in her lap but she remained staring at the monitor.

Inside his head, Luke screamed, 'They'll have heard already, everyone knows, you don't have to write!' But he realised she wanted to write about it, to try to write out the hurt. Nor did she really need reminding about the notoriety, not after the episode of the cameraman that morning.

'I'm going on to bed,' he said. 'It's all locked up. There's only the burglar alarm.'

'That's all right, dear. I'll set it on when I come up.' She took up her keyboard activity again.

Against the rattle of the keys and the distracting hopping of the characters on the screen, Luke said, 'You won't sit up very late, will you, Mum? Promise me.'

'I promise,' she said.

He left her to it, dissatisfied at that as at everything else.

It could hardly be expected that he slept well. He dozed fitfully for a while, only to awake to the muffled darkness of a house at night. Luke sat up, switched on the bedside lamp and swung his legs to the floor. He tugged on old jeans and a sweater and pushed his feet into disreputable plimsolls. What was the use of trying to sleep? He was wound up like a clockwork spring. The illuminated face of his watch told him it was a little after midnight but there was usually an old film on TV.

The alarm control panel was at the foot of the stair. He ran down to switch it off before it started shrilling, only to find that his mother, after all, had forgotten to set it. Luke hissed in annoyance, but he didn't blame her. He should've waited up and done it himself.

He set out first for the kitchen with the intention of making a hot drink. Luke made his way along the passage in the dark, pressing against the wall to minimise creaks from the old oak floorboards. The house was as familiar to him as his own skin. He didn't need lights any more than a blind man would've done.

However, when he reached the kitchen he switched on the hob

light which gave just enough illumination to let him see what he was doing. He set the electric kettle to boil and took down a mug and a jar of Nescafé from the cupboard above the worktop. Suddenly it struck him that he was following a similar set of actions to his father's very last. Dad had been messing about in the kitchen, filling a hot-water bottle apparently, when something had impelled him to open the back door and walk out into the night and to his death.

He supposed he believed Kate's version of events that night. That she'd returned, but fled before attracting his father's attention, frightened off by a shadowy figure lurking in the gardens. His mother believed it. As far as anyone could tell, the police also seemed inclined to believe it, since they hadn't arrested Kate. To be honest, Luke couldn't imagine Kate wielding a weapon with sufficient force . . .

He blanked out the picture. Then, unbidden, the words leaped into his mind: *What if she weren't alone? If she'd had a confederate out there in the darkness?*

Luke paused with spoon in mid-air, horrified. Then he tried to tackle the problem with something of the academic discipline his tutors had tried to instil in him. He lined up the arguments for and against. It was a possibility no one seemed to have considered. That didn't rule it out. So, then, who else could have been there that night? Who else might have a reason, or could have been offered a bribe, to help? What about that lawyer of hers? He'd been quick off the mark to get down here. He seemed to have an interest which was more than just professional. Perhaps, Luke thought, he ought to ask the police if they'd considered questioning the fellow Green.

Then he reflected dismally that he oughtn't to be thinking something like that about a girl who was his half-sister. Despite his challenge to Kate to prove it, he didn't doubt the relationship. He knew it was true. The really bad things, which hurt the most, generally were.

Luke took his mug of coffee to the Windsor chair in which, though he didn't know it, Kate had sat on her early visit that fateful night. He let his gaze travel around the kitchen with its fashionable country look – or what glossy magazines imagine to be a country look. What a splendid array of Le Creuset pots, Italian faïence plates, gadgets and utensils and every cook's aid were dimly discernible in the gloom. It struck Luke that the whole thing was pseud. No one had ever done a lot of cooking here, not in his entire lifetime that he could recall, unless you counted Irene with her batches of fancy cakes or her pots of vegetable soup. His mother got out of cooking anything if she could, although she didn't mind popping something ready-prepared into the microwave, as they had done that evening. Delicatessen meats and salads, cheese and biscuits, were the staple of her culinary efforts, but they'd survived well enough.

His first encounter with the traditional daily 'meat and two veg', laboriously roasted, boiled or braised from scratch, had come at boarding school. He remembered the shock with which he'd regarded his first platefuls. The wet heaps of vegetables, gristly beef, greying mashed potato and thick gravy, these he could smell and taste now in memory. And as for those old-fashioned puddings, bread and butter, canary, steamed jamcap, all dished up in generous portions doused in bright yellow powder custard! He'd never seen such sights before and it had seemed to him an altogether peculiar way to eat.

Luke eased himself out of the chair which was a tight fit, took his mug to the sink, rinsed it, and placed it upside down on the draining board. Then he switched out the hob light and prepared to cross the kitchen to the hall door. But as he moved forward, he thought he heard voices.

Had his mother not gone to bed? Or had Kate come downstairs intending, as he had, to watch TV? Luke went into the hall but the voices ceased immediately and there was no sliver of light beneath any door. Despite that, he checked the TV room and study. Both were empty. His mother's computer was switched off. The plastic dustsheet had been placed carefully over the keyboard. All her papers and writing materials were neatly stacked away. She was a tidy soul. So, had he imagined it?

Hesitantly he returned to the kitchen and stood in the darkness, listening, straining his ears. There it was again. A low distant murmur, not in here, but outside in the garden.

The hair bristled on the nape of his neck. He couldn't make out any words, nor even tell if a man or a woman spoke, just that persistent shu-shurring of furtive speech. He went to the window but it was dark out there, no moonlight tonight, and he could distinguish little. He wished he could see something, anything. Yet a foolish superstitious fear touched him as he remembered that old story of the Cavalier and his Puritan beloved. Housebreakers he could deal with, but apparitions from the past were something else. Luke pulled himself together. Irene Flack might believe that sort of nonsense. He didn't.

He strode to the nearest electric switch and pressed it. Light flooded the room and beamed out through the window to splash bright bands across the back lawn. The garden was transformed in an instant from impenetrable darkness to a spotlit stage set, picking out bushes in ghostly silver, the tree trunks beyond an eerie backdrop. But no flesh and blood thing showed itself. It was a stage which the actors had quitted. After a moment, Luke switched the light off again.

The transition back to night was so abrupt as to be shocking. He wondered whether to fetch a torch, go outside, and check round. But the garden offered almost limitless hiding places and if there were still someone out there, he wouldn't find them. The intruders, on the other hand, would locate him easily as he stumbled around with his torch, just like Dad . . .

Luke uttered a stifled groan as the reality of loss struck him a painful blow in the chest. Nausea swept over him. For a moment he even felt he might do what he never done in his life and pass out. He'd thought he knew what his father's death meant to him, but he hadn't realised the depth or permanency of it at all, not till now.

He stumbled back upstairs and threw himself down in his clothes on his bed. He quite forgot, in his misery, the burglar alarm, which remained a useless silent witness at the foot of the stair, just as it had been on the night of his father's death.

CHAPTER FOURTEEN

Despite the improvement in the weather, investigations now promised to sink into that slough of despond to which they were prone after the first rush of interviews and collecting of obvious evidence. Forensics were taking their time, as they'd warned, over examination of the tools removed from Sawyer's workshop. So far none had turned up any traces of blood, skin or other suspicious matter. There was absolutely no sign that they'd been used for anything other than fixing cars. Markby was now sure they were barking up the wrong tree there.

At Tudor Lodge, relations remained strained. By Thursday, they were all visibly seeking to escape the pressure. At breakfast, both Carla and Luke announced they'd be out all day.

'I've got to go up to London,' said Carla. 'I must follow up discussions about the new programme.'

'Can't it wait?' Luke asked crossly. 'They know – they know the situation here, don't they?'

'They know it perfectly well, darling. But the world of TV doesn't stop because of one person's problems. I'll have to go. I've had three faxes all on the same subject. It's best if I go up and sort it all out.'

Luke pushed a piece of burned toast to one side of his plate. 'I had thought of driving over to Cambridge today and having a word with my tutor. I mean, like your television people, he knows what's happened here, but there are things I'll have to sort out. But if you're going to be out too . . .'

He looked at Kate who said calmly, 'I shall be all right. You both go.'

She couldn't fail to notice how relieved they both looked.

In fact Kate wasn't sorry to be alone in the house. Alone, that was, except for Mrs Flack. It gave Kate an opportunity to make a 'safe' call to Freddie Green.

'I've been in touch with the Probate Registry and lodged a *caveat*,' he informed her.

'What's that?' she asked. A movement outside the door caught

181

her attention and she added quickly, 'Hang on!' After a moment, she said, 'It's OK, go on. It was just that old bat of a housekeeper on her way upstairs. The door's shut but I wanted to be sure.'

'Basically, it means that we've declared an interest in the will and they can't go ahead and grant probate without keeping us informed.'

'Luke's talking about my having to prove who I am. I told him I was prepared to take a DNA test.'

'It needn't come to that. In my view, your father clearly showed by his behaviour throughout your childhood that he regarded you as his daughter. His widow, by inviting you into the family home, has implicitly recognised your status. More importantly, Penhallow was actually making you a regular allowance at the time of his death, maintaining you, and you are certainly entitled to request for that maintenance to be continued.' Mr Green paused and asked with slightly less assurance, 'What are the plods doing?'

'God knows, I don't. They've been down to the garage near here, turning out the poor guy's workshop.'

'Good, keep 'em occupied. Clearly they've not got a case against you. But just to be on the safe side, I still think I ought to have that informal chat with Sir Montague Ling.'

Kate snapped, 'You're a great help!' and hung up.

The phone shrilled for attention almost at once. 'Don't get depressed, Kate!' Freddie Green urged. 'It will all be fine. But we've got to cover every possibility.'

'Thanks, Freddie,' she said. 'Sorry I bit your head off, but it's getting to me.'

'It's going to be all right, Kate,' he repeated. 'It's going to be all right, believe me.'

Following this conversation, and with her offer of help with domestic chores politely rebuffed by Mrs Flack, Kate walked into the town centre. It was probably only imagination, she told herself, but she felt people were staring at her. This was a small place and the murder big news. Kate retreated to the security of Tudor Lodge.

'What about lunch?' Mrs Flack greeted her, standing foursquare in the doorway in her overall.

'I got something in town,' Kate lied.

'Oh well, then,' Mrs Flack said. 'I'll go on home. Coming in last weekend's left my own chores not done. You'll be all right, then?'

'I'll be all right.'

Kate watched Mrs Flack depart. She went into the kitchen and made a cheese sandwich and a cup of coffee and took them to the TV room. She'd just settled down when the doorbell rang.

She peered out of a window before opening the door. There was a man standing on the doorstep but the porch prevented her identifying him. He might be press. She slipped the chain across, opening the door the permissible crack and then, with a muttered, 'Oh, sod it!' unhooked the chain and pulled the door open wide.

'Hullo,' Alan Markby said. 'The very person I want to see.' He held up a paper package. 'I've brought back your clothes.'

'I can make you coffee, if you want,' Kate said. 'Or there's a drinks cabinet over there.' She pointed at Andrew's bar set up in the corner of the TV room.

She'd been obliged to invite him in. He would turn up today, while both Carla and Luke were out. Or did he know that he'd find her here alone? She didn't know what he knew, that was the trouble. Just seeing him standing there on the doorstep in that awful old Barbour which had lost nearly all its wax, holding a brown paper packet tied up with string. What sort of police officer looked like that? And managed, she had to admit, to look irredeemably upper class at the same time? But this, after all, was a man who'd been at public school with her own father. To say he didn't look like a policeman was putting it mildly. What he looked like was the lord bloody lieutenant of the county on his day off.

Markby had settled down in an armchair and now smiled at her as he stretched out his long legs. His shoes were well polished but ancient, with the leather uppers threatening to crack. Nevertheless, Kate knew you didn't buy shoes of that quality and fit in high street shoeshops.

'No need to cater for me, and don't let me put you off your lunch.' He nodded towards the cheese sandwich and cooling cup of coffee.

'OK.' She sat down and took a nervous bite from the sandwich. 'Does every suspect get this service?' she asked indistinctly. 'Senior coppers running errands?'

'No, but I was passing so I thought I'd drop it off.'

'You didn't find anything on any of it, then?' she said drily.

He shook his head. 'No. Oh, we've still got the yellow scarf. You'll get that back later.'

Kate drank her coffee slowly, thinking things over. She'd abandoned the sandwich after the initial bite. Food had lost its appeal. She put down the empty cup. 'They'll neither of them be back till tonight. Carla's gone to London, Luke to Cambridge.'

'I came to see you. I know you don't like formal interviews and I thought, well, perhaps an informal talk.'

He still looked irritatingly at ease and Kate, who well knew how such an attitude on her part unsettled others, was annoyed to find that now she, in turn, was becoming unsettled. She chose attack, as she usually did in these circumstances.

'I thought it wasn't just to bring back my things. What else do you want?'

'I wondered if you'd been in touch with your solicitor again.' If he'd noticed the aggression in her voice, he didn't show it.

'Yes, I have, but it's none of your business.'

'I've also been going over your story,' Markby told her. 'It's a small point, but something occurred to me and I thought I'd check it out.' He saw caution enter her face. 'It's to do with the party in Cambridge earlier this year, the one you gate-crashed in order to scrape an acquaintance with Luke Penhallow.'

A rush of annoyance made her forget caution. Kate snapped, 'I didn't gate-crash. I was invited by someone I'd met at the match earlier. I told you I wangled it but that's not the same as gate-crashing. I actually went there with someone!'

'And some photographs were taken? Flashlight presumably. They came out well enough for you to decide to bring them here and show them to your father.'

'That's right.' The memory caused her to flush deeply.

'How did he take it? Seeing the photos?'

'Not very well,' she said honestly. She glanced at the little drinks cabinet. 'Look, I can pour you a sherry or something.' She got to her feet.

'Where are they now?' he asked.

Kate paused, halfway to the cabinet, and stared at him. He looked bland enough, just mildly interested. His fair hair had fallen forward over his forehead. With his narrow face, unlined but for the faint crowsfeet tracing at the edge of the bright blue eyes, there was a perennial youthfulness about him. It suggested something of the school group photograph, she thought. The cricket team, perhaps. Nevertheless, as a contemporary of her father's, he must be in his late forties.

Gently persistent, he said, 'I'd like to see the snaps you showed your father. You still have them?'

Frustrated and angry, Kate stamped upstairs to seek out the photos. She was alarmed, despite not knowing what possible interest he could have in seeing them. They'd show nothing he didn't already know or had been told about. Was he simply verifying their existence? Was he that thorough? Yes, she thought waspishly, he probably was.

She didn't like being reminded about the photographs or the ploy of showing them to Andrew, which had been such a failure. She hadn't looked at them again, ashamed of them in some way. She didn't relish seeing them now. Kate thrust her fingers into the bag and hunted about. Then she pulled the haversack open wide and finally tipped all its contents out on the floor. For a moment, she crouched over the spilled items, puzzled. Then she got to her feet and looked around the room. She had few possessions and to check them was the matter of seconds. She pulled open the one drawer she was using to store her meagre supply of underwear and riffled irritably among the garments, only to slam it closed in frustration. She picked up the stack of paperbacks on the bedside cabinet, just in case.

'Shit!' she muttered. She made her way downstairs, rather more slowly than she'd stormed upstairs.

He was still lounging in the chair, looking as if he lived in the place. Generally, Kate felt she could handle the police. Well, certainly handle that sergeant who'd bought her tea. But this man, Markby, was different. He frightened her. Not that he had behaved unkindly so far. In fact, he'd been courteous to a fault. But it didn't fool her.

From the doorway, she announced defiantly, 'They're not there. I don't know where they are. I put them back in my bag after showing them to my father. I'm sure I did. Perhaps I left them at The Crown.'

'You showed them to someone at The Crown?'

'No!' She fought for control of her voice, fearing she was beginning to sound shrill. 'I don't – I can't recall taking them out of the bag while I was there. But that doesn't mean I didn't do it. Perhaps, when I took out my sponge bag and hairbrush, I might've taken out the folder and put it on one side.' A thought struck her. 'I just hope that—'

She stopped herself but too late. He was raising a questioning eyebrow. 'You hope what?'

She could refuse to reply. She could try and pass it off with 'nothing'. But he wouldn't accept that. He was a man whose questions were answered. She said as calmly as she could, 'I hope that creepy barman didn't get hold of them.'

'Lee Joss? Why or how should he? Why do you call him creepy? Did he come up to your room?'

'No!' she snapped. 'But he was nosy. He wanted to know about me and tried fishing for information. Of course he was trying his luck. They always do. I soon let him know how far that'd get him! Nowhere and fast! Or there was a chambermaid who snooped about the place. She was curious about me, too. They might have hatched something up between them. She could have taken them to show him. I wouldn't have put it past her. Look, why do you want to see them?'

'It was just a thought, filling in the gaps, you know.'

'The pics wouldn't fill in any gaps.'

'But you are obviously disturbed at losing them.'

'I'm annoyed,' Kate said coldly. 'It's irritating. But it doesn't have to concern you. If they're lost, that's my problem.'

She was relieved to see Markby get to his feet but the relief was short-lived.

'By the way,' he observed casually, 'we still haven't been able to talk to your lorry driver. As far as we can make out, he's on his way back from Turkey.'

Kate shouted, 'You're looking at every single little bit of evidence supporting my story, aren't you? You've pawed over my clothes and didn't find anything wrong with them. Now you want to see harmless photos and talk to that stupid trucker! What do you think you're going to find? Proof? Proof of what? *I didn't kill my father!* That's what you want to prove, isn't it? That I murdered him? You won't. You can't. I didn't do it and you can't make it look as if I did. Freddie's on to you. Freddie will sort it out. He's talking to Sir Montague Ling.'

That was a mistake. She knew it instantly. She shouldn't have mentioned the barrister. She thought he might ask why, if she were innocent, she was making contingency plans against being in court. But he didn't.

'Don't worry.' He had that considerate look on his face again. 'And don't forget, will you, that evidence clears as well as convicts. No one is going to make out you did anything you didn't do. We have to check, that's all. That's why we'll have to talk to the truck driver, when he gets back, any day now.'

Markby smiled at her but it called to mind the phrase 'the smile on the face of the tiger' and she wasn't comforted.

In fact Markby was wrong about Eddie Evans' schedule, for it was about to meet with serious interference. Not even Eddie was aware of the imminent change – though he was just about to become aware of it.

He was, at that very moment, steering his rig round the bends in a crawl up a Greek hillside, heading for the border into the former Yugoslav republic of Macedonia. To his right, the bare hillsides were dotted with scrub and baked in the sunshine. In tiny terraced fields, black-clad women toiled with mattocks. They worked bending stiffly from the waist with straight legs. Whitewashed villages and domed churches looked down on the road. He passed the ruins of an old Turkish fort, more ancient than the Turks, if its foundation stones could have told their tale. Eddie liked this part of the world. He whistled to himself cheerfully. And then he turned a corner and was forced to brake by a stationary vehicle ahead.

It appeared to be one of a long queue. Foreboding closed on Eddie's heart and his whistling petered out. After a few minutes, he climbed from his cab and made his way to the head of the multinational column to find out the cause of the delay. He soon discovered it. He rounded a corner and found the entire road blocked by closely parked tractors and a small army of militant Greek farmers.

Eddie approached a group of men, clearly stranded truckers like himself. They were sitting in the shade of a patch of olive trees by the road and playing cards. A battered tin kettle sat atop a Butagaz stove, providing the necessary mugs of tea.

'What's it all about?' he asked.

'Search me,' offered the nearest card-player. 'But a couple of them have got guns and they're all pretty edgy. I'm not arguing with 'em. They say stop, I stop. Something to do with the Common Market.' He poured a treacly brew into an enamel mug and handed it up. 'Have a cuppa.'

'Thanks.' As he sipped, Eddie took a cautious look at the nearest moustachio-ed brigand, perched atop his tractor and drinking from a leather-covered flask of no doubt potent homebrew. A rifle was slung from his shoulders. The man's clothing was patched and dusty, his battered cloth cap shapeless, but the rifle gleamed. Eddie had no doubt its owner, drunk or sober, was a crack shot.

'How long have you been here?' he asked the card players.

'Since early this morning. The police drove up, took a look, and drove away. We could be here days.' His informant was remarkably cheerful dishing out his gloomy prophecy. 'You got perishables?'

'Dried fruit,' said Eddie, 'figs, dates, raisins and stuff.'

'You'll be all right, then,' said the other. 'At least you won't starve.'

The demonstrator on the tractor belched, wiped his moustache with the back of his hand, and raised the flask genially in Eddie's direction. '*Yassou!*' he called. '*Oreksi!*'

'Cheers, mate,' returned Eddie. He sat down under the nearest olive and took out his cigarettes. It was going to be a long day.

CHAPTER FIFTEEN

Carla Penhallow arrived back from her London trip shortly before six that evening. Dark smudges circled her eyes and she was clearly exhausted. Kate's enquiry as to how the day had gone was brushed away with scant attempt at courtesy. Any further attempt at conversation was cut short by Luke's own arrival back from Cambridge, equally tetchy. Another tense meal followed, this time a deep-frozen concoction, which arrived via the microwave, purporting to be Thai stir-fry vegetables.

Neither of them asked how Kate had spent her day and she was relieved at it. It meant she hadn't to mention Markby's visit, something she'd been wondering how to explain. Partly because of the tension in the air and partly because if she'd stayed downstairs one or other of them might remember to ask her what she'd been doing, Kate went up to bed early. She thought both Penhallows looked relieved to see her go.

She picked out a book from the stack on the side table and began to read. Her days at Tudor Lodge already threatened to settle into a pattern and it wasn't an encouraging one. The paperback was a romance, an old Georgette Heyer, escapist fantasy which she hoped would take her away into a different world. But it failed. It was difficult to care about the fate of some Regency moppet, who would certainly be rescued eventually by the masterful hero, when what Kate herself needed was a knight in armour to ride in on his white horse and get her out of what was feeling uncomfortably like a quicksand.

No one was going to do it. No one ever did that for you in Kate's experience. Other people dropped you in it, but never gave you a hand out of the mess. You got out by yourself.

'And it wasn't meant to turn out like this, dammit!' she muttered. It had all bloody gone wrong from the start. She'd planned it badly and screwed it up. Now she had to sort out the mess.

She reviewed her options. For practical purposes, she could rely on Freddie Green up to a point. But Kate was under no delusions as to the real reason for Freddie's interest. Freddie never did anything unless he thought there was something in it for him. Kate didn't blame him for that. She quite understood – even, in her own way, approved. It came back to the same fact every time: if you didn't look after yourself, no one else would.

People could, however, sometimes be bribed, led, persuaded or manipulated into making themselves useful. She wasn't overlooking that impressionable young detective sergeant.

Kate managed a wry smile. Sergeant Prescott was hardly a trump card, but a card in her sleeve of a sort. She might need to play it if things didn't work out. But they ought to work out. You couldn't always get everything right at the first attempt. But if you learned by your failures, you got it right next time. Kate meant to make no more mistakes. One by one she would tidy up the loose ends and then sit back and enjoy what was hers.

'And it is mine!' she whispered aloud in case the house, which already seemed to her to have a personality of its own, had any doubts about her right to be there.

She put down the book, switched out the light and dropped off to sleep.

Luke lay awake in the darkness and thought about his day.

Funny, he thought, as he listened to the familiar creak and sigh of old wood settling in the house around him, a funny sort of day.

In his mind he relived it all, the conversations, the faces of the people. The word which came to mind was 'awkward' closely followed by 'embarrassing'. It wasn't a word he would have associated with murder before this. Murder was many things but he wouldn't have said embarrassing was one of them. Yet undeniably it was the word now. People had been awkward in their condolences and their advice. Given half a chance they'd have preferred to avoid him. It wasn't easy to console a bereaved person at the best of times and the relative of a murder victim . . . well, what could they have said?

In the end, it had seemed to Luke that the sympathy had flowed in the wrong direction, not from them to him, but from him to them. He had felt sorry for them, for their distress and embarrassment. On their part they'd looked at him less with sympathy than with nervousness, even fear, as if being a victim's relative were catching, like chickenpox. There'd been curiosity, too, on the part of some. The interest had been both open and veiled. People who were unable to repress the urge to stare and pry had grown garbled in speech and shifty-gazed. He'd gained the status of a freak. On his tutor's part, despite a stream of platitudes and a manner which would have sat well on a Trollopian prelate, Luke had detected a distinct irritation. Through Luke, a breath of coarse reality, blood and crushed bone, meaningless violence and cruelty which mocked the word civilisation, had been brought into the groves of Academe.

The tutor had been anxious to be rid of his awkward visitor. Luke hadn't been able to get away fast enough. But sooner or later he was going to have to go back, pick up the reins, and start again. Life had to go on. He hadn't approved of his mother's trip to London, and still thought it had been made unwisely early, but he understood why she'd made it. The world was sorry for you but it didn't stop for you. If you stepped off, it rolled on and left you behind.

On this sober note, he drifted into sleep.

Luke awoke to find himself in the full throes of a panic attack. He sat up, sweating, senses in chaos, his heart pounding. The room was ablaze with light but not the cool pastel tones of daybreak. This light had an unnatural ruddy glow varying between orange and blood red. Shadows flickered wildly on the walls, dancing, jumping, snaking towards him with pointing fingers. There was a distant roaring as of a giant furnace. For a dreadful moment he thought he must have died and been whisked in payment of some unknown heinous sin to a gothic inferno. But this nightmarish scene was his old bedroom with familiar furniture, books, clothes tossed on to a chair. What terrible thing had gone wrong with it?

He leaped up and ran to the window. The sky behind Sawyer's garage was a lurid pink and when he flung the window open, the furnace-like roar was joined by the crack and crash of breaking glass and snapping wood.

Luke raced out into the corridor and hammered on the door of his mother's room. 'Mum! Mum, get up and dressed! Any old clothes, be quick! There's a fire over at Sawyer's bungalow and the whole bloody garage could go up! We've got to get away from here!'

He ran on down the corridor to Kate's room, thumping at the door and yelling the same message as behind him, his mother stumbled out into the corridor in her nightdress.

Her frightened questions were drowned out by the approaching sirens of the fire engines.

It was the insistent yodel of the fire engines which awoke Meredith Mitchell. At first she merely turned over and attempted to go back to sleep. But then the first was followed by another and it was clear a major emergency was underway.

She got out of bed and padded barefoot to the window. She thought initially that it must be dawn because there was a rosy glow to the sky in the east. But a glance at the alarm clock revealed it was a little after three. The rose haze hung above the fire and if she calculated aright, it was located approximately in the area of Tudor Lodge.

Meredith switched on the light and began to drag on jeans and a sweater. All the fears she'd stifled since this business began now rose up in a tide of panic which she struggled to control. She'd known disaster would follow Kate Drago's move to Tudor Lodge. Had it struck so soon?

Driving through the town's dark, deserted streets, Meredith told herself that it was foolish to suppose she could pinpoint the source of the fire so precisely from her window. There was no reason why it should be Tudor Lodge at all. When she reached her destination, she saw – at first with relief – that it wasn't. The fire was beyond the terrace of cottages and must be at Sawyer's garage.

The relief didn't last long. An organised evacuation was underway here amid scenes of controlled chaos. Not only were the fire crews present, but the police and an ambulance. A uniformed police officer flagged her down.

'You can't go through, miss, sorry. You'll have to go back, and make it quick, eh?'

'I've friends at Tudor Lodge, at the big house!' she shouted back at him through the open window. The roar of the flames, the hiss of water and steam and the shouts of the firemen threatened to drown her voice.

'We're getting everyone out, don't you worry! Everyone's being taken down to the church hall. You'll find your friends there.'

He was impatient and with good cause. Meredith didn't need to be told what a fire at a petrol station meant. She shouted one last question.

'Is it the garage itself?'

'No, the bunglalow behind – but the whole ruddy lot can go up. Will you leave the area immediately? I gotta insist!'

Meredith backed down the road and drove to the church hall. It beamed with light. She was greeted by James Holland, the vicar, who stood on the threshold in corduroys and a shapeless Guernsey sweater, probably one of the steady supply of such garments knitted for him by a grateful parishioner.

'Ah, Meredith!' he yelled, as if seeing her there at that hour were the most natural thing in the world. 'Come to lend a hand? Good! You can make the tea. They'll want a cuppa when they get here.'

Before she knew it, Meredith found herself struggling with a gigantic kettle and rooting about in cupboards for cups.

The refugees from the fire straggled in moments later, looking dazed and frightened. Meredith's anxious gaze checked off Carla, Luke and Kate, so that was all right. And there was Mrs Flack, her hair confined in a net but otherwise dressed much as normal in her overall, though quaintly teamed with Wellington boots. She carried a voluminous ancient handbag apparently stuffed full of documents and, under her other arm, a large framed portrait photograph.

Of all the arrivals, Irene also seemed the most unfazed. She made straight for the kitchenette, put her handbag on the worktop, set up the photo frame (a picture of the late Mr Flack) and set to work putting sugar in bowls and biscuits on plates.

'I can't tell you, I'm sure,' she said in reply to Meredith's questions. 'All I know is, I woke up sudden, hearing a really funny noise. A sort of *boom*!' She looked up at Meredith. 'You know?'

'An explosion?' Meredith asked.

Mrs Flack frowned. 'Not quite that, well, I don't know much about explosions. A sort of thud, then a rushing noise, *whoosh*, a bit like the noises you hear on Fireworks Night, when the blue touchpaper's lit. To tell you the truth, I thought for a moment that some silly kids were fooling around with fireworks, though it's not the time of year for it. Then the sky went all pink and orange, just like one of them blood oranges we used to get and you never seem to see in the shops now. One of my bedroom windows overlooks the garage. I ran and looked out and saw it was Harry's place.'

She paused in her tea-pouring. 'I haven't seen Harry. Have you?' She sounded worried. 'I was hoping he'd be here.'

Meredith hadn't. 'But he might still arrive,' she assured Mrs Flack. She was remembering the ambulance, however.

'I phoned the fire brigade and I got dressed quick,' Irene went on. 'I thought I could run over there to Harry's and make sure he was out of it and all right. But it was too hot, so fierce. Then the fire brigade came and the police and they said we had to all clear out quick.'

Meredith took a tray of tea mugs and returned to the main hall. Still no sign of Harry Sawyer and it didn't look good. She didn't recognise the other people who'd arrived, except for the ancient woman with a long pigtail of hair, Mrs Joss, accompanied by a mixed gaggle of figures, male and female, of assorted ages, who appeared to be members of her family. A spiky-haired youth among them was demanding the right to bring a motor cycle into the hall for safety, something Father Holland was vigorously contesting. The others were engaged in a bad-tempered argument which was centred on a cardboard box. The box had been set down on the floor and from within it came a desperate yowl followed by a frenzied scrabbling of claws.

'It's old Mrs Joss's cats,' a voice at her elbow, Irene Flack's, informed Meredith. 'Two of them anyway. She wouldn't leave without them. One of them's run off and is probably halfway across the county by now! We stuffed the other two in that box, not that Dan Joss was very keen.'

Meredith assumed Dan Joss must be the beer-bellied, unshaven hulk who was consoling his mother with the kind words, 'Will you shut up for a bit, Ma? The bloody cats are all right and they're not what I'd have wanted to save from a fire, I can tell you!'

'Pixie's run away! He'll be too afraid to come back!' wailed Mrs Joss. 'He's gone over the fields and them foxes will get him!'

'Can't one of you take care of her?' demanded Dan Joss of his womenfolk.

A couple of them descended on Mrs Joss. They were strikingly alike, though one was older and more raddled. Meredith supposed them mother and daughter. They hovered around the old woman shouting, 'It's all right, Grandma!'

Meredith took her tray of mugs across and urged tea on them. They each grabbed a mug with scant ceremony including the spike-haired biker. And then, looking up, Meredith found herself staring into another face, one she recognised well enough, but had certainly not expected to see here.

There was a moment of mutual recognition. Round and pale, topped by a crest of ginger hair, the face stared back, eyes popping with surprise. Then discomfiture was replaced by a wary sullenness. Before Meredith could say or do anything, Luke Penhallow appeared at her elbow, distracting her. The owner of the face took the opportunity to slip away towards the back of the hall.

'How did you get here, Meredith?' Luke didn't wait for an answer but went on quickly, 'Look, can you take Mum over to your place? The police say we've all got to wait here until they say we can go back, which won't be before morning if then. They don't know how long it will take to put the fire out and then the area's got to be declared safe.'

'Of course you can all come over to my house!' she exclaimed.

'Have some tea. Look, take these for Carla and Kate.' She pushed the tray of remaining mugs at him. 'What's actually happened, Luke? Is anyone hurt? Irene's asking after Harry Sawyer. I saw an ambulance down there . . .'

'You were there? It's Harry's bungalow. It's gone up like a bonfire. I haven't seen anything of Harry. I hope the poor bloke's all right. The fire crew are worried about the fuel storage tanks, although they're underground. But there's enough vapour around the place to set up an almighty explosion.'

'Action stations, Meredith!' boomed Father Holland at her elbow.

He had staggered in with the first of several boxes of bedding from the vicarage. Luke jumped up and went to fetch in the rest.

'It's our emergency store,' puffed the vicar. 'It's a bit fusty but I don't think it's damp. Give 'em a sleeping bag or a blanket each.'

The Josses weren't waiting to be served. As soon as the boxes of bedding were set down, they dived forward and made off with the bulk of the contents.

'Hey!' shouted Meredith indignantly, rescuing with difficulty a well-worn sleeping bag and threadbare green blanket.

She carried them over to where Carla and Kate sat, huddled together, sipping tea from the mugs in their cupped hands.

'Wrap these round yourselves. You must keep warm. Shock . . .' Meredith shook out the blanket and draped it round Carla's shoulders. 'Just hang on here a bit and as soon as I can get away, I'll drive you all over to my place. You can sleep there.'

'I'll stay here,' Luke, who'd joined them, said quickly, 'so that I know what's going on. As soon as we get permission to go back, I'll come over to your place and let you know. Take Mum and – Kate.'

Kate Drago said in a tight little voice, 'No, thanks anyway, but I'd rather stay here.'

Luke gave a hiss of exasperation. 'Well, take Mum. And don't argue, Mum.'

'I'm not arguing,' Carla said plaintively, her fingers plucking at the threadbare weave of the blanket. 'I don't want to stay here, certainly not with all the Josses. Where's poor Irene?'

'In the kitchen,' said Meredith. 'She can come too, if she likes.'

But Mrs Flack, when asked, declared she'd rather be at the hall, if they didn't mind, lending a hand and being useful.

Eventually, around four forty-five in the morning, Meredith drove Carla Penhallow to her little house in Station Road. Behind them at the hall, the Josses had settled down, rolled up in blankets like so many pupae, and forming a circle with their toes all pointing inward in a daisy pattern. Mrs Flack was washing up mugs and appeared quite at home, though still worried at the lack of news of the garage owner. The cats had squirmed out of the box, but being Joss cats, had joined the family encampment and settled down with the rest.

'You take my bed,' Meredith said. 'Don't argue. I'll just slip a clean pillowcase on.'

'What will you do?' Carla asked dully, sitting on the sofa and staring up at Meredith with confused eyes.

'I won't go back to bed, not now. Or I'll doze down here. I'll call my office in the morning and explain there's been an emergency overnight and I won't be coming in. It's Friday, anyway.'

She bundled Carla upstairs and managed to settle her before returning to put her feet up on the sofa. Only then did she get a chance to glance at her watch and see that it was five thirty and before long would be time to get up again.

Alan arrived at eight.

'All right?' he asked anxiously, dropping a kiss on her forehead.

'I'm fine and just made coffee. Carla's asleep. You don't want to talk to her, I hope? She was fit to drop when I got her back here.'

He shook his head, took the coffee mug she held out, and they went back into the sitting room.

'Is the fire out?'

'It was well under control when I last heard. "Out" is a word the fire service is wary of. They'll be coming back and damping down for a few days, they reckon. The heat builds up in the embers and fires can reignite spontaneously at almost any spot.' He sank back in an armchair, stretching out his legs with a sigh of relief.

'So when will all the people in the houses there be able to go back?'

'Certainly not before tonight, perhaps even not until tomorrow morning. It's because of the fuel storage tanks.' Alan sipped his coffee, his hair flopping untidily, his face thin with strain.

It distressed her to see him look so worried. She leaned forward with a hand outstretched in consolation and asked quietly, 'Is there any news of Sawyer?'

'They got him out but unconscious, badly affected by smoke. Burns too. The fire officers had difficulty because the three-piece suite in the sitting room must've been stuffed with horsehair and that makes a lot of smoke. They've taken him off to a special unit.' Alan's voice was still muted. 'We won't be able to talk to him for days.'

After a moment's silence, Meredith said, 'It seems – odd.'

'Odd things happen.' He gave a hiss of annoyance. 'But you're right. It's too odd. Last Sunday his workshop and bungalow were both searched. Thursday night his bungalow is – goes up in flames.' She hadn't missed the hesitation. 'Was it accidental, Alan? Irene heard a noise, not exactly an explosion, more a bump and then whoosh! That doesn't sound like a domestic gas explosion.'

His blue eyes met hers, then his gaze flickered aside. 'The fire service will send in its own investigators as soon as they can get in there safely. But I've had a word with the senior officer on the scene and he's given his opinion, though as yet it's unsubstantiated, that this is a case of arson. The seat of the fire is in the area of the back door. He thinks that perhaps fuel-soaked rags were stacked against it and fired, possibly using some kind of incendiary device. There would be plenty of oil- and fuel-contaminated rags in the workshop or chucked out in the waste bin for anyone to fish out. That bungalow was very old, built late 1920s. All the window and door frames are – were – wooden, the interior doors of wood. The kitchen furniture was all wood – table, chairs, cupboards that sort of thing. No fitted units. That's what Pearce remembers. He says there were wooden parquet floors in the place covered with a few old carpets, dry as tinder. The whole thing was just a pile of kindling as far as fire was concerned.'

'He didn't have a dog?' Meredith frowned. 'Most people with their business premises alongside their homes would keep a dog.'

'He had a dog but they haven't found it and we assume it perished in the flames. Pearce saw it last Sunday. It was as old as the hills and as deaf as a post. No use as a guard dog, certainly.'

Meredith pushed back her brown hair in an impatient gesture. 'But why? Why Sawyer? Could it have been revenge? If he'd quarrelled with Penhallow he might have quarrelled with other people. Perhaps someone held a grudge?'

'Why indeed? After you told us that he'd had a dispute with Penhallow, we'd even pencilled the fellow in as a possible suspect. Now, it seems, he's a victim. Damn it, Meredith!' Alan suddenly leaned forward in his chair, his face flushing in anger. 'We already had one body and we damn nearly ended up with two! Sawyer might yet die.'

'It's a dreadful thought. I just hope and pray he doesn't!' Meredith said softly.

He looked up and caught her expression. 'What's up?'

'I feel guilty,' she confessed. 'I told you about the dispute between Andrew and Harry. That sent you over to the garage to search the place. Perhaps that had something to do with last night's fire. Even if it didn't, I still feel as if I put a match to poor Harry's place myself.'

'That's plain silly!' He shook his head vigorously. 'There's no reason at all why you should feel that way. There's probably no connection at all. Until the fire service comes in with a proper report, we don't even know it was arson. Perhaps old Harry smoked in bed. Perhaps he dropped a smouldering match or cigarette end into a waste bin or left a coal fire overnight without a guard. Wait and see.'

Alan got to his feet. 'You can keep Carla here with you, can you?'

'Sure. I'm not going to work today.'

'Good, good. I'll see you later . . .' He sighed. 'At least, if I don't see you before, I'll call for you Saturday night to go over to Laura's place. We've been invited to dinner, remember?'

'Oh Lor—' she said, quickly amending it to, 'I mean, oh good. Paul's a great cook.'

'He is,' Alan told her. 'But you had it right the first time. I can't say I'm in celebratory mood. Sawyer's lying in intensive care and I've no idea what's going to happen next. "Oh Lor" is putting it mildly. I'd express it in a considerably stronger way!'

From her sitting-room window, Meredith watched him drive away. She didn't feel as tired as she ought to, but later, probably, weariness would come. Thoughts buzzed in her head. With guilt she realised that one of them was – in the circumstances – almost ignoble. She was thinking that the fire and Sawyer's hospitalisation had put all other ideas out of Alan's head. He hadn't referred to his proposal of marriage again, or her promise to give an answer this time, once and for all. And she was pleased that his attention had been diverted.

'Selfish of me,' she mused aloud. She pushed up the sash window to let in the morning air. A noise of traffic from the main road could be heard. Cars passed by as people set out to work or took children to school. Bamford was awake and about its business. At the hall, Father Holland would be organising breakfast for his unexpected guests. Irene Flack would take care of that. Poor Irene. It had been a near miss for her, living so close to the fire. So much distress and tragedy for so many people, Meredith thought, and here am I, worrying about myself and what I'm going to say to Alan.

What am I going to say to Alan?

CHAPTER SIXTEEN

Luke arrived at ten that morning looking tired, dusty and dishevelled. His hair stood on end. Overnight he seemed to have regressed to a ten-year-old, if admittedly an outsize one.

'Do you want to take a shower?' Meredith asked, ever practical.

'Thanks, I'd love to. It was a dire night, what was left of it!' He grimaced. 'All the Josses snore, even the damn cats! Kate and I sat up talking to the vicar. Or he did most of the talking and I managed to reply. Kate didn't have much to say. Irene Flack dozed off on a chair in the kitchen there. She didn't look very comfortable but at least she got forty winks. How's Mum?' His sandy eyebrows formed an anxious steeple.

'Still asleep,' she told him. 'Better leave her. Have you had any breakfast?'

'The vicar organised baked beans and tinned sausages and a local bakery sent over some bread rolls. Irene got the tea kettle going again. It was a bit like being at scout camp.' Luke managed a smile at the memory, then shook his head.

'But certainly not all beer and skittles, to quote the vicar! He meant the proximity of the Josses slurping beans, and their cats swarming up the hall furnishings like wild things because they wanted to go out. The old woman wouldn't hear of it in case they ran off. The vicar's a really good bloke to have on your side. He found a litter tray for the moggies and a discreet corner where they could go and do what cats do out of sight and smell of the rest of us. But I tell you, Meredith, it's not a pretty sight down there!'

Meredith was heartily glad to have been spared it. 'No news yet of when you'll be able to return home?' she asked.

'Not before tonight or even, if they have trouble damping down the embers, tomorrow morning. Could you put Mum up for a second night if necessary, Meredith? I can book Kate and myself into The Crown but I think Mum would be better off with you, out of it, if you see what I mean. Kate's going ballistic down there at the hall. I thought she was going to punch Dan Joss on the nose. He sat there scratching his beergut and then lit up a foul cheroot. She sorted him out pdq. She didn't like The Crown when she was there but now she's quite longing to get back to the place. Honestly, on top of everything else, this fire is the straw to break any camel's back.'

Meredith wondered whether to tell him that there was a possibility of the fire being started intentionally. She decided against it.

Luke had a question of his own. 'Have you heard any news of Harry Sawyer?' His blunt begrimed features crumpled anxiously. 'Poor old Irene is worried stiff. She's been Harry's neighbour for years and he used to fix up her old car for free.'

Meredith could tell him something about that, though little enough. 'He was brought out alive. Alan was here earlier and told me Sawyer was taken to a specialist burns unit. He was unconscious when rescued. Certainly no one will be able to talk to him for some days. That's all I know.'

Luke looked down at his hands. 'Is the poor bloke going to die?'

'I don't know, Luke. I don't think anyone knows that yet, not even the hospital. There's the shock and loss of fluids, the smoke inhalation and burns. It can't be good. He's not a young man.'

'Seems odd,' he said, echoing her words to Alan. 'As if the place was suddenly jinxed. First Dad, then Kate turning out to be who she is, now Harry's bungalow. Problems go in threes. They say that, don't they?'

'Did you hear anything, Luke?' Meredith asked curiously. 'Before the outbreak of the fire?'

He looked up sharply and for a moment seemed astonished but then his expression turned wary. 'What sort of thing?'

'Irene Flack heard a muffled thud, bump, mini-explosion, she's rather imprecise as to what it was. It was followed by a whoosh, as she describes it. Rather like a firework going off.'

'Oh, did she . . . ?' Luke settled back and, for a moment, looked, or so Meredith fancied, almost relieved. 'No, nothing like that. The fire had taken hold when I first got to know of it. The light in my room woke me, I think. I didn't know where I was for a minute. It was like being awake and still in a bad dream with that weird red glow and the crackle of the flames.'

Meredith bit her lip and considered whether it was worth asking more questions now. She decided against it. 'Go and take that shower. I don't think you'll waken your mother. I'll brew up fresh coffee.'

He came back twenty minutes later, his face red and hair tousled, but looking refreshed. He sat at the table and admitted to hunger having returned. Meredith cooked sausages, tomatoes and egg.

'You really can doss down here,' she said as he tucked in to the food, 'Kate as well, I suppose, if she'd like to. Though frankly, I don't see why Kate can't go back to the hotel, especially if she's quite keen to do so, as you said. In my view, she ought to have stayed there. I never thought she ought to go to Tudor Lodge.'

Luke swallowed a lump of bread. 'It's been sticky, having her there. Sort of awkward.' He looked thoughtful. 'This whole thing has turned out surprisingly awkward, Meredith. I went to Cambridge yesterday. Everyone was kind, a few were curious, some downright nosy, but most just embarrassed.' He looked straight at her across the table. 'You've dealt with murder before, haven't you?'

'Yes, I have,' Meredith admitted. 'Though it doesn't make me any kind of expert and I'd hate you to think I was! *I'd* hate to think I was!' She thought of Gerald. 'Someone at work made a crack about that. Things happen when I'm around, he said. It made me sound like a Jonah.'

Luke shook his head. 'No, it's because you don't stand aside, Meredith. You pitch in.'

'Interfere?' she asked wryly.

'No, not interfere!' He looked shocked. 'But some people go out of their way to avoid nastiness, even when it's right there under their noses. You're not afraid to face unpleasantness. It's a rare quality. I admire it.' He paused. 'Before all this happened, I'd have said I wasn't afraid to face the nastier side of life. But I only thought that because I'd never been called upon to do it. Actually having to do it, that's much more difficult. I suppose none of us knows how we'll react in a really sticky situation until it happens. I've found out I'm not as tough as I thought I was. I don't think I'm even as tough as you—' He broke off to apologise. 'I don't mean you're an old boot, Meredith. Far from it! You're strong. That's what I mean. Don't take offence, please!'

He looked so worried that he might have put his foot in it that Meredith grinned and said, 'Thanks for what I think was a compliment! Of course I haven't taken offence. I know what you meant about the awkwardness of murder. The aftermath is not what you think it will be. Worse than one imagines in some ways and it's always going to take one by surprise. Don't feel bad about not being able to cope. We're talking of a death and in this case it's your father's which makes it so much worse. Because it's a violent death, all the usual ways of coping aren't there for us. We flounder about. What I'm trying to say is, murder is outside of most people's experience and they don't know what to do. In addition, they're afraid. Somewhere in their community a killer is on the loose. They start looking at neighbours and friends in a way they didn't before. As for the victim's family, no one knows what to say. Nothing's adequate.'

Luke speared the last piece of sausage. 'That's exactly it. Does it ever come right again? I mean, in your experience of these things, once it's all sorted out and the – the murderer is behind bars, do things go back to normal?'

Meredith thought about that one carefully. 'I wish I could say yes, but I don't think they do. Not really, no. Superficially, perhaps. But it's like any experience, good or bad, it's entered in your memory bank. Press the right button and you'll call it up again.'

'I'm worried about Mum, you see,' he said, glancing up at the ceiling and the direction of his sleeping mother.

'Your mother's strong, Luke,' Meredith said. 'She needs support but she's not about to break apart. She'll tackle it.'

When Carla came downstairs at lunchtime, Luke had left to book himself and Kate into The Crown.

'I'm glad he called round,' Carla said. 'And thanks for letting him shower and feeding him.'

'I'm concerned about feeding *you*. You've got to eat. We can go out and get lunch somewhere or I'll produce something primitive here. I'm not a cook,' Meredith grimaced. 'And Luke's eaten the sausages. I've got frozen pizza, tinned tuna, tinned soup and some salad stuff.' She got up and rummaged in her kitchen cupboard. 'Oh, some pasta and a jar of pesto.'

To her surprise, Carla began to laugh. It started as a low chuckle and then developed into a full-blown shout of merriment.

Catching Meredith's alarmed eye, she subsided. 'Sorry – I'm not hysterical, not going off my rocker with strain or anything. It's just, you sounded just like me. I mean, your kitchen is like mine. I haven't cooked properly for years. But I used to be quite a dab hand, you know. When we were first married, I used to make a pretty nifty curry and really good lasagne. It's just that, as time went by, there was less and less time for that sort of thing and well, other more interesting things to do.' She paused. 'I mean, of course, I got myself a career. Threw out the garlic press and bought a fax machine.'

'Sounds reasonable to me,' Meredith told her.

Carla put her elbows on the table and leaned forward confidentially. 'I'm going to make more of an effort. When we get back into the house, I'll cook something for the kids, a sort of "now we're back in our own home" dinner.'

'Luke will appreciate it, but don't count on Kate's gratitude,' Meredith said. '*Are* you taking her back with you? Luke's booked them both into The Crown and if I were you, I'd leave her there this time. Tudor Lodge is *not* her home, though I'm sure she'd like to make it so. It's not fair on Luke, Carla, taking her in like that. She's not a poor lost kitten. She's a tough little number, that's my opinion. She had some sort of run-in with Dan Joss down at the hall, so Luke told me, and Joss definitely came off worse!'

Carla sat back and looked obstinate. 'Of course it's not fair. It's not fair on Luke and it's not fair on me – but when has life ever been fair? It wasn't fair of Andrew to leave us all this as a legacy, but he did. I've got to accept it and so has Luke, poor love. The young adapt. Maybe, after this business of having to camp out in the Church Hall and so on, he and Kate will get along better.'

Meredith thought she personally wouldn't count on it. But it didn't surprise her to find Carla obstinate under that elfin exterior. She'd made up her mind.

'Lasagne,' Carla said, her mind running ahead. 'Andrew brought some really good red wine from France just before Christmas and we didn't drink it all. We'll have that and lasagne. On Saturday night. Can you and Alan come?'

'Afraid not, though thanks. We're invited to his sister's place.'

'Oh yes, her husband is a professional chef, isn't he?'

'He writes about food, not exactly a chef, but a first-class cook, certainly.'

'How useful,' said Carla thoughtfully, 'to be married to a man who can cook.'

As things turned out, the fire service wasn't prepared to allow people back into their homes until Saturday morning, when Luke collected his mother, and Meredith had her house to herself again. She'd been glad to be able to offer Carla shelter, but she was pleased to have been given a free hand once more, because there was something she had to do. She had to go back to the scene of the blaze and do it urgently before she saw Alan that evening.

To follow the returning refugees back to their homes on the same morning would have seemed too obvious. Moreover, the fire brigade would probably still be there. Despite her impatience, Meredith left it until the afternoon to make her visit.

Not wanting her car to betray her, she walked. It was a longish walk from where she lived but a pleasant afternoon and she needed the exercise.

As she approached the edge of town where the garage was situated, the smell of burning, wet smoky wood and the acrid stench of melted plastic hit her nostrils. The garage forecourt was smothered in dried foam. The site of the bungalow was cordoned off and a warning notice advised the public to keep clear.

The bungalow's walls were still standing but the windows were gaping holes and the roof had caved in. The roof timbers formed charred skeletal ribs. Meredith ducked under the tape. Puddles of water lay about on the ground and a black oily film covered the scene. Everything was still hot after forty-eight hours. The heat seeped through the soles of her shoes. The atmosphere was akin to a steam bath and from time to time, the debris crackled ominously within as the fire fought back, struggling to re-establish itself. Meredith picked her way carefully through the wreckage and, as she'd hoped, discovered she wasn't alone.

A boy of about thirteen was poking around in the ruins of the bungalow with a stick, so engrossed he didn't hear her approach. She'd learned his name now, back there at the hall on Thursday night, and called it out.

'Sammy!'

He jumped and whirled round, his foot slipping on a wet piece of timber. When he saw her, he looked at first as if he would flee, but changed his mind and stood his ground.

'Sammy Joss,' she said, 'son of Dan Joss, right?'

'So what?' he retorted.

'You should be careful in there, Sammy. The wreckage is unsafe.'

'What you doing here, then?' he retaliated, edging a little further away.

'Actually I came looking for you. But you won't be surprised to hear that, will you?'

'Don't know what you're talking about.' Sammy glanced across the distance between himself and the terraced cottages where he lived, calculating how long it would take him to get across it and whether she'd head him off before he got home and found sanctuary.

'I think we should have a talk, Sammy. Don't panic. I'm not proposing to go to the police.'

He relaxed, then looked wary. 'What's the police got to do with me?'

'Come on,' Meredith told him sharply. 'You tried to break into my kitchen and I believe you're the kid who pinched my neighbour's purse.'

'You're daft, you are. You don't know what you're talking about. I didn't do nuffin' and you can't prove it, there!' Sammy believed aggression the best form of defence.

'I don't have to. I only have to tell the police I believe it was you and they'll be down here asking questions. I don't think any of your family would like that.' It was a shot in the dark, but her brief study of the massed Josses had made Meredith fairly sure of that. 'Have you been in trouble before, Sammy?'

'You mind your own bloody business!' he yelled at her.

'And you mind your language when you talk to me!' she snapped back. 'I said I wanted a talk and it might be better to talk to me than to the police, right?'

Sammy thought about this. He rubbed his face, his fingers leaving sooty trails across it, and squinted at her. 'All right, whatcha want, then?'

Meredith looked across the wasteland towards the fields on the further side. A thin line of trees edged them; one had fallen or been felled and left on the ground. 'We can go and sit over there,' she said. 'Better than standing around here. Safer, too.'

He followed her unwillingly across the sodden, filthy mess of the fire site until they arrived at the trees. Meredith spread her handkerchief on the dusty log and sat on it. As her fingers scraped the bark, black soot which had drifted from the fire stained them. Sammy scrambled on to the trunk and walked like a gymnast on a beam to the far end, where he balanced, one hand held above his head to grasp the overhanging branch of the neighbouring oak. If he felt it necessary, he could swing up there like a youthful Tarzan and be out of her reach in seconds.

'What were you looking for over there in the ruins?' she asked conversationally.

'Dunno, nuffin'. Anything. I found his dog.' He imparted the last bit of information with pride.

'Sawyer's dog?' Meredith was startled.

'It's dead, all burned. There's just bones and bits of black stuff, all shrivelled.' Sammy described his find with some relish. 'I thought I'd take the skull home and clean it up. I could keep it in my bedroom.'

Nice kid, thought Meredith. She kept her tone conversational. It would be easy to alarm him and he'd be off. He didn't trust her and she didn't expect him to, but so long as he didn't see her as an immediate threat, he might be prepared to talk.

'You've heard all about the murder at Tudor Lodge, of course.'

'Yeah, exciting.'

'I'm interested too. We could talk about it.'

Sammy's fingers tightened on the overhead branch. 'I didn't have nuffin' to do with that!'

'I'm not saying you did. Mrs Penhallow is a friend of mine.'

'Oh, yeah?' He was distracted, reaching up into the tree above him and trying to shake something loose. 'Gotta bird's nest,' he said.

'Well, don't shake it!' Meredith was unable to keep her tone casual. 'It'll fall out!'

'It's only an old one. Birds is only just starting to build this year. They're late, see. Everything's late. It's been cold.' He stared at her as if regarding someone whose ignorance was scandalous.

Meredith supposed that at school Sammy was probably labelled an underachiever, destined for the euphemistically named Progress Unit. But he was a country boy and his knowledge of the world around him doubtless considerable. Years ago, the Sammys of the world would have found work as gamekeepers, kennel- and stablemen, farmhands and woodmen. Countryside jobs had dwindled to the few, and the modern technological world offered nothing to replace them. She wondered whether Sammy would ever 'work' as society would deem it, or whether he was destined to a life on the dole supplemented by petty crime.

'What do you do in the evenings, Sammy?'

'Watch telly. Go over the fields . . .' He jerked his head towards the landscape behind them.

'When it's dark?'

'Sometimes.' He released the branch, dropped on to his heels and then swivelled to sit on the branch, swinging his legs. His jeans and trainers were filthy from his exploration of the bungalow. She wondered what his mother would make of that or whether she would simply accept the state he was in as normal, and chuck everything, trainers included, into the family washing machine.

'There's a way over the wall into the gardens of Tudor Lodge,' Meredith said. 'By using the low branches of trees on either side. I've done it, climbed out of the gardens that way.'

Sammy eyed her with interest, clearly judging her general athletic ability. She thought she might have gained a few plus points on whatever scale he rated her.

'Have you ever explored the gardens of Tudor Lodge at night?' Sammy took his time before deciding to answer that. She feared he was going to deny it, but eventually he nodded. 'Yeah, I've done it. Sometimes I've hid out in the bushes and watched 'em all through the windows. They never seen me.'

So much for the Puritan maid who'd frightened Mrs Flack. No ghosts, but Sammy Joss lurking about spying on the alien world and lifestyle of the Penhallows. And who could blame the kid? thought Meredith in sympathy. The sort of life Sammy had glimpsed through the windows of Tudor Lodge had only ever been seen by him before in TV soap operas of the glossier kind.

There might, of course, have been a less innocent side to his spying. There would be plenty worth stealing in such a big house, but like Mrs Crouch, Meredith wondered how Sammy would get rid of any item of rare value.

She leaned forward. 'It's important, Sammy. Don't just deny it if you were there, it's much too important for that. Were you in the grounds of Tudor Lodge the night Mr Penhallow died?' Seeing that he was about to leap off the log and flee she added quickly, 'I know you didn't have anything to do with his death, but were you there?'

Sammy was silent for a few minutes. Then he said carefully, 'I never tried to get into your kitchen and I never pinched the old woman's purse, right?'

'If you say so, Sammy.'

'Then I was there, but I didn't see no murder.' Sammy sounded regretful. A dog's skull was a trophy but to witness an actual murder would have been a rare coup. Was it TV or video nasties which had scrambled Sammy's sensibilities, or was he simply unworried by death? Did he subscribe to the countryman's view of nature, red in tooth and claw? Meredith didn't know.

'What did you see?' she asked him.

'I never saw nothing. I didn't get no chance because *he* was there.'

A tingle ran up her spine. 'Who was there, Sammy?'

'Him, of course.' Sammy pointed towards the burned-out shell of the bungalow. 'Old Harry. He was snooping around in the gardens and I nearly walked straight into him. He must've got in over the wall like I did. It was dark and I didn't see him first off. Then I nearly bumped into him. But he didn't notice me. He was too busy watching that girl.' Sammy began to pick at a loose piece of bark and found a beetle underneath. He picked it up carefully and balanced it on his palm.

Please, prayed Meredith, *don't let him decide not to tell me.* He might, at the last minute. He was getting fidgety. 'What was the girl doing, Sammy? Was it a girl you recognised?'

'Not then, I didn't. But I did after. She was at the hall. She was with them Penhallows. They called her Kate.' Sammy scowled. 'Seemed funny to me, if they knew her, that she was spying on them through the window like it. Why'd she do that?'

He held out the beetle for her inspection. It was a fearsome thing and when prodded by Sammy's finger, reared its nether abdomen threateningly like a tiny scorpion. 'Devil's coach-horse, that's called, so my Gran says. Good name, isn't it? You gotta matchbox?' When she shook her head, he set the beetle back on the log and it scurried away.

'When you saw her, she was looking through the window?'

'Yeah. The kitchen. Watching someone inside. And old Harry, he was watching her.'

'What then?' Meredith held her breath.

But disappointment was to follow. 'I cleared off. I didn't want old Harry to see me. He don't like me. He's a miserable old sod, is Harry. He's always reckoning I'm hanging around his garage trying to nick something. So when I saw he was there I sneaked off back over the wall. That's all I know.' He stared at Meredith with frank curiosity. 'Here, you reckon she did it?'

'Nobody knows who killed Mr Penhallow,' Meredith said.

'I reckon she did it,' Sammy told her. 'She's got a real old temper, she has. She went for my dad, down at the hall, just because he lit up. My dad says he feels sorry for any man gets landed with her. She's a right nutter, my dad says.'

Sammy slid from the log to the turf. 'I don't know no more. I can't tell you no more. You're not going to the police?'

'I'll have to tell them you saw Harry that night, Sammy.'

He scowled again then shrugged. 'That's all right. Don't make no difference to me. But you're not telling 'em about me being in your kitchen? Not that I was!' he added hastily.

'I won't tell them that. But you promise me there'll be no more stealing from old people, right! My neighbour only has her pension, I dare say, and it really hurt her to lose her money, no matter how little. You wouldn't like it if someone pinched money from your grandmother, would you?'

Sammy looked sullen. 'I'd never have took it if she hadn't left it lying on her shopping basket like it. It didn't have nothing in it, only some change and a library ticket and I don't read books. Oh, all right, you don't have to start moaning on at me. I won't do it again. Provided,' he added artfully, 'you don't go telling on me this time. You promised.'

'Yes, I did.'

There was no way of telling whether Sammy would keep his side of the promise, but perhaps he'd try, and it was the best one could hope.

Sammy considered the matter closed and in the manner of his traveller ancestors sought to seal the bargain in visible form. 'You want one of the bones from Harry's dog?' he offered generously. 'I want to keep the skull, but you can have any of the other bones. You can have his tail.'

'Thank you,' she told him. 'But you can keep the lot.'

CHAPTER SEVENTEEN

Meredith hadn't forgotten the dinner party. Although her first impulse was to ring Alan and tell him what she'd discovered, time had passed while she'd been talking to Sammy Joss, and Alan would be arriving to collect her in less than an hour, anyway. Inevitably, she stank of the fire debris. She had to clean up and more than that, make herself presentable. Laura was always stylish. Meredith didn't want to be outdone or look as if she'd made no effort.

Glamour didn't come easy. Meredith had never been a fashion slave. It wasn't because she was tall, five-ten. The supermodels were tall. It wasn't because she was by nature untidy or sloppy. She was, if anything, inclined to be overorganised. Even with a mortgage, she couldn't blame extreme poverty. It was, quite simply, the physical and mental torture involved in shopping for clothes.

There were so many things she disliked about the exercise that it was hard to see how she'd ever overcome the problem. To begin with, there was the fluorescent lighting in the stores which always managed to make her complexion look livid, throw shadows under her eyes, and lend an air of Hallowe'en to any attempt at dressing up. This was made worse after several sessions 'trying on' which left her hair on end, her make-up runny and her expression wild.

There was the inexorable conclusion, reached after riffling through innumerable racks of garments, that all of them had been designed for people with totally different proportions to her own and that she must, *ergo*, be some kind of freak. Add to that the inescapable fact that, whichever colour she'd fixed on before setting out, it turned out not to be in fashion this year or, worse, to have been in fashion two years ago.

Time without number she'd emerged from a store at the end of the day, hot, dishevelled and bad-tempered, to discover on getting home, that she'd parted with a large sum of money for something which didn't fit, didn't suit, carried a label which, read too late, informed her the garment was only washable by hand with extreme care, and was a shade which could only appeal to someone under the influence of hallucinatory drugs.

So it had been with extreme reluctance that she'd allowed herself to be dragged around the London sales earlier that year by an enthusiastic colleague. She'd returned from the expedition with a dress severe enough in style to please a nun but for a split side seam designed to reveal flashes of leg.

'It's a very stylish,' said the colleague knowledgeably, adding the *coup de grâce*, 'and it'll be *useful*. It's the sort of little number which, you know, you can wear anywhere.'

Despite the gnawing fear that it would prove to be the sort of little number one could wear nowhere, Meredith succumbed. She'd taken it back to the office and unpacked it from its tissue to display it to Gerald. Not that Gerald's opinion was especially to be valued, but the feeling she'd made another mistake was gaining rapid hold and she needed an independent view.

'Sexy,' said Gerald. 'I approve.'

Gerald's unqualified approval was, if anything, worse than Gerald saying he hated it. Meredith gazed at the dress, appalled. 'How on earth can it be sexy? It's got a high neck and long sleeves, regulation buttons and no waist and it's dark navy. It looks to me like the sort of thing hospital matrons used to wear in the days when they were dragons. All it lacks is a little watch pinned on the bosom. And look at this split in the side. The sales assistant called it a feature. It looks like the stitching's come undone.'

'Believe me,' said Gerald, ever politically incorrect. 'That dress plays on two male fantasies, women in uniform and women with long legs. You can't go wrong.'

'Oh God . . .' groaned Meredith, and stuffed the dress unceremoniously back into its bag.

She'd taken it home, hung it up, and there it had stayed. Until now. She took it out and studied it. If she never wore it, it'd be a complete waste of money. She tried it on again. Two things became immediately apparent. She'd need a decent pair of tights without ladders or cobbled repairs and she'd need high heels, something she normally avoided. Meredith extricated a pair of black patents from the back of the wardrobe and blew the dust off them.

She managed to shower, wash her hair and be ready by the time Alan arrived at seven, but only just.

'Damp,' Alan observed, patting her thick brown hair as he kissed her. 'New dress? Nice.' He sniffed. 'And new perfume?'

The dress had cleared the first hurdle. Meredith relaxed. She saw no need to explain that the faint aroma of perfume was actually from a furniture polish spray, aroma 'Flowers of the Meadows', which she'd used to buff up the patents.

'The hair's damp because I just got out of the shower,' she explained. 'I was smelling like a kipper before.'

He frowned. 'Why? Oh, from the remains of the fire. You've been over to Tudor Lodge, have you? Are they settled back in?'

'I suppose they are, for better or worse but I've not been there to see. I went to where Sawyer's bungalow was. It's a terrible mess. The smell of smoke and wet wood hangs over the entire area and will do for days yet, blighting the return home of everyone nearby. Poor Irene Flack's home is blackened outside with soot and general muck. Having seen the ruins, it's a real miracle the fire didn't spread. I suppose Harry is insured? Though it's probably the least of his worries right now.'

Meredith knew that by introducing Harry to the conversation, she was trying to deflect Alan's inevitable next words, and that it wouldn't work. She saw that slightly exasperated and slightly reproachful expression in his face which always annoyed her. He was going to say she oughtn't to have gone over to the site of the fire. He was forever saying she ought not to have done things, which was one reason she tended to do them first and tell him afterwards. Not that he wasn't often right, but knowing he was right usually made it worse.

And if we were married, she thought suddenly, he'd know everything I did and I'd see that look a dozen times a week . . .

'That area's dangerous, Meredith!' he was saying severely. 'The ruins are unsafe and the fire could spring up again. The fire service will be going out tomorrow, damping down. What on earth were you looking for?' Without waiting for her to answer, he went on, 'Now I don't normally object to your ferreting around—'

'Hey!' she interrupted indignantly. 'Don't you just! Nor do I ferret around. I might chat to a few people, and that, as it happens, was what I was doing this afternoon. A very interesting chat it was and I'll tell you about it if you're polite, but if you're going to be pompous, I won't.'

'Chatting to whom?' he asked suspiciously.

She allowed herself a smile, knowing he would be surprised. 'To Sammy Joss, as it happens. He's the younger son of Dan Joss. Dan Joss is the one who bears a strong resemblance to the Incredible Hulk—'

'I know about the Joss clan!' Alan cut in. 'When I was at Bamford

I had run-ins at various times with Solomon Joss, Ezekiel Joss and Jericho Joss. All likeable rogues when not fighting drunk. Just to be fair, the Joss women are pretty good scrappers. Salome Joss, on one notorious occasion, demolished the front desk of Bamford Police Station all on her own.'

'Do they all have biblical names?' Meredith was diverted.

'Either biblical or patriotic. When I was a youngster, there used to be an old fellow, a local character, called Waterloo Joss. He had a rag-and-bone business and was occasionally picked up and charged with being drunk in charge of a horse and cart. What led you to talk to young Sammy?'

'I saw him at the church hall the night of the fire and it occurred to me that now they were all allowed home, a kid like him wouldn't be able to keep away from the site of the fire. So that's where I went and that's where I found him.' A note of triumph sounded in her voice which didn't go down well.

'Then I hope you told the wretched kid to keep away! What was he doing there?'

'Poking around. He'd found the remains of Harry's dog. He was tickled pink about it, the little horror.'

'Look here!' Alan burst out. 'The fire service hasn't finished looking into the cause of the blaze and now you tell me that young pest is out there interfering with evidence!' He scowled. 'Why did you want to talk to him, anyway?'

'Let's have a drink,' said Meredith, seeing that the mood of things wasn't going her way. 'We've got time. Would you like a gin or a drop of whisky?' She sidled towards her modest drinks cabinet.

'I'll have a sherry if you've got one, but only very small. Paul is bound to be lavish with the wine.' Alan sat down on the sofa and relaxed. He said no more until the sherry was handed to him, then raised it in salute.

'Cheers, so are you going to tell me what young Joss had to say for himself? Or why you supposed he would have anything of interest to say?'

Meredith sat down beside him, displaying the split seam.

'Oh yes?' he said. 'Who's that for?'

'For you, surprise, surprise! Look, Sammy Joss is the sort of kid who roams around unsupervised – no one ever asking where he is or where he's been or what he's been doing, right? Nor is he the sort of child who's sent off to bed at a reasonable hour. You remember the way over the wall into the gardens of Tudor Lodge? It seemed to me that Sammy, living so near, had

214

probably been over that wall any number of times, just curious, you know.'

'Possibly.' Alan was looking thoughtful. 'Or casing the place, as you choose, either on his own behalf or someone else's. But then, I know the Josses rather better than you.'

Meredith chose to ignore this suggestion. She'd made a bargain with Sammy and she meant to try to keep it. 'So I wondered if he'd been hanging around Tudor Lodge on the night of the murder.'

Alan set down the sherry. 'And?'

'It took a while to persuade him but eventually he admitted it. He's been in the habit of watching the family through the windows. Or at least through the kitchen window which faces the back of the property and no one bothers to shield with a curtain or blind after dark. That night he'd slipped over the wall as before, meaning to hide in the bushes and watch, but he got a shock instead. Someone was there ahead of him, playing the same watching game. Harry Sawyer.'

'Was he indeed?' Alan exclaimed. 'Perhaps Dave Pearce is right, after all.'

Startled, Meredith asked, 'Does Pearce think Harry's the killer?'

'Let's say Pearce has a theory and it's a plausible one.'

'And you go along with it, this idea of Pearce's?'

'It was a distinct possibility before and now it seems even likelier. Dave's a good man, keen to make his mark. I fancy he'd like to crack this case and get the credit. Nothing wrong with that. He might turn out to be right, especially as we've now got a witness who places Harry right there at the scene.'

Meredith thought it over, rubbing distractedly at her mop of hair and destroying the careful arrangement created before the mirror a little earlier. 'Well, that would stymie me and *my* bright idea!'

'Which is?' Alan smiled and slid his arm round her shoulders. 'Believe me, I really want to know. I have a lot of respect for your bright ideas, although occasionally they're—' he caught her eye and amended his next words to – 'they fall into the category of difficult to prove. The trouble with police work is, we have to have proof. At the end of the day, it's got to stand up in a court of law. A copper doesn't go on gut instinct, no matter how strong it may be. He goes by the evidence or pretty soon he's in trouble.'

She nestled into the crook of his arm. 'Hum, well, I'm a member of the public and I go by gut instinct. Unlike Dave Pearce, I don't think Harry is your man! I do think Harry knows who *is*. Sammy nearly walked straight into Harry in the dark. He and Harry don't get along, so he didn't want Harry to catch him on someone else's property, even though Sawyer had no more right to be there than he did. Harry didn't notice Sammy because his attention was taken elsewhere. He was watching a girl whom Sammy can now identify as Kate Drago, having seen her with the Penhallows at the hall.'

Alan sipped the last of his sherry and put the glass down carefully on a side table. 'What does Sammy say she was doing?'

'Spying on the house through the kitchen window, which Sammy thinks odd, if she's a friend of the family.'

'It bears out her story, though,' he pointed out. 'She says she watched her father filling his hot-water bottle. After that she thought she saw someone watching her and it frightened her off. We had some trouble accepting that as she couldn't prove it. But now you tell me Sawyer was doing that, so Kate's telling us the truth. Did your informant see what happened next?'

Meredith sighed. 'Unfortunately, he didn't. The kid was worried about being caught by Sawyer so he slipped away back over the wall.'

Alan leaned his head back and stared up at the ceiling. 'Perhaps by Monday we'll be able to speak to the man.'

'Suppose the killer caught a glimpse of Harry,' Meredith said thoughtfully. 'Or suspected Harry'd seen him? He'd want to shut him up, wouldn't he? The fire came very close to doing that.'

'Damn the wretched Sawyer!' Alan muttered. 'If he knew or saw anything, why on earth didn't he tell Dave Pearce when he had the chance? Why must people always insist on keeping things to themselves? Dave says all the man did was grumble about his rights. Said he knew what they were and wasn't going to be done out of them by anyone. He accused poor Dave of sending in "the heavy mob", if you please!'

Meredith laughed. 'Somehow I can't imagine Dave putting the frighteners on anyone. Unlike that sergeant, the one who looks so terrifying – I've forgotten his name. He'd give anyone the jitters.'

'You mean Steve Prescott and you're being unjust. He's suffering a bad bout of love's blues at the moment.'

There was an awkward silence. Meredith hoped he wasn't going to start talking about their own personal situation again. She still hadn't sorted that one out for herself.

Fortunately, Alan went on, 'I don't mean Prescott doesn't have his mind on his work. If anything, it's rather concentrated his thoughts.'

'You don't mean – not Kate Drago?' Meredith was startled into forgetting her problem.

'She's a striking girl and she's got an unsettling way with her. I don't think Steve Prescott's the only one to find that out. I could have taken him off the case, but that would have been a drastic thing to do and, frankly, he's got to learn to handle this sort of situation. Nor did I want to demonstrate lack of trust in him. I'm fairly confident he won't do anything silly and I don't suppose for a moment she's given him any encouragement. I certainly hope not. Look, do you mind if I use your phone?' Alan sat up abruptly and took his arm away from her shoulders. 'We'll have to put a guard on Sawyer in the hospital. If Dave's right, he's a killer. If you're right, then having tried and failed, the killer may be desperate enough to try again.'

'It's been a long time,' said Laura, raising her glass. 'Too long, Meredith. Super dress, by the way. I really don't know why we haven't got together for ages. We used to see more of you and Alan. But time flies these days. I've been busy, you've been busy, Alan's *always* busy . . .'

'Keep your clients from getting bumped off, then!' said her brother crossly.

'Hey, protecting the public and keeping the peace is your job. How's it going, any progress?'

'Some,' was the guarded return. 'What have you done with all the kids, by the way?'

'Emily and Vicky are asleep. Matthew's at school, of course, and Emma's gone to a Pony Club weekend camp. It'll be all plaiting manes and polishing tack and eating burned sausages. I hope they remember to wash their hands,' concluded Emma's mother, slightly worried.

From the kitchen came a clatter of utensils and sound of the cook swearing.

'Don't worry about Paul,' said his wife serenely. 'He's happy. Is there any news of poor Harry Sawyer, Alan?'

'Doing as well as can be expected. We haven't been able to talk to him. I hope we shall soon.'

'Can you imagine it?' Laura turned to Meredith. 'There some poor soul is, lying in a hospital bed in plaster or whatever, and a leaden-footed copper arrives, unfurls his notebook, licks the end of his Biro and starts taking a statement. It's enough to send anyone into a relapse.'

'Our techniques have somewhat improved on your description,' Alan said mildly.

'Frankly, I don't think police techniques have changed a jot, except to lose what little charm they might ever have had. What happened to the days when the plod on the beat touched the rim of his helmet respectfully when telling the public to mind how it went?'

'We have community policing and it works very well. I tell you what, Laura, you come over the Regional HQ for a day and just sit in. Then you'll see what we do and how we do it!'

Paul arrived at that moment, a glass of wine in hand, and collapsed on the sofa beside Meredith. 'Cheers!' he saluted them. 'All's going well and we should be able to eat soon.'

'What are we having or is it to be a surprise?' Meredith asked. 'I start drooling as soon as I know I'm going to eat here.'

'Good. That's the idea. I'm making a version of *alouettes sans têtes*, otherwise known as *moineaux sans têtes*. You're supposed to use veal but that's expensive and a lot of people still have ethical objections to it. So I've devised a version using turkey escalopes and it works very well. I add a little crumbled crispy-fried bacon to the forcemeat just to pep it up a bit.'

'It'll be delicious,' she said. 'I'm now salivating like one of Pavlov's dogs.'

Paul beamed at them all. 'And are we discussing Bamford's celebrity murder?'

'Talking shop, you mean,' said his brother-in-law. 'Yes, but only in the most roundabout way. Your wife has ideas on policing which went out with Dixon of Dock Green.'

'I'd have thought by now,' Paul observed with a grin, 'that you knew when your sister was winding you up!'

'Always so easy . . .' murmured Laura with a wink at Meredith.

'But seriously,' Paul went on, 'you nearly had another body, didn't you? Poor old Harry Sawyer, he's a touchy character. He either likes you or he doesn't. If he likes you he goes out of his way to be helpful. If he doesn't he won't give you the time of day. He's a good mechanic and not a bad businessman. A pity his wife moved out. I think he started getting surly after that. I hope he pulls through. Is that girl still around?'

'If you mean Kate Drago, yes, she is,' said Meredith.

Laura crossed a shapely leg and tucked a wisp of blonde hair back into its neat pleat. 'You sound as if you don't like her much, Meredith. You did meet her, didn't you?'

'I did indeed. I delivered her, literally, to the door of Tudor Lodge and I've had good reason to fear since that it was one of the worst day's work I ever did!' Meredith told her gloomily. 'I feel as if I deposited a changeling on the doorstep.'

'Ah,' said Paul. 'You think she's a wrong 'un!'

This statement rather put Meredith on the spot, she had to admit. She didn't want to be unfair to Kate, but the gut instinct she'd spoken of earlier to Alan was strong. She didn't trust Kate, but there were degrees of distrust. One could believe a person to be self-seeking and manipulative – and Meredith suspected Kate Drago of being both of those – without believing her a murderer. It was a big hop from shiftiness to homicide and not an accusation to bandy about.

'Depends what you mean by that!' she said carefully. 'If you mean, do I think she killed her father, I hope she didn't and I've no evidence she did. What I do think is she's a catalyst. She's one of those people who, once they arrive on the scene, make things fall apart or provoke other people into doing things they'd never have dreamed of before. I think,' Meredith added slowly, 'that once upon a time people might have thought her a witch!'

'Hey, that's a bit much!' Alan protested.

'No. Witches were always believed capable of turning themselves into beautiful maidens. She has an effect on people as you were telling me earlier. No one's impervious to her. She's unsettling. There was a time when people might have termed that witchcraft.'

'She does unsettle people,' Alan admitted to his sister. 'She's got Pearce rattled and young Prescott's showing alarming signs of being smitten. Have you heard any more from Green, her solicitor?'

'I have, but if you want to know the content of his letter, you'll have to ask him. All I can say is, he's written.'

From the kitchen came the sound of the timer singing out a welcome message that the main course was ready. Paul disappeared in answer to its call and the others removed themselves to the dining table in happy anticipation.

'You did enjoy it, didn't you?' Paul asked anxiously about an hour and a half later.

They'd retired to the sitting room and were relaxing over coffee and brandy. Conversation had centred chiefly around the children and their latest achievements or crises, although Markby, a devoted uncle, for once showed little interest but glowered into his brandy balloon.

'Of course we did!' Meredith assured him. 'It was all delicious.'

The cook fidgeted. 'Thanks, Meredith. I, er, actually I was asking Alan.'

'Me?' His brother-in-law looked up, startled. 'What? Oh yes, first class! Always is. Why are you asking? I did say, didn't I?'

'Well, yes, but I did wonder because – now you won't mind me remarking on this, will you?' Paul's expression verged on panic. 'But I was thinking of demonstrating this particular recipe to a women's group next month and I want to know if there's anything wrong with it in any way at all. I mean, including the way it looks. Only, sorry, Alan, but you sort of poked at it and scrutinised it and looked very perplexed. I – I was going to remark on it then but at the table, it seemed well, I didn't want to embarrass anyone or have everyone peering at their plates. And since dinner, you've been rather *quiet*.'

'My dear chap, I'd no idea!' Alan sat up, looking stricken. 'It wasn't anything to do with the food . . . I mean it was, no!' Paul had shown great alarm. 'The meal was perfect. Demonstrate away next month, they'll love it. But could you tell me how you made it?'

His sister and Meredith regarded him with some surprise.

'Going to have a go, Alan?' Laura asked.

'No – look, I didn't realise I'd made it so obvious and I apologise. It was nothing to do with the taste or appearance – well, it was something to do with the appearance but nothing which would interest anyone but me. Bear with me, Paul, tell me how – I don't mean a list of ingredients, but *how* you made it. What you actually did when you put it all together. Pretend I'm one of your old dears.'

That gained him an old-fashioned look from Laura. 'Who said the audience would be composed of old dears?'

'They'll be a mixed bunch, I think,' Paul said, diverted. 'Oh, the *method* you mean, Alan? Well, you prepare the forcemeat stuffing, sausagemeat, chopped mushrooms, the bacon bits as I told you. Then you spread out each escalope and beat it out as thin as you can. Put some forcemeat on each piece, roll it up and fix it with a cocktail stick or tie it round with thread—'

'Hold it there!' Markby held up a hand. 'Beat the escalope with what? I may sound dim, but remember, I'm a copper not a cook. I noticed, you see, the meat had a sort of dimpled surface.'

'With a meat hammer,' Paul said bewildered.

'Can I see it, this meat hammer?' Alan got to his feet eagerly.

'I think he's flipped,' said Laura in a loud aside to Meredith. 'It's all that police work.'

'Sure,' said the good-natured Paul. 'Follow me.'

They made their way to the kitchen where Paul produced not one, but two meat hammers of differing sizes and proceeded to demonstrate their attributes and differences.

'This small one is your usual standard British meat hammer. The head is too small to do much good and if you beat too much you risk breaking up the meat. Now this—' Paul hefted the other hammer. Markby eyed it. It was a much more formidable affair, a real mallet, long of shaft, one end of the heavy solid wood head armoured with a blunt-toothed steel plate.

'This is your genuine central European schnitzel mallet, as bought by me in Prague last year when Laura and I went on that trip!' enthused Paul. 'You can beat a schnitzel as thin as paper with this and it won't break. Whereas this dinky little hammer here, overdo it and you end up with a lot of mashed meat shreds.'

Markby stretched out his hand and took the larger hammer. He weighed it and made a striking movement with it. 'You ever read a story, I think it's called "The Purloined Letter", Paul? No matter, it's an old detective yarn about an attempt to retrieve a compromising letter. The villain's apartment is searched to no avail until the detective realises that the letter in question is under their noses, stuffed into a letter rack with all the usual daily post. He, I may say, was a better detective than me. I've been looking for a murder weapon, and all the time it's been hanging on a kitchen wall with a lot of other utensils, staring us in the face!'

He turned and dived out of the kitchen. 'Can I use your phone? Sorry to break up the party and I'll do whatever I have to to make amends but this, no exaggeration, is really a matter of life and death!'

He was tapping out the number as he spoke and shouted into the receiver, 'Hullo? Superintendent Markby here. Who's still there? Prescott, good, get him to the phone. Steve, that you? I want you to go to Tudor Lodge and meet me there. Yes, now! I'll see you in,' he glanced at his watch, 'I'll see you in twenty minutes.'

By now Meredith and Laura had crowded into the hall and were brimming with questions.

'I have to go, sis, I'm sorry and I'll crawl round the garden fifty times on my knees or whatever it is I'll have to do to atone, but I've got to get over to Tudor Lodge.'

'I'm coming too!' Meredith said promptly. 'I can come, can't I, Alan?'

He hesitated but only briefly. 'Yes, you'll come in useful. I'll need someone unofficial but reliable to be a guard.'

'To guard who?' asked Laura ungrammatically.

'Carla Penhallow!'

CHAPTER EIGHTEEN

'Going to tell me what it's all about?' Meredith asked as they sped through the night. 'And slow down, you've had a few drinks and the last thing you want is to be stopped and breathalysed!'

'I've finally worked out what's going on. I was worried earlier the killer might try again and, of course, would try again. But I was looking at the wrong victim! When we get there, no matter what happens, I want you to stick by Carla Penhallow. Don't leave her side.'

'She's cooking a family meal tonight!' Meredith remembered Carla's plan. 'She wanted to make a home-coming dinner for herself and the two youngsters so she decided to dust off the cookery books and make a curry or a lasagne or something.'

Markby said nothing but scowled in the darkness and pressed his foot on the accelerator.

Fortunately they met little other traffic. However, speedily as they made the journey, Prescott had been quicker. He emerged from the shadows by the gate of Tudor Lodge as Markby drew up.

'What's wrong, sir?' Prescott's normally healthy complexion was bleached in the inadequate street-lighting here at the edge of town, and his features were drawn with tension. 'Is everything all right in the house? You said meet you here, so I didn't ring the doorbell. I wondered if I should . . .'

'No, we'll all go in together.' Markby marched briskly up the path and rang the bell with gusto.

Luke opened the door, peering out suspiciously. 'Who – oh, you, Superintendent – and Meredith! Come in. We've finished dinner and Mum and I—'

At that moment, Luke caught sight of Prescott's impressive form looming up in the dusk and realised that this visit wasn't just social. His cheerful welcome was wiped from his face. 'Sergeant? Why – why are you all here?' He blinked at them in the hall light. 'What do you want?'

'Mind if we come in, Luke?' Markby was already over the

threshold and Luke stepped back to let him pass. 'I haven't got a warrant, and you can stop me if you like, but in the circumstances I could insist.'

Prescott had shouldered his bulky way indoors by now and was looking around eagerly in the dim light in the hall.

Not spying the person he sought, he turned to Luke and demanded, 'Is everything all right?'

'What circumstances?' Luke had rallied and flushed. He glowered at Prescott. 'Look here, we've just had dinner—'

'In the circumstances,' said Markby, 'that I have reason to believe a crime is about to be committed on these premises. OK, Prescott, the kitchen!'

Luke pursued them as they set off down the hall, uttering protests, but before the kitchen was reached there was a diversion. A shaft of light suddenly broke into the hall from a nearby door and Carla appeared.

She too had dressed for a party and wore loose-fitting tan crepe trousers and jacket over a silk shirt in a golden caramel colour which complemented her short fair hair. Bunched amber beads dangled at her earlobes. Her eyes were wide open and bright with alarm. 'What on earth's going on? Alan?'

'Don't you worry, Carla. Meredith's come to see you,' said Markby, pushing Meredith forward. 'Why don't you and Carla go back in the room there and have a chat and we'll be with you shortly, right?'

'I don't know what it's all about, Mum,' said Luke, exasperated. 'But he's right. You go on back and sit down and don't worry about it. I'll sort it out and we'll – well, we'll find out what it is that's got everyone in such a tizz! There's obviously some mistake—'

'Come on, Carla,' urged Meredith, taking Carla's arm and piloting her back into the room behind them. 'Let's leave them to it.'

Prescott had reached the kitchen and was standing in the middle of it looking around him at the pile of unwashed dishes, his expression puzzled. 'Sir?' he looked questioningly at Markby.

Luke seemed to think he had to apologise for the state of the place. 'We haven't got around to clearing up. I was going to stack the dishwasher in a minute. Mum cooked a celebration meal.'

'What was it?' Markby asked with more sharpness than usual for such a domestic enquiry.

'If you must know, lasagne. Mum made it.' Luke sounded both surprised and proud at his mother's foray into the kitchen. 'It was great, nice and spicy, not squishy and bland like some you get. Hers was really good.'

Markby was at the wall where the kitchen implements hung in their impressive row. 'This one, Sergeant. The meat hammer. Bag it up.'

'Yessir.'

'Look here.' Luke's ruddy countenance had paled and in his eyes showed a flicker of fear. 'I don't know what's going on but if you don't tell me soon, there'll be hell to pay. You can't just—'

Markby was also casting an eye over the dishes. 'Separate portions? She didn't cook it in one big dish?'

'What?' Luke looked quite bewildered. 'No, in separate dishes, it crisps up better round the edges – look, what the hell is this? A cookery lesson?'

'Where's Kate Drago?'

At the sharpness in his voice, Prescott's head snapped up and alarm re-entered his face. Luke stood his ground and stuck out his jaw pugnaciously.

'Kate? She went to bed and if you think I'm going to let you wake her up—'

'Already?' Prescott moved forward, arms hanging by his sides but fists clenching. 'Bit early for her to turn in, isn't it? You said you just had dinner.'

'If you must know, she felt tired. Well, she would, after two nights with virtually no sleep, one spent in the church hall and one at The Crown! We had rather a lot of wine with tonight's meal and it just about finished her off. She was dozing off in her chair—'

Markby swore and strode back into the hall. 'Which room? Come on, Luke, move! Which is your sister's room?' He was already halfway up the stairs as he spoke.

Prescott pounded up the creaking wooden stair behind him. 'Kate!' he shouted desperately. 'Kate, where are you?'

'Along the corridor to your right – at the end . . .' Luke was close on their heels. 'But why – look, she's probably asleep—'

Markby threw open the bedroom door, stretching out his hand for the lightswitch, but letting it fall back as he saw it wasn't required. There was light already in the room, from the bedside lamp which had been knocked from the table and lay on the carpet, sending a muted gleam across the huddled form collapsed beside it.

Kate Drago was propped up by the side of the bed. The duvet had been thrown back as she'd climbed or rolled out, dislodging the lamp, and dragging the quilt down on to the floor. She sat with her back half turned to it and slumped at an angle. Her magnificent bronze mane of hair cascaded as a backdrop to her pale profile. She wore an elaborate, ribbon-trimmed nightgown of rose-pink silk in Empire style.

By a stroke of irony, a paperback novel which had fallen to the carpet and lay face down and open, showed as cover illustration a damsel in a dress of similar fashion, together with a gentleman in breeches and topboots. *Sprig Muslin*, read Markby, by Georgette Heyer. He guessed the nightgown had been borrowed from Carla Penhallow and wondered briefly if it had been one of the luxury presents bought by Andrew for his wife, to salve his conscience. Markby hoped it wasn't to prove a shroud for Andrew's daughter.

Kate was as serene in repose as a marble statue and might have been modelling for one of the Pre-Raphaelite brotherhood, had they not been able to observe now from the rise and fall of the gathered pink silk that she was sleeping as soundly as the enchanted Beauty in the fairytale. Even the arrival of three heavy-footed males in the room didn't make her stir.

Prescott was first off the mark. He reached the girl and stooped to grasp her shoulders and shake her vigorously. 'Kate, wake up. Oh hell . . .' His voice rose in a wail of despair.

Markby pushed him aside, hunkered down and pushed up the girl's eyelids. 'Doped. Get an ambulance. Luke, help me get her on her feet. We'll try walking her.'

Prescott pounded back down the stairs. In the distance, women's voices could be heard asking him what was wrong. Luke, silent and with his expression frozen in horror, helped Markby haul Kate's inert body upright. She hung between them like a lifeless rag doll.

'Come on, Kate!' Markby ordered in her ear. 'Come on, we're going for a walk. Come on . . .'

'It's no use . . .' Luke gasped.

As he spoke Kate moaned softly and her head, which had flopped forward, rolled to one side.

'Atta girl!' urged Markby. 'Good kid, now – walk . . .'

As they part dragged and part trundled her up and down the carpet, she began to moan more loudly and then coughed and spluttered. Her eyelids flickered.

'We may be in time,' Markby breathed. 'But I hope that ambulance gets here quickly!'

'But what's she taken?' Luke asked. He sounded young and frightened. 'And why should she do it? It was a great dinner party. We were all so happy . . .'

'At a guess, sleeping pills. The wine's hastened the effect.'

Prescott reappeared, panting. At the sight of Kate lolling between them, he started forward, fiercely protective.

'OK, you take over then.' Markby released Kate's arm to Prescott. 'Just keep her moving. Don't worry, lad, she's got a good chance.'

At that, Kate gave a loud gasp, retched, and threw up all over the sergeant.

'Thank God for that,' said Markby, disregarding Prescott's plight. To do him justice, Prescott was clearly just as relieved.

The ambulance arrived moments later and bore Kate away and they all made their way to the sitting room.

It was much as Markby had seen it when he'd met Carla here to pay his condolences and tell her he was in charge of the case on the morning Andrew's body had been discovered. It had that comfortable, rumpled family look. A wood fire crackled in the grate. The Cornish painting was still above the fireplace. The onyx lamp was glowing and threw its light over Carla who sat on the sofa, as hunched and silent as Kate had been upstairs. The difference between the two being that whereas Kate had been in repose, Carla was as tense as a strung violin string. Meredith, beside her, put an arm round her shoulders as she saw the expression on Alan's face.

'Mum—' Luke started towards his mother, but Prescott caught his arm and held him back.

Markby pulled out a chair and sat down in front on Carla. She looked up and fixed her huge wild eyes on his face.

Very gently, he said, 'It's over, Carla.'

She moistened her lips with the tip of her tongue and asked in a toneless, dispassionate way which sent a chill up his spine, 'Will she die?'

'Not if you help us. We want to know exactly what she took. Were they the sleeping pills you told me you had in the house?'

'Don't say anything, Mum!' Luke said loudly. 'Not until you get a lawyer here!'

Markby turned his head and said sharply, 'If the hospital knows what the girl was given, then they can give an antidote.'

Luke looked as if he'd burst into tears. Then he said in a stifled voice, 'Yes – yes, of course. My mistake. Tell them, Mum. If you, you have to . . . Please.'

Carla looked across the room at him, met his gaze and dropped her own eyes. Without a word, she put a hand in the pocket of her crepe jacket and took out a small bottle. She held it out to her son.

There was a moment when no one moved. Then Luke, as if

sleepwalking, went to his mother and took the bottle in his broad hand. He stared down at it, as if unable to figure out what it was. His fingers twitched as if they'd close on it and crush it. Markby made to move forward but Luke looked up, his eyes clearing. He asked, 'Shall *I* call the hospital?'

'Why don't you?' Markby replied.

Luke left them and after a moment his voice could be heard from the hall, speaking on the phone. Carla gave a sigh and Meredith put her hand gently on the other woman's forearm.

'That was the right thing to do, Carla. Luke had to know.'

'I thought, she'd just go to sleep,' Carla said almost inaudibly. 'I'm not cruel. She wouldn't suffer. But I couldn't let her hurt us any more. She wanted Andrew's money. She'd no right to anything of Andrew's! Nothing! She'd already taken Luke's father from him. Now she wanted to take what his father had left him.'

With a childlike candour, she went on, 'I put crushed pills in her lasagne. We drank a lot of wine tonight and it must have hurried things up, because she started to doze off at the table. Luckily she put it down to having spent two sleepless nights and Luke accepted that. I went upstairs with her and saw her settle down. She was quite happy, you know. She thought she'd won, got everything she wanted.' Carla's voice hardened. 'And that's what she wanted, everything!'

Markby replied so harshly that Meredith started: 'But she didn't just go to sleep, Carla. She woke, realised something was wrong, tried to get out of bed and seek help. Her last conscious moments were of terror.' Carla flinched but he was unrelenting. 'You tried to kill her. You tried, and pray God we found her in time and you've failed.'

Carla said in a small tight voice, 'Why shouldn't I kill her? She'd destroyed everything. Even Luke's memory of his father is sullied. Why shouldn't I mete out justice?'

'Carla?' Meredith asked. 'I don't understand. Are you telling us that, after all, Kate killed Andrew?' As she spoke she glimpsed Luke through the open door. He was sitting on the lower staircase, his head bowed.

Carla could see him too. Her eyes fixed on the stiff, silent, hunched figure of her son, she said, 'No, she didn't kill him. I did that.' She wrenched her gaze from Luke and stared up at Markby. 'That's what you'll say. Others will say you're right. But everything decent in Andrew was already dead, had been dead for years. He had no thought for anyone but himself. He had no compassion. He had no honour.' She leaned forward and hissed, 'If I'd stepped on a cockroach it would've been the same!'

A pity, thought Markby, she'll never say that in court!

CHAPTER NINETEEN

It was damp under the trees but cool, rather than cold. The close-packed vegetation excluded the wind and the canopy above had protected the previous autumn's mulch of fallen leaves which still lay unrotted on the path. There were primroses growing under a mossy log, the first Meredith had seen this year and she pointed them out to Alan.

'That proves it's spring, real spring, not just a date on the calendar.'

She had seen little of him since the eventful visit to Tudor Lodge. They'd not discussed what had happened. She knew from the newspapers and local gossip that Carla Penhallow had been remanded for psychiatric reports, Kate Drago had made a good recovery and Harry Sawyer was reported to have turned the corner. In the town opinion was vigorously divided over Carla but unanimous with regard to Harry Sawyer. Harry was one of themselves. He had his faults, as Mrs Crouch put it, but he was a good worker and you don't expect to be burnt alive in your own bed, do you?

With Harry in mind, Meredith asked now, 'Is he still making good progress? He'll be in hospital for a good while yet, I suppose, poor man.'

Alan nodded. 'In addition to the burns and the damage to his lungs from the smoke, he's deeply traumatised. We've been able to talk to him for short periods only. We've been able to get the gist of it, however. He saw her, of course, on that fatal Thursday night. He actually saw Carla strike Andrew down. He'd sneaked over the wall as a shortcut to the back door of the house. He was hoping for a chance to speak to Andrew about that piece of land. But when he got there, he saw another visitor had arrived before him. It was Kate Drago and she was looking through the kitchen window in a very furtive way. Harry realised something was up, so he waited in the shadows to see what she'd do. He didn't hear the boy, Sammy Joss, come up behind him or make off again.

'Harry must have made a noise or drawn attention to himself

somehow, because Kate realised someone was there and took fright. She ran off and Harry went up to the window and took a look himself. He saw Andrew and the opportunity for a talk seemed to offer itself. Harry rapped at the window. But almost the moment he'd done so, he saw the door from the hall into the kitchen open, and just glimpsed a woman in a blue dressing gown. Andrew had heard Harry's rap but mistook it for a knock at the back door and set off to open it. He hadn't realised anyone had opened the door from the hall.'

Markby paused to glance at Meredith. 'The dressing gown Carla wore was a blue chenille housecoat. We found blue fibres under his fingernails and they match up.'

Meredith said, she was surprised to hear how bitterly, 'A jury will like that. Simple to understand forensic evidence, placing the accused at the scene of a crime.' She shook her head. 'I'm sorry.'

He was looking at her in concern. 'I know how you feel. But I'll be honest and yes, we're lucky to have got hold of the garment in question. She tried to get rid of it by giving it with other castoffs to Irene Flack. But Irene's car is out of commission, so she left the bin bag of clothing in the utility room at the Lodge, where we found it. Although it's been washed, we hope forensics will still manage to find blood traces.'

Meredith said nothing. There were more primroses on a bank but their sunny yellow faces had lost their charm.

'For her part,' Alan said, still watching her, 'Carla was concentrating on her husband and didn't see Harry at the window. Andrew, as I said, hadn't realised his wife had arrived. Harry decided three was a crowd. He changed his mind and made his exit before Andrew opened the door and saw him. He scurried back to his clump of bushes. From there, he saw Andrew come outside and heard him call for Kate. Then he saw Carla come out. She held what Harry calls a mallet in her hand. He saw the attack and he saw Andrew fall . . .'

'Couldn't he have done something?' Meredith interrupted indignantly.

'He was paralysed with shock, so he reckons, and I believe him. He thought she'd gone mad. Perhaps in a way she had, though whether that's a clinical diagnosis remains to be seen. Anyhow, she went back indoors, shut the kitchen door. The light went out. Harry ventured out and went over to Penhallow. With only the moonlight now to help him, he couldn't see well enough to make a proper examination. He tried for a pulse at Andrew's wrist and temple, and couldn't find one in either place. He did realise, when he touched Andrew's head, how much blood there was and that he was getting it on his hands. Up to then he'd been scared. Now he panicked completely. He didn't want to touch the body again. As far as he could tell Andrew was dead. Harry didn't want to be found with a corpse or with the dead man's blood on his hands or clothing. He'd have to explain what he was doing there. He might be accused of having killed the man. He'd had what some people might have called a quarrel with him and the police might've thought it motive enough. Murder has been done for less. Harry did as Sammy Joss had done, retreated hastily back over the wall and went home. Irene Flack saw him return. She thought he'd been in his garage or workshop. He often worked late. She'd heard Andrew's last cry but she hadn't been able to identify it and thought it might be the screech of Harry's workshop door.'

'Sawyer should still have phoned for help. He could have done it anonymously,' Meredith burst out. 'Andrew might have been saved, if he had. He left Andrew there to die. I'm sorry for what happened to Sawyer later, but it seems to me if he'd done the right thing in the first place, he mightn't be in hospital now.'

'You're probably right, but we can all be right after the event,' Alan pointed out. 'At the time the instinct for self-preservation was uppermost. Harry was in a spot. He insists he believed Andrew dead.' Alan swished at a clump of frost-blackened nettles with his walking stick. 'This was my father's, you know,' he said of the stick.

'You told me before.'

'So I did. Well, later Harry got his nerve back and decided he could turn all this to his advantage, or so he thought. Harry knows all about the garage business, but he's an unsophisticated man and women like Carla have never figured in his life. It led him to underestimate her. He got in touch and suggested they meet as he had information she wouldn't wish him to give to the police. A classic ploy and a classic mistake! You can't do business with a murderer. A murderer has everything to play for, and nothing to lose!

'Carla realised there was only one thing he could mean. Somehow, he knew the truth, but she had to find out exactly what he had on her, and whether he was likely to have confided in anyone else. So she arranged to meet Harry secretly, out in the garden one night. She'd taken care, she says, to be sure the burglar alarm was off. She didn't want to touch the doorbolts for fear someone would come downstairs after her, see them drawn, and shoot them back – locking her out! So she climbed out a drawing room window. Harry let her know what he'd seen. Then the idiot told her he'd forget all about it, if she'd sell him the land. Carla told him she was sure they could come to some arrangement, but she would need to talk Luke round. Harry went off happily, thinking he'd pulled off a clever bit of business.

'But Carla had decided Harry was too dangerous to be left alive. She had won herself a little time and used it to plan a fire. She knew his bungalow would go up like tinder. She's a chemist, don't forget, and as her first job, before she got into telejournalism, she worked at a Ministry of Defence research establishment. It was simple enough for her to rig an incendiary device with a delay mechanism which would allow her to get back to Tudor Lodge before the fire broke out. She counted on the old dog being deaf and that it wouldn't raise any alarm while she was fixing up her deadly little box of tricks. After that, the speed at which the flames took hold would prevent escape.'

'So cold-blooded,' Meredith said slowly, 'like her attempt to kill Kate. But Andrew? She loved him! Nothing will convince me she meant to kill him. She must have had some kind of a brainstorm.'

'She had the strongest motive of all,' Alan said. 'Kate and Sawyer both needed Andrew *alive* in order to get what they wanted. But Andrew alive was about to destroy Carla's world and Luke's, or so she believed. Don't forget, she loved her husband, but he'd betrayed her, and she loved her child more.'

The interview was fresh in his mind and he didn't think he'd ever forget it. They'd sat in the same interview room in which they'd talked to Kate Drago, only now Carla Penhallow had been sitting on the uncomfortable wooden chair, with her lawyer alongside her.

Markby didn't know the lawyer, a London man, plump, Savile Row suit, silk tie, dark hair silvering at the temples. His hands, resting on his leather briefcase had been smooth, white and manicured. He wore a signet ring and a gold Rolex wristwatch. He was probably the sort of solicitor Freddie Green aspired to be one day. Markby had expected Carla's story to undergo a subtle change and it had. The lawyer insisted his client had given way to intolerable stress. Whatever she might have done, it had been done whilst she'd been temporarily unhinged. She wasn't responsible either for that or for anything she might have said on the night of her arrest.

As for Carla herself, she seemed hardly aware of the interview room or of her situation. Markby had the impression she'd switched off. He didn't think it was an act. Perhaps her mind had tipped over, at that. It wasn't something he had to decide. The doctors would do that. He just had to get her story.

Carla told them, as she'd told Meredith, how she'd discovered Andrew had a mistress and a child.

'But I left things as they were because of Luke. Luke loved and trusted his father. I believed Andrew loved us both, loved us both more than – than Helen Drago and her daughter. If he hadn't he'd have left us. But he stayed with us, he'd made his choice.'

Carla had paused to sip from a tumbler of water. The legal man watched her carefully. He was getting ready to jump in and put a stop to her statement at the slightest sign of distress. Markby hoped Carla didn't break down.

But she'd gone on, quite calmly at first, though gradually growing more agitated.

'About a year ago, the situation changed in a big way. Nothing was said, but I realised something had happened, something major. Andrew was jumpy, acted strangely, very much out of character. He was morose, clearly very worried even depressed, but refused to admit it or discuss anything. Instead he adopted a horrible false cheerfulness and he was never a very good actor, poor Andrew. I knew instinctively it had to do with the setup in Cornwall. I went down there as soon as he went back to Brussels, and did a little detective work. I found out she'd died, his mistress. So that was why he was upset. My first thought, I admit it was selfish, was that it was all over. She'd gone and was out of our way, Luke's and mine, for ever. Then I remembered the girl and with a little trouble, I managed to get a look at her. The shop her mother had run was closed, but there were still things for sale in the window, and I could see someone in there tidying up. I hung around looking interested until she noticed me and came out and told me they weren't doing any more business. I don't think – in fact I'm sure – she didn't know who I was. She wasn't paying much attention but I'd taken trouble to change my appearance. I wore a wig and sunglasses.'

Carla had smiled wanly at the memory. 'Just like all the best spies in the thrillers! But a wig does make a difference. I didn't doubt for a minute she was Helen Drago's daughter. She looked like her mother – or how I suppose her mother looked when Andrew – when their liaison began. She was so beautiful, but with such a sharp, closed little face. She reminded me of a trapped wild animal. I could see she was trouble. Still, so long as Andrew kept her out of the way as he'd always done, we'd manage. I trusted him to do that. After all,' here Carla's voice had become scornful, 'he'd had enough practice! But he messed it up. He was a fool, really.'

The legal man shifted in his chair. He wasn't sure he should let his client go on.

Markby said, 'Take your time, Mrs Penhallow.'

'Thank you,' she said gravely. 'Well, earlier this year I went down to Cambridge for the weekend to see Luke. He was playing in a rugby match on the Saturday afternoon but he offered to give up the after-match party to have dinner with me. But I said, of course not. I'd come along to see the match and after that, he should go to his party and I'd be fine at the hotel. The next day we'd meet up for lunch. It was cold on the touchline.' Carla managed a faint smile. 'I walked up and down to keep warm. That's when I saw her—'

The speaker's voice echoed the dismay she'd felt at that time. 'She was with some other youngsters, but there was no mistaking her, even though the grief had gone from her face and she was laughing. I was horrified. She couldn't be there just by chance. There was nothing I could do. I was on hot coals until the next day, lunchtime, when Luke came over to the hotel for our lunch together. But he didn't say anything about her. He had a bit of a hangover, poor lamb. He said it had been a great party but he couldn't remember much about it! So I thought, fine, if she was there, he's forgotten her.'

Carla shook her cropped fair hair. 'I'd overlooked how easily she must have been able to get round Andrew. I suppose she played on his conscience, always his vulnerable point. That day – the day I came home with the migraine . . . That bit's quite true, by the way. I did have migraine. I went to bed. But I didn't take the sleeping pill, I went off to sleep without it and when I woke up, most of the symptoms had cleared up. I felt a bit woozy, a bit nauseous, but the headache had gone. I was pleased because sometimes it lasts as long as three days. I thought I'd go downstairs and tell Andrew I was better and we'd have a cup of tea.'

She bit her lip. 'I went down to the kitchen. Andrew was walking towards the back door and didn't see me in the doorway from the hall. He opened it and went out into the garden. I couldn't think why. It was night-time. He was in a dressing gown and carrying a hot-water bottle. Then I saw – I saw the photos on the kitchen table. They must have been taken at that post-match party. They showed Luke and Kate together with others. Then I heard him call her name! He was out in the garden, shouting *Kate! Kate!* Telling her to come in, to come in to our home, our *family* home!'

The solicitor patted her arm. 'Can you go on, my dear?' he asked unctuously.

To Markby's relief, she nodded. 'Yes. I'm all right.' She looked up and full at the police officers in the room for the first time and her voice rose and became clearer. 'I don't remember what I did next. I realise what I must have done, but I don't remember doing it. I must have taken the meat hammer from the wall. It's a big, heavy one. I got in from a continental kitchenware place in Soho, years ago when I was first married and had ideas about homecraft. The next thing I remember, I was outside, in the garden. I felt very cold. Andrew was lying on the ground, bathed in the ribbon of light from the open kitchen door. He didn't move. I realised I was holding the hammer. I kneeled over him and saw the blood and that he was dead. I went back indoors. I couldn't take it in. I must have killed him. I locked the door and went upstairs and sat for about an hour in my room, just numb. Then I saw I had blood and dirt on my dressing gown. So I went downstairs and put everything through the washer-dryer, and put the clean things in a bag for Irene's handicraft group. I washed the hammer and put it back, because if it was missing, Irene might notice. I burned the photos. It was morning by then. I went outside and sat by his body and waited for Irene to arrive. I sat with Andrew, because I didn't want to leave him alone. I talked to him while I sat there and told him how badly he'd treated us, how wrong he'd been. And I cried because I'd loved him and I still loved him, but he oughtn't to have treated us like that.'

Meredith listened in silence to this sad tale. They'd reached the edge of the wood by the time he'd finished it. There was a broad farm-track here, deeply rutted, and beyond it a threadbare hedge and five-bar gate. They leaned on the gate, side by side, and gazed out over the rolling farmland. It fell away into a deep valley and rose on the far side to another coppice, like the one they'd just traversed. No longer sheltered by the trees, their faces were stung by the breeze, which came across the open land.

Rooks wheeled far above their heads, uttering discordant cries. When the landowner died, so country lore had it, it was important to visit any rookery on the land and tell the birds, Meredith recalled. Bees too. The bees had to be told or they would leave. Death disturbed things. It called an end to the old order and the new order was as yet unknown. The old order at Tudor Lodge had gone and the new order, Luke and Kate, what would they make of it?

'The thing puzzling me,' she said, 'is why she left it so late before

237

she tried to kill Kate. If she'd tried earlier, say after she saw her at the rugby match, it would've made more sense. Carla must've realised then Kate was trying to strike up an acquaintance with Luke. But she left it until the police were all over the place and there was a fresh investigation beginning into the fire.'

'In fairness,' Alan told her, 'she's not a killer by nature. To have plotted to kill Kate earlier in the year, after seeing her at a rugby match, would have been a cold-blooded thing to do. Nor could she know what Andrew's reaction would be to his daughter's death. So Carla went away and brooded about it. She hoped, I suppose, that Andrew would sort things out as he'd done until then. It was when she heard Andrew call out to Kate and believed that he was about to invite her into the family home, that she struck first at him.

'But with Andrew dead, the cat was out of the bag as far as his double life was concerned, so a damage limitation exercise was called for. She took the girl into the house to keep the press away from her and to have her under her eye while Carla decided what to do next. Then Kate signed her own death warrant – or Freddie Green did it on her behalf! He lodged a *caveat* with regard to probate of the will. Andrew was a wealthy man and there was enough to go round, but Carla didn't see it that way. She saw what Kate was doing as an attempt to steal Luke's inheritance from his father. It was then she decided Kate must die. She was going to say, after the event, that Kate had seen where Carla kept the pill bottle and had emptied it. It would've been a plausible tale, given Kate's volatile personality. We might have believed it.'

Meredith said quietly, 'I felt in my bones that something dreadful would come out of Kate's move to Tudor Lodge.'

Markby was forced to an admission. 'OK, you were right and I was wrong. I should have prevented it. But I didn't expect anyone else to die! I was making an elementary mistake. The first kill is the difficult one. After that it's so much easier for the killer. There's nothing to lose and the gamble seems worth it. The killer starts to feel invincible. I've seen it before yet I didn't recognise it when I saw it beginning in this case.'

In the silence which fell between them, Meredith noticed spent cartridge cases on the ground by her feet, red, green, blue. She wondered what the farmer shot up here, pigeons, perhaps, or rabbits. There was so much death in nature, and so much death in the way of the countryside. Even the cattle browsing down there some distance away, looking like toy beasts, were destined for the slaughterhouse and the table.

Unexpectedly, in the midst of her gloomy thoughts, she heard Alan beside her chuckle. Meredith looked up in surprise.

'I was thinking of the old lady, Mrs Joss,' he said. 'She heard Andrew's car go out and come back and the headlights strafed her window. That was the trip he made to deliver Kate to The Crown. She also heard Irene's car returning from town. Its engine made a distinctive noise she recognised. But the next morning, to her great alarm, she learned that Penhallow had been murdered in his garden. The Josses have an uneasy relationship with the law and when things go wrong, suspicion readily falls on them. Mrs Joss didn't think any kin of hers had done murder! But she thought one or other of the clan might get caught up in the inquiries and there was a chance one might have something to hide. So she told the first policeman she saw that cars had been coming and going all night! She was spreading a false trail to take the hunters away. But when Prescott interviewed her, it was clear that she could only swear to those three instances of car noise. That was significant, because it meant that any killer had either arrived on foot, or had already been there in the house. She also said, shrewd old biddy that she is, the way the Penhallows lived was asking for trouble. If her husband had been continually going off for long periods, she said, she'd have wanted to know what he was doing! As Carla eventually did. Mrs Joss suspected something was going on. She was right. We have charged Lemuel Joss, by the way. Or Lee, as he calls himself.'

'What!' Meredith cried. 'What did he have to do with it?'

Startled by her cry, a wood pigeon erupted from the trees behind them with a clatter of wings. It flew low over their heads and landed in the field beyond where it began a stately waddle on its short legs, its plump body cumbersome, its head jerking back and forth with its white collar enhancing its resemblance to a well-fed cleric.

'Nothing at all to do with the murder. But in the course of investigations, we checked him out as his grandma feared we might. He's the local fence, a middleman who disposes of stolen goods through contacts in the bar where he works. All pretty routine stuff. Mostly stolen televisions or video recorders, that sort of thing. I don't suppose having been caught will deter him long term. He'll carry on doing it and graduate to other things, most likely firearms. We'll have to watch Lee Joss.'

Alan turned and leaned back against the gate. 'So that's it. It's up to the doctors and the Crown Prosecution Service. My job's done.' He paused. 'And we can think about us.'

Meredith leaned forwards so that her hair swung over her face.

She could feel her cheeks burning and it angered her to think she couldn't control a stupid girlish blush.

'I do love you,' she said, the words coming out more in a defiant mutter than with passion. 'I wouldn't say it if I didn't.'

'I know you wouldn't and I know you do. I love you. It makes me wonder what the problem is.' He sounded rueful. He knew there was a problem and he probably knew what it was.

She tried explaining, anyhow. 'I've always been on my own. I've never had anyone to please but me. Until I met you I'd never had anyone to help out when there was a crisis. My parents were older than many of the parents of my contemporaries. I was always good friends with them. But I never felt I could bother them with my problems. So I got used to dealing with things on my own quite early on. I never learned to share my life, Alan. It's something which has to be learned, you know. It's not instinctive. I suppose, to be honest, I mean I'm too selfish.'

'You know this is nonsense,' he said gently. He was shaking his head slowly in a puzzled way, but there was resignation in his eyes.

'Don't say that!' She hadn't meant to sound so sharp. 'I can't make the sort of commitment you want from me, Alan, and I'm truly sorry. It's got nothing to do with how I feel about you. It's how I feel about myself.'

'Perhaps I've more faith in you than you have in yourself?' he suggested wryly.

'Don't have.' Her words echoed bleakly off the wall of tree-trunks behind them.

In the ensuing silence he swished the walking stick back and forth through the air until in a wilder sweep it caught the edge of the gate with a crack. The wood pigeon took flight immediately.

'I frighten things off,' he said. 'That creature, you.'

'It's not your fault,' she said wearily.

'Look,' he prepared to put up an argument. 'You've said yourself that you don't think you'll get another overseas posting, so your job wouldn't—'

'It's nothing to do with my job.'

'Then is it to do with that fellow, Mike?'

For a moment Meredith was lost for speech. She had once, in a rash moment, told him about that long-ago, doomed affair. She oughtn't to have done. She'd imagined Alan had listened and filed it with the lost causes which litter everyone's career. He had a failed marriage, she a failed love affair. But he hadn't dismissed it so easily.

To her horror she realised he had, in his own way, been brooding on it and now it came leaping back into her life out of nowhere to bedevil things even more. 'No, of course it isn't! That's – it's long ago, over and done. I was a kid. I'm a different person now.'

The wind rustled the leaves behind them. Alan tucked the stick under his arm in military fashion. 'I apologise. I shouldn't have issued an ultimatum. I had no right to do that. You're entitled to turn me down. It would be boorish of me to persist.'

'You don't have to apologise, for God's sake!' She stared at him, appalled. 'I'm the one who should do that and I'm looking for a way. Your being so nice about it isn't helping.'

'Lose my temper and shout a bit, that would be better?' He had a quizzical look on his face now.

'It would make me feel better,' she confessed.

'Do you think,' he asked slowly, 'that you might feel differently at some future date?'

'Yes, I might. But I can't see into the future, so I can't swear to it.'

'I accept that. But so long as you're not ruling it out for ever.'

He's obstinate, Meredith thought, wanting to laugh and cry at the same time. He won't give up. But perhaps he will, one day, as Carla warned. Perhaps he won't wait for ever.

'What do we do now?' she asked. It had suddenly occurred to her she hadn't a clue what they did from now on.

'In the short term, go and find a decent pub lunch. In the long term, wait and see?'

They linked hands and walked away down the track together.

CHAPTER TWENTY

Steve Prescott stood in the front porch of Tudor Lodge, his attitude very much that of a Victorian suitor, a mixture of hope, bashfulness and a secret resolve that if the worst came to the worst, he'd behave like a gentleman. He didn't have a hat, but if he'd had one, he'd have been picking nervously at the brim.

As far as the police were concerned, the affair of Tudor Lodge was over until the trial. It was in the hands of others now, the Crown Prosecution Service, the lawyers, the medical experts and Uncle Tom Cobbleigh and all. It wasn't over for Prescott. For him there was still unfinished business.

He raised his hand to the bellpush, hearing the insistent buzz echo inside the house. He didn't know who would open the door, and he hoped it would be Kate, because to have to explain himself to anyone else would be embarrassing. Yet to face Kate held out the possibility not only of embarrassment but of humiliation. To be fair, she'd never given him any encouragement and he was probably acting like an idiot in coming here at all. But he couldn't stay away. He had to know. He pressed the bellpush again.

The door flew open almost at once to reveal Mrs Flack, breathless and indignant.

'I was on my way, you know. I'm not deaf. What do you want?'

It was clear she recognised him and took it he was on police business. He didn't imagine she normally greeted callers like this.

'I'd like to see Miss Drago, if she's here,' he said firmly.

Mrs Flack glanced him over. 'It's not more statements and trouble, I hope? I thought we'd got through all that.'

'It's a private matter,' Prescott said, reddening.

This earned him fresh scrutiny. 'Oh yes?' said Mrs Flack, investing this simple phrase with a wealth of innuendo. 'I'll see if she wants to see you. She's busy, packing.'

'Packing?' exclaimed Prescott in alarm.

Mrs Flack took pity on him. 'Come in. I'll see if she'll come down for a minute.'

He stood in the hall and watched her plod purposefully upstairs. He glanced round him while he waited, remembering the last frantic visit here with the superintendent and Meredith Mitchell, Kate collapsed on the floor, the dramatic scene in the drawing room with Carla Penhallow and Luke. There was no sign of Luke and Prescott was glad of it. He had no wish to distress Luke any further and the sight of the sergeant would surely do that.

Voices sounded faintly above his head and he raised his face ceilingwards. A door opened and shut. Footsteps, too heavy for Kate's. Mrs Flack was coming back.

'She'll be down in a tick,' she said. 'You just hang on here, I'm in the kitchen if needed.'

Prescott nodded, his voice sticking in his throat. He watched her as she made her way down the hall and disappeared. Distracted by this, he missed the most important moment of all, Kate's own arrival.

Without warning, her voice, close by his ear, said, 'Hullo?'

He spun round and saw her standing on the lower part of the staircase, leaning over the banister and looking down at him. Her face was a few inches above his as he looked up. The ends of her glorious mane of hair brushed the top of his head and the effect was like an electric charge going through him.

'Hullo,' he replied hoarsely.

This got no reply, she just waited. He was forced to plunge on, 'I came to see how you were.'

'I'm fine – or as fine as anyone would be in the circumstances. Do the police always pay follow-up calls like this?'

'It's nothing to do with the police!' Prescott was suddenly irritated. 'I came on my own account. I mean, on your account.'

She straightened up and came down the remaining stairs to stand beside him in the hall. Now she looked up into his face and he thought how tiny she was, really. The force of her personality had somehow made her seem taller, fuller, than she was. But now she looked as fragile as one of those bits of china on old Ma Joss's mantelpiece. Then he met her direct, resolute gaze, and he was the one who felt insignificant.

'I don't need anyone chasing after me, asking how I am,' she said sharply. 'I'm fine, I told you. The hospital cleared out the drug she fed me. I'm fit – and I'm also busy, so if there's nothing special . . .'

He swallowed. 'The housekeeper said you were packing. That means you're going?'

She gave a little hiss of impatience. 'Yes.'

'At once, today?' He didn't mean to sound dismayed but knew he did.

'There's nothing here to keep me hanging round.' If she was aware of the cruelty of this sentence, she didn't show it. 'I only came back to the house to pick up my gear. I can't get out of the place fast enough, believe me.' There was bitterness in her voice and he thought he understood it. She'd come here with such hopes.

So had he, come with hopes. 'I thought you might like to go out for a meal or something.' This sounded lamer than he'd have wished, so Prescott added with a touch of truculence, 'I'm not just a copper, you know.'

He was rewarded with a grin but before he could take it for encouragement, she was shaking her head. 'Thanks. I appreciate it and all you and Markby did for me the evening Carla tried to finish me off. But I just want everything to do with Bamford right out of my life. Do you understand that?'

He did. He couldn't blame her and he didn't, but a cold fog of depression settled over him. 'Can I give you a lift to the station or anything?'

Even that was to be denied him, as he heard her say, 'No need.'

A thought struck him. 'You're not planning to hitch again, are you?'

She pushed her pale face close to his. 'Look, this is my life,' she said, 'and I've had enough of coppers in it. I don't want to be rude, but whatever I do, it's no concern of yours, right? There was a time you all thought I'd murdered my father.'

'I never thought it!' Prescott protested.

Her attitude softened. 'Well, thanks for that, anyway.' Without warning, she put out her hand and touched his. 'Go on,' she said. 'It was nice of you to come, but there really wasn't any point in it, you know.'

'I know,' Prescott said. 'Good luck. Take care.' He stooped and bestowed a chaste kiss on her cheek. He hadn't known he was going to do it and was overcome with his temerity when he had.

She didn't react, just opened the front door silently. He managed half a smile and and walked past her and out.

Much later that afternoon, as the light was beginning to fade and the air turn chilly, Kate Drago swung her khaki haversack over her shoulder and turned away from the lorry at which she'd just asked for – and been denied – a lift. It'd been another curt, unsmiling refusal such as she'd received at all five trucks parked here.

It wasn't the lay-by in which she'd encountered Eddie Evans, but an almost identical set up, with a similar fast-food van selling greasy sausages and burgers and scalding cups of tarry tea to the same clientele. It had taken her far longer than she'd anticipated to get this far and if she didn't get a long-distance lift soon, she wouldn't get home before dark.

She knew what it was, of course. She should have foreseen it. She hadn't given her name and they didn't have her photograph but they didn't need it. Truckers had an efficient bush telegraph of their own and they all knew who she was. She was a harbinger of misfortune who carried with her the stigma of violent death. She would have to rely on a private car driver picking her up and she disliked accepting lifts in cars. Truckers were a safer bet in her experience. Of course there was always the risk of a rogue one, but generally they had timetables to keep, families at home, jobs or business which might be jeopardised, and they didn't want trouble. Not wanting trouble, this time they'd turned her away.

She walked away, head held high, step assured. The tougher things got, the more you had to act as if you owned the world and didn't give a shit. That she'd learned long ago. Like a sick wolf, if you showed weakness, the encircling pack smelled the fear and you were done for.

She moved out of the protection of the lay-by and set off on the grass verge by the road. It wasn't intended for walkers. There was no proper path. Up ahead the grass petered out and soon she'd be walking on the tarmac surface. It was dangerous in good light and in poor light would be suicidal. Perhaps, if she were lucky enough, she'd come upon a bus stop. She'd wait there for the scheduled service and get on it, any bus, going anywhere.

'I can go *anywhere*,' she murmured to herself. Because no one cared where she went or what she did or what became of her. It was freedom of a sort, or total isolation, whichever you cared to call it. Her plan, in that she had one, her present intention at any rate, was to head for London. She'd go back to college, finish the course – supposing that Freddie got the money from the Penhallow estate to allow her to do that.

Cars sped past but none slowed. She didn't signal. What the hell. For the first time since her mother had died, she felt near to tears.

Now at last a car did slow and pulled over, just up ahead, waiting for her. She approached it cautiously with a mixture of hope and resentment and stooped by the passenger window.

The driver leaned over and wound it down. 'God, Kate, I thought I'd never find you!'

'Luke?' She was so startled she could only gape at him. 'What are you doing here?'

'What the hell do you think I'm doing? I've been looking for you. Here, get in, for Chrissake!' He pushed open the door.

She had little option but to fall in with his request. Kate tossed her haversack on to the back seat and slid in beside him. The car pulled away from the verge and rejoined the mainstream of traffic.

'Irene said you'd been to the house, picked up your stuff and gone,' Luke said, glancing up at the mirror and mindful of the TIR transporter pulling out to overtake him. 'Why isn't that bloody thing on the motorway? And why didn't you tell me you meant to leave?'

The heavy vehicle roared past. Kate thought it had been one of those which had turned her down, back at the lay-by. She wondered if the trucker had seen a car driver pick her up, and if so, what he was thinking. That Luke had got himself a packet of trouble, most likely.

'He had a local call to make, I suppose,' she said in answer to the first part of Luke's question and, in answer to the second part, added, 'would you have wanted to know?'

Then she thought, yes, he probably would, so that he could speed her on her way with a well-chosen curse or two. He'd wanted her to go from the start. Had he followed her along this road, determined not to be cheated of his chance to have his say? Perhaps she owed him that much.

'I had to work out where you were heading.' He sounded more aggrieved than angry. 'I guessed London. I went down to the rail station but the booking clerk didn't remember anyone answering your description. I thought you might be hitching again. Why do you do it?'

'Do what?'

'Hitch? Haven't you got any money?'

'Not much. Anyway, it's not the money – it's – you wouldn't understand.'

It was a game. Herself against the rest. Getting them to do what she wanted. She'd played it all her life. Not from choice, she told herself, but from necessity. It was called survival.

'*Are* you going to London?'

'Yes.'

'Then I'll drive you.'

She looked at him in surprise. 'What, all the way?'

'Well, I might as well!' he snapped.

Kate said carefully, speaking slowly, 'I don't need you. I don't need anyone.'

'Talk sense,' was the blunt reply. 'It's getting late. We can go back to Bamford if you prefer.'

With a spark of her old spirit, she riposted, 'I don't prefer. I don't want to go near that dump of a town ever again.'

'I don't blame you. I'm beginning to feel the same way about it,' Luke muttered.

She found these words, from him, shocked her. 'You shouldn't. It's your home,' she protested.

'That's what I thought.' His voice was savage. 'Now I don't know. I don't know anything for certain. Everything's upside down, higgledy-piggledy, inside my head. Nothing's what I thought it was. I thought I was an only child and I wasn't, I'm not. I thought I knew my father and I didn't. I thought I knew my mother even better—' He broke off, biting back the words.

They drove on for a while. The evening was drawing in fast. All the cars had their headlights on now. She was lucky that Luke had picked her up. There probably wasn't a bus. She might have had to sleep in a hedge. She supposed she ought to feel grateful and thank him, but she couldn't find the words. Gratitude, thanks, these things stuck in her throat.

Luke too was struggling to find words. 'You know Mum is – is in a place where they can look after her.' Not hearing any reply, he glanced sideways and saw her frozen profile incline slightly.

'She didn't mean – that is, she's ill. She wouldn't have done it if she hadn't been ill, not tried to kill you or attack Dad. She broke down. She adored Dad. It was the shock.'

'Why not just say it's my fault?' Kate asked him. 'I made her do it. If I hadn't come to Tudor Lodge, he'd still be alive.' She turned her head to look at him and asked challengingly, 'Don't you think that? Really, in your heart of hearts? Don't lie.'

'I won't lie. It's what I did think at first. But I know now it's not that simple. Mum had known about him and your mother, about you, for years. She kept it from me and from everyone. It must have just eaten away at her. I never even suspected. But she *had* known. She didn't find out because you turned up. She knew and sooner or later she would have snapped. I suppose it was Dad's fault, if anyone's. He was selfish and careless and stupid. But I know he didn't mean any harm. He wasn't a cruel man, just a weak one, I suppose. He told himself he could have it all. He didn't want to hurt her. He didn't want to hurt anyone.'

Kate heard herself say, 'My mother had cancer. It ate away at her. Perhaps your mother had a sort of emotional cancer. I'm sorry. I'm sorry if I made it worse.'

'It's not your fault nor mine. Neither of us created any of it. They didn't think about us when they started all this. What I mean is, I've been trying to think it out. I'd just about got it worked out, what I wanted to explain to you, when I came home and found you'd scarpered. So I had to find you because it has to be said and it can't wait. We didn't ask for our parents to mess things up. You're my sister. I'd like us to be friends. Or at least, not enemies.' His voice sounded anxious.

'We're not enemies.' Kate grimaced in the gloom. 'In fact, you're the one person in this whole thing who can be truly said to be blameless. You didn't do anything.'

'So we'll call it quits and start with a clean slate, right?'

'All right,' she said cautiously. 'We can try. I'm not going back to Bamford, though, at any time in the future. You can come and see me in London sometimes.'

'You're going to finish your college course? I think you should.'

'I suppose I will. Will you finish yours?'

He sighed. 'I suppose so. I seem to have lost interest at the moment, though. Have the police finished with you?'

'I think so. They said I could leave. I'd have gone anyway. Apart from anything else, there's that sergeant. I had to extricate myself from that.'

'Hey, what's he been up to?' cried Luke indignantly.

'Nothing. I don't mind having you for a brother but you don't have to act the heavy. I can look after myself. I'm used to doing that. The sergeant was rather sweet but not my type. I don't need him now. I thought I might, but I don't.' Crisply, Kate added, 'I'm not a nice person, by the way.' After a moment she added, 'It'll be late when we get to town. You can doss down at my place. I've got a sofa.' She grinned. 'I'll tell the landlady you're my brother, but she won't believe it.'

The lights were on at Regional HQ. The neon strips flickered and cast their pitiless glare over abandoned desks, filled waste baskets, trays of untouched paperwork, blank VDU screens and, because technology cost money, the manual typewriters which were still a feature of the place. The night shift was coming on, joshing or complaining outside in the corridors, according to circumstances. Their feet clattered on the tiled floors.

Sergeant Prescott was packing up for the day. He'd cleared his desk as far as possible and left the rest for the next man. He swept a clutter of sweet wrappers, plastic sandwich containers and polystyrene beakers into the basket, stretched and got cumbersomely to his feet. Yawning, he reached for his coat. The phone chose that moment to ring.

He glared at the offending instrument and fought a brief struggle with his conscience. It had been a long day and he'd had enough. It shrilled again. He sighed and picked it up. 'Prescott.'

'That you, Sergeant?' The voice was male, unknown and uncertain. 'You there?' it persisted and there was a noisy clearing of a throat. 'I want to talk to Sergeant Prescott.'

'Speaking,' said Prescott, tucking the receiver under his chin and struggling to get his arms into his sleeves.

'My name's Evans. Eddie Evans. I'm a truck driver. My wife says you wanted to talk to me about that girl. Not that I can tell you anything. Sorry I picked her up. Never would've done if I'd known all the trouble she was going to cause. Well, not to me, but to others, you know. Thing is, I've just come back from taking a load over to Europe. I drove down to Turkey and on the way back I got stuck in this Greek farmers' private war. That's why I couldn't get in touch with you before. Anyway, I'm here now. How can I help? Do you want me to come in?'

Prescott rescued the receiver from beneath his chin and stood with it in his hand for a moment. The receiver squawked, prompting him.

'Thank you, Mr Evans,' he said slowly at last. 'It's good of you to get in touch. But there's nothing. We don't need to talk to you now. That line of inquiry is closed.'

He set the receiver gently back into its cradle.